ONE CHILD

To
Kim Knudsen,
Thanks for your help with
the technical details in
the book.
All the best.
Jeff

JEFF BUICK

This story is based on a mixture of fictional and true events. The true events, however, have been fictionalized. All fictitious characters presented in this novel have granted the publisher their exclusive biographical and personality rights. Any resemblance to real people, living or dead, is entirely coincidental.

Some of the companies in this book are real and some are not. When real companies are presented, their details have been fictionalized and any resemblance to real persons within those companies is entirely coincidental. All fictitious company's rights, including their common law trade-mark rights and domain names, are hereby owned exclusively by the publisher.

Contact the publisher Enthrill Entertainment Inc. at legal@enthrill.com for any queries or comments you may have.

First Edition
ISBN: 978-0-9866199-0-8

Printed & Bound in Canada by Blitzprint Inc.
Book Layout & Cover Design by Francomedia.com
Cover Photo by A.J. Valadka & IStockphoto LP
Published by Enthrill Entertainment Inc.

Acknowledgements

One Child would not have been possible without help from numerous people. This book has many different plot themes woven together, and I'm the first to admit that I'm not an expert in any of them. So here are the people who kept me accurate and on track. Any errors that made it through to the final print run are entirely mine.

Jill Klacza
Laura Rushford
Bill Schultz
Janis Rapchuk
Matthew Gow
Cade Seely
Michael Hornburg
Bryan Taylor
Kim Knudsen
Wayne Logan
Celia Rushford
Kevin Franco
Cameron Chell
Cory Cleveland
Robert Greenwald

and

The entire team at FrancoMedia
Christina, Colin, Dave, Sandor, Nicholas & Ryan

Jeff Buick

Dedication

To the memory of Harvey Chan

The tyranny of distance was the greatest threat to our enduring friendship. But every time I picked up the phone and heard your voice, it was like we had spoken only yesterday. Though your time on earth was short, you left a legacy of smiles and warm-hearted acts of kindness in your wake. You worked hard at being a good friend, a loving husband and a devoted father – now it's time to rest.

Jeff Buick

Prologue

Kandahar, Afghanistan

A harsh wind attacked the room on the top floor of the dilapidated building, tearing at the loose fabric over the solitary window and driving tiny particles of sand into even the smallest gap. It stung against exposed flesh – a thousand angry bees attacking in the darkness.

A man was huddled inside the tiny apartment, treasuring the last shreds of the night. The sun would be up soon and the relentless heat would return. Every day, without fail, the temperature rose until it threatened to suck the oxygen from the air. He was at the mercy of the elements – in a country mired in constant turmoil by an endless stream of would-be conquerors. Some days he loved his native Afghanistan. Some days he hated it.

Kadir Hussein reached out with gnarled fingers and pulled together two pieces of torn cloth that covered the window. For a moment the onslaught of sand ceased. The young girl asleep in his arms twitched as he moved, and he stopped. She slept so little. She was so small, so frail. She needed to sleep. Her body shuddered – mild convulsions that accompanied hunger pangs.

Hunger. More relentless than the heat.

He glanced down at the worn tile floor, at the two younger girls sleeping under threadbare blankets. At least they ate yesterday. He and Halima had gone without. He was the father and she was the older sister. They sacrificed so the young children could have something in their bloated stomachs. Eleven years old and Halima was already well versed in the harsh lesson of poverty. He wondered if she remembered the days before they lived in the small room atop the apartment building. She said she did, but it was so long ago. Almost two years. He hoped her memories were more than a collection of blurred images.

Light filtered through the gap in the curtains. The cool night air wouldn't linger long once the sun rose. Today would be difficult. They had no food, which was usual, but they had drunk the last of their water, and surviving the heat without it was impossible.

Kadir stared at his youngest daughter. Only five years old. A mere baby when they had arrived at the dusty, bleak building on the outskirts of Kandahar. Much too young to remember her mother or their life on the fertile banks of the Arghandāb River. He closed his eyes and envisioned a time when their lives had been different. His wife was at the *tandoor*, baking naan for their evening meal. Kids running about the small hut on the edge of the pomegranate field. The family goat trying to push its way into the house. She was smiling, amused by the goat's persistence. Always smiling, despite a hard life providing meals and clean clothes for her husband and the girls.

The vision slowly dissipated. Their home faded and was replaced by a side street in Kandahar city. His wife's expression changed, first filled with apprehension, then horror. He could see them clearly – the soldiers rounding the corner – the Taliban fighters spraying the street with bullets – his wife caught in the crossfire. He, screaming and running toward her. Her body jerking as the bullets cut into her flesh. The food and water she was carrying spilling across the broken pavement.

He opened his eyes and the images were gone. But not the sting of the memory. Holding her, cradling her head as warm blood trickled over his bare arms onto the dusty ground. Feeling her last breath against his skin. He cursed the vividness of the scenes that played out in his mind. And cherished them. It was all he had left of the woman he had loved.

Halima stirred and opened her eyes. She looked up at him, focusing on his rugged face, creased with worry and hope. A hint of a smile passed over her lips and disappeared. She closed her eyes and snuggled tighter to his body, her thin fingers grasping at his tunic.

"Sleep," he said quietly, his voice a pleasant break from the incessant wind.

Her eyelids flickered, then opened. Large brown eyes stared at him through strands of tangled hair. "We have no water. I should go to the well before the sun is up."

"I can fetch the water today," he said. He knew she wouldn't allow it. Her sisters were too young and weak for him to be gone so many hours.

"No, father." A small hand appeared from one of the folds of his tattered tunic and pushed back her hair. "I'll go."

"It's so far," he said. "More than a kilometer." *And the streets are not safe*, he thought.

"I've walked it lots of times." She pulled tighter to her father. "No one bothers me. Sometimes I think they don't even see me."

A ray of sunlight poked through the hole in the curtains and illuminated Aaqila. She was tiny for five, half the size of the children who lived in the city and had food on the table two or three times a day. Sleep was the best part of her day, when the hunger pangs were bearable and her body was cool and rested. Her chest rose and fell slightly with the rhythm of her breathing and her eyelids flickered as the sunlight touched them.

"I had a dream last night," Halima said, her eyes locked on her youngest sister.

"Dreams are good," her father said. "Do you remember what you dreamt?"

"Yes, I do." She licked her cracked lips with a dry tongue. "I was someone important. I'm not sure why, but people were talking about me. Many, many people. They had pictures of me."

"You *are* important, Halima."

"No, father. Not just to you. To hundreds of people. Maybe even thousands."

"How are such things possible?" Kadir asked.

She shrugged, her shoulders pressing into his chest. "I don't know. But they were talking about me. Saying that I changed the world."

Kadir tilted his head so he could see her eyes. They were shining with excitement. "You changed *my* world, Halima. You made it so much better."

Her eyes dimmed and the smile slowly faded. “Do dreams come true?”

Kadir considered the words. They were thoughtful words, and an important question to an eleven-year-old girl. His answer was equally important. He was her world and what he said and how he said it would help form the woman she would become.

“Yes, they do come true.”

The light crept back into her eyes.

He pushed at a few errant strands of hair with his weathered fingers. “But dreams may not always appear exactly as we saw them. Sometimes they find other ways of showing themselves.”

“Will I know when it happens?” she asked uncertainly.

“Oh, yes, Halima, you'll know.” There was confidence in his voice and it satisfied her natural curiosity.

Aaqila stirred and opened her eyes. Confusion prevailed for a few seconds, then she rolled over and crawled to Kadir and Halima. She wrapped her arms around her sister and lay still and quiet. Sunlight streamed into the room and the temperature rose sharply. A new day had arrived. With it would come intense heat, hunger and thirst. Satisfying the most basic needs meant getting food and water. And if they were successful, there was always someone else nearby who needed food and would use violence to take it.

Their world was about survival. Kadir knew that was the key. Nothing more than surviving, day by day. He was a common man. His dreams had nothing to do with changing the world. His dreams were to have food and water. To have a house with thick walls, where there was relief from the blistering summer sun and the bitter cold of the Afghan winter. He wondered when, if ever, things would change? He had no answers. He had nothing but an unwavering will to survive and to protect his children.

Every day, without fail, he prayed that would be enough.

CHAPTER 1

Midtown Manhattan, New York City

The computer screen glowed softly, bathing the polished wood desk in an eerie blue. Beyond the wall of windows lay the lights of Manhattan, and to the north, a massive black rectangle defined Central Park. A lone figure sat at the desk, staring out over the city.

His city.

William Fleming had seen much of the world, moving about when he was young, but New York was where he had settled. He had staked his claim to the American dream and built a fortune while millions of others treaded water. They lived in the world they created – he lived in his. And William Fleming's world was one of privilege and excess.

The Forbes List for 2010 had ranked him as the 35th richest person in the world, with an estimated net worth of ten-point-three billion dollars. Not bad for a kid who had delivered groceries from his father's store on the back of his bicycle in his native Hungary in the early sixties. Life under communist rule was difficult, especially for a teenager with a head full of opinions that went against the ruling party. He stayed below the Soviet's radar until 1975, when he was seventeen. Then everything changed.

He and his sister were on their daily route home from the family store on a warm June afternoon, bicycling past the palace in their hometown of Kormend. It was more of a cluster of three main buildings with six smaller ones than a real palace. Janka was two years older and wearing a skirt with a white blouse. As they passed the group of buildings, a middle-aged man dressed in a crisply-pressed suit rushed out. He insisted they stop and come in for something to drink. He had seen them riding by numerous times and wanted to show them around the grounds. Both of them were suspicious, but it was the era of communism and nothing good would have come from denying an important man a simple request.

The man had been drinking and within fifteen minutes was trying to seduce Janka. When he pulled up her skirt and yanked down her panties, Fleming hit him. Hard. The man went down and didn't move. Fleming checked for a pulse. He was alive, which was lucky for Janka. If the man was dead, she would have been an accessory to murder, but with him simply unconscious, it meant Janka could still remain in Kormend with the rest of her family. For Fleming, however, it was a different story. He was a marked man, and jail awaited him if he remained in Hungary. He immediately fled his homeland, going over the nearby Austrian border, never to return. He emigrated from Austria to the United States and changed his name legally from Laszio Farkas to William Fleming.

As he settled into his life in America, one thought burned through his mind a hundred times a day. *If his family had money, and if they had used it to pay off the official, he could have stayed in Hungary.* He vowed that would never happen to him again. That he would always have enough money to buy his way out of trouble. It had proved to be a very valuable lesson over the years.

Fleming looked away from the cityscape and stared at the newspaper article he had clipped from the *Times*. The Irish rock band, U2, was playing Luzhniki Stadium in Moscow on August 25th. He could care less. He liked their music, but other than that, they were nothing more than a collection of musicians who had hit the big time. What he did care about, and the reason he had kept the article, was the person who was bringing the band to Russia.

Dimitri Volstov.

Fleming's jaw clenched tighter and his temperature rose at the thought of the charismatic Russian. To Fleming, he was nothing more than a black-market street-trader who had befriended the Russian political hierarchy and rode on their coattails to incredible wealth. Volstov's company, Murmansk-Technika, was one of the largest energy producers in Russia. It held substantial oil and gas leases in Siberia and was active in building nuclear facilities in six regions of the country. Its net worth ran into the hundreds of billions of dollars. All this owned by a man who had actually owned pig farms at one time. Worked with pigs – in their pens.

"A travesty," he whispered to the empty room. "Makes The List look like nothing but a damn joke. Old man Forbes would be sick." He crumpled the newspaper and threw it in the small wastepaper basket under his desk.

To William Fleming, Volstov was more than some upstart pig farmer. Volstov was a thief. The man who had stood between him and a pipeline deal in 2002 that was ultimately worth a quarter of a billion dollars. The money was substantial, and important, but it was not just the money that Fleming cared about. Volstov had humiliated him, and that he *did* care about. The Russian had invited a select group of influential men and women to his country dacha in Konsha-Zaspa. During the party, he quieted the group and made an announcement. He listed his partners in a pipeline that stretched from Turkmenistan to Russia, via Kazakhstan. It was a deal worth six billion dollars and one that identified the major players on the world stage. Despite a promise to bring Fleming in on the deal, Volstov reneged, due to complications with the government in Kazakhstan. Fleming was left standing alone in a room filled with people who knew exactly what had just happened.

Then, instead of simply cutting him out of the deal and letting it die quietly, Volstov had brought in the media and issued press releases detailing who the major players were. And who was left out. The world of the ultra-rich was a small community and Fleming was branded as an outsider. It took years to wriggle his way back in. And even now, despite his incredible wealth, there were still many European families and businessmen who considered him damaged goods.

Eight years wasn't enough time to soothe the anger. It roiled inside him, a relentless sea of hate that some days threatened to consume him. All time had done was magnify the loathing and the desire for revenge. He had no doubt that the Russian would pay. The only questions were – when and how.

He leaned forward and retrieved the paper from the wastebasket. He set it on his desk and smoothed the creases, then reread the article in its entirety. The editorial slant was easy. Volstov was being hailed as a hero for organizing the event and bringing the world's most popular band to Moscow. The concert date was August 25th and he did the math. Twenty-nine days. Fleming stared at the scrap of paper, wondering if it was an opportunity.

He checked his watch and switched off his computer. Other business called. The soft Italian leather soles on his shoes made no sound against the ebony hardwood floor as he approached the door. It opened automatically and he walked through without breaking stride. On the other side, grasping the handle, was a stocky man dressed in Armani. He fell in behind Fleming and they took the private elevator to the underground parking garage. A Lincoln Navigator with tinted windows was waiting next to the elevator shaft. Fleming slipped into the back seat. His bodyguard settled into an identical vehicle parked immediately behind Fleming's.

"Kellari," Fleming said to the driver.

The vehicles entered the traffic – oddities among the surge of yellow cabs. The drive between his office on the Avenue of the Americas and the Greek restaurant was less than five minutes. The driver parked at the curb and Fleming got out without a word. The maître d' greeted him by name and walked at a quick stride through the packed dining area. A few people nodded as Fleming passed and one man stood and offered his hand. The maître d' motioned to a table tucked in the back of the restaurant. A thin man dressed entirely in black was seated in one of the chairs. Fleming sat opposite him.

"I'm tired, Jorge. I hope whatever you have is worth my time."

Jorge Amistav leaned forward. The Armenian, with his olive skin and black hair, could easily have been one of the Greek businessmen having a late dinner. In reality, he was an arms dealer.

"I don't think you'll be disappointed."

Their waiter appeared at the table. "Can I get you something to drink, sir?" he asked, setting a menu on Fleming's napkin.

Fleming asked for Maker's Mark bourbon, then turned back to Amistav. "What do you want?"

"I have another warehouse filled with armaments. All of them are next to untraceable."

Fleming shook his head. "We've done this before. I didn't like the risk then. I like it even less now."

"These ones are almost free." He smiled, revealing crooked teeth. "The profit margin is much better than the last deal."

Fleming traced his finger across his napkin. "What's the bottom line, Jorge?"

"Thirty-five million in your pocket. After expenses."

Fleming sat back in his chair and stared out over the room. For a moment he was a ten-year-old, on his bicycle, bags of groceries in the basket. The summer Hungarian sun was warm on his arms as he pedaled along the bumpy road, delivering milk and bread and other staples to the elderly people who couldn't make it to his father's store. Two cents a delivery. Thirty deliveries a day. Ten hours of pedaling to make sixty cents. And now, this man sat in front of him offering thirty-five million dollars if he financed and invoiced one deal.

"What's your end of things?" Fleming asked.

"Two million for my contact at the warehouse and three for my fee."

"Thirty-five is good," Fleming said slowly. "But there's usually a downside to deals like this. What's the risk?"

Amistav smiled. He knew the question was coming. Fleming wasn't stupid. Far from it. "The weapons are rejects. They didn't pass the necessary testing. They were slated to be destroyed, but I have a contact inside the warehouse who..." he paused to choose the right word, "saved them."

The waiter returned with the bourbon. "Your drink, sir." He set it on a coaster.

"Thank you," Fleming said. "So you're suggesting that I supply our troops with defective weaponry. I'm not sure I like that idea. The last time we sold the US military weapons, at least they worked properly."

Amistav shook his head. "The military standards are ridiculous. I don't know the exact figures, but it's something like a one or two percent fail rate and they toss it in the reject pile. That means the gun is firing at 98 to 99 percent efficiency.

I think that's pretty damn good."

"What's the rate of fire for an M-4?" Fleming asked.

Amistav shrugged. "I'm not sure."

"Ninety rounds per minute. So if the soldier in the field keeps the trigger depressed for a full minute, and the gun is firing at 98 percent efficiency, it will jam."

"Nobody fires for a minute without stopping. The magazines don't hold enough bullets."

"The magazine holds 30 bullets." Fleming sipped his bourbon and set it back on the coaster. "And M-4s no longer have a fully automatic setting. Single shot or three-round bursts are the only options." He settled back into the leather chair. "The fact is that at 98 or 99 percent efficiency, the gun will fail at some point in time."

"Probably."

"No, Jorge, not probably. Definitely. Don't ever try to bullshit me on armaments," Fleming said.

"Sorry."

A roar of laughter from a table of eight shot through the room and most people glanced at the origin. Fleming didn't. He simply looked irritated at the noise. He took another sip of bourbon.

"Leave it with me. I'll let you know tomorrow."

"Okay." A bead of sweat ran down the arms dealer's forehead. He picked up his napkin and dabbed it away. "Should I call you?"

"I'll call you."

Fleming finished his drink and walked back through the restaurant. His Lincoln was parked directly outside and the second one appeared from down the street in seconds. The man in the Armani suit followed him and jumped into the tailing vehicle. They disappeared into the New York night.

CHAPTER 2

Soho, New York City

The beeping from the alarm began as a low gurgle, then increased in cadence and volume until a hand hit the snooze button. The room sank back into silence. One of the figures stirred under the covers, then bare feet touched the floor.

Carson Grant shuffled across the worn hardwood into the kitchen and touched the brew button on the coffee machine. He returned to bed and pulled the woman under the covers close to him. She mumbled something incomprehensible, but contented. They lay unmoving for ten minutes, then he roused himself again and returned to the kitchen. He added cream and sugar to the brew and padded back to the bedroom. He opened the shades on the window and slipped into bed, sitting in the dark with his back against the headboard, staring out the window. Across the street, the windows of the four-story warehouse lofts were still dark. Above the building the last remnants of a full moon lit the early morning sky. The woman rolled over on her side, snuggled up to him and dozed off.

A light breeze pushed through the open window. Carson sipped the coffee, his mind growing alert as the caffeine kicked in. Below him, Soho was slowly coming alive. The sounds of traffic from Spring Street picked up and a large truck drove past, the roar from its diesel motor reverberating off the brick buildings. Low voices carried up to the third floor window, the words muted and indistinguishable. Cans clanged as a garbage truck hauled away the last of yesterday's trash.

New York was waking up.

The woman shifted slightly under the covers and coughed. She clutched the duvet until her fingers turned white. Her body was wracked with convulsions – muscles tensed and contracted as the shock waves rolled through her thin frame. The coughing fit lasted almost a minute, then she settled back into the pillow and her grip on the covers relaxed. Tiny spasms shook her body for another minute, then she lay still, her breathing labored and shallow.

"You okay, Nicki?" Carson asked.

"Fine," she answered. Her voice was strong for such a small frame. "Business as usual."

"Yeah," he said quietly. He hated it when she said that.

He sipped the coffee and stared out the window, listening to the growing wall of white noise. The alarm clock flipped over to 6:00 and he slid out of bed and started the shower. The water was cold – invigorating – and his mind ran through his daily calendar. The two o'clock meeting trumped everything. In fact, it was the meeting that could change his life. Or not.

The water dripped for thirty seconds after he turned it off, then petered out. Carson couldn't help smiling. Everything about the third-story flat was like the shower and had some sort of quirk. The heat register thumped six times before it kicked in and the electrical outlet the television was plugged into would only work if the bathroom light was on. Two years was enough, it was time to move on. Maybe that would happen today.

"It all comes down to one meeting," he muttered to himself as he stripped the plastic off his freshly pressed suit. He knew he was ready.

He dressed and checked his look in the mirror. Perfect. Never better. His light brown hair was exactly the right length and was behaving itself. None of the usual cowlicks or unruly tufts. He smiled and was rewarded with the sight of even white teeth behind full lips. His eyes, pale on the grey days, were vibrant blue. He ran a sponge over his black leather shoes and returned to the bedroom.

Nicki was awake and sitting up in the bed.

"I should have gotten up this morning," she said. "Made you breakfast." She was thin – too thin – her clavicles jutting out from her shoulders. The natural beauty in her face was accentuated by her leanness. Like freshly fallen snow – a simple white blanket with no blemishes. Nothing to detract from the perfection of the place and the moment. Short black hair framed her striking features.

He sat beside her. "It's okay. I'll grab something at the deli near the office."

"Big day for you," she said. She adjusted his tie.

"Big day for us."

She nodded. "For us. Of course."

He hugged her, longer than usual, then left the apartment and locked the door behind him. Spring Street was already busy. Delivery trucks filled with early morning shipments pulled in at the curb and an occasional yellow cab trolled, looking for fares. He stayed on Spring Street to the Avenue of the Americas and caught the 1 Line subway at the Canal Street station. The train was crowded, but not unbearable and he rode it past his building to the 50th Street Station rather than getting off at Times Square. He liked the walk coming back in from the north better.

The lobby of 1177 Avenue of the Americas, home of Platinus Investments, always amazed him. A grand piano sat just inside the doors and the ceilings soared five stories above the marble floors. He cleared security and took the elevator to his office on the eighteenth floor. Getting through the morning was hell. A problem with the latest algorithm was waiting on his desk and needed his attention. But his thoughts and focus were already in William Fleming's office, facing the man across his desk. He finished lunch and checked his watch. 1:20. Forty minutes until he was due for the most important interview of his life. He felt a tinge of wetness in his armpits and willed his sweat glands to stop. Nothing was going to ruin this.

It was three weeks ago to the day when he found out he had been shortlisted for the job of heading up the High Frequency Trading division of Platinus Investments. It wasn't a title that was to be taken lightly. In addition to overseeing two hundred highly educated men and women, the job description included advising the CEO on a daily basis. That meant one-on-one contact with William Fleming, a man who stood among the ruling elite on Wall Street. High Frequency Trading was enormously lucrative for the firm, and it was Fleming's baby. Fleming wanted opinions on how the firm could maximize profits and keep the other HFT firms at bay. Carson would have influence over the computer programs that were the engine of the global financial markets. It was Nirvana. And he was one of five who had made the shortlist.

Almost double his current salary plus bonuses. It would easily run over a million a year. If Fleming chose him for the position, he would move up the wedding and get a new place in Midtown. Soho was nice, but couldn't compete with an apartment overlooking Central Park.

It was so close. Everything he had worked for. So many years of college, all for this moment.

Carson switched off his computer and took the elevator to the forty-seventh floor. It opened with a swooshing sound and he wondered if it did that on every floor. He strode across the foyer to where a mid-forties woman sat at a sleek metal and glass reception desk.

"Carson Grant to see Mr. Fleming," he said.

"He's ready for you," the woman replied. She motioned to the door behind her with one hand and touched a button on her computer with the other. "No need to knock."

"Thank you," Carson said.

His knees almost buckled. He moved past the desk and glanced at his watch. Was he late? It wasn't possible. The minute hand on his Omega was exactly on eleven. Five minutes before the hour. He was early. He wasn't sure what to think as he pushed open the solid wood door.

The corner room was spacious and sparsely furnished. An average-size desk, dark wood with pewter accents, faced the bank of windows looking north toward Central Park. William Fleming sat on one of a pair of sofas that faced each other in front of a second wall of windows. He was reading the contents of a file folder. He set the folder on his lap and pointed to the other couch. He was dressed in tan slacks and a dark blue shirt open at the neck. His dark hair was pushed back behind his ears and framed a thin, intense face. His eyes were deep brown, almost black.

"Sit down, Carson," Fleming said.

"Thank you, sir." Carson tugged his trouser legs up slightly as he sat, then adjusted the material so it sat properly on his legs.

It was the fifth time he had met William Fleming. If anyone asked, he could tell them where each encounter had taken place and what was said. Conversing with one of the richest men in the world wasn't something that was easily forgotten.

"You have an MBA from MIT," Fleming said.

"Yes, sir."

"Did you like the school?"

Carson considered his answer. The examination was underway. No foreplay with this interview. "Yes and no. I found the professors to be the best I had ever encountered. But the student body was a different thing altogether."

Fleming tilted his head to one side. "Why is that?"

"There were some students on scholarships, but there were a lot more from wealthy families. Most of them had attitudes of entitlement."

"And you didn't." It wasn't a question. It was a statement.

"No," Carson said. He wondered if the $375,000 student loan he had taken out to attend the prestigious campus was noted in his file. He suspected it was. No, he *knew* it was.

Carson was ready for the questions. He had studied everything he could find about William Fleming prior to the interview. Born Laszio Farkas in Hungary in 1958, he was the younger of two children. He had a late October birthday, which made him a Scorpio. His father had dropped out of school in grade eight and spent his life running a small grocery store. His mother helped with the store and cooked the meals. There was some sort of trouble with a communist party official in the summer of 1975 and Fleming had left the country the same night the incident had happened. He changed his name to William Fleming and settled in Wisconsin, where he excelled at math and statistics. He enrolled in business at the University of Wisconsin - Madison, maintained a 3.85 GPA for two years then dropped out and headed for New York. Fleming spent the next nine years with a handful of investment companies, then started Platinus Investments in 1989. The rest was logged in the Wall Street history books.

Fleming locked eyes with the younger man. "Thursday, May 6th, 2010. A computer glitch erases 723 points off the Dow in sixteen minutes. What is your immediate response to counteract the drop?"

The questions continued for over an hour. Easy ones that lulled him into a false sense of security, followed by staccato bursts that tested him on industry knowledge, his integrity and decision-making ability. There was no rhythm, nothing to indicate what question might be next. To Carson, it was an hour that redefined stress. Finally, Fleming closed Carson's file and set it on the table.

"Can I ask you a personal question?"

Carson nodded. "Yes."

"You're engaged – getting married soon."

"Yes, sometime later this year, maybe early in 2011."

"Why are you marrying a woman who is dying?"

Carson's mouth opened, then closed. His mind was racing. Somehow, instinctively, he knew that the outcome of the interview rested on this one answer. The obvious one, and the truth, was that he loved Nicki and that it didn't matter to him how much time they had together. But this moment wasn't about truth. It had nothing to do with Nicki or with love. It had everything to do with his dedication to William Fleming and to Platinus.

"I committed to her," he said. "A commitment – a promise – is everything."

Fleming leaned forward. He stared coldly at the younger man. "Are you committed to this company? To running a High Frequency Trading department that outperforms every other firm in the world?"

"One hundred percent."

Fleming remained motionless for fifteen seconds, eyes locked on Carson. Then he relaxed into the leather cushion and touched a small black button embedded in the arm of the couch. A pleasant voice answered.

"Yes, Mr. Fleming?"

"Cherise, I'd like you to cancel the interview with the final applicant. The position has been filled."

"Yes, sir."

Fleming smiled. "Welcome to the inner circle, Carson."

CHAPTER 3

Boston, Massachusetts

Russell Matthews closed the lid on his camera case. Then he opened it and checked his lenses, batteries and memory cards. For the sixth time. It was a habit – and a good one. Forgetting one piece of specialized equipment when heading to a country like Afghanistan could be disastrous.

"Are you ready?" a woman's voice asked.

Russell slung the bag over his shoulder and grabbed his backpack. "Ready as I'll ever be." He faced the woman in the doorway.

"You're crazy. You can still back out." She was leaning against the doorjamb, dressed in tight jeans and a white T-shirt. Long curly hair fell past her shoulders and tiny worry lines creased her skin near her eyes. They hadn't been there when she married Russell in Punta Cana three years ago. Living with a photojournalist who covered the world's hot spots wasn't easy.

Russell set the pack on the floor and pulled the woman close to him. At five-eight she was still six inches shorter than her husband. He pushed his blond hair back from his face and gave her his patented one-sided grin. Disarming to most women, but it didn't work on her anymore.

"It's only a month, Tina. And I'm embedded."

"I don't like it. Not with you traveling in the trucks with the soldiers. Most of the injuries in Afghanistan are caused by IEDs."

"I won't be in a truck. I'll be in an armored vehicle called a Stryker," Russell said. His face darkened slightly. "You're right about the Improvised Explosive Devices. I think they're a coward's way to fight a war."

"Well, cowardly or not, they work. Look at the body count." Tina Matthews pulled back from her husband and held him at arm's length. "It may be a good assignment, Russell, but I have a bad feeling about it."

"I'll be spending most of my time behind the wire – some in the villages. Anita wants the story on what it's like to be a soldier in Kandahar, but it's more than that. She's pushing for stories on the Afghan people and how all this is affecting them."

"Anita Greenwall is behind a desk at the television station. She's not the one with her life on the line."

"Anita's cool. You know that. She's the reason the network is footing the bill for this. And she talked them into having me cover more than just the troops. She pushed for the humanitarian angle."

"Sorry," Tina said. "Just venting." She sunk in against his chest. "I want you intact. Not with your legs blown off. Or dead."

"Man, you really know how to sweet talk a guy."

She was trembling now. Enough for him to feel her chest pulsing against his. She clutched him tighter. "I love you, Russell. I don't want a phone call in the middle of the night."

They stood entwined for a minute, then Russell said, "I'll miss my flight."

The mid-morning drive from the eastern edge of Cambridge to Logan International was easy – by Boston standards. Less than forty minutes from door to door. They alternated between banal conversation and prolonged stretches of silence. Two minds processing the same information. Both of them touching on the reality of what was happening and neither of them wanting to talk about it.

"How long until you're embedded?" Tina asked as they approached the Sumner Tunnel. She slowed for the toll and threw a handful of change into the basket.

"About five days," Russell answered. "Today's the 28th, so I should be in the field by August 1st or 2nd."

"And you're flying back on August 30th."

He tapped his camera bag, which doubled as his carry-on. "E-ticket is in here. Confirmed. I'm back about six at night."

"Good," Tina said, navigating the Saab through the thickening traffic. She slipped into an opening near the departures door and set the transmission in park. "Promise me something."

"Sure," he said.

"Come back alive."

Tina was crying. She dropped him at the airport every time he left on assignment. It was their routine. She was emotional, but never like this. Never tears. It shocked him into a sudden realization of the danger he would soon be plunged into. He was thirty-six years old. No longer an invulnerable twenty-something who couldn't see the frailty of life. Maybe it was time to rethink his career path. Maybe. He wasn't sure. One thing was certain. If he left the war and disaster zones to the younger pups, he'd miss the adrenaline rush.

"I'm coming home," he said. "My life is with you, and I'm not giving that up."

"To them – you're faceless. Just another white guy in their country messing up their lives. They could care less about the life you left behind. Or about me. I don't exist. Keep that in mind."

He kissed her and joined the throng of people in the Lufthansa line for the flight to Frankfurt. Security was a nightmare, with the line snaking all the way from the scanners to the main terminal. He made the gate eight minutes before his scheduled departure. The attendants had closed the flight, but reopened the computer file and ran his boarding pass through the machine. More and more people late for their departure times. In one way, the terrorists were winning by impacting millions of travelers every day.

Russell settled into the flight and played the mental tape of his meeting with Anita Greenwall. She had pushed for the network to take him on as a contract journalist to ferret out why the American involvement wasn't working. Why was Afghanistan a rat's nest of death and disappointment? Somehow, she figured, the answer lay with the civilians. He liked the angle. It was new and fresh. America was getting tired of seeing coffins draped in the stars and stripes on their local television stations. What they didn't see, were the coffins being unloaded off transport planes arriving at Dover AFB in Delaware. They didn't see the bodies being taken into the mortuary units for autopsy. There were a lot of things the American public didn't see. They needed a different perspective and it was up to him to deliver.

Usually he didn't mind the danger, but Tina was right, this time felt different. No reason – it was the same as Iraq or Somalia or Haiti after the earthquake. Places he had been and had survived. Mogadishu was the worst. A failed government, militia serving all-powerful warlords, and street thugs with loaded guns. Nothing nice about the Somali capital. *Blackhawk Down*, one of his favorite movies of all time, had portrayed it for what it was. A total clusterfuck.

He had faced irate men armed with guns and had seen people die violently. His memories harbored injustice beyond what any normal person could imagine. The worst of what he filmed was deemed too offensive and never aired on the major networks. This was the footage that got buried in the vastness of the Internet, where the government had trouble sterilizing things. He wondered if the film from this trip was destined for the digital bone yard, or if it would be edited for the six o'clock news. He had mixed feelings about that. Part of him wanted it on the major network – part of him wanted the story that could never be told. It was the stories that never made the news that held the most impact.

Anita was the reason he was on the plane. She was a veteran newswoman who knew the industry and pushed for the truth. He respected her and knew she would do everything she could to get the best stories on the air. But even she had her limitations. The American people could take only so much truth. At least that was the network's logic.

A flight attendant passed by and offered him snacks and a drink. He thanked her and ripped open the small bag of pretzels. Such a simple thing, having a bite to eat on an airplane. Yet in five days he would enter a world where opening pretzels was a treat and flying to another continent was unthinkable. Where war had raged continuously for twenty-five years and survival was the order of the day.

He'd seen it before. The vile acts of murder and rape, always perpetrated on the weak and vulnerable. He hated it. The scenes haunted him while he slept and even when he was awake. The eyes – the stares of those about to die – burned into his soul. There was no escaping the horror. And now he was heading directly into the storm.

He asked himself the same questions he did every time he left the comfort and safety of Boston and climbed aboard a plane destined for a war zone. Why? Why did he do it? Why risk his life to give the world such sad images? Why did he care? The answer was always the same. The oppressed deserved a voice and if he didn't do it, who would?

He finished the pretzels, pulled the window shade down and settled in to sleep.

CHAPTER 4

Soho, New York City

"When do you start?" Nicki asked.

"July 29th," Carson said. He stirred a touch of cilantro into the spaghetti sauce and tasted it. Perfect. He spread it on the steaming noodles and sat opposite Nicki at the rickety table.

"That's tomorrow." She broke a piece of bread and dipped it in the sauce, then bit into it and rolled her eyes back, a smile on her face. She touched her napkin against thin lips. Her hand unconsciously traced the bones above her gaunt cheeks. "This is good. Really good."

He smiled. "I'm not trying to take over the kitchen. It's still your domain."

She toyed with the strands of pasta for a minute, then said, "It's getting harder, Carson. I don't know how much longer I can cook."

He reached across the table and touched her hand. She had never asked to be born with cystic fibrosis. The disease was genetic. It just happened. "We can deal with it."

She grasped his hand and squeezed. "Why are you marrying me?" she asked. "You know this isn't forever."

"I'll take whatever time I can have with you." He looked around the cramped room, at the peeling cabinets and scratched laminate. The wallpaper had teapots on a floral background and the curtains were striped polyester. Two years was too long. Twenty-four months of living in a rental that needed work while they saved every extra dollar toward a place of their own. He was done with the apartment. Nicki deserved more than this for the waning years of her short life. "Let's hand in our notice and move."

"When?"

"Now," he said. "We have the down payment for a small place in Midtown. The new position is almost twice my salary and the bonuses will push it to four times. I'll check around the office and see if anyone knows a good Realtor."

Nicki set her fork on the side of the plate. Her breathing was shallow and she coughed, bringing up liquid into her napkin.

Carson stood and came around to her side of the table. He knelt on the chipped lino and pulled her against him. She shuddered and sucked air into her damaged lungs, tears running freely. This was the hardest part of their relationship. Making Nicki understand that he didn't want to be with anyone else. That there was no pity in the gamut of emotions he felt for her. Love, caring, adoration – but not pity. Not an ounce.

He wanted to tell her that he had lied to William Fleming about why he was marrying her. It had nothing to do with commitment. It had everything to do with love. But that was one secret he would take with him to the grave. He would never repeat those words again. Ever. He'd assessed the moment and guessed at what the man wanted to hear. The reward was a job almost every Massachusetts Institute of Technology MBA would kill to have. High Frequency Trades accounted for over seventy percent of the daily stock trades in the US. And he was running the division of a major player. It was an opportunity to influence business on a global scale. The chance of a lifetime. Telling Fleming he was marrying Nicki because he had committed to her was a white lie with no downside.

If that was the truth, he wondered why did he feel so dirty.

Carson lifted her chin and wiped a tear from her cheek. "You and I," he said quietly, "are going to find a nice, cozy place close to the park. We'll get a dog and call it some stupid name that means something to us and no one else. And we'll walk the little guy every day."

"Every day," she repeated. The tears had stopped. "Dogs need walking every day."

"Except when it's brutally cold."

"Okay."

"And raining or sleeting or snowing. Or too hot. We can't walk him if it's too hot."

She smacked him on the arm. "Let's get a wiener dog. A little brown one. They're cute."

He shook his head. "No way. They take too long to let in when it's cold outside."

"Funny," she said. She kissed him and pushed him away. "Go back to your side of the table and eat your dinner. You're only over here because you're after my spaghetti sauce."

Nicki finished her dinner and headed for the living room. She plopped into her favorite spot on the couch and flicked on the television. A news program was on but it didn't register. She was thinking about Carson – and her disease.

The CF was progressing. Attacking whatever healthy cells were left in her lungs. Making it almost impossible to get enough air. It was like breathing through a tiny tube – constantly feeling like she was asphyxiating. Which she was. Not quite enough to kill her. Not yet. But that was coming, and faster than she had hoped. She was a realist and had long accepted that she wouldn't live a long life. No children, few plans for the future, and until a couple of years ago, no partner. No one to share the days and nights with. Until Carson.

She glanced into the kitchen. He was at the sink doing the dishes. She wanted to help, to wash or dry, but it wasn't possible. The effort was too much. The last time she had tried to stand for long enough to clean the kitchen she had collapsed. Broke her finger when she threw her hand out to cushion the fall. That was the last time he had allowed her to stand at the sink for any length of time. Most days he came home from work, cooked dinner, served it, ate and cleaned the mess. Then he sat on the couch with her and held her hand as they watched a movie or one of their favorite programs. She teared up watching him. He was so kind, so thoughtful, so loving. And he was hers.

He wanted to marry her. A woman with end-stage cystic fibrosis. On the list for a lung transplant. Waiting. Enduring each day, hoping for the call that might extend her life. She had no idea why he loved her. He did though, and that was good enough.

"What's on?" Carson asked, joining her.

"Good movie on HBO."

"Romantic comedy?"

"Boy movie." She snuggled in against him. "You deserve it. Big promotion at work, excellent spaghetti sauce, and you cleaned the kitchen. I think you should have a movie with guns and stuff."

"You're the best," Carson grinned.

* * *

Midtown Manhattan, New York City

Fleming dialed Jorge Amistav's cell phone and waited. He hated waiting. Line-ups. Traffic lights. Ringing telephones. Waiting on things or people cost him money. He had calculated the rate his net worth was increasing, then broke it down to the second. If he added an additional five-hundred million a year to his bottom line, and there were 31,536,000 seconds in each twelve month period, then he was earning $15.85 every second of every day. He counted silently as he waited. Amistav answered after five rings – twenty-seven seconds. Waiting for the arms dealer to answer the phone had cost him $427.95 in lost time.

"I have a couple of questions about the deal," Fleming said.

"Go ahead."

"Where will the arms be deployed?"

"The 5th Stryker Brigade, 2nd Infantry Division is entrenched in Spin Buldak. It's in Afghanistan, about 60 miles from Kandahar. The delivery works well for them."

"Why?"

"The Stryker is an eight-wheel armored combat vehicle that carries six to eight Javelin shoulder-fired anti-tank rockets. The soldiers accompanying the Strykers can blow up buildings where snipers or Taliban troops are hiding. Problem is, the Javelins cost eighty grand each, so the military brass only put two, maybe three, on each vehicle. The infantry hate that. So we come in with two hundred and fifty of these things and they love us. That puts a cool twenty million in your pocket."

"You can reroute the Javelins to Spin Buldak?"

"Easily. We make sure it's a normal shipment, with a couple of 81mm Mortars, some M134D mini guns and the M-4s."

"M-4s?"

"The M-4 is an M-16 with a shorter barrel and a collapsible stock."

"Okay. So is that the entire shipment?"

"That's it. We'll throw in a few cases of ammo so the thing looks legit."

"What's the cost on the mini guns and the large bore mortars?"

"The mortars are one-point-five each and the mini guns run about a quarter million."

"Two hundred and fifty thousand for a mini gun?"

"That's not a very accurate name. They fire three thousand 7.62mm rounds a minute. Nasty machines."

"What about the M-4s? They're cumbersome. Can we eliminate them?"

"The small arms are part of the deal. It's all or nothing. My guy won't ship the big-ticket items without including the rifles. He's adamant on that."

Fleming toyed with the idea of simply hanging up and getting on with the next deal. There was risk associated with Amistav's proposal. What bothered him most was the bulk of the shipment. The M4s didn't add much profit to the bottom line. Still, thirty-five million and no tax. It would buy him a house and yacht in St. Bart's. He didn't have a place in the Caribbean. Hadn't since he'd sold his Cayman Island estate in 2006. He liked the Caribbean. A new place would be nice.

"If I can invoice the Pentagon through a shell corporation I have in the Caribbean, you have a deal," he said.

"That's between you and the Pentagon."

Fleming ran through the paper trail in his mind. The shell corporation was registered in the Cayman Islands, and it was linked to a second numbered company in the Seychelles. The board of directors for the Seychelles company was six men spread over four Eastern European countries. All of them fictitious. The money coming in to both the companies was forwarded through a chain of offshore bank accounts. Providing the money was legitimate, each bank was protective of their client's identities. And few things were more legitimate than a check from the US military. He could make it work without the trail leading back to him.

"My net is thirty-five million US dollars, after expenses?"

"Yes."

"Okay. I'll wire you three-point-five million to cover half your fee and the cash to purchase the weapons." There was a pause and Fleming knew the man was deciding whether or not to complain about not getting his entire fee upfront. "You still there?"

"Yeah. That's fine. You have my account number?" Amistav tried to sound upbeat but irritation clouded his voice.

"Probably, from the last deal we did. E-mail it to me just in case. Send it to my private e-mail, not my Platinus one."

"Okay," Amistav said.

Fleming hung up and walked over to the window. New York was a different city from forty-seven floors above the sidewalks that ran along the Avenue of the Americas. Quieter. More refined. It lost the raw edge that the street injected. The constant bombardment of noise and activity that saturated every pore of Midtown Manhattan. He liked the city both ways. It depended on his mood. There were times when he walked the streets, another worker among a throng of similar faces and suits that crowded the concrete, enjoying the congestion. Other times, like tonight, he preferred his perch far above the streetscape. Sterile. Removed from the mundane world.

Dusk was throwing long shadows over Central Park, and he turned back to his office. His desk was clean, only one sheet of paper left from the day's business. The cover page on Carson Grant. The young MBA was a good pick. He was bright and ambitious. But the defining trait that had won Carson the coveted job was his detachment from emotion. It would serve the job description well. He pushed the paper to the side of his desk and touched the computer mouse. The screen lit up and he searched for a phone number in his directory. Trey Miller. Florida area code. He wondered why this particular man lived in Florida. It seemed so out of character. He dialed the number and lifted the phone from its cradle.

"Yes?"

Fleming liked Miller. His one-word greetings and answers. Decisive and intelligent. "Trey, it's Bill Fleming."

"Good evening, Mr. Fleming."

"I have something I'd like you to look into."

"Where and when?" Miller asked.

"Moscow. The latter part of August."

"I can make that work."

"We should meet," Fleming said.

"I can be in New York by Friday."

"Ten in the morning. The east side of Bryant Park."

"Between the library and the lawn?" Miller asked.

"Yes. There are lots of tables and chairs. Shouldn't be a problem finding an open one at that time of day."

"Fine. I'll see you there at ten o'clock."

Fleming ended the call and set the phone back in its cradle. Trey Miller was ex-CIA, a covert operative who was tied into the underbelly of American interests throughout the world. He refused to talk about the twenty-one years he had spent with the agency, other than to say it was an interesting time in his life. Fleming had spent over a million dollars digging into Miller's past and had managed to piece together a hazy picture of the agent's time with the agency. None of it was pretty.

Miller had left a trail of dead foreign agents across the Baltics and the breakaway republics of Uzbekistan and Tajikistan. He spoke six languages fluently, including Russian, and could enter and exit countries without leaving a trail. Trey Miller was a very dangerous chameleon. And perhaps the man who could derail the concert and disgrace Dimitri Volstov. Just thinking about yanking Volstov down a few notches on the world ladder brought a smile to his face. He harbored few grudges, but this was one that refused to die. It was time to do something about it, and Moscow was looking to be the place. He'd find out on Friday when he talked to Miller.

Revenge. Served cold. He liked the sound of that.

CHAPTER 5

Kandahar, Afghanistan

The hunger never left. Never.

Kadir Hussein shuffled through the market, his mangled hand tucked under his tattered robe. His stomach contracted and he tasted acid in his back of his mouth. He swallowed it back and felt the burn in his throat. Three days without a proper meal was too long. Even for a belly used to going empty. Any food he had earned or begged had gone to the children. Aaqila and Danah had eaten and slept well, but Halima had refused to eat any rice or naan bread until her younger sisters were finished. Only scraps were left. Not enough to nourish a growing eleven year old girl.

Today would be better. Kadir had a chance to work and the pay was good. A crew from the Iranian Red Crescent was working on a new well in a small square located in the oldest section of Kandahar. They needed men to move bricks and mortar through the labyrinth of narrow streets by hand. They were paying three American dollars a day. More than he could hope to earn sweeping stalls in the market. Enough to buy some onions, rice and bread for the evening meal. Maybe there would be some for him after his daughters had eaten.

Maybe.

Halima was watching her sisters and he was confident they would be fine for the day by themselves. The Taliban never entered the town anymore. At least, not in force. Kadir knew they were among them, walking about with the impunity that came with having Pashtun heritage and speaking the language. It was almost impossible to tell who was Taliban until they let it be known. And that was usually by violence or cruelty. He didn't care if they shared the same street or the same water fountain. He only cared if they hurt him or his children.

When that happened, the hate surfaced.

It burned deep inside him, a simmering fire that would never be extinguished. Time healed some wounds, but not all. And there was one wound in him that would never fade into the past. It was far too deep, and penetrated beyond muscle and bone. It resided in a tiny space in his mind. The spot reserved for things too horrible – too unthinkable – to ever happen. Except to him. And countless thousands of other Afghans.

God how he hated the Taliban. But it hadn't started with them. It had started with the Russians.

Kadir rounded a corner, his robe brushing against a mud wall that had seen countless invaders enter Afghanistan. And the same number leave. He was only fourteen when the Russian army descended on Kabul and the nightmare began. In his mind, nothing worse could happen. He could still taste the diesel fumes from the tanks as they rumbled down his street, and when he closed his eyes to sleep, the soldiers were everywhere, their Kalashnikovs slung over their shoulders and cigarettes dangling from their lips.

They took what they wanted. At first it was the nicest homes and newest cars. But there was only so much luxury in Kandahar and after three years they were at his father's door. The family house held little of value. His father was a merchant in the Kabul Darwaza, a market filled with trinkets and second hand goods, and they lived a simple life. The soldiers didn't care. They smashed open the cupboards and kicked the furniture into worthless piles of splintered wood. They grabbed the meager bits of food and shattered the solitary window. When his brother told them to stop, they beat him with their rifle butts until he was unconscious and bleeding on the floor. He watched, his fists clenched, wanting to rip a rifle from their hands and kill them. His father sensed his thoughts and silently shook his head. Resistance meant death.

Three weeks after the first visit the soldiers returned. This time they simply took his father and left. One of their neighbors, a man who was in the favor of the commanding officer, discreetly inquired into the disappearance. He was told they had taken the elder Hussein to Pul-i Charkhi prison near Kabul. No charges were pending, but he was being held in a twelve by twelve cell with twenty-five other men. None of them were charged with a crime, but punishment was being doled out. Slowly, by some sort of diseased attrition, they vanished. One at a time. The jailer opened the cell door and called out a name. The man walked out the door and didn't come back. To the men inside, it was a sign that freedom was possible. That if their name was the one that passed over the jailer's lips, they would feel the sun on their face. That was true, but only for a moment. Then a single bullet in the back of their skull ended the misery.

Kadir had no idea how long his father survived in the dank, horrid space. It didn't matter. He had died at the hands of the Russians, and for that, he despised them. His older brother had left the family home and joined the mujahedeen before his father died and he too found a shallow grave in the cold, unforgiving hills. But the day the Russian soldiers raped and beat his mother to death was the grimmest day of his life. They had taken so much, and left nothing.

He gave thanks to Allah every day for the horrors his native country had inflicted on the Russian armies. Extreme temperatures, rugged and unforgiving terrain, and the incessant attacks by the mujahedeen. But of all the hardships that Afghanistan could throw at the Russians, their slow and inevitable slide into drug addiction was the worst. Hashish, laced with heroin and opium, cracked open the door, and once the soldiers had tasted the high of Afghanistan's poppy-derived drugs they couldn't get enough. It dulled the drudgery and enhanced the danger. It was no surprise to anyone when the Soviets turned their tanks around and slunk back to their own borders in February of 1989. But ten years of war had left a terrible scar – one and a half million Afghans dead and six million in exile.

Kadir's father was one of the faceless dead.

Three years of relative calm slipped by, then Kabul fell to the mujahedeen and that triggered two years of civil war. The country was tearing itself apart at the seams. Kabul was constantly under siege from one faction or another. Once the capital fell, the US and its allies forgot about the decade of misery the people had suffered under the Soviets and turned their backs on the Afghans. The country was left on its own to struggle with its demons. To Kadir, life with or without the Russians wasn't much different. The warlords who controlled the southern third of the country were merely other violent dictators sitting atop broken thrones. They exacted a heavy toll on the locals, and Kadir learned quickly to keep his head low and his voice even lower.

But neither the Russians nor the warlords could have prepared him for the brutality of the Taliban. They were in a class of their own when it came to hateful behavior. Kadir focused on the dusty road at his feet and forced any thought of the Taliban from his mind. Today was a good day and the black-turbaned monsters deserved no part of it.

The Old City was crowded, street vendors hawking everything from mobile phone cards to opium poppy scrapers. The odor of spicy *karai* was strong, the mutton and chili mixture available on almost every street corner. None of the vendors paid Kadir any attention. His shalwar kameez had frayed sleeves and was a glaring testament to his lack of money and low position in society. At one corner, three members of the Afghan National Police leaned against one of the low, stone buildings and he averted his gaze. They sucked on their cigarettes and watched him with disinterested eyes. He reached the square and walked tentatively across to an Iranian attired in western dress. The man smiled as Kadir approached.

"Kadir?" he asked.

"Yes."

"Can I see your identity card, please?" the man asked in fluent Pashto. His black hair was cut short and the Iranian Red Crescent insignia was embroidered on his shirt.

Kadir fumbled with his identification, keeping his right hand under his robe. He finally found it and passed it over. The man surveyed it closely, then handed it back.

"You are forty-five years old?" he asked. Kadir nodded and the man said. "Maybe that is too old for this work."

"There is nothing bad with me. I can work. Very hard."

"What's wrong with your hand?" he asked.

"Nothing," Kadir said. He showed the man his good hand.

"The other one. The one inside your shirt." He pointed. "Show me."

Kadir pulled his right hand from his shirt so it was visible.

The Red Crescent worker stared for a moment, then said, "How did this happen?"

The memories of the incident flooded his brain. The tall, heavily-bearded Talib accusing him of stealing an orange from a vendor's stall. He, muttering that he had done nothing wrong. That he was not a thief. The Talib had simply smiled and told him that he could take his punishment now or in the soccer stadium on Friday. Kadir knew that option. Every Friday afternoon thieves and adulterers were ushered onto the field in front of a somber crowd. The thieves were the lucky ones. They had one hand sliced off with a saber. The adulterers – almost always women – were not so fortunate. Screaming their innocence, they were put to death by volleys of stones thrown by young Taliban fighters. That most of them had been raped was an irrelevant detail.

Kadir told the Talib he would take the punishment on the spot. He put his hand on the rough stone road and closed his eyes. He felt the rifle butt hitting his hand, his fingers, his wrist. Crushing the bones into dust. He wanted to scream in pain but knew that one sound and he would die. He thought of his father and tried to remember his face. It had been fifteen years since the Russians had taken him from the house and dragged him through the dark streets to prison. No matter how hard he tried, he couldn't conjure up an image. Only blackness.

Any tears he cried that day were not from the savage mutilation of his hand. They were tears of sorrow for the unjustified murder of his father.

Kadir looked down at his hand. "An accident," he said to the Iranian. "It was caught in a piece of machinery."

"Can you carry bricks?" the man asked.

"Yes," Kadir replied confidently. "For hours, without a break. I am very strong and work hard."

Kadir forced a brave face as the Iranian studied him. Three US dollars hung in the balance. A week of food for his children. Seconds ticked by. A fly landed on his face but he didn't flinch.

"Of course you can carry bricks," the man said with a gentle smile. He turned to a Pashtun standing to one side. "Kadir will be working with us today. Show him what to do."

"Thank you," Kadir said. He felt the tears coming and willed them to stop.

They didn't.

CHAPTER 6

Midtown Manhattan, New York City

Platinus Investments was a monster.

Not a huge monster if you compared it to the other Wall Street firms in the number of people on the payroll or the total square footage of leased office space. Platinus stood out where it was important. On the profit/loss side of the ledger sheet. They made money. A lot of money. And more than half of it came from their High Frequency Trading division. The same division that Carson Grant assumed responsibility for on Thursday, July 29th.

It was familiar territory. He had worked in the HFT sector of Platinus for three years, first as a programmer, coding other mathematicians' works, then later, designing the algorithms. The algos, as they were called in the industry, fueled the lightning-fast computers that bought and sold hundreds of millions of shares every day on the US stock market exchanges. It was the algos that were crucial to trading in the high frequency world. If your program was one millisecond – one one-thousandth of a second – slower than the guy down the street, then you were the first loser in making the trade. They were the winner. And in the algo trading industry, you were first or you were out of business.

The computers were one of the keys. They had super-fast CPUs and weren't restricted by input-output at any stage of the game. They performed on a level that NASA dreamt of. Locating the computers close to the stock exchanges was another key. The time delay in transmitting signals across Manhattan at the speed of light was enough to add a millisecond to the data transfer. Platinus had their systems located immediately next to the NYSE and NASDAQ. Alongside their hardware were the supercomputers that churned out data for their main competition, Citigroup and Goldman Sachs.

But the computers were nothing without the algorithms. Programs that analyzed hundreds of thousands of offers to buy or sell and predicted which direction a stock was headed before it started down the road. Once the program anticipated what was going to happen, it jammed the market with thousands of orders that were withdrawn before they could be filled, providing further evidence of what other investors were willing to pay. Within a second, the algo sampled every bit of available data, correlated it against the numbers from the previous day's trading tape and determined exactly what was going to happen in the immediate future. And once they knew how things were going to play out, they pulled out their trump card. The thirty-millisecond delay.

Thirty milliseconds is far less than a blink of the eye, but it's enough time for the HFT algorithms to determine the direction a stock is going to move and send out buy and sell orders. The faster the system and its algos, the quicker it can flood the market with orders. All of this happens before non-HFT firms looking to sell are even aware of the buy orders from the other, slower traders. While the markets are supposed to be a level playing field, nothing could be further from the truth. The thirty-millisecond delay completely destroyed that myth. It gave the fast traders an advantage that simply could not be measured. If you were a firm that engaged in high frequency trading, and paid the exchange a fee, the delay was all yours. As was a rebate paid by the NASDAQ or the NYSE to the traders who brought the lion's share of their business to that particular exchange. It was nothing more than salt in the wounds suffered by the slower traders.

And it was unregulated. No laws existed to stop the HFT firms from paying the fee and accessing crucial information before the other 18,000 trading firms that played by the rules. The Securities and Exchange Commission was under fire from politicians like Senator Charles Schumer who was threatening to enact laws to bring fairness back to the business of trading stocks. But to date, nothing was in place. Which meant Platinus Investments was raking in cash faster than they could count it. Billions of dollars a year.

Billions. Unregulated.

It still amazed Carson Grant that something so fundamental could be so screwed up. Americans embraced democracy and capitalism, so long as everything was fair. Every American had the right to own a house, to start a business, to live the dream. Many chose the safe route and worked for a company, drew a wage and went home at five o'clock and forgot about the job. They were fine with the system, because no one was cheating. At least, they weren't getting caught. But Carson knew that assumption was absolutely false. Platinus, Goldman Sachs, Citigroup and the rest of the HFT firms were exploiting a loophole. Legally. But it was exploitation nonetheless. And it was very profitable.

It bothered him. But not enough to say anything. Or refuse his bi-weekly paycheck or yearly bonus.

Thursday, July 29th dawned sunny, and Carson caught a cab from his Soho apartment to the office. The subway was so crowded. So mundane. The taxi gave him time to think about his first day as the head of the HFT department at Platinus. He reached inside his suit pocket and withdrew the folded 8.5 x 11 sheet of white paper. An e-mail from William Fleming. It was simple and to the point.

Carson,

Hope you enjoy your first day as division head. There is something I'd like you to look at immediately. Somebody is gaming us and we need to front-run them. Probably Goldman. Trim the algo. Beat them at their own game.

~Bill

He tucked the memo back in his pocket and stared out the window as the congestion of Manhattan slipped past. One of the big players was running a faster algorithm and sniffing out the buy/sell orders from the slower traders quicker than Platinus. Then they were offering flash orders on a specific exchange for a few milliseconds, making them a poster, not a responder. Being a poster was a much better position to be in, especially if another trader jumped in and grabbed the order. If they did and a sale went through, the flash-order trader was in a position to receive the rebate. And although the rebates weren't huge, if a company had millions of them coming in every year, they were making serious money.

Bottom line was – another firm was making the money. Something Fleming wanted stopped immediately.

The cab pulled up in front of 1177 Avenue of the Americas. Carson paid the driver and took the elevator to the forty-sixth floor, one level below Fleming's private domain. The top of the financial food chain was coming into focus, and he liked what he saw. The elevator opened and he glanced about. It was different from the eighteenth floor, where he had been sequestered with nine other mid-level players in the HFT division. The eighteenth floor was where the algos were devised and written into computer code, and it was a bullpen-style office, with desks scattered around a central group of whiteboards. Here, on the forty-sixth floor, where the code was applied to the real world and turned into gains and losses, soft music played on the sound system and the floors were covered in thick carpet.

"Good morning, Mr. Grant." The woman was young, maybe twenty-five, and dressed conservatively in a white blouse and mid-length grey skirt. Her shoes were polished and her fingernails painted a light shade of blue, which matched her belt perfectly. "I'm Nadine Strang. Welcome to forty-six."

"Thanks."

"Your office is this way," she said, not extending her hand, nor expecting him to offer his. She pointed down a hallway to the right and started walking. "The coffee room is tucked in behind this false wall, but if you want anything, just call me and I'll bring it to you. We have a latte machine if you prefer. There are sandwiches, muffins and salads brought in every day. If you want lunch delivered from a local restaurant, let me know the day before and I'll put in the order."

They reached the end of the hall and Nadine continued into the corner office. The opposing wall looked north and had the same view of Central Park as William Fleming's. To the right of the door, the wall was fitted with ebony bookshelves. Carson glanced at the books and pictures that filled about half of the shelves. There were six pictures of Nicki and him and his math and physics texts were neatly arranged by category. He looked at Nadine and shrugged.

"We had everything moved up from eighteen last night," she said.

"Very efficient."

She smiled. "You have no idea."

"What's that?" he asked, pointing to a door on the wall to the left of the entrance.

"Your private bathroom."

Carson walked across the soft carpet and poked his head through the doorway. It was far more than just a sink and toilet. An open closet butted up against the oversize shower. Three suits hung over polished shoes, with six shirts of varying colors next to them. He turned and looked at Nadine.

"These are mine?"

She nodded. "Mr. Fleming has a tailor who can custom fit suits from your image on the security camera. Overnight. Not really rocket science, but impressive."

"Very," Carson said. He returned to the office and sat in the leather chair behind the desk. A flat screen monitor and a pad of paper with a pen were the only items on the surface. He looked out the bank of windows. The view of the park was stunning.

"Is there anything else?" Nadine asked.

"Yes," Carson said. He slid the paper in front of him and jotted down six names. "Could you have these people meet me at nine tomorrow morning in the boardroom?" He handed her the sheet of paper. "We do have a boardroom on this floor, don't we?"

Another smile. "Yes, we do. I'll reserve it for you for nine o'clock tomorrow morning. How long will you need it for?"

"Probably one to two hours."

"I'll slot you in from nine to twelve. That way you won't have to worry about hurrying."

"Thank you."

Nadine disappeared into the hall and Carson leaned back in the chair. Yesterday he had walked into William Fleming's office, nervous and hopeful. Today, his dreams had gelled. The countless thousands of hours spent hunched over math and physics books at MIT. Stressing out at exam time. Eating poorly, driving a rusted-out Toyota with no spare tire. All memories now. This was his new reality. Forty-six floors above the congestion and noise of Manhattan. A million a year in salary and bonuses. This moment justified the rigor of seven years in one of the nation's most prestigious and demanding schools.

He reached out and dialed his home number. There was little doubt that his first call, from this new perch in his life, would be to the woman he loved. Nicki answered the phone and he smiled. He was happy. Truly happy. And that was something not everyone could say.

CHAPTER 7

Midtown Manhattan, New York City

Five men and one woman were seated at the table when Carson Grant entered the boardroom at precisely nine o'clock Friday morning. He greeted each of them by name and shook their hands. Then he took the chair at the head of the table and opened a thin file.

"I'm glad you could all make it," he said.

One of the younger men, Asian with a thick thatch of jet-black hair and a wide face, said, "You're the boss now, Carson. You ask, we come."

"We're still a team, Chui," Carson said. "In fact, you guys are lucky. If one of those other guys had snagged this job, you'd be in deep trouble. Nobody from outside the group could ever understand how you guys think." He looked at the lone female. "And by guys, I mean you too, Alicia. Especially you."

"Same old Carson," she said. "Except you're dressing a bit better and..." she looked around the ebony and glass room, "...living in some kind of nice digs."

Alicia Crane had been with Platinus three years longer than Carson, and they had worked alongside each other almost every day. She was Harvard educated and second only to Chui Chang in her skill at cutting math-based code, but her biggest challenge was fitting into the nattily dressed Manhattan landscape. Carson had told her on more than one occasion that she resembled fashion road kill. She couldn't have cared less.

"If you think *this* is nice, you should see my office," he grinned.

"Are you inviting me to your office, Carson?" Alicia asked. She was a fit and vibrant African-American woman with a sharp mind. And she liked to tease. "That could be grounds for a monster sexual harassment lawsuit."

"Dream on," Carson said. "You and I have spent a thousand hours together in one office or another and nothing happened. I don't think you stand much of a chance of milking any easy money out of the firm. You're going to have to earn it."

"Damn," she said.

Carson scanned the people at the table. In addition to Chui and Crane, who were whizzes in pure and applied math, there were four men, all between thirty and forty-five. Dan Loewen was a programmer who analyzed the tapes from the previous day's trading on the NASDAQ, BATS, Direct Edge and the New York exchange. NASDAQ alone generated fifty gigabytes of data on any given trading day. It was measured in nanoseconds, which is a billionth of a second. The amount of data was staggering, but it revealed other firms' trading strategies. Knowing what the competition was doing was crucial. As was Dan Loewen's legendary expertise.

Arthur Black was a forty-year-old bachelor who lived at Platinus. They all kidded him that he didn't have a place in Manhattan, and the couch in his room was actually his primary address. He spent his waking hours at Platinus reviewing Dan Loewen's reports and structuring their trading strategies accordingly. His group, totaling thirteen people, issued flash orders and immediate or cancel orders, or IOCs, to help establish Platinus as a market-maker. By being recognized as a market-maker – a firm that drove the market valuation – they were considered to be one of the big fish in the pond. A highly important role to play in the cutthroat trading business.

Allan Dannos and his team operated in the dark pools – exchanges where almost every order was iceberged. Iceberged orders were entirely anonymous, and it was in the dark pools that gamers sniffed out the large orders by using a mathematical equivalent of sonar to ping them. Once they located a large incoming order, they initiated a series of trades to front-run it, and grabbed the stock before the larger order, submitted by a slower trading firm, had time to close. If one was to compare Platinus to the US government, Allan Dannos's team was the CIA. Covert and dangerous.

What Ray Moore did at Platinus was much more visible. His team monitored global trends. They analyzed the tapes from Toronto, Tokyo, London and every other major exchange. Global positions were becoming increasingly important in the commodities and derivative markets, and Platinus was on top of every trend. Usually before the trend showed itself.

"Fleming thinks we're being gamed," Carson said to the group. "That someone is beating us to the punch." He let the words sink in for a few seconds. To the people in that room, being gamed was the equivalent of an Olympian running a good race and coming in second. Silver wasn't the goal. Silver was the first loser. "They're seeing the patterns and initiating their algos before ours kick in. We're losing somewhere in the range of six to twelve million shares a day. That's about twenty to forty million a year in lost revenue, not counting the lost rebates from the exchanges. And that's only one other trader beating us by a millisecond or two. I'm sure we're being gamed in more than one arena right now." He looked around the silent table. All eyes were on him. "Fleming feels we're losing about a hundred million a year. We need to stop the bleeding."

"What's the approach?" Allan Dannos asked.

"Multi-pronged, as I see it. You guys are welcome to share whatever strategies you have, but I think the key to getting competitive is the algorithm."

"We have the best in the business," Dannos argued.

"We *had* the best," Carson corrected him. "Someone built a better mousetrap. We need to catch them."

"Who is *them*?" Ray Moore asked.

"We suspect it's Goldman."

"Thought so," Alicia said tersely. "It's hard to keep up to them. They throw a shitload of money at research."

"So do we," Carson shot back.

"You said the approach to fixing this is multi-pronged," Chui said. "What else, aside from the algos?"

"Trading strategies. We need to front-run more. To sniff out the big orders and jump in front of them."

"The algos cover that," Chui pointed out.

"To some degree," Carson said. "But there's a human factor here that we need to address. We need to point the computers in the right direction. Identifying the highest liquidity is a key. And the lowest latency. Nothing replaces the human mind for seeking the big picture. We're looking for trends that are too big for the algos to see."

"I guess that's me," Ray Moore said.

"That's you, Ray," Carson said.

"Shit. I wanted a week off with the girlfriend."

"Well, you can have one. But not until November."

"It's July, Carson." Moore rolled his eyes and shook his head. "It looks like Fleming picked the right guy to crack the whip."

Carson grinned. "If you need a break, Ray, you let me know. The same goes for everyone at this table. We're going to kick some Goldman ass, and we can't do that if you're not at the top of your game."

The meeting ran for fifty minutes, then Carson shut his file. "That's it, we're done." He glanced at Alicia. "Can you hang back for a couple of minutes?"

They filed out and when the door was closed, Carson said, "I need you to strip a millisecond off the algo."

She looked confused. "We talked about that. It's a process-driven thing. Chui and I and our teams will work through it."

Carson toyed with his pen. "I want you to shave off a couple of iterations. Streamline it."

Alicia stared at him. The edges of her mouth curled down slightly. "That's a quick-fix, Carson. And it's dangerous. It'll attack the integrity of the whole thing and possibly destabilize it."

Carson rose from his chair and dropped into the one next to her. "Maybe, but I doubt it. We use seven iterations now. We sample the data seven times and take the average. Like a bell curve. If we cut it down to five we have the same curve.

And we're a millisecond faster."

"It'll save a mil, but five iterations is sketchy. The algo needs seven to properly sample the data. A couple of glitches and we'll be basing our trades on erroneous information. You know this, Carson, I don't need to tell you. This algorithm is your baby."

Carson waved his hand. "Like you said, it's a short term fix. We'll find another way to save time. But for right now, I need you to take two iterations out of the loop."

She was silent, her eyes boring into his. "Are you *telling* me to do this?" she finally asked.

"Yes."

Alicia gathered up her papers from the meeting and slipped them into her briefcase. "Anything else?" she asked.

He shook his head. "When can you have the changes made and implemented?"

"Today is Friday. I can spend some time working on it over the weekend and if there are no problems, it'll be modified, tested and functioning by Monday morning."

"Perfect," he said, then added. "I know this isn't the best fix, but it's temporary. We'll have a new, faster algo in no time. It's not like we're cutting back to three iterations. Slicing two out of the algo isn't the end of the world."

She managed a small smile. "I hope not."

Carson watched her leave, then walked over to the window. The view of the park was from a different perspective than the one from his office, but equally as impressive. There was something about being forty-six floors above the sidewalk that gave him a warm feeling. It was difficult to define. Detachment. Entitlement. Power. Maybe just knowing that he had arrived. That he was part of the inner circle that shaped the financial lives of countless millions. That he had finally achieved the privileged position he had dreamt of for so long. He remembered one of his professors at MIT talking about privilege. That many of the school's graduates would find some degree of that in their lives. The man had linked another word to privilege. Responsibility. One didn't arrive without the other.

Carson glanced down at his watch. Five minutes to ten. Not bad. Six teams of highly educated men and women were scrambling to find a solution to the problem he had laid out in the boardroom a scant fifty minutes ago. This was power. And privilege. He liked it.

"Responsibility," he said quietly to himself. "I'll get on that next week."

He left the boardroom, a smile on his face.

CHAPTER 8

Bryant Park, New York City

Bryant Park was quiet. An oasis in the giant slab of concrete and glass that was Manhattan.

A handful of the tables and chairs between the lawn and the library were taken, but at ten in the morning, most were empty. In two hours, the lunch rush would descend on the park and finding a place to sit on anything but the grass would be tough. A thick wall of trees blocked out most of the buildings that towered over the park on three sides. To the east, the massive windows of the New York Public Library reading room watched over the park. That was the direction William Fleming approached from.

It was precisely on the top of the hour when Fleming entered the park and scanned the rows of metal tables for Trey Miller. He spotted the ex-CIA operative sitting next to the stone railing overlooking the grass. Miller was late forties and resembled a host of other similar-age white men in Manhattan. His off-blond hair was cut short, but not military, and he wore camel-colored dress pants and a dark blue shirt. He was average height, between five-ten and six feet, and carried little extra weight. The one feature that set Trey Miller aside from the slew of stock traders and book publishers that roamed the streets were his eyes. Incandescent blue and unblinking. They took in every detail – every potential threat – every weakness. They missed nothing. They were the reason Miller had survived twenty-one years in covert ops.

Fleming's shoes tapped out a steady cadence on the concrete as he cut past a group of men setting up a piano adjacent to the bar. Fleming glanced at the sky. Blue, without a trace of clouds. A good day to risk a bit of outdoor music. He reached Trey's table and sat without offering to shake hands.

"Hello, Trey."

"Bill."

Trey Miller was one of the few people who were thick enough with Fleming to call him by the shortened version of his first name. Their history was an interesting one, including how they met. When Miller left the CIA in 2005, he took an extensive mental dossier of names and places, and most importantly, incidents, with him. The agency was aware of the depth of knowledge Miller possessed and had to make a decision whether to kill him or leave him to flap in the breeze. Cool heads prevailed and they decided Miller wasn't the kind of man to kiss and tell. After a year of silence, one of the division heads decided to link Miller with William Fleming – a reward of sorts for keeping his secrets locked away. After all, Fleming was a man who paid well for professionalism and anonymity. Those were two things he could always expect from Trey Miller.

Miller had been firm at their first meeting. He didn't kill people anymore. He caused them some distress perhaps, but didn't kill them. Fleming had agreed and so far they had managed to stick to the rules. Miller handled sensitive issues for the billionaire, many related to Fleming's sexual appetite. Shutting up women who decided to chase the golden egg by blackmailing Fleming was a regular occurrence. Not that it really mattered if the details hit the trash mags – Fleming was single and could sleep with whomever he chose. Nonetheless, it didn't look good. So Miller dug up dirt on the women and their families, packaged it nicely and sat down with them over coffee. The results were predictable. They backed off and Bill Fleming went on to the next woman. Fleming's indiscretions were a good source of revenue for Trey Miller.

"What's up?" Miller asked.

Fleming leaned back against the metal chair. It was still cool, the sun had yet to clear the buildings and begin heating the park. "I have something interesting for you."

"I figured as much. Moscow in August isn't the usual gig."

"A Russian mobster, Dimitri Volstov, cheated me on a deal. Tens of millions of dollars. I'd like to repay the favor."

Miller eyed the man sitting opposite him. There were two ways this could play out. One was to feign ignorance about Volstov, the other was to be honest. He chose honesty. He always did with Fleming.

"Volstov isn't tied in with the Russian mafia," he said.

A touch of color showed in Fleming's face. "Not now," he said.

Trey didn't argue the point. He knew of Dimitri Volstov and the simple truth was, the man had never been allied with organized crime. He was one of the oligarchs who fed on the breakup of the Soviet Union. A well-connected businessman who was allied with other billionaires like Roman Abramovich and his circle of friends. Trey knew they were a lively bunch with their fingers in everything from steel mills to world-class football teams, but they weren't the mob.

"He stole money from me," Fleming hissed, leaning forward.

"Maybe. Probably. But that doesn't make him part of the Russian mafia. He owns the controlling share of Murmansk-Technika, which is a perfectly legitimate business operating out of Russia."

"Why is it so important that you correct me on this, Trey?" Fleming asked, settling back in his chair.

"Because if he *was* in the mob, I wouldn't touch this. Not a chance."

Fleming's eyes narrowed slightly, his interest piqued. "Why not?"

Miller shrugged. "If I cross paths with the Russian mafia, someone is going to die. It could be a few of them, it could be me. But people would get killed. And I stopped doing that. Remember?"

"Of course. The one rule you brought to the table." Fleming smiled, but there was no warmth in it. "The Russian mob, they scare you."

"Damn right. I'm telling you, Bill, people will die if you stir up that nest."

"All right. Back to Volstov. Will you deal with him?"

"He's on my list of approved Russian billionaires. What do you need done?"

Fleming ignored the sarcasm. It was refreshing in a way. No one else dared to talk to him like Trey Miller. "Volstov is the promoter for the U2 concert coming to Moscow on August 25th. I want you to ruin the concert. Take it apart. Embarrass him."

The ex-CIA man looked out over the park. He watched a couple throw a blanket on the grass and lie down next to each other. They sipped on coffee in paper cups and talked. The scene was banal to the point of making him sick. He glanced back at Fleming.

"Volstov is well-respected. He's competent and organized. He'll bring those qualities to the table with the concert."

"Probably," Fleming said. "But he's not a concert promoter. This is all new to him."

"Still, he'll surround himself with a good team. My guess is that he'll pull this off and the concert will be a resounding success."

"Unless we cause things to go wrong," Fleming said.

Slowly, Miller's head bobbed up and down. "I can probably do that." He was quiet for a few seconds, then said, "I'll need help. At least one person here and an entire crew on location in Moscow. That gets expensive."

"Money is no object."

Miller smiled broadly. "That makes things so much easier. Especially with such a tight time frame. August 25th is only twenty-six days from now."

"How much do you need?"

Trey pulled a small pad of paper and a pen from his pocket and jotted down a few notes and numbers. After the better part of thirty seconds, he said, "Let's start with seven hundred thousand. I'll probably need more, but I'll pay it out of my own pocket and bill you later."

"I'll wire you an even million." There was a long pause, then, "I don't want this traced back to me."

"Absolutely no chance."

"Excellent," Fleming said. He stood and looked down at Miller who didn't bother standing or offering his hand. "If you send me an e-mail in the next few hours, you can expect the money this afternoon."

Trey nodded. "I'll call you if I need anything, but I highly doubt that will happen."

Fleming turned on his heel and strode back across the concrete to West 40th, where a Navigator was waiting for him outside the Bryant Park Hotel. Two men in well-cut suits who had followed him into the park and watched while he talked with Trey Miller, slipped into a dark-colored car behind the Lincoln. A careful observer might have noticed the slight bulge in the men's jackets under their left arms. Fleming took his personal safety seriously. The vehicles pulled away from the curb and melded into the sea of yellow cabs.

Inside the Navigator, Fleming allowed himself a rare smile. Trey Miller was an asset without a tangible value. The man's ability to take on any task and find a solution was brilliant. He made a mental note to call his contact inside the Central Intelligence Agency – the man who had introduced him to Miller – and convey his thanks. Again. It wouldn't be the first time. Perhaps a week at his villa in St. Tropez would be a nice touch. His phone rang and he checked the call display. It was Jorge Amistav.

"Good morning, Jorge," he said. "What can I do for you?"

"Good morning. I received the three and a half million and forwarded the necessary amount to my contact. The merchandise is being crated in Germany and is being tagged for delivery to Kandahar. I e-mailed the info to you. I'll advise you when it arrives so you can send your invoice to the Pentagon."

"Is that all?"

"That's it for today."

"Good work. Thanks for calling." Fleming killed the line.

Thirty-five million dollars for a single arms shipment. More money than almost every person on the planet made in his or her lifetime. His for knowing the right people and having a paltry five million dollars in cash lying about. God he loved money. He loved what it bought. The respect it commanded. Money didn't care who owned it, and a lot of it had found its way into his accounts. Now he lived by the golden rule.

The person with the gold ruled.

It was his variation on an old adage. One he liked much better than the original.

CHAPTER 9

Kandahar, Afghanistan

Venturing into the streets of Kandahar was an adventure, even for the men who wore the traditional long *pirhan tonban* and carried a gun concealed beneath the flowing robes. For an eleven-year-old girl, with her little sisters in tow, it was insanity.

Halima peered out the tiny window that overlooked the city from their deteriorating room on the top floor of the abandoned apartment building. An endless mass of squat mud houses, few higher than two stories, stretched out toward the desert mountains that framed the distant horizon. A handful of kites fluttered above the labyrinth of twisting alleys, adding color to the bland, brown palette. Today she had to leave the security of their house and visit the market to buy fruit and vegetables. Her father had entrusted her with two US dollars, most of his pay from the previous day, with the understanding that she would barter with the merchants and bring home enough food to last for at least a week. Her hands shook as she tucked the money inside her loose shirt. So much money. Her father had worked so hard for it.

"Aaqila, Danah," she called. "It's time to go. Are you ready?"

Her younger sisters were dressed and anxious to get out of the house. To them, the streets and the market were an outing. Something to anticipate and treasure. At seven and five years old, they were too young to truly understand the danger. It was everywhere. The dusty streets were breeding grounds for insurgents and Taliban, and soldiers from the International Security Assistance Force were never far away, their automatic rifles tucked against their chests as they watched the foot traffic suspiciously. Bombed-out buildings lined the roads – piles of mud bricks that were houses at some time before the war. Unexploded shells lay under the rubble, a constant threat to children who foraged through the ruins searching for hidden trinkets. Landmines were always a problem, but more in the countryside and villages outside Kandahar than in the city itself. Still, one had to be cautious.

"Let's go," Halima said. She adjusted her headscarf and straightened Danah's as well. She tucked two ratty canvas bags under her arm. If it was a successful trip, they would be full on the return home.

They navigated the staircase with care. There was a stone wall on one side and a steep drop to the courtyard below on the other. Errant pieces of broken bricks made their footing treacherous. Halima had offered to clean the stairs, but her father had told her that if she did, scavengers would suspect someone was living in the building and climb up to see if there was anything of value on the upper floors. She understood all too well. In the last place they had lived, men with guns had kicked in the door and taken their food. The leader of the gang pushed his pistol against the side of her father's head. The way he held the gun – the look in his eyes – Halima knew he wanted to pull the trigger. But he didn't. The memory of her father after the men had left, hugging her and her sisters and crying, would never leave.

Aaqila and Danah reached the courtyard and Danah scampered across the uneven bricks. She hesitated at the arched entrance to the courtyard. Halima grasped her sister's hand and they walked into the empty street together. A steady wind blew down the narrow street, whipping the sand and grit from the road and stinging their eyes. They turned away from the wind and headed toward the market, ten blocks to the north.

Their house, south of the Old City in the Shakpur Darwaza Chowk-e area, was one of many that had been destroyed by the fighting between the Taliban and the foreign soldiers. The battles had been so intense that the Afghans moved out, leaving their homes and eking out meager existences in safer neighborhoods. Or leaving Kandahar altogether. Large tracts of the city were rendered uninhabitable for most people. Unless you were one of the unfortunates who had nothing, then a roof over your head in a damaged building was better than a tent in the desert. That's what her father said, and he knew best.

As they approached the corner, a rickety jeep filled with armed men cruised by the crossroad. All heads turned and they stared at the three young girls for a few seconds, then they were gone, leaving a putrid trail of diesel exhaust in their wake. Halima reached down and pulled Danah's scarf over her mouth. Inquisitive brown eyes stared back at her.

She knelt down. "It's not good for you to breathe the smoke," she said quietly. She smoothed the child's windswept hair. "I'll buy you a candy today if you're good."

Danah hugged Halima's arm, then held her hand as they continued down the road to the market. Traffic picked up as they moved north, into the city. Boys on bicycles, bearded men on whiny mopeds and women clad in traditional blue burqas shared the road, dodging smoke-belching vehicles. A foot patrol of ISAF soldiers with red maple leafs on their shoulders passed the girls. One of them smiled and offered candy. Halima thanked the man in Pashto, took three pieces and divvied them up among her sisters.

"They're nice to give us candy," Aaqila said when the patrol had passed.

"That's because you smile and make them feel welcome." Halima clutched Danah's hand a little tighter.

She hated the guns. Not the men who carried them, but the guns themselves. It seemed that everyone in Kandahar was armed. The soldiers. The Taliban. The Afghans who tended the shops and farmed the land just outside the city. Rifles slung across their shoulders. Pistols strapped to their thighs. Bullets draped over their chests. She had never known a day in her life without seeing a weapon. They were as much a part of Afghanistan as the mountains or the desert.

One of her father's friends, a shoemaker in the Old City, had traveled to America to visit his daughter. She sat quietly next to her father as the man told stories of his adventure on the other side of the world. His description of the buildings, the cars, the clothes all fascinated her. The women were so elegant, the men so handsome. She worked up the nerve to ask him a question – whether there were guns in America.

"The police carry guns," he said, stroking her head gently. "But they never use them. They never even take them from their holsters."

She wished Afghanistan was like America.

The streets were crowded now, thick with noisy vehicles and people pushing past each other. They reached the madness of the market and Halima gripped her sisters' hands tightly. Tea boys ran through the narrow alleys and open squares, delivering fresh pots of steaming jasmine and mint to the vendors working in their stalls. Women in ankle-length burqas emerged from side streets, bought their daily vegetables from one of the many merchants, then blended back into the web of alleyways. The heavy odor of mutton hung in the air as orders of spicy *karai* were spooned onto freshly baked naan bread. In the rear of the stalls, out of the scorching midday sun, turbaned men smoked *sheesha* pipes and sipped on *chai*.

Halima scrutinized the produce carefully. Her father would expect her to buy onions and rice for *pulao*, and almonds, carrots and raisons to flavor the mixture. Bread was a staple and despite the intense heat, there were many tandoor ovens fired and churning out naan. Getting fresh bread for the family would not be a problem. She walked past at least twenty merchants, watching how they dealt with the other customers. Whether they were polite or belligerent, and if they smiled or scowled when they handed across the vegetables and took the money. She didn't want to deal with a difficult man. She stopped at the corner of two narrow lanes to give Aaqila and Danah a rest. A merchant wearing a pale blue turban and a colorful shalwar kameez was doing a brisk business. For good reason. His fruit and vegetables were the choicest she had seen since they entered the market. Halima approached the stall and stood in front of the bright red tomatoes. The seller looked at her with indifference – until she asked about his prices.

"They are the best in the market," he said. "If you have money."

"I have money." Halima pointed to the onions. "How many can I get for ten Afghanis?"

"Six," the man replied after thinking for a moment.

"Six is not enough."

The merchant eyed her more closely. He scratched the side of his head and crossed his arms over his barrel chest. "How many do you think you should get?"

"Ten," Halima said without hesitation. "And I get to pick which ones."

"You'll take the biggest," he said.

"Of course I will. My sisters and I are very hungry and we need to eat."

The man smiled. "I will lose money if I let you pick the ten biggest."

Halima shook her head. "Not if I buy carrots, raisons and rice as well. You could make some money on that."

He raised a thick eyebrow. His pale blue turban moved with the motion. "And I get to choose how many carrots to give you."

Halima shook her head. "No, I get to choose."

"Then I'll probably lose money on them, too."

"If you're concerned about losing money, then I'll talk to another seller. I need to find someone who has good prices on all his vegetables."

"Why is that?"

"I have US dollars, and I want to buy all my food from one stall."

The man gave her a closer look. "You have dollars? Where did you get them?"

"From my father. He is paid in US dollars."

"How many do you have?" the man asked. The tone in his voice had changed. It was much more serious. The young girl with two sisters in tow was a paying customer.

"More than one," Halima answered.

His eyes softened a touch and he said, "Where is your mother, little girl?"

"Dead."

His head turned slowly on his thick neck, his gaze locked on his youngest customer of the day. "That is a common problem." He leaned forward over the tomatoes. "How many dollars do you have to spend at my stall? If you tell me, I can put together a selection of fruit and vegetables for you. More than you would get if you went to a different merchant."

Halima hesitated. "I need some money for naan."

He nodded. “That’s a good point. I will allow for that. Make sure you have some change to take with you to the baker.”

“I have two dollars.”

“All right,” he said. “Let’s see what you can buy for two dollars.”

Ten minutes of wrangling netted Halima two big bags of food. They were so heavy she could barely lift them. The merchant sent his son, about the same age as Halima, to buy her bread. When he returned, the merchant wrapped it in paper and handed it to Danah.

“What’s your name, girl?” he asked as she turned to head home.

“Halima.”

“Patience,” the vendor said, then added when she looked confused. “That’s what your name means. Patience.”

She smiled at him, then turned and pushed into the throng of people in the narrow street. The bags were heavy and the weight hurt her shoulders. She couldn’t hold Aaqila’s hand, and had to keep reminding her youngest sister to grip one of the bags tightly. It would only take a moment to lose her in the congestion. Ten minutes of pushing through the crowd brought them to the edge of the market. They retraced their steps home, Halima growing increasingly worried that someone might try to take their food as the streets grew less busy. A couple of men in their twenties riding a motorcycle slowed down as they passed, then hit the gas and were gone. Halima breathed easier as they turned the corner onto their street.

Above her was the burnt-out shell of mud and brick that kept the rain and sand off them. Some days she hated it – and thought of it as a prison. It kept her from playing with her friends and going to school. Other days, like today, it was a beautiful sight. She climbed the stairs, knowing that her father would be pleased with her. It was a wonderful feeling. The best in the world.

CHAPTER 10

Soho, New York City

Nicki knew she had to eat. She was sick, and for a CF'er not eating was pretty much a death sentence. She pushed the plate back and collapsed into the chair.

It was impossible. She couldn't do it.

Nicki rose and walked to the living room on unsteady legs, then sank into the overstuffed chair that looked out over the street three floors below. She stared at the window of Crocs, the shoe store on the corner of Spring and Wooster, and squinted to see if they'd put any new models in the display case. It was hard to tell and she gave up after a couple of minutes. She glanced at her watch. Eleven o'clock on Saturday morning. Carson would be home from the gym soon. And angry at her if she hadn't done her exercises. She corrected that thought. Not angry – disappointed. He was her biggest cheerleader and she could read his emotions when she strayed from the routine leading up to her surgery. Nicki hated letting him down, but the regimen was so extreme.

The thought of having her lungs removed and another person's inserted into her ribcage scared her. To hell with that – it terrified her. Of all the transplant surgeries, lungs were the toughest. But without the surgery, she was on her last legs. Dead within six months. There really wasn't much of a choice.

The lung transplant would grind the disease to a halt. For a while. Since it was genetic, the new lungs would never succumb to the disease. She could live for a number of years, breathing like a normal person, until some complication from the CF finally killed her. But the transplant was a double-edge sword. Following the surgery, she'd be on immunosuppressant drugs forever. Trading one disease for another. The post-transplant crap every CF'er suffered. And they were the lucky ones. She couldn't imagine where she'd be without the transplant.

Getting on the list was tough. Symbiatic, her health care provider, had been honest with her all the way through the process. There were only so many spots. Only so many lungs became available and you had to be one of the sickest to be slotted in. But there was a caveat to that. You had to be sick, yet still stand a good chance of surviving the transplant. She had fallen into that narrow category and been awarded another chance at life. There wasn't a day went by that she didn't give thanks for her good fortune.

Preparing for the transplant was tough. Four hours a day of cardio and weights, which couldn't be considered exhaustive exercises. At least, they wouldn't be exhaustive to most people. To her, they were like running a marathon then pumping a ridiculous amount of iron. Simply thinking about her exercises was tiring her and she reached for her oxygen. She tucked the plastic tubes in her nostrils and pulled the strap tight around the back of her head. She turned on the oxygen flow and almost immediately felt the uplifting effect of the increased O^2 to her body. Relying on oxygen bothered her, as did how she looked with tubes sticking out of her nose, but it was a necessary evil.

The door opened and Carson stepped in. He grinned and headed straight over and kissed her on the forehead.

"You look like you've been exercising," he said, sitting beside her on the arm of the chair.

"I tried," she said. She left the oxygen tubes in, despite desperately wanting to pull them out and look nice for him. "I didn't get through the whole thing."

He stroked her hair. "You need to stay strong. We could get the call any day now."

"I'm trying, Carson. It's so hard."

"I know," he said. He slid off the arm and squished his butt onto the chair beside her. She pushed into the faded leather, giving him a bit more room.

"You're doing great."

"And how are you doing at work?" she asked. "Mr. High Frequency Trading guy."

"Fantastic," he replied. "Had a meeting yesterday morning. It went really well. The whole team is behind me." He paused, then added, "At least, I think they are."

"Why would you wonder? They either are or they aren't." She brushed an errant hair from his forehead. "You know all these people. You've worked with them almost every day for two years."

"I had to push Alicia Crane a bit and she pushed back."

"Alicia's brilliant," Nicki said. "Every time I see her I'm so impressed. I love talking to her. She seems to know a little bit about a lot of things. Makes for great conversations."

"She's smart, all right," Carson said. "Too smart sometimes."

Nicki pushed back in the chair and gave him one of her looks. "What's going on, you?"

"Nothing. I asked her to streamline the algorithm a bit."

"What's wrong with your algorithm?" Nicki asked. "You designed it, along with Alicia and Chui."

"We're being gamed. Probably by Goldman Sachs. We need to speed it up by a millisecond or two. I asked her to take a couple of iterations out until we find a better fix."

Nicki stared at him. "How many times have you told me that stripping down the algo threatens its integrity?"

He shrugged. "We're still running the data through five iterations to predict the market direction. It's fine."

"Is it?" she asked.

"Sure," he said.

"Carson, high frequency trading is dangerous. You need to be careful with what you're doing. The last thing the market needs is another meltdown.

"Dangerous is a little harsh, don't you think?"

"No, I don't. The Immediate or Cancel orders you and Goldman and all the other players use are driving the market." She wagged a finger at him. "You're not supposed to be a market-maker. The stocks should find their value based on tangible assets, not the market liquidity you guys inject into the system."

"High frequency trading represents almost 80% of the daily trades on the US markets," Carson countered. "Of course we're market makers. We should be. We drive the market and deliver liquidity."

"Based on what?" Nicki said. "Your computers issue sell orders for small lots until the buyers stop biting, then you cancel and sit back. That's not liquidity, that's driving stocks to their absolute max, maybe beyond. You do that every day with thousands of stocks and the market is overvalued. And the next thing you know...," she looped her hand down in a long arc, "...we have another crash. Remember 1987?"

"You're being a pessimist."

"I'm being a realist. The games you guys play are scary. When they backfire, people get hurt. They lose their life's savings."

"Why are you attacking me?" he asked. "I'm only doing my job."

"Don't use that excuse," she said quietly. "It doesn't fly. If you know what you're doing has the potential to cause harm, then you should back off. Economics shouldn't trump ethics."

His eyes were serious – sad, almost. "But it does, Nicki. You know that."

They sat in silence for a minute, then Nicki touched his arm and said, "I'm not attacking you, Carson. But privilege doesn't come without responsibility."

He managed a smile. "I should never have linked up with another MIT grad. Too smart."

She punched his shoulder. "That's a horrible thing to say. Shame on you."

"Fact is, you *are* smart," he countered. "It's tough to get away with things. I always get caught."

She grasped his hand and clutched it as tightly as she could. "I don't need to tell you what's right and wrong, Carson. You already know."

He hugged her and they embraced for a full minute. Her body shook with every shallow breath. She was right and he knew it. Stripping down the algorithm was like outfitting a downhill ski racer with faulty equipment. Speed was dangerous, whether it was on the side of any icy mountain or in the CPU of a supercomputer designed to trade on the world's stock exchanges. But if a downhill racer crashed, he only injured himself. If the computer made a grievous error, millions could be hurt.

For a moment, he considered calling Alicia and telling her to back off.

He didn't.

CHAPTER 11

Paris, France

There was no reason for Trey Miller to stay in New York. Paris and Moscow held the key to bringing the Russian down a few notches.

He walked through Charles de Gaulle and hailed a cab outside the airport's main doors. He gave the driver the address for Hotel de Seine in St-Germain-des-Prés, then settled back as Paris flashed past his window. He enjoyed Paris more than any city in the world. The raw beauty of the buildings, the passion of its people, the elegance of the museums and monuments. And most importantly, men and women who operated in the shady world of covert ops. The ghosts who, like him, could appear or disappear at will.

He reset his watch to local time. Ten-eighteen on August 1st. Mid-morning was the best time to arrive to avoid the usual congestion on the roads, but it was Sunday and the volume was light. Traffic was flowing on the Boulevard Périphérique and the signs giving estimated times to off-ramps were dark. The Eiffel Tower poked through the maze of buildings intermittently, and overhead the summer sun warmed the city as it had done for countless centuries. A handful of clouds, white puffballs against a striking blue background, floated lazily on the breeze.

What a wonderful day for a little treachery, he thought.

The cab reached the hotel and he paid the driver and wheeled his lone piece of luggage into the lobby. Like many upscale Paris boutique hotels, it was small but filled with quiet elegance. The main reception desk was paneled wood with a wall mural depicting a jungle scene on the back wall. Miller had always thought that piece of the hotel to be out of sync and wondered why someone didn't notice and change it. He approached the desk, which was attended by a middle-aged man in a freshly pressed suit.

"Reservation for Ambrose. I made it on the Internet yesterday afternoon," he said in fluent French. He placed an American passport with his picture and the name Roger Ambrose on the marble counter. Anonymity started with never letting anyone know who or where you were. He dropped a Platinum VISA card next to the false passport. Same name. Deception worked best when all the details were taken care of.

The clerk smiled. "Yes, it's here. Welcome back, Mr. Ambrose. We've upgraded your room to a suite. Our thanks for staying with us on so many occasions."

"My pleasure," Miller said. "I like your hotel."

What he really liked was the we-could-care-less-who-you-are attitude. Pay the exorbitant rates, tip well and the staff left you alone. He found his room, opened the door and threw his suitcase onto the bed. The hotel provided free wi-fi and he switched on his computer and Googled *Details Matter*. The website for U2's security provider didn't even make the first page of Google. It was number thirteen. That bothered him more than if it had been number one. Successful companies that preferred to remain in the background were the ones that built their reputations on quality. Clients came looking for them, not the other way around. And if Details Matter was handling the security for U2 while on tour, they were guaranteed to be good at their job.

It took a few minutes of searching to discover the person behind the company. Julie Lindstrom. He read her bio – sketchy – but enough information to tell him that she was American and at some point had been involved with either the CIA or the FBI. She didn't have to come out and say it, he could tell. The more he read, the more he was convinced she was ex-FBI. Warning bells started going off. Lindstrom was a woman who had excelled in the male-dominated world of high-level security. She was not a person to dismiss lightly. He sent a quick e-mail to Fleming before packing up the computer.

Assembling team. P today. M tomorrow. Worried about Lindstrom.

The curtains were open and he checked the view. Across the street was a white stone building, conspicuous in its cleanliness, and below him was Rue de Seine, one of the more famous arteries in the Left Bank. Miller used the hotel phone to call a local number. A woman answered and he set a meeting in ninety minutes at the city's oldest church, a few blocks away. He showered and changed into a clean pair of jeans and a crisp dress shirt that he left untucked. He slipped a set of drawings into a thin leather briefcase, then wandered out into the street and headed for the Café des Deux Magots, a favorite hangout of Picasso and Rimbaud. A double espresso and a quick look through the daily newspaper revitalized him and he set out through the heavy pedestrian traffic at a brisk pace for St-Germain-des-Prés.

Trey loved the church. It was a Romanesque marvel, rising harshly over the brasseries and cafés that littered the square and the web of narrow streets that spun off in all directions. It had stood since the 11th century, destroyed and rebuilt more times than the history books could record. He reached the base of the buttresses that supported the bell tower and opened the door. Inside, the church was dimly lit and quiet, a world apart from the busy street scene. The Sunday service was over and only a handful of stragglers remained, lighting candles and sitting silently in the empty pews. Trey recognized her hair from the back and made his way up the left-side aisle to where she sat, facing the chancel.

"You're early," he whispered, sitting next to her.

"A church on Sunday morning," she answered. "Really inconspicuous. Brilliant place to meet." Her voice was laced with sarcasm. Maelle Robichaud was mid-thirties and kept herself well toned. Her deep-brown shoulder-length hair matched her eyes, and her skin was unblemished and tanned. Her face was lean and nicely proportioned, but not pretty. There was a tinge of hardness to her eyes and her movements that made most men wary.

"I forgot it was Sunday," he said easily. He shrugged. "Whoops."

"It's over a year since the last time we met," she said. "How have you been?"

"Very well. Better than that, actually. Fantastic."

Maelle raised an eyebrow. "Seriously, or are you simply trying to impress me?"

"Serious. But impressing you is probably a good idea." He let his eyes roam over her body. "You want to have sex?"

She shook her head. "Well, it's nice to see that you haven't changed." He was the same Trey Miller who spent two decades globe-trotting on a CIA expense account.

"See, stability counts," he said. "What about my question?"

She hesitated, then said, "Maybe. If you're a good boy. And if I like whatever job you have on the go."

He grinned. "I think you'll like this one." He pulled the drawings out of his briefcase and handed one set to her. "U2 is playing Luzhniki Stadium in Moscow on August 25th."

Maelle set the papers on her lap, out of view, and unfolded them. They were rudimentary plans of the stadium. "I like U2, but what's the gig? I'm sure your client isn't paying us to watch the concert."

"He wants us to derail it. Take it apart, piece by piece."

"Why?"

"The Russian who is promoting the concert pissed off our client," Trey said. "The idea here is to discredit him. The nice thing is, nobody gets hurt."

"What's the plan?" she asked.

"We take out the infrastructure. My first inclination is that we key in on the electricity. Take down the power grid. No electricity, no concert. We make it look like someone dropped the ball. But we need to be careful. If we sabotage things so the investigators can find evidence, then the finger gets pointed elsewhere and we've failed. But if everything crashes because they overloaded the circuits, then the promoter takes the heat for not being prepared."

"Interesting," she said. "Not the kind of thing that gets dropped in your lap every day."

"No, it's different. Planning is important, but execution is crucial. We have to disguise whatever we do so well that it never gets uncovered."

"Do you still speak Russian?" she asked.

"A bit, but it's rusty. Certainly not good enough to get us through this."

She shrugged her shoulders and stuck her head forward a bit. "So..."

"So we'll have to pick up a couple of Russians to help us."

"Who?"

"Alexi Androv and Petr Besovich."

She shook her head, sending her hair flying back and forth. "I don't like Besovich. I worked with him in Prague once and we didn't see eye to eye on things. He's a cowboy and caused everyone grief."

"He's a bit of a hothead," Trey agreed. "But he's also the best guy I know at tracking electrical systems and finding the right places to cut the power."

"If he's in, then I'm out," she snapped. "Find someone else."

"No," Trey replied evenly. "Besovich is the man I want and the fuse is short on this one. Twenty-five days, including today. We need more detailed plans of the stadium so we can figure out how to crash the systems. And we have to get it done in a little over three weeks. There isn't time to find a substitute for Besovich."

"He talks too much, Trey," she said. "A few vodkas and he'll give it up. The Russian newspapers will know what we're up to."

"One word and he's out," Trey said. He waited a few seconds for it to sink in. "One word to someone outside the group and he's out. You okay with that?"

Maelle mulled it over for the better part of a minute. "One word," she said.

"And he's gone."

She finally nodded. "Okay, but you'd better keep your dog on a tight leash. Especially once the job is done."

"So you're in?" he asked.

"What's the pay? I need to know how much I'm getting paid before I say yes."

"Eighty thousand US, which works out to about thirty-two hundred a day. And most of those days are easy. Reading blueprints and cracking computer access codes – figuring out how to do this."

"I'm worried about the days that aren't easy," she said, then nodded. "Okay, I'm in."

"So you like the job."

She smiled. "I do. Moscow during the summer. And nobody gets hurt."

"So what about my question?" Trey asked.

"You still have to be a good boy." She tucked the drawings in her bag and stood up. "I'll study these. When are we leaving for Moscow?"

"Two days. I'll call you on your cell phone."

"I'll clear my calendar." She stepped over him and shuffled between the pews to the nearest aisle. "Good seeing you, Trey."

He watched her leave the church. Memories flooded back from the previous jobs they had worked together, he with the agency and she on loan from Interpol. Maelle Robichaud was brilliant at manipulating computer systems and getting them to do exactly what she wanted. Some people called what she did hacking, she called it a learned skill. Maelle was about ten years his junior in age, but that was unimportant. What mattered was the depth of her skill set. She was the best and he had her. Getting the Russians on board would be easy. All it took was a handful of money and the promise that what they were doing was highly illegal.

The wheels were in motion. The gig was underway.

CHAPTER 12

Kabul, Afghanistan

Russell looked up from his newspaper and mint tea. The noonday sun was directly overhead and cooking Kabul under its blistering rays. An employee of the Gandamack Lodge was standing on the grass in front of him. He held an envelope in his left hand.

"This just arrived, Mr. Matthews," the man said in halting English.

"Thank you," Russell said. He dug into his shirt pocket and handed over a tattered ten Afghani note. The messenger inclined his head in a polite nod and returned to the hotel.

Russell took the envelope and ripped it open. It was the communiqué he had been waiting for. His documents ensuring safe passage from Kabul to Kandahar. At least, as safe as possible in a country constantly under attack. He memorized the itinerary, folded the envelope in half and tucked it into his back pocket. Two days in Kabul was enough. He was ready to join the troops at their Forward Operating Base in the southern province. He finished his tea, signed the chit and left a generous tip for his waiter.

He took one last look at the quiet garden that had been his refuge from the onslaught of Kabul's traffic and street boys for the past forty-eight hours. The tract of worn grass tucked behind the lodge was so peaceful. If only the rest of the city, the country for that matter, could be like this tiny enclave. Relaxing. Quiet. Safe. These were expected things in so many places, yet so elusive in Afghanistan.

His itinerary was straightforward, but he knew that even simple things in countries like Somalia or Afghanistan could become complicated very quickly. A driver was to pick him up in thirty minutes at the hotel and take him to Kabul's main airport. A local agency had arranged for him to join a plane flying supplies for a Non-Government Organization to Kandahar. It left at two o'clock. The flight was less than two hours, which meant it would still be light when he arrived. Someone from the brigade was scheduled to pick him up at the airport and take him to the Forward Operating Base. If everything went as scheduled, he would be inside the wire and chatting with the soldiers of the 2nd Infantry Division before dark.

If everything went as it should.

"Sure, and the pigs are fueled and ready to fly," Russell mumbled to himself.

He packed the few items he had taken out of his suitcase, looked over his camera gear and computer, then headed for the front desk. Checking out took fifteen minutes – problems with translating between Dari and English and getting the credit card to work in the machine – and by the time Russell arrived at the car, his driver had been waiting long enough that he was sleeping. The ride to the airport was complete chaos. Traffic laws simply did not exist in Kabul. It was every man for himself and the timid were quickly overtaken and forced onto roads they had no intention of taking. Air quality was poor – the thick brown pollution choked even the heartiest Afghans.

Street boys swarmed the car at every intersection with offers of freshly filled balloons on strings. Some of them waved smoking cans, promising that for a small fee they could ward off the evil spirits in the car. With sixty thousand of them working the inner city, there was hardly a block that passed without one of the children banging on the door panels.

"Are they orphans?" Russell asked the driver.

He shook his head. "No, most of them have a mother or a father. The lucky ones have both." His English was heavily accented but understandable. "Their parents are very poor, and too sick or injured to hold a job. So the children work the streets. It's very bad for them. They get no education and end up working for nothing all their lives. Very sad."

Russell nodded. He understood sadness. Inevitably, it permeated the family unit, the one piece of closely-knit fabric that tied war-ravaged countries together. It challenged pride and wiped out ambition. It haunted children's dreams and destroyed hope. Sadness was something Russell Matthews had seen many times. He never became accustomed to it. He never wanted to.

"What's going on?" Russell asked as the car slowed almost to a stop. Directly ahead was a series of concrete barriers spanning the road.

"This is Wazir Akbar Khan. There are many embassies here. Security is very strict."

Outside the car soldiers were scanning the occupants as vehicles drove slowly through the twisting maze of concrete slabs. They were placed to impede traffic flow so any speed above five miles per hour was impossible. One of the soldiers, a Union Jack on his shoulder and an automatic weapon tight to his chest, nodded to him as they passed. No paperwork, no passport, just off-blond hair, blue eyes and white skin and you merited a nod. It should have made Russell feel better. It did exactly the opposite.

The driver navigated the Mercedes through the barriers and resumed a reasonable speed. Russell watched Bibi Mahru Hill slide past on his left, a favorite district of Kabul for expats and the site of the city's only Olympic-size swimming pool. He'd heard stories from more than one journalist about how the mujahedeen used the diving board for daily executions during the war.

They reached the airport and the driver pulled into Zone A, the most secure of the three zones and the one reserved for VIPs and foreigners with status. Security forces surrounded the car, guns ready. Always guns. Russell's driver leaned back and told him that they were the elite guard of Afghan National Police, well trained and trustworthy. And that he had arranged for Russell to enter through the most prestigious zone. The initial security was not as stringent and coming in through Zone A meant fewer headaches once inside the terminal.

Russell shouldered his bag and handed the driver a generous tip. "Good work," he said, looking at the chaos in the other two zones where the security lines were massive and the guards much more difficult to get by without having your suitcase and body searched. "You did well."

His driver pocketed the tip. "Someone from the NGO will meet you in the terminal. Have a good flight."

Inside, Russell spied a man in western dress holding a sign with his last name and angled over to him. The man introduced himself, then helped the journalist through the secondary security checkpoint and to the plane. It was an older model DC-9 that had been partially converted to handle supplies, but still had about twenty seats near the front of the craft. The pilot checked his ID and pointed to the cloth-covered seats.

"Sit anywhere you want," he said. "No in-flight service here, but we'll get you to Kandahar on time. Sort of. That's more than most of the commercial airlines that fly out of Kabul can say."

"Thanks."

Russell picked a window seat and settled in. The plane pushed back at twenty after two and was airborne by two-thirty. Below him, Afghanistan spread out like a giant brown carpet, stained with tinges of green and blue. Few main roads crisscrossed the massive steppes directly below the plane, and to the northwest the Hindu Kush mountain range rose harshly on the distant horizon. The paths leading through the mountains, where there were any, were too narrow to be seen from the air. The rugged and unforgiving landscape was part of the reason the ISAF troops were still hunting the Taliban. Rooting out the black-turbaned insurgents was a problem that wasn't going away soon. Understanding the other factors, aside from the geography, was why he was in the country.

The topography changed as they neared Kandahar. On the western edge of the city were the fertile farmlands of Helmand province, the world's number one source of opium. The Arghandāb River snaked its way through Helmand into Kandahar province, bringing vibrant green with it. Groves of olive and date trees clung to the riverbanks and fields of grapes and pomegranates spread back from the life-sustaining water. Villages came into view as the pilot decreased his altitude, the mud and brick buildings melding into the dusty brown soil.

Horse and ox-drawn carts traveled slowly on the bumpy, unpaved roads. Men and women, many burdened with firewood and food, shared the roads with the rudimentary vehicles. A convoy of ISAF tanks rumbled toward Helmand, small clouds of dust rising from their tracks. The plane banked sharply to the left and dropped fast as it approached the runway. The tires touched and the plane bounced, then settled onto the asphalt.

Kandahar.

Russell sucked in a deep breath. Five days had taken him from the safety of Boston to one of the most dangerous places on earth. And simply being in the city wasn't enough. He was going to be embedded with the soldiers on the front line. As vulnerable as any of them. Perhaps more so. At least they had guns. All he had was a camera. A wave of nausea washed over him – the same one that hit him every time he landed in a war zone. Tina's face materialized for a second in the dust swirling about the plane, then dissipated into a random jumble of whipped-up sand. He wondered if he would ever see her again. The thought hit him hard. It had never occurred before.

They taxied to a position close to the terminal and the pilot cut the engines and opened the cockpit door. "Are you ready?" he asked.

Russell nodded. "Sure." He grabbed his bag and exited the plane. The heat hit him at the door. Kabul was hot and the air quality poor, but the bone-dry superheated air of Kandahar scorched his lungs and left him gasping for breath. He took a few breaths and started down the thin metal staircase. A man in a military uniform standing near the terminal caught his eye. He was focused on the plane, and on the man exiting. Russell walked toward him. At ten meters, the man raised his hand and gave the approaching reporter a small wave.

"Russell Matthews?" he asked.

"Yes." He reached the man and they shook hands.

"I'm Darcy Plotkin. 5th Stryker Brigade."

"Thanks for coming in from the base. I appreciate the ride. It'll be good to get out with the troops."

"Sorry, sir, I can only take you to a hotel tonight. It might be a day or two before you get to the Forward Operating Base."

"What's up?" Russell asked.

"I really can't say," Plotkin said, taking Russell's bag and shouldering it. They started walking. "Security problems on the road between Kandahar and Spin Buldak. It might not be safe to try today."

"How are things in Kandahar?"

"Stable right now. The Taliban are mostly in the hills, but they come into the city to keep an eye on us."

"That's always a problem," Russell agreed. Foreign soldiers were easy to identify, making them targets. The insurgents, in Somalia, Iraq or Afghanistan, looked like the locals. You never knew who the bad guys were until they started shooting at you.

"This way, sir. I have a vehicle."

Russell fell in beside Plotkin. *Almost made it,* he thought. The pigs almost got off the ground – but not quite.

CHAPTER 13

Kandahar, Afghanistan

The man wore a dark turban and stared at Kadir with black eyes. His hand rested on the Kalashnikov, his finger caressing the trigger.

Kadir focused on the sidewalk and pushed gently on the back of Halima's scarf. Aaqila and Danah trundled ahead of their older sister, staring at the man, not knowing any better.

Please, not today. Leave us in peace. Let the soldiers show themselves so you will creep back into the ruins, the coward that you are.

The Talib didn't move as they passed and Kadir and his daughters turned the corner without feeling the sting of the man's anger. Kadir's hands shook as he steered Halima across the street toward a doorway in a mud building. They were near the outskirts of Kandahar, a part of the city where the Taliban occasionally showed their faces, then disappeared into the cracks when the foreign soldiers showed up. Here, in this remote district, the dirt road was pockmarked with small craters. He stumbled in one of the larger holes and almost fell into the cracked wall. He threw out his crushed hand to keep from going down. His younger daughters stared at him, but Halima looked away, saving him the embarrassment.

A man with a flowing white shalwar kameez appeared in the door and waved at Kadir. "You are here, my friend," he said, greeting Kadir with a respectful peck on each cheek. His face was clean-shaven and lined with deep creases from the constant onslaught of sun and wind. Dark, compassionate eyes peered out from under thick eyebrows. "You and your beautiful daughters must come in. We have naan and *shorwa*." The odor of freshly baked naan and the sharp tang of the oily soup escaped out the door into the street.

"Thank you, Ahmad," Kadir said, bowing his head ever so slightly. "You are a gracious host and your *melmastia* is the most regal in all of Kandahar."

Ahmad shook his head. "My hospitality is that of a pauper," he said. "We are not men of wealth, you and I. Come in. My house is your house."

The girls scampered into the single room and through the door in the back that led to a rear courtyard where a small *tandoor* was cooking the naan. The girls peered into the clay oven, intent on the food, until Ahmad's wife shooed them away. They busied themselves with an old doll with one arm, one leg, and a bright red dress.

"How is the job?" Ahmad asked, pouring two cups of *chai sabz*. The green tea was steaming and had an aroma of pungent herbs. Ahmad offered his friend sweets in a clay dish and pushed back his unruly, thick hair. "The one in the old city, working on the well."

Kadir waved his good hand and sighed. "It's finished. I worked for two days, then the Iranian Red Crescent packed up. They had two more wells to dig, but the Taliban threatened to kill the supervisor so they headed back to Iran. Maybe they will return." He looked doubtful.

"The Iranians are good people. They have helped us many times."

Kadir took a sweet and popped it into his mouth. It had been so long since he had tasted sugar. He tucked it under his tongue so it would last longer. "My family stayed in an Iranian refugee camp when the Taliban were in power. They were kind and welcomed us into their country."

"What will you do now?" Ahmad asked.

Kadir shook his head. "I don't know. I have no food, no house, no furniture to sell. I am a damaged man with no wife and three daughters. The job building the well paid six American dollars, but that will be gone soon. Things are very difficult."

Ahmad stroked an eyebrow and asked, "How old is Halima?"

"Eleven, almost twelve. Her birthday is in two weeks."

Ahmad sipped his tea and gave Kadir a thoughtful look. "Maybe there is a way for you to feed your children."

Kadir leaned forward. "How is this possible?"

"I know of a man, a Pakistani who lives in Peshawar, who travels to Afghanistan to find girls to live with rich families in his city. The girls must work to earn their keep, but they get a small room with a bed, all their meals, and a chance to attend school."

Kadir looked confused. "Why does he come to Afghanistan? Why not find girls in Pakistan?"

Ahmad laughed and the sound reverberated off the thick, mud walls. "The girls in Pakistan are spoiled. They are not at war like us. They think nothing of having new clothes and food on the table twice a day. This man travels to Kandahar because the girls who live here understand that such things are luxuries. They don't mind working hard, scrubbing the dishes and changing the bed linens to earn their keep and live in a nice house."

Kadir nervously licked his lips. "Would this man be interested in taking Halima to such a house?"

"Maybe," Ahmad said. "I could ask. I have only seen him once. He came for a girl whose family lived in a tent on the south edge of Kandahar. He was very nice, and the girl's parents received pictures of her at her new house in Peshawar. I saw the pictures. She was very happy, smiling and wearing a nice dress. And the house they live in – it is beautiful."

Kadir frowned. "But how does that help me feed Aaqila and Danah?"

Ahmad grinned. "This man receives money from the family in Peshawar for finding good, hard-working girls, and some of this money is paid to the girl's parents."

Kadir's hands were shaking and he set his tea on the sturdy wood table to keep it from spilling. "How much money?" he asked through dry lips.

"The family living in the tent received one thousand five hundred American dollars."

Kadir's head swam at the thought of such a fortune. He could find a small apartment and feed Aaqila and Danah for years if he had that kind of money. And Halima would be safe and well fed. With an elegant roof over her head. He may not have many chances to see her, and Halima would not be part of watching her younger sisters grow up, but those were small considerations given the opportunity. He took a second mint from the clay dish and picked up his tea. He sipped the steaming liquid.

"Is it possible to meet this man?" he asked. His voice was different, like it was in a tunnel. It didn't sound like him. He hoped that his words and his tone weren't giving Ahmad the impression that he was desperate. Even though he was.

"Perhaps. I can talk to the family of the girl who moved to Peshawar. They only live a few blocks from here in a small house they bought with the money."

Kadir's heartbeat quickened. This was a dream. Halima safe and living a good life and his other daughters living in a house with their father, a landowner. A dream that could come true.

"Could you please try, Ahmad?" Kadir asked. "It would be greatly appreciated."

"Of course."

Halima and Safa, Ahmad's daughter, came running in from the courtyard and the small room was filled with laughter. Aaqila and Danah remained in the back portion of the house with Ahmad's wife. The older girls had the family goat tethered to a short section of rope. The goat, and the girls, were anxious to leave the house.

"Can we play in the field by the stone wall?" Safa pulled on the rope, trying to keep the goat in the house. "The goat needs some exercise."

Ahmad wagged his finger at her. "It isn't the goat that needs exercise, it's you and Halima. We can't hear ourselves think with all this racket."

"Can we?" Safa begged.

Ahmad looked at Kadir, who shrugged that he didn't care.

"All right," Ahmad said sternly, "but Kadir and I will come and watch. We don't want the goat to get too much exercise."

The girls ran out the front door and down the street toward the open fields on the edge of town. The men followed behind them, their steps slow and deliberate. They talked as they walked the deserted roadway, about the weather and their common friends and the young people who were leaving Kandahar for Kabul, where it wasn't as dangerous and work was easier to find. Although Kadir wanted to talk about the situation with Halima, his friend had said he would look into it and it would be rude to broach the subject again. They reached the stone wall, a meter high and equally as thick, and watched the girls chase the goat about the dusty pasture, bordered on three sides by the wall and the fourth by a crumbling, abandoned building.

"I'm glad they never knew the Taliban," Ahmad said. "Life is so much better for girls and women now that the soldiers are here."

Kadir stroked his damaged hand. The agony of each crushing blow shot through his brain. Painful memories were always the most enduring. Nothing about the Taliban was pleasant. Their mark on the country – on the people – was a swath of misery and brutality that refused to fade. And despite being driven out of the cities and back to their caves, they were still omnipresent. A stain that couldn't be washed out. He wished the soldiers could end the terror. He prayed for them to end the terror. Daily.

"So much better," Kadir agreed.

They turned their attention to the girls, who had fashioned a game with the goat and an empty tin can. Every time they kicked the can, the goat would bolt toward it, then lose interest when it stopped bouncing. Halima and Safa squealed every time the goat charged the can. Halima bent over and scooped up the can, then threw it as hard as she could. The goat took off the second it hit the ground.

The small, fragmentation landmine was Russian, and had sat just under the sand for over twenty years. Many feet had trod over it, never causing it to explode. But the force of the goat's hoof as it veered sharply toward the can was at exactly the right angle to depress the switch and trigger the jammed detonator. The mine exploded, sending shrapnel in all directions. The upward force of the explosion tore the goat's torso in half, shredding its vital organs and killing it instantly. The lateral spray of hot metal, designed for maximum collateral damage, sliced through the air, slamming into mud and stone.

Safa went down screaming and holding her side and her face. Halima buckled under the force of a red-hot sliver cutting into her calf muscle. Both girls lay writhing in the sand and rocks. Kadir and Ahmad jumped over the fence and raced to the girls. Neither were doctors, but it was obvious that Safa had taken the worst of the shrapnel. Her cheek was a mess, the metal still protruding from her skin. Another piece had punctured her skin above her hip. Kadir turned his attention to Halima. He grasped her leg and pulled at the metal. It was scalding hot and burned his fingers. He ripped off his shirt, wrapped it around his good hand, grasped the metal and pulled. Halima screamed as it wrenched free.

"Does it hurt anywhere else?" he asked.

She shook her head, her eyes wide and scared.

"I need to help Ahmad. Safa is badly hurt," he said.

"Yes, I understand," Halima managed through tears and gritted teeth.

Kadir slipped his hands from under her and turned to Ahmad and his daughter. She was in shock and bleeding from numerous cuts. Her father was holding her, unsure what to do.

"We need to get the metal out." Kadir touched the piece protruding from her cheek. "It's hot and it's hurting her."

"Then pull it," Ahmad said. "I will hold her." He grasped the girl's arms and pinned them to her side and wrapped one of his legs over hers. "Do it," he yelled.

Kadir yanked on the shrapnel, but it stuck. It was implanted in her jaw. He gripped it tighter and pulled again. This time it came free. Safa passed out from the pain. Blood was staining her blouse and Kadir lifted it so he could see her side. Another piece had cut through the flesh immediately above her hipbone. He rewrapped his shirt on his hand and pulled. It came free. A small trickle of blood followed, then stopped.

"The heat of the metal has cauterized the wounds," Kadir said. "She shouldn't bleed much."

Ahmad nodded that he understood and checked Safa for any other wounds. He found none. "We need to get her home. To clean the cuts and dress them."

"Yes," Kadir agreed. "Halima as well."

Ahmad lifted Safa and started for the fence. The remnants of the goat were splayed out over the ground, the blood staining the dirt a dark purple. He stepped over the carcass and onto the street. Kadir was behind him with Halima in his arms.

"We were lucky today," Ahmad said as they walked quickly up the street. "The girls could have been killed."

Kadir simply nodded. Visions of Halima living in a nice house in Pakistan flooded his mind. He had to get her out of here. To give her a chance at a good life. Kandahar was their home, but the dangers were too great. He needed to make it happen. And when it did, when Halima was safe, then he would take the money and move to a quiet part of Afghanistan, where Aaqila and Danah would be safe as well.

Nothing could stand in his way. Nothing.

CHAPTER 14

Midtown Manhattan, New York City

Tuesday, August 3rd dawned sunny and clear in New York. Carson was in his office and poring over printouts at seven-ten when William Fleming appeared at his door.

"I saw Monday's tapes on the NASDAQ and BATS. We led the market yesterday."

Carson allowed a slight grin. That was exactly the information that was sitting in front on him on his desk. "Yes, we did."

Fleming walked into the office and stood near the window. "You like it here?" he asked, staring out over the park.

"Very much. Especially the private bathroom."

Fleming nodded, then turned away from the view to face Carson. "First week on the job and you nailed the bid-ask spread on sixty-one stocks."

Carson knew the teams at Goldman and Citigroup would be racing to catch up. "The other firms will notice that they were tapped by odd lots," he said. "They will be looking for us."

"Let them look," Fleming said. "If we're faster, we can keep pinging them with small orders, then front run them. It's all about the algorithm."

Carson didn't answer. Fleming was right and they both knew it. The firm with the fastest computers and slickest algorithm controlled the new trading floor. The one that existed in cyberspace. The one where almost eighty percent of America's stocks were traded every day.

"Do you know how much money we made by being the fastest yesterday?"

Carson shrugged. Those figures weren't on his daily reports. "No idea," he said.

"Including the rebates from the exchanges, one-point-seven million." Fleming let the figure sink in. "If we continue to run a mil or two faster than the other firms, these numbers will be the norm. That's eight-point-five a week. Four hundred and forty-two million a year." Fleming flashed a wide smile. "Imagine your Christmas bonus."

"They'll catch us," Carson said. "If we're beating them by a millisecond, they'll find a way to shave two off their algo."

"Then we shave one off ours."

"I have Chui working on it. Yesterday's trading was with a band-aid fix. Alicia stripped the iterations. But we should have something solid up and running within the month."

"How many iterations did she take out?" Fleming asked.

"Two. We went from seven to five. I don't think it compromises the program."

Fleming nodded his agreement. "Five is fine. For now. I don't think we want to run five forever. Remaining stable is crucial. We don't need a meltdown."

Carson felt a bit of wind pull back from the sail. Shortcuts were risky. The sub-prime fiasco came to mind. Packaging the sub-prime mortgages in bundles and selling them as asset-backed securities to the banks was the con of the century. It was a moneymaking strategy that had collapsed when the housing market stalled. Part of the blame fell on Wall Street and the MBA's who had been willing to take risks with other people's futures. Being part of the group that had orchestrated the downturn was a bitter pill – one that he often choked on. Fleming's voice cut through his thoughts.

"How is your fiancée?" he asked.

"Nicki is doing so-so, not great. She's on the list for a double lung transplant, though."

"Will she be okay when she gets new lungs?"

"Maybe. Cystic fibrosis is genetic – the new lungs will never get the disease and her breathing should be normal. But there's always the possibility of rejection. She'll be on a lot of immunosuppressant drugs."

"Nasty disease."

"You have no idea," Carson said quietly.

Fleming glanced out the window, then walked to a wingback chair in front of Carson's desk and sat down. "I want to expand your department and I have a shortlist of candidates for you to look over. I think you're a bit light on the technical side right now. Another programmer or two would help. What are your thoughts on that?"

"Chui and Alicia and their staff are running hard," Carson said. "Extra bodies are appreciated." He paused, then qualified that statement. "But not just *any* bodies – we need the best minds on the market."

"We pay well. We'll steal them. You can look over the shortlist and arrange for interviews. I'll sit in on the last interview with the final three candidates if you don't mind."

"Love to have you there."

Fleming smiled. "Well, good work, Carson. Let me know when Chui gets the new algorithm up and running. I'll be interested to see how much faster it is."

"Sure, I'll do that."

Fleming retreated from the office and into the hall. Carson watched him leave, then swiveled around in his chair and stared out the window. This is where all the late hours at MIT, alone with his books in the study hall, or at his tiny desk in the corner of his dorm, had gotten him. His dedication had propelled him forty-six floors above the mayhem that ruled the sidewalks of New York. Forty-six floors above minimum wage and subsistence salaries. A world above mundane.

He spun back to face his desk, picked up the phone and called his home number. Nicki answered. "Hey, you," he said. "How are you doing?"

"Okay." Her voice was strained. Weak. "Having breakfast," she lied. The thought of food made her violently ill. Typical for end-stage CF patients.

"Good. You need to keep up your strength. I was thinking of calling a Realtor and setting up some showings. Are you up to looking at some places?"

"Sure." She didn't sound sure.

"Fleming was just in my office. He was talking bonuses. He said mine could be pretty substantial if the numbers keep up."

There was silence on the other end of the line. A disapproving silence.

"Yesterday's numbers were good," he continued. "Fleming is impressed."

"That's one day, Carson. We can't make a decision to buy a condo in Midtown Manhattan based on you having one good day at work."

"Two good days," he replied. "Yesterday we made a ton of money. Today Fleming came into my office and told me I'm doing a great job. That's two good days."

"Okay, funny guy." She coughed, a thick sound that came from the depths of her chest. It continued for almost a minute. When she was finished, she said, "We can look at a couple of places, but not right away. I'm not a hundred percent on this yet."

"Okay. We'll wait a few days. Talk to you later."

"Later."

Carson heard the coughing as he set the phone back in its cradle. Nicki's lungs were getting worse. Much worse. Without the transplant, she would be lucky to make it for another six months. The nagging doubt returned. What was he doing? He was on the top of his game, thirty-six years old and set to pull down an income of well over a million a year. He could have his pick of intelligent, attractive women. Manhattan was full of eligible girls in their early thirties who would date him in a minute. Sleep with him. Marry him.

He pushed the thoughts aside. Nicki was everything to him. He loved her, and Nicki and he were forever. Whatever forever was.

* * *

Soho, New York City

Nicki hung up the phone and gasped for air. She pushed the oxygen hose tight against her nostrils, closed her mouth and breathed through her nose. The oxygen-rich air satisfied her body's craving and she slumped back into the chair.

She was dying. Her lungs were filling with phlegm and mucus faster now than even a month or two ago. Even with the physiotherapist beating on her chest and back to loosen the thick liquids, she was going downhill at a horrific rate. She needed a lung transplant or she wouldn't see Christmas. She didn't need a doctor to tell her that. The cystic fibrosis was winning. It always did.

A tear spilled from her eye and started down her cheek. She wiped it away. Her parents would have to know soon. They were living in the family home of thirty-three years in Michigan and blissfully ignorant of how quickly she was deteriorating. She only called them on the phone when her breathing was good and she had enough stamina to talk for a couple of minutes. And close to dinner so when she was too exhausted to speak she could lie to them that Carson had food on the table. Another tear caressed her cheek and she ignored it. This one was for her mother. For the woman who had always felt guilt for bringing a child into the world with a fatal disease. CF was genetic. She didn't get it from making bad choices or living a questionable lifestyle. It was embedded in her at the cellular level. Forever.

How could she marry Carson? Marriage was for life, but when life meant a few months that vow took on a completely different meaning. She wasn't sure if she could go through with it. Playing fair was important, and marrying a man and dying less than a year later certainly wasn't playing fair. The tears were coming now. She always cried when she considered telling Carson she wouldn't marry him. No, that wasn't right. Not wouldn't – couldn't. That she couldn't marry him.

The transplant would change everything. If it happened. A fresh set of lungs meant a new lease on life. They would give her a chance to look ahead and see a future for her and the man she loved. She stared at the phone. One call. That's all it would take. The phone only needed to ring once, with the right person on the other end saying the words she needed to hear.

We've found a match. We need you at the hospital.

But that call had yet to happen, and her life was hanging by an immeasurably thin thread. The tears started again. It seemed that these days they never stopped.

CHAPTER 15

Moscow, Russia

"We'll need more accurate blueprints of the stadium than these," Maelle said.

In the distance, visible from the balcony of the room in the Korston Hotel, Luzhniki Stadium was tucked into the lush green on the north side of the Moscow River. She cleared the table and laid out the rudimentary set of drawings Trey had given her in Paris. They showed the circular structure of the building, its support columns, seating diagrams and many of the major features, like concourses and stairwells. Conspicuous in their absence were the electrical, plumbing and heating/cooling systems.

"I should have better ones in a day or two." Miller opened the bar fridge and took out a beer. He checked the label, shrugged and popped off the lid. A swig, a thoughtful nod on the quality, then he sat on the couch. He watched Maelle as she poured over the schematics of Moscow's largest sports stadium, then checked his watch. "Dinner in an hour. No blue jeans. We're going to the Sky Lounge."

"I'll be ready," she said without looking up. "Did you tell Androv and Besovich that I was coming?"

"No," Trey said. "Things are always so much more fun when there is a surprise involved."

"You're childish," she snapped.

"You like it."

She looked up from under her hair, which fell down across her eyes. "I like it when we're having fun. This is business."

Miller didn't bother responding. There was no reason to. Maelle would let him know when the time was right for them to play. If ever. He had let her know he was willing to blur the lines between the job and pleasure when they had met in the church, now it was in her court to make the next move. He picked up the Mac laptop, keyed in his password for his international bank account in the Caymans and checked the balance. It was a touch over three million. Yesterday the dollar figure was a bit over two, so Fleming's million dollars had arrived. He clicked on the transfer icon and sent eighty thousand US to Maelle's account in Jersey, where he had deposited large sums of money many times.

So nice dealing with professionals, he thought. He sent Fleming a quick e-mail about meeting with the team before closing the computer.

"We're going to be late," he said.

"Fashionably," Maelle replied. "Nobody ever eats in Moscow before nine o'clock."

The drive from the Korston Hotel, set in the picturesque green district of the Vorobyovy Hills, to the Sky Lounge was less than fifteen minutes. The restaurant was in Gargarin Square, set atop the building housing the Russian Academy of Sciences and almost directly across the river from Luzhniki Stadium. The late evening sun reflected off the building's gold windows.

Two men were sitting at the corner table on the outside terrace. The river, and the stadium, were easily visible to the west, tucked into one of Moscow's most eco-friendly zones. On the east side of the bridge and the freeway was a solid block of concrete apartment buildings. Spreading out directly below the ornate sciences center were the Leninsky Hills, an undulating wave of trees punctuated by red tile roofs. Moscow at its best. Neither man was enjoying the view. They were both watching Trey and Maelle approach.

"Petr. Alexi." He offered his hand. They both stood and shook.

Petr Bẹsovich was short and thick, his chest so wide it forced his arms to hang at a twenty-degree angle to his body. He had no neck to speak of, his head appeared directly attached to his broad shoulders. His features were crude – the flattened nose and protruding ears common to professional boxers, which he had been in his youth. He was early forties with a thick thatch of jet-black hair and dense eyebrows to match. A scar sliced across his lower right cheek and disappeared below his jawbone. Every time Besovich shaved he remembered the look on the face of the man who had cut him – as he died from a severed trachea.

"Trey," Besovich said, his eyes focused on Maelle. "I see you brought some pussy with you. What's wrong with Russian girls?"

"I see you haven't changed," Maelle said. "You're still a pig."

Besovich grinned. "Pig or not, girls like me."

"Not this one," she said, sitting. She acknowledged the other man. "Hello, Alexi."

"Maelle," he said, retaking his seat. Alexi Androv was the other end of the spectrum from Petr Besovich. He was average height and slender, stylishly dressed in camel-colored slacks and an untucked black silk shirt. His shoes were pointed and well polished. Androv's face conveyed kindness, soft brown eyes and an easy smile framed by nicely coifed, blond hair. Of the three men, his look was the most sophisticated and benevolent. The sophisticated part was true – he had lived in Moscow all his life, attended the ballet and enjoyed art galleries. The benevolent part was a lie. Alexi Androv was skilled in weapons most people had never even heard of. And he was ruthless. Androv was the man Trey Miller went to when someone had to die.

"You look wonderful," Androv said. "Life in Paris must be agreeing with you."

"It is. It does," Maelle said. She smiled, but it was detached. She knew Androv's true nature. Knew it all too well. She had seen too many men die at his hand to ever see him for anything other than what he was. A vicious, psychopathic killer. His presence as one of the team members didn't resonate well with her, but Trey had picked the men for specific reasons.

Trey sat down in a chair facing the river and the stadium. The sun was setting and thousands of streetlights were blinking on. A shimmering glow settled in over the massive city. After five minutes of small talk, the group ordered dinner and got down to business.

"Thanks for coming," Trey said. "I have something that I think will interest you."

"Your jobs always interest me," Besovich said. His beer arrived and he drank half and waved to the server for another one.

"This is strictly confidential, as always," Trey said, and when they had all nodded, he continued. "I have a client who wants to disgrace the promoter of the upcoming U2 concert."

"Dimitri Volstov," Androv said matter-of-factly. The event was big news and Volstov's name was linked to it as the man who had made it happen.

"Yes, Volstov. They dislike each other intensely, and my client is incensed that Volstov is a hero to the Russian people for bringing U2 to Moscow. So, we need to be inventive here. This needs to look like the promoter screwed up. That he didn't think about the immense draw the concert would have on the electrical systems. We need to crash the grid – cause the lights to fail just as the concert is starting – but do it in a way that will never be discovered. It has to look like an overload on the system from a lack of planning."

"I doubt Volstov would take on any project without proper planning," Petr said. "He built Murmansk-Technika from one gas well into Russia's leading energy provider. Volstov is all about planning. He's brilliant and he doesn't make mistakes."

"I'm sure he makes mistakes," Trey said. "He never lets anyone see them."

Alexi was looking the calendar on his phone and he shook his head. "The concert is on the 25th. Today is the 3rd. That's twenty-two days. Today is pretty much over and we'll have no time to do anything inside the last twenty-four hours. So that means we have less than three weeks. It's impossible."

"Difficult, but not impossible," Trey said. "And the pay is good."

"How much?" Besovich asked.

"Eighty thousand US. Each."

"What sort of risks are we looking at?" Androv asked.

"We'll be in the sewer system cutting into the electrical conduits, which means it will be dark, wet and cold. There might be an occasional city worker around. And we need to get in and get out of the sewers without being seen. It's probably best if we rent an apartment or main-floor business from which we can access the underground. We have to be careful that no people come into the space we rent and see the hole. And there will be some level of security around the concert itself. A firm named Details Matter handles the security for the band while they're on tour. They'll have people on the ground in Moscow in advance of the show, but most of the muscle will be local guys hired to stand around in T-shirts and look tough."

"That's it?" Besovich asked skeptically. "Pay seems pretty good for such an easy gig."

Trey shook his head. "No such thing as an easy gig. I'm not telling you anything you don't already know. We've both seen the wheels come off and everything go wrong on assignments that looked easy. We need to be ready for anything."

"What will we be doing?" Androv asked.

"Petr will review the schematics and identify where we need to splice into the main lines to maximize the damage. Then all of us will work on getting that done. Alexi, in addition to building the equipment we need to cut the power, you will ensure we have drawings of the sewers and the stadium. Preferably in English."

"What do you care?" Androv said. "You speak Russian."

"It's rusty. I haven't used it for a while."

Androv shook his head. "I don't think we'll find them in English. I'll have to translate."

Trey smiled. "Well, there you go. That's the reason I'm paying you eighty large."

Besovich asked, "What happens when the lights fail? People could get trampled if they panic."

"If we take the lights out early enough, there will still be some daylight. Moscow is pretty far north and it stays light late in the evening. In fact, I checked and sunset is 8:42 pm on August 25th."

"Still, the sun will be low and the stadium will be darkening."

"To some degree," Trey agreed. "The emergency lighting is on battery packs so it will kick in. But there's still a degree of risk."

"What about backup generators?" Alexi asked. "A band the size of U2 probably has backup systems for the sound and lights."

"Good question," Trey said, raising an eyebrow. He hadn't expected anyone on the team to think about that. "U2 has built three stages for their tour and they leapfrog them from place to place. Each stage is accompanied by a massive generator mounted on a dedicated truck."

"That's a problem," Alexi said.

"Not if the truck breaks down," Trey said.

"Which it will."

"Yes."

Their food arrived and Besovich turned to Maelle as the waiter set the plates on the linen tablecloth. "You're quiet," he said.

"I have nothing to say," she replied.

Trey dug into his meal. Sea trout on buckwheat noodles. "Are you guys in?" he asked between bites.

Androv nodded. "I'm in."

Besovich grinned, crooked teeth poking out from behind thick lips. "Hell, yes. Easy money and a hot chick. It doesn't get any better."

The sun dipped below the western horizon and a sudden wave of darkness swept over the city. "No such thing as easy money, Petr," Trey said. "It's fool's thinking to be expecting that."

"Whatever," Besovich said.

An uneasy calm settled over the table.

CHAPTER 16

Outside Spin Buldak, Afghanistan

"I have an assignment for you." Captain Brian Hocking, thirty-one and on his third tour in Afghanistan, handed a single sheet of paper across his desk to the soldier on the other side. "I think you'll like it."

Specialist Andrew James took the paper and scanned the typewritten text, his icy blue eyes moving quickly from side to side. His military records indicated James was exactly six feet, but every person who met him assumed he was at least six-two. He stood perfectly straight, with a wiry body, gaunt cheeks and a determined jaw line. His blond hair was long by military standards, short when compared to his surfing and clamming buddies who were still hanging around his hometown of Pismo Beach, California. When he was finished, he said, "Why me, captain? Taking care of embedded reporters usually goes to men with sergeant stripes."

Hocking reclined in his wooden chair. His office was the remnants of a shipping container that had served as a shower until half of it was blown up in a mortar attack in early July. Hocking had commandeered the useful half and reconfigured it into a workspace with phones, faxes and computers. The open side backed onto an eight-foot-thick wall of heavy-duty canvas bags with wire frames filled with sand called HESCO bastions. The welders had cut a front door into the opposing wall. The plywood floor creaked under the weight of the chair.

"Because you spent time working on the newspaper in high school, and you're the best man for the job," he replied. He rubbed a thick hand through the military-style stubble on his head. "You can get this guy interested in what we're doing here. Let the world know what it's like to be in a Forward Operating Base."

"Babysitting a reporter," James said. "Great. Thank you, sir."

Hocking checked the time. "He's waiting in Kandahar. You should probably pick him up. There's a chopper heading in this afternoon. Hurry and you might make it by air rather than on the road."

"He's not at KAF?" James asked.

"No, he arrived at the airfield on August 1st and headed into the city. Nothing was moving on the road between KAF and here on the 1st and we didn't have access to a chopper."

"The 1st was Sunday – the day they attacked the convoy when they were crossing the bridge," James said.

Hocking nodded. "That's right. So he got the opportunity to spend a few days in the city. Now it's our turn to take care of him. Show the man around, Andrew. Give him an idea of what we do here. And don't let him get himself killed."

"I'll try, sir."

Andrew James spun and walked out the door into the August blast furnace that was southern Afghanistan. He didn't mind the heat all that much. His first tour had been at high elevations during the winter and he'd frozen every conceivable body part with the exception of the one he considered to be the most important. Least used these days, but that would change when his second tour was done and he was back in California. He took the quickest route back to his bunk, skirted the HESCO walls and pushed open the door. The room was empty, with most of the men out on a mission. He'd been held back and now he knew why. He changed his socks and checked the magazine on his M-4, then headed for the chopper.

The pilot had the rotor moving and was already into the pre-flight check. James waited until the pilot spied him and waved him to approach, then ducked under the wash from the rotor on the UH-60 Blackhawk and ran across the landing pad. He slipped into the back section and settled into a seat by the window, immediately forward of the gunner. He plugged his ear buds in his iPod and turned it on. Coldplay flooded through the earpieces.

The chopper lifted off and banked to the north toward Kandahar. Below them was a series of ridges and flatlands, crisscrossed by intermittent riverbeds, now bone-dry. A vast plateau of wasteland stretched off to the west – thirty-foot-high sand dunes running to the horizon without a break. No roads, no villages, no life other than scorpions and vipers. Even the Taliban ignored Dasht–e Mārgow. No poppies, no opium, no villagers to lean on for taxes. Why bother.

Ahead, to the northwest, was Kandahar, the center of everything in the south of Afghanistan. The city Alexander the Great had founded early in the 4th century BC still held enormous power over the entire southern portion of the country. *Control Kandahar and you'll control Afghanistan* was an ancient Pashtun proverb with great relevance. The problem was, no one had figured out how to do it. Not the Mongols, led by the butcher Genghis Khan, or the Russians with their tanks and MIGs. Now it was the International Security Assistance Force that was bogged down fighting the Taliban for control. A fight the ISAF was not sure if they were winning or losing.

Andrew stared down at the bleak landscape. Identifying the river systems was simple – look for trails of green snaking through the desert. How anyone could survive in the massive stretches of rocks and sand was beyond his comprehension. But they did. The Taliban were there, in the cracks and fissures, waiting for the windows of opportunity to embed Improvised Explosive Devices in the roads. They were good at it. Give them twenty minutes a night for three or four nights and they would have an IED in place that was capable of taking out a tank. Huge charges that killed and maimed indiscriminately. The men in the black turbans didn't care. When someone died they celebrated.

Kandahar came into view. From the air it appeared peaceful. Kites cut through the air on summer breezes and traffic moved on its boulevards and streets. The Old City was congested with street markets and thick with people on foot and bicycles. Life on a normal day. The only problem was, normal in Kandahar would be considered insanity in any other city of half a million people. Arms deals, drug dealers, insurgents, soldiers and a wary civilian population shared the same space. Everyone carried weapons, many of them hidden under loose-fitting robes, and the guns were loaded. The view from the chopper was a lie. People died violently every day in and around Kandahar. And that world of deceit and treachery was the one Andrew and the rest of the ISAF soldiers lived in.

The helicopter hovered over the landing pad and dropped slowly to the ground. The rotor wash whipped up a cloud of sand and small pebbles and the military personnel working the landing area covered exposed skin to keep from being sandblasted. The rotors slowed and then stopped. Andrew pushed open the door and stepped out into the quiet as the dust settled. A thin man dressed in civilian clothes was leaning against one of the mud buildings adjacent to the landing area. He had blond hair, was tanned and wore sunglasses. At his feet were two bags. Andrew recognized one of them as a reinforced camera case. He had his journalist. As Andrew walked toward him, he could feel the man's eyes focusing on him. Evaluating him.

"Russell Matthews?" Andrew asked when he reached the man.

"Yes." Matthews removed his sunglasses.

"I'm Specialist Andrew James. I'll be taking care of you while you're in Kandahar province."

Matthews extended his hand. "You. Personally?"

"Yes, sir," Andrew said. He shook the writer's hand, surprised at the strength in the man's grip.

"Please," Matthews said. "Do me one favor."

"Of course, sir."

"Do not call me sir. Not ever. It's demeaning."

"I refer to all my superiors with that word. I don't think it has a demeaning connotation."

"Not to me," Matthews said. "To you."

Andrew studied the reporter. He was squinting to keep out the blinding sun, but had angled himself so that even with his sunglasses off, he could still see. There were small crow's-feet at the edges of Matthew's eyes – premature for a man in his mid-thirties. His eyes were observant, and without fear or panic. Andrew knew that look. It was the same one that was in his eyes. The look of someone who had seen more than anyone should see in one lifetime. Someone who wore those memories in quiet solitude. Russell Matthews was a player.

"You got it." He motioned toward the chopper. "You ready to get out of the city?" he asked.

Matthews nodded. "Please. I need a break from all the noise. I'm looking forward to a little quiet time at the FOB."

"Yeah, it's pretty quiet," Andrew said. "Aside from the mortars."

"Damn things wake you up," Matthews said. He picked up his bag and walked toward the chopper. "Shotgun."

Andrew grinned at the man's back. He liked Russell Matthews already.

CHAPTER 17

Kandahar, Afghanistan

Halima ran her finger over the bandage on her leg. She had seen bandages on other people lots of times, but had never felt them against her own skin. The texture was strange, like the shell of one of the small, green turtles that lived in the reeds by the river. The wound from the shrapnel didn't hurt – rather it was more of a constant throbbing. Mostly, for the past three days, she had ignored it. She was too busy fetching water and cooking *qorma* and *kachaloo* for her family to fuss over a cut on her leg. With her father not working, there was no meat to supplement the potato and vegetable dishes, and no money to buy any more food. She could see the worry etched in his face.

At least she was okay. Safa was still in bad shape from the landmine blast. The metal that pierced her cheek had broken a bone in her jaw. Ahmad had taken her to the hospital in Kandahar and had waited sixteen hours for a doctor to stitch her cheek and the gash above her hip. Halima had visited her friend once since the accident and didn't want to go back. Not until her face healed and she could speak. Halima hated sitting beside her in silence, listening to her moan in pain. Her father, who had left at an unusually early hour, returned and sat on a blanket. He was quiet, careful not to wake Aaqila and Danah.

"Can you fetch water today?" he asked.

"Yes, of course." She studied his sun-drenched face. He looked worried, but recently he was always worrying about something. "Is everything all right?" she asked.

The look faded and he smiled. "Everything is fine." He dug inside his tunic and pulled out a small wad of dog-eared bills. "I have seventy Afghanis. Enough for some vegetables and *pulao*. Maybe some naan. Does a trip to the marketplace interest you?"

She brightened. "More than fetching water."

"Do you enjoy bartering with the merchants?"

"I do. They're very nice and there is one man who always gives me the best tomatoes on his cart."

Concern washed over his face. "Does this man ever touch you?" he asked. She looked puzzled by the question and he said, "Like to pat you on the head, or adjust your scarf so it covers your hair."

Halima shook her head. "No. Why do you ask?"

"No reason, Halima." He handed her the money.

Kadir closed his eyes and imagined a world where there were no Taliban or foreign soldiers and young girls were safe. Where poppies grew for their natural beauty, not for opium. Where fathers didn't have to sell one of their children to feed the others. Where his wife was still by his side and their children had a mother. That world existed somewhere, but not in Afghanistan. Maybe that world would return to his country, but it had been so long since they had known peace that it was hard to imagine living without death and pain as neighbors. He opened his eyes as she slipped the money from his fingers.

Seventy Afghanis. Enough to feed them for a couple of days. The last of his money. After this, there was no more. Nothing to sell. No way to feed the girls. He needed Ahmad to make the connection to the man in Peshawar who arranged to have girls work for rich families. Halima would have a better life, with a bed and a good diet. And school. He could not even fathom sending Halima to school to learn mathematics and reading. Books and paper and pens cost money, and he needed her to fetch water and watch Aaqila and Danah on the few days when he could find work.

"I'll go now," Halima said, rising and stretching. "Before it gets too hot."

"Yes. That is a good idea."

She collected the canvas bags and tucked them under her arm. Chances were good that with seventy Afghanis to spend she would only need one bag, but she took both, just in case. Halima glanced back from the door and waved to her father, who gave her a tired smile. The strange look had returned to his face. She carefully navigated the stairs and made her way through the courtyard. Outside the wall, the street was empty. She headed toward the Old City, a spring in her step.

Her father was giving her more responsibility now. She was tired of watching her sisters and the trips to the market were fun. It was a long walk, and the bags were heavy on the way home, but she was helping with her father's burden and that was important. She liked bartering with the merchants, especially with the man with thick eyebrows who wore the pale blue turban. He gave her more tomatoes than he should. Probably because she didn't have a mother. She saw the look in his eyes when she told him that her mother was dead. It was a look she had seen a hundred times. The brief moment when the mask that concealed hidden emotions was stripped from the person's eyes and the pain of loss escaped. Everyone in Afghanistan had lost someone close to them. It was the ugly product of three decades of war and unrest.

Halima rounded a corner and walked into a group of girls playing a pickup game of soccer with a bright plastic ball. Three of them broke off and came running over to her. She knew two of them, sisters from the neighborhood and had talked a few times to the oldest one, who was about her age. She had even joined in on some of their games. But not today. She was entrusted with an important job and having a good time wasn't part of it.

"Halima," Jahenn, the older girl, gasped. "We heard you and Safa exploded a landmine."

Her sister, Ramin, and the other girl stared with wide eyes and Ramin asked, "Did Safa lose her leg?"

Halima shook her head. "No, she still has her leg. A goat set it off. Safa and I were close enough to get hit, though."

The third girl pointed at Halima's bandage. "Is that from the mine?"

Halima nodded. "Yes. A big piece of metal was sticking out of my leg. My father pulled it out with his bare hands. He said it was very hot and burned his hands."

"Did it feel hot?"

Halima thought about the question. "No, not really." That surprised her. It was the first time she'd really comprehended that the metal that had been embedded in her leg was too hot for her father to grasp. She hadn't thought about it until she said it out loud. "It hurt a lot."

"My brother lost a leg when he stepped on a mine," the nameless girl said. "He used to be a tea-runner but he can't do that anymore. He sits at home now and doesn't go outside much."

"My uncle was driving to visit his sister in Helmand Province about a month ago and he hit a mine in his car," Jahenn said.

"What happened to him?" Halima asked.

"He died," she replied. There was no emotion in the words. The tone was the same as if she was asking a merchant for two apples. No spark fired in her eyes. No anger at her uncle dying in a mangled wreck of twisted metal on a road to nowhere. No hate for the men who had planted the bomb under a thin covering of sand and rocks with the sole intention of killing or maiming a completely random person.

"The shells that don't explode scare me," Ramin said. "I crawled in a bombed-out building and I saw one. A big one. It was jammed between two stones. I wanted to touch it but I wasn't brave enough."

"You don't have to be brave to touch them," her sister said. "Just stupid. The boys like to touch them."

"Boys are dumb," the other girl stated.

A man appeared in a doorway and yelled at the girls that it was time for school. They wished Halima a speedy recovery and asked her to say hello to Safa. Then they scampered off and picked up their books and pencils and fell in behind the man as he walked briskly down the street.

Halima clutched her canvas bags. "And I have to do some shopping at the market," she said to the deserted street. She was surprised at the feeling of emptiness that swept over her when she thought about the other girls attending school. On rare occasions she thought about sitting in a classroom and working on lessons. Learning to read and write and add numbers together to make bigger ones. Passing exams and becoming a teacher, then standing in front of the class as the children stared at her with inquisitive eyes. She knew it was a dream, and when the thoughts floated through her mind she chastised herself for wasting time. Nothing tangible was to come of such farfetched thinking. She had other things to do. Shopping for the family was a job. A real job with great importance attached to it. Something she took very seriously. Halima started down the street.

A tiny wave of pride surged through her as she walked. Maybe this was how the shopkeepers felt when they stood behind their piles of rugs or goods and customers strolled past looking at their wares, ready to buy. Working and making money. She wasn't tending a stall like the merchants – she was only taking money to the market and spending it on things, but to her it was a job. Without her effort, the family would go hungry and thirsty. Which gave the job a tangible importance.

The sun was high enough now to find its way into the cracks between the single-story buildings on either side of the street. It was already blistering hot, a precursor of what was coming. When September rolled around it would cool down and her daily outings to the well for water would be easier. Two women in burqas passed her and Halima wondered how uncomfortable it was inside the garment. It must be awful. Already her father was talking about buying her one and seeing which boys were available for marriage. She didn't want a burqa and she certainly didn't want to get married. Boys made no sense to her. They played silly games and they all wanted to carry guns. None of her girlfriends were interested in guns. Only the boys. They wanted to shoot things. Some of them wanted to shoot people. One boy who lived near the Old City and walked with a limp wanted to kill the soldiers. He hated them and wished he had a gun every time they walked past, rifles on their chests. He took the candy they offered, but swore behind their backs that when he was old enough he would perform his own *jihad* and take as many heads as he could before they killed him. Halima steered clear of him as best she could, but he always came running to talk with her. Being near him made her nervous.

She didn't mind the soldiers. Her father told her that until they came, the Taliban were monsters. They still were. Halima could sense the fear in his voice when he spoke their name.

She was nearing the market now and there were more people on the street. A group of soldiers passed her, single file and spaced far apart. Even she knew why they walked like that. One of them smiled at her and she smiled back. Something twigged in his eyes and inexplicitly she wondered whether he had children. She looked around and noticed that most Afghans who were on the street were busy with their daily activities and ignored the soldiers. Everyone ignored her. The soldiers filed past and disappeared around the corner. A dark-skinned man in a deep burgundy turban stared at her as he passed, a hundred meters behind the soldiers. His eyes were black and intense. She sunk back into the wall, trying to make herself small. He turned the corner, still following the soldiers. Halima wondered if he was Taliban. It was hard to tell.

She pulled herself away from the rough stone wall and wove through the people to the edge of the market. Maybe her favorite merchant would be working his stall today and she would get an extra tomato. But he still had to earn her business. She only had so much money and she needed the best deal possible. No friendships here, this was business.

She entered the market, clutching the ratty cluster of bank notes tightly in her tiny hand.

CHAPTER 18

Midtown Manhattan, New York City

"The weapons are at the Kandahar airfield," Jorge Amistav said.

"Yes, I received your e-mail," Fleming replied. "That's excellent news." He glanced at the date on his copy of the *New York Times* – August 5th – then set the paper on his lap and looked out the car window. Midtown Manhattan flashed past. "That was fast. When I talked to you about a week ago they hadn't shipped them yet."

"They came in by air from Germany. It's an established route and we have people at both ends. It doesn't take much time to load the plane and fly it in from Europe. The paperwork is fairly easy and it gets e-mailed directly to the logistics people at the Pentagon. I think it's best if you give it another couple of days to make sure the shipment has been logged in, then send the invoice."

"Sounds good," Fleming said.

He pushed the end button on his cell phone and dropped it on the seat next to him. Thirty-five million for doing absolutely nothing. Aside from having the seed money to cover the payments to Amistav and his contact who had amassed the cache of substandard weapons. Money attracted money. Money didn't care who owned it. He figured it might as well be in his bank account instead of someone else's.

The limo began the climb onto the Queensboro Bridge, Manhattan in the rearview mirror, La Guardia the destination. His corporate Gulfstream V was on the apron, fueled and a flight plan to Houston registered with the tower. Houston in August held little appeal to him, but he had a meeting that he needed to attend in person. Most times he could delegate business meetings to his staff, but not for this one. He didn't mind too much – his share of the hostile takeover and dissolution of the board of directors was twenty million. The lawyers had taken care of the details and all that was required now was his presence and his signature. The upside was that he was only in Houston for six hours before heading to his private villa in Cabo San Lucas.

Fleming pulled his Blackberry from its perch on his hip and checked his daily schedule. The fourth item caught his attention. It was the shortlist of candidates for the HFT positions. He had meant to send it to Carson Grant but had left it sitting on his desk. He swore under his breath and dialed Carson's line.

"Carson Grant," the voice said.

"Carson, it's Bill Fleming."

"Mr. Fleming. What can I do for you?"

"The shortlist of candidates is on my desk. I'd appreciate it if you could pick it up and look it over. Set up some interviews and pare it down to the top three before I get back to New York."

"That's not a problem," Carson said. "When are you back?"

"On Friday, the 13th."

"I'll have it ready."

"Fine. Arrange for interviews the following week. And check my schedule with my secretary."

"Yes, sir."

Fleming hung up without saying goodbye.

The limo reached the east end of the bridge and touched into Queens. This was a different world from Manhattan – the cheap seats in a world-class arena. Three-story apartments overlooked the freeway, dirty curtains hanging at odd angles in the windows. Fords replaced the BMWs and jeans with T-shirts were the choice of clothing. Queens always brought out a quantum shift in his thinking. He wondered what sort of life it was to work fifty hours a week to pay the bills and have enough left over for a movie and a tub of greasy popcorn.

People with no money talked about the importance of the struggle. It was a fallacy. The struggle wasn't necessary. If they were motivated and set their minds to becoming rich, they could eliminate eking out a living and have a good life. A great life. But they didn't. They settled for mediocrity in a world where opportunity surrounded them. And at the end of the day, they sat staring across the river to the island with sad eyes, wishing they could be part of that world.

He glanced out the window at the traffic, all the lanes moving in unison. A woman was a passenger in the car in the adjacent lane. She was overweight and her face was a mix of bland features. The visor was angled down and she was applying eye makeup. Fleming watched as she carefully traced around her eyelid with a pencil then blinked a few times and checked her look in the mirror. The traffic flow in his lane slowed slightly and the other car pulled ahead. He shook his head.

"Why bother," he muttered.

The limo took the exit for La Guardia and he relaxed in his seat, knowing a fifty million dollar aircraft was waiting for him. And that he was going to make more money in the next five hours than most people would make in a lifetime. Simple thoughts, but ones that made him feel good.

Really good.

* * *

Midtown Manhattan, New York City

Carson phoned ahead to Fleming's office and let his secretary know he was coming. Fleming had already called her and she was expecting him. He considered slipping on his suit jacket, decided against it, then took the elevator from forty-seven to forty-eight – the doors from the stairwell were locked on the upper floor. You either belonged there and used the elevator or you didn't. Simple. That was one of the things that Carson liked about his boss. William Fleming was a simple man in some respects. He let the people around him know what he expected and gave them the leeway to get it done, or to fail. Your salary and bonuses were commensurate. It didn't get much clearer than that.

The elevator door opened and he strode across the tile to the reception desk. He addressed Fleming's private receptionist by name. "Hi, Betty."

"Mr. Grant." She smiled and waved at the door to Fleming's office. "I'll buzz you in from here. The file is on his desk."

"Thanks."

Carson entered Fleming's inner sanctum and walked slowly across the ebony hardwood to the desk. It was only one floor above his and the view was essentially the same, but there was a difference between his office and this one that couldn't be measured on any scale. His was nice, opulent even, but it was a working space for a man who made an enviable salary. This was the mother lode. The big dog's lair. Even without the billionaire in the room, there was an energy coating every object. It was in the air, like static electricity, and he felt the hairs on the back of his neck rise. Carson reached the desk and touched a finger to the polished wood. Another surge of energy coursed through him. He lifted his finger and it stopped.

The file was sitting on the desk next to the mouse pad. He reached down and picked it up. The pad moved slightly and the screen flashed to life. Carson thumbed through the papers in the file and turned to go. He hesitated, wanting to look at the screen, but knowing it was improper. Curiosity won the battle and he glanced at the screen. Microsoft Outlook was running and e-mails were popping up now that the server thought the owner was back at the computer. Fleming had his private e-mails set up so the communiqués opened as they arrived and displayed on the right side of the monitor. The final one beeped and opened. Carson couldn't help looking.

It was from TM and the message was brief.

Received your fee. Team in place. Time frames are tight but should be okay. Crash inevitable.

The final line froze Carson on the spot. *Crash inevitable.* What the hell did that mean? The bottom was going to drop out of the market? And if it was, who was TM and why was he telling Fleming that a market crash was coming? Why was there a team involved?

Carson was sweating. His underarms were already damp and getting worse. It would be no time before the stains showed on his shirt. He cursed himself for not putting on his jacket. He was out of time. He took one quick look at the screen and read the e-mail address where the message had originated.

tm5397@gmail.com

He tucked the file under his arm and headed for the door. It opened when he was halfway across the floor. Betty poked her head in.

"Oh, good, you found it," she said.

"Yes," Carson smiled. He kept moving. The room seemed even more expansive than when he entered. "I had to take a minute and check out the view. See if it was better than mine."

"Is it?" she asked.

He shook his head. "Nope. The very same. Makes me feel kind of special."

It was her turn to smile. "Well, you are. He's given you the vote of confidence." She scanned the room, hesitating briefly as her gaze passed over the desk.

"I'll e-mail Mr. Fleming my thoughts on these candidates," Carson said, holding up the file.

Betty shook her head. "Don't bother. He refuses to check his e-mail when he's in Cabo."

"Okay, I'll wait until he's back."

Carson reached the door and continued on into the anteroom. Betty followed him and Fleming's outer door swung shut behind her. He caught a glimpse of her glancing back into the room a split second before the door closed completely. Had she seen the computer screen? Did she know he had spied on Fleming's personal e-mail? Would she go back into the room and check things out after he left? He had no idea what the answers were and he couldn't wait around to find out. His underarms were drenched from the stress and his hands were shaking. He punched the button for the elevator.

"Are you alright, Mr. Grant?" Betty asked.

"Yes," Carson said, wiping his brow. The elevator dinged and the down light illuminated. "I feel a bit flushed. Maybe I'll go out for some air."

He slipped into the cage and pushed the button for forty-six. Get to his office and change shirts. Relax. Then process what he had just seen. The doors closed and he slumped against the wall. Christ, what was going on? What was William Fleming up to?

CHAPTER 19

Outside Spin Buldak, Afghanistan

They were ready to roll.

A line of Strykers wound out of the Forward Operating Base onto the road leading from Spin Buldak to Kandahar. Each eight-wheeled light armored vehicle was topped with either a .50 Caliber machine gun or a 40mm grenade launcher. The two-man crew, driver and commander, was augmented by six infantry troops in each vehicle. Light for a vehicle that could comfortably fit nine. Two Javelin shoulder-fired anti-tank rockets were strapped to the sides. Inside the Strykers, the men were serious.

The target was the Taliban force in the medium-size village of Dabarey, about sixteen kilometers northwest. Dabarey was positioned mid-way between the main highway linking Spin Buldak and Kandahar and a secondary road to the south. The Taliban were using the secondary road as a fast and safe way of moving men and supplies for their attacks on the ISAF forces. 5th Stryker Brigade was in charge of changing all that.

Andrew was in the sixth Stryker from the front. Seven more of the fast-response vehicles were lined up behind his. He was settled in against the armored plating, his M-4 resting comfortably on his chest. Five other soldiers mirrored his image. Russell Matthews sat next to Andrew, near the back, dressed in cargo pants, a tan shirt and a flack jacket, his camera case on his lap. The Strykers rolled out of the FOB and onto the main road. They reached forty miles an hour and kept a tight formation.

"I knew they were using these in Iraq," Russell said above the road noise. "I didn't know they had Strykers in Afghanistan."

"We brought this Brigade in last July. Great vehicle, but not as good here as it was in Iraq," Andrew replied.

"I heard about that," Russell said. "Something to do with having a better road system over there."

"Exactly. Here, if there's one road that's better than a goat path, we use it, so the bad guys know our route. It's not hard for them to sneak in at night and plant an IED or two."

"Big problems, IEDs," Russell said.

The Stryker hit a larger-than-average pothole and the men inside the vehicle bounced high enough to bang their heads on the ceiling. They picked themselves up and retook their seats. The interior was heating up and the air conditioning unit was straining to keep the temperature in check. Each soldier had a water bottle in hand and drank often to keep hydrated.

Andrew pushed his helmet back off his forehead. "No kidding. They're getting better at it. Some of the charges they're burying are large enough to flip one of these things or take a track off a tank. You try to go around a disabled piece of equipment and there's another IED in the rocks and crap beside the road. While you're sitting and waiting for a recovery vehicle, they pepper you with small arms fire and lob in a few mortars."

"How often does that happen?" Russell asked.

Andrew smiled. "Pretty much every time we go outside the wire."

"You expecting it to happen today?"

"Chances are about nine on a scale of ten. We're not just driving around waiting for them to fire at us, we're going after them. But we're not expecting big numbers today, or the CO would have put nine or ten guys in each Stryker."

"You think they know we're coming?"

Another smile. "They always know we're coming."

The Stryker slowed and the road surface changed. They were on the unpaved secondary road running south of the main highway. IED heaven. The ride inside the Stryker was rough and the noise levels somewhere close to pandemonium. Rocks banged off the undercarriage, a constant barrage of loud, sharp pings. Russell focused on the soldiers. They didn't seem to notice the small bumps and showed little reaction to the bone-jarring reverberations when they hit large holes in the road. Their faces remained impassive – unconcerned by the unimportant stuff. No sense getting upset by a few potholes when no one was shooting at you.

Russell had seen it before. Somalia was the worst. The troops were outnumbered and outgunned by the locals to the point where each day held the promise of being overrun and slaughtered. At least in Iraq and Afghanistan the logistics were better. Or so he'd been told. He'd find out soon enough if it were true.

"What sort of resistance do you think we'll hit today?" he asked.

"Sixty to eighty tier three, maybe a handful of tier two. We're not expecting any tier one bad guys on this run."

"Tiers? What's that?" Russell asked.

"Tier three are basically farmers with rifles. They get recruited because they need the money. They're dressed the worst, so sometimes you can tell who they are. It doesn't stop us from shooting them. But if you kill one, it gets all the relatives pissed off and the next day there's more of them with guns." Andrew took a sip of water and continued. "Tier two are the Afghan religious nutcases. They think they're fighting a *jihad* of some sort. They're still getting paid way more than they could earn doing anything else, but they have a bit of ideology left in them. If I was low on ammo and had the option of taking out a tier three or a tier two, I'd take the tier two every time."

"What about the tier one guys?"

Andrew's face steeled and his eyes grew cold. "Mercenaries," he said. "Former professional soldiers from Chechnya or Iran, sometimes Bosnia. These guys know what they're doing and they're dangerous. They're all about the money. And they like to kill us. Nasty fuckers. You get one of those guys in your sights, you take him out."

"Do they ever come after you?"

"Nah, not often." Andrew shook his head. "We always have reinforcements reasonably close and the chances of the Taliban putting together a well organized attack are slim. It's not their MO. Sneaking about planting IEDs and taking pot shots from the hills are what they're good at. They're pests. Very dangerous pests." He grinned and his eyes shifted from cold to mischievous. "They tried attacking the FOB one night but that didn't work out very well for them."

"Makes sense. The FOBs are well protected," Russell said.

"Yeah. The COPs, on the other hand, get overrun all the time."

"Combat Outposts?" Russell asked and when Andrew nodded he said, "I haven't heard any reports of us taking casualties from that."

Andrew shook his head. "It's mostly Afghan National Army guys manning those posts. If the bad guys know we're there they tend to leave them alone. They wait until the ANA are alone, then they take it out. If they kill a handful of US or Canadian soldiers, it's like stepping on an anthill. We're all over them. They don't like getting us too mad."

Russell looked dubious. "Are you saying that you don't care if the ANA guys get killed?"

Andrew shook his head. "No, not saying that at all. OMLT works really hard to get the ANA self-sufficient, so it's a bad day when they get overrun. But not quite the same as having US or Canadian troops on site when it happens."

"What's omelet?" Russell asked, pronouncing the acronym like the word, as Andrew had.

"O-M-L-T." He spelled out the letters. "Operational Mentor and Liaison Force. It's a Canadian program and we picked up on it. OMLT mentors the Afghan National Army and trains them to take over once we're gone."

"So it's our exit strategy."

"Yeah. We're kinda hoping it works."

"*Contact. Out.*"

The voice came over their headsets on the frequency reserved for the Tactical Operations Center in Kandahar. *Contact* meant someone in the line of Strykers was taking fire from the enemy. *Out* signaled the TOC that the Stryker commander who had called in did not expect, or want, a response. A Contact Report would be coming over the radio in a minute, detailing what sort of fire they were taking and estimated enemy strength. The line of Strykers kept moving and the report followed thirty seconds later.

"Small arms fire coming from the ridge at seven o'clock. Four to six shooters. Keep rolling to Dabarey, about three clicks."

Andrew leaned in toward Russell. "We've got a handful of bad guys with rifles firing at us from a ridge. Not worth stopping for. We're heading into the town."

"Okay," Russell said. He adjusted the camera bag, even though it didn't need it.

The Strykers were moving slower now, almost at a crawl, and Andrew noticed concern spreading across Russell's face. He said, "The secondary road we traveled on to get here was cleared this morning before we left the FOB. They checked the culverts for IEDs, so we could move a bit faster. This short stretch from the road to the village hasn't been cleared, so we have to go a bit slower. The first vehicle is at the greatest risk and he sets the pace. The drivers coming up behind all follow in exactly the same track, so in a way, the road has been cleared for them."

"How do you get to be the lucky guy in the front?" Russell asked.

"Piss someone off," Andrew said, then grinned. "Just kidding. Sort of."

Russell wasn't sure whether Andrew James was kidding or not. He was two days into his assignment, on his first trip outside the wire, and he was already feeling the incredible stress that the soldiers manning the FOB felt every day. It was the same as Somalia and Iraq, and he wondered how they managed. How they distanced themselves from everything they'd known as teenagers and young men and women in their twenties, living in John Mellancamp's America. The lyrics floated through his mind as the Stryker commander came over the radio and told them to be ready. They were rolling into Dabarey.

Little Pink Houses. Ain't that America.

Man, America had changed.

CHAPTER 20

Moscow, Russia

Friday afternoon and Moscow was teeming with life. Traffic was impossible and the heat was stifling. It almost made Trey Miller wish that U2 had booked their concert during the winter. Almost. Until he remembered Russia in the dead of winter – bone-chilling cold and everything frozen. It shocked him back to reality. August was just fine.

Alexi Androv had secured moderately accurate drawings of the stadium, showing some of the conduits that housed the electrical wiring and most of the water mains entering the structure and the sewers leaving. His contact inside the local office at MosEnergo had promised him more detailed drawings of the electrical system by the following Wednesday. That was five days away – too long to sit and wait. They needed to make significant progress in the next week if they hoped to be successful. Which meant they had to start with what was at hand.

Androv laid the plans on the table in Miller's suite in the Korston Hotel. All four members of the team were comfortably seated with a clear view of the schematics. Laid alongside the new plans were the ones Trey had brought with him from Paris that showed the structural components of the stadium.

"Luzhniki was built in 1956, so its basic infrastructure is getting old," Androv said. "There have been six major upgrades to the services over the last fifty-four years. Four of these were to bring the electrical systems up to date with the latest advancements in technology. The events in the stadium these days draw more power than they use to, so they've upped the voltage coming in and have used numerous incoming lines to ensure the power can't fail simultaneously across the stadium."

Trey leaned back in his chair. "Does that make it easier or harder for us?"

Androv shrugged. "A bit of both, I think. I don't know if we can knock out everything at the same time. A lot of that depends on Petr. He's the one who has to identify where we cut into the system." Androv lit a foul-smelling cigarette and continued. "We can trip the relay networks or breakers or whatever you want to call them, and shut everything down, but that doesn't work if you want to have the blame passed on to Volstov. He'll simply deflect it and say some terrorist group targeted the concert. The problem we have is making this look like incompetence, not sabotage."

Trey nodded in agreement. "That's the key to this whole thing. Tripping the circuits is not an option."

Petr Besovich studied the plans showing the utilities. He pointed to the entry points for the electrical lines. Six of them in total. "This is a problem," he said, his voice heavy with a Russian accent. "We need access to the sewer system in six different places. Then we need to find the main lines and splice in contactors. These are switches that we can open and close to allow or disallow the electrical flow. But there is some good news. Since the incoming power is split into six separate lines, the voltage and amperage on the lines is much lower than if the stadium was being fed by one line." He pointed to another section of the drawings. "Six hundred volts and three hundred amps in each line. That means the wires won't be too thick, which makes attaching the contactors much easier."

"Well, that's good news," Trey said.

Petr held up a finger. "But having six lines complicates things. Since we can't work on live wires, we need to cut the power on the incoming lines in order to make this happen. To do this once is difficult. To do it six times in such a short time frame is crazy. Someone at the stadium will notice the power losses and report them."

Trey considered the words carefully. "Good point, Petr. Maybe there's a way around that. What if there was an advisory from the city to the stadium that they were conducting upgrades to part of the grid and needed to take the power down in different sectors at specific times. Always late at night, maybe two in the morning. And only for a short period of time. Half an hour, max. That way the guys working the night shift at the stadium are ready for the interruption."

"That might work, but how do we get the city to send out that memo?" Androv asked.

Trey grinned. "They don't send it. We do. We create a profile for a fictitious department head and e-mail the stadium. Then we set it up so any response from the stadium comes directly back to us."

Besovich nodded. "That could work. If we had success with one interruption, the other five would probably be a run in the park."

"Walk in the park," Trey corrected him. "It's a walk in the park, not a run in the park."

Besovich looked confused for a moment, then turned to Maelle. "Maybe for most guys, but for me, it's a run." He tapped his barrel chest. "The girls like it when their man is in good shape."

Maelle rolled her eyes.

"Ahh," he grinned. "You want me for my mind, not just my body."

"Oh, Christ," Maelle said.

"We need an entry point to the underground system," Trey said, bringing the conversation back on track. "A safe place to cut through the concrete and brick so we can get into the storm sewer."

"I've already thought of that," Androv said. "There's an empty retail space on Usaceva, just across Hamovniceskij Val on the north side of the stadium. I think it's the closest we're going to get. The space around Luzhniki is all parks and grass or parking lots, and the river is to the south, so there's no chance of coming in from that direction."

"Can we access the storm sewer from there?" Trey asked.

Androv nodded. "It runs directly underneath the building. The only problem is, getting from the entry point to the stadium is a fair distance."

"How far?"

"Between 150 and 200 meters."

"That's doable," Trey said. "Once we're underground and moving there should be little to keep us from making good time. We'll be going in at night, so we won't have to worry about running into any maintenance workers."

"There could be security gates," Besovich offered.

"In the sewer system?" Trey asked. "That's pretty anal, don't you think?"

"It's Moscow," Besovich shrugged. "You never know what you're going to run into here."

"Okay, we can figure out how to get through them if it becomes a problem. I'm not going to worry about it right now." He turned back to Androv. "What are the chances of getting this place on Usaceva?"

Androv dug into his leather briefcase and pulled out a legal-size document. "I think they're pretty good. This is a six-month lease. All we need to do is sign it and give them a bank draft for a hundred thousand rubles. We can get the key tomorrow."

"A hundred thousand rubles," Trey said. "The conversion rate is about thirty to one right now, so that's around $3,200 US dollars. Reasonable for a deposit."

"I thought so."

"Okay, good work," Trey said, taking the lease and quickly scanning it. He glanced up at Androv. "We're putting in a chocolate shop?"

"Seemed harmless."

Trey handed the lease back to the Russian. "I'll give you the money in dollars and you can convert it and pay for six months. We'll need equipment to cut through the floor and the top of the sewer pipe."

Petr Besovich said, "I'll get whatever equipment we need. We should make a list."

"Sounds good." Trey turned to the lone woman in the group. "Maelle, once we're inside the sewers and have access to the electrical conduits, that will give you a direct link to the city and stadium computers. Once you're tied in, you'll be able to manipulate them as we need."

She nodded. “Yes. That shouldn’t be a problem.”

“She speaks,” Besovich said.

“Petr, you’re going to fuck this up,” Maelle snapped at him. “I don’t want things going wrong because you’re distracted, so get your mind out of the gutter.”

A tense silence settled on the table, until Trey said, “She’s right, Petr. We need you focused. Wait until we’re finished, then see if you met Maelle’s criteria.”

Besovich measured the words for a minute, then smiled. “All right, that’s a deal. No more comments until I take care of things, then I collect my reward.”

Maelle looked disgusted but didn’t disagree.

“Alexi, you get this lease signed and cover the front windows with construction paper. Petr, you secure the equipment we need to cut into the sewers. Maelle, I need you to go over every scrap of information we have on the city and stadium computer systems so you’re ready when we need to hack into them.” He folded up the plans and slipped them into his briefcase. “It’s August 6th. We have nineteen days to do this. Let’s get to it.”

One Child

CHAPTER 21

Dabarey, Afghanistan

Andrew grabbed Russell by the arm and yelled at him over the roar of the Stryker engines and the incoming small arms fire as they entered Dabarey.

"We're going in hot. I want you to stay in the vehicle."

Russell shook his head. "No way. I'm more of a target in this thing than on the ground with you guys. I'm coming with you."

Andrew made an instant decision. "Okay, but they're shooting at us. You understand that?"

"Yes."

One of the crew members threw back the rear hatch and the men piled out of the vehicle. Andrew scrambled out and took a defensive position against the side of the Stryker, then yelled to Russell. "Let's go. Now. Now." He pointed to a six-foot mud wall on the right side of the road. "Get flat against that. Hurry."

Russell jumped off the Stryker. The impact when he hit the ground sent a shock wave from his knees through his body to his skull and jarred his teeth. He almost collapsed but stayed on his feet and ran to the wall. He hugged the hot, rough-textured mud, his hands shaking so violently he hitched his thumbs under the camera-bag straps to keep them from vibrating. Andrew scurried up beside him.

"Here's the deal. We're coming at these guys from three different angles. Left flank, right flank and the center. We're in the center. Got it?"

"Got it."

"There's an irrigation canal about a hundred and fifty meters ahead and we expect them to be dug in behind it. But we're going to get face-to-face with them as we move through the streets. We want to engage them before they can drop back and regroup behind the canal wall." Andrew glanced both ways on the street. "Stay behind me. Don't get ahead. We won't push too hard or too fast or we'll be like a thumb sticking out of a glove and they'll come in behind our platoon and cut us off."

"I understand."

Andrew adjusted his helmet and snugged his M-4 tight to his chest. He indicated to the rest of the men from his Stryker that he was ready and the lead man started down the narrow street. Behind them the Stryker backed off far enough that it wasn't vulnerable to any RPGs coming from the nearby buildings. Inside the vehicle, the gunner checked the optics on the remote weapons station for the .50 caliber gun, ready to provide cover fire. They fell into formation, one of the soldiers taking up the rear so Russell wasn't the last man in the line, and moved down the street.

It was quieter after the roar of the Stryker engines diminished. Still omnipresent was the steady crack of automatic gunfire and a constant wave of explosions. The two-way radios in their helmets crackled with short reports from the three platoons – their positions and what sort of resistance they were facing. Left flank, totaling twenty-three men, had the easiest route through the town. The spaces between buildings were wider, giving the enemy fewer hiding places. The thirty-eight men working the right flank had the toughest slogging. The roads leading through the town were narrower and shaped like crescents. The soldiers were constantly rounding corners and dealing with thin crossroads, not much wider than their shoulders. Enemy fire was steady and according to the radio, three troops were already injured. The talk coming back from the point men on all three platoons wasn't good. They were meeting fiercer resistance than expected. Intel had pegged the number of Taliban way too low.

"Get the Strykers to circle the town and lay down some grenade fire on the irrigation canal," Captain Conroy, the officer in charge of the company, ordered over the radio. "Close the back door on these guys. Don't let the ones inside the village get into the canal. Target some of the shells on the back edge of town."

Verbal affirmatives came in from the lieutenants in charge of the platoons. The Strykers were on the move, seven to the west, six to the east. The first Stryker to hit an IED was detouring on the left flank. The explosion tore off two wheels and it leaned precariously to the right. The commander and gunner were uninjured and they radioed in what had happened. Another of the light armored vehicles hit an IED a couple of seconds later. The Taliban had laced the ground surrounding the town with caches of explosives with pressure triggers. The disabled vehicles still had their firepower and the commanders set up firing positions from where they had been hit. Word came across the radio for the rest of the Stryker drivers to find a firing spot ASAP and pull up. They were caught in a minefield and moving anywhere in the area near the town was too dangerous.

The three Strykers with the MK19 grenade launchers settled into position and the commanders input coordinates to the computers. They targeted the narrow band between the village and the canal, and the canal itself. Six minutes after the order to pull back and set up a barrage, they were lobbing grenades onto the rearmost Taliban positions.

Fighting inside the town was intense. Of the seventy-eight men who had entered the town, six were wounded, two severely, and the entire right flank was pinned down by stiff resistance in the narrow alleyways that dominated that side of town. The left flank was moving ahead, but cautiously so that they didn't run ahead of the main force and allow themselves to be cut off from behind. The center force was under the most intense fire, from Taliban entrenched behind the walls bordering the canal and in the houses skirting the main road.

Talk on the radios was confirming something they already suspected. They had been set up. The Taliban had brought in hundreds of men under the cover of darkness. Some of the soldiers had tried ducking into houses for cover and found some of them occupied by scared women and children hiding from the fighting, other buildings were crammed with Taliban. Training, and their ability to react immediately to the volley of fire coming at them, had saved them from being killed. Calls for MEDEVACs were coming in from every squad. They were bogged down and in the fight of their lives.

"RPGs."

The voice came over the radio a second before the first Rocket Propelled Grenade hit one of the Strykers. It bored into the armor between the driver's hatch and the turret, knocking out their communications and disabling the gun. Additional RPG fire came from the canal, peppering the Strykers as they laid down a withering barrage of cannon fire.

Russell was tucked up tight to Andrew, in a small compound just off the main road. A Talib manning a machine gun at the north end of the street, about fifty meters from the canal, had them pinned down. Russell slipped his video camera around the corner and focused it down the street, shooting footage that he couldn't see. Andrew grabbed him by the shoulder and he pulled the camera back.

"Here," Andrew said. He pulled his 9mm Berretta from its holster and handed it to the reporter. "Do you know how to use one of these things?"

"Yes," Russell said, taking the gun.

"When this is over, you hand me the gun and I put it back in my holster. This never happened. You understand?"

"I understand."

Andrew's grip on the reporter's shoulder strengthened. "We're in trouble. Serious trouble. If you see a bad guy, shoot him."

"Got it."

Andrew and two men from his Stryker conferred for a minute, then he took a couple of deep breaths and ran out from behind the wall. The two soldiers ducked out and laid down covering fire on the machine gun. Andrew's legs pumped hard and he wove from side to side toward the Taliban position. He started taking fire and ducked into a doorway. He disappeared inside the house and there was more gunfire from his M-4. Then silence.

In the distance the grenades from the Strykers were targeting the Taliban positions at the canal. Deadly accurate, the rounds were decimating the entrenched Talibs with hot shrapnel. The amount of fire coming from the canal was lessening. Another RPG hit a Stryker, destroying the gun turret. The casualties were mounting – quickly. Radio talk indicated they were down to eight functioning vehicles out of thirteen.

But the tide was beginning to turn. The artillery fire from the Strykers had the Taliban pinned down behind the canal, allowing the soldiers to move up the streets without taking as much fire. They were clearing each house they came to, finding Taliban in many of them. Training in how to enter occupied buildings surpassed the advantage of being dug in, and the US troops cleared the houses with almost no casualties. Both right and left flanks were moving fast now. The problem was in the center where the men were bogged down by the machine gun positioned in the house at the end of the street. They needed to take out the gun, a tough job considering how well entrenched it was.

Andrew's voice came over the radio. "Drop smoke on the street in front of the gun."

Seconds later two plumes of red smoke billowed across the road ten meters in front of the machine gun nest. The heavy thumping of the machine gun followed as the Talib shooter panicked and blindly sprayed the road with lead. Andrew waited until the gunfire stopped, then sprinted toward the smoke. He wove hard left and right in case there were other shooters in the neighboring houses. Nothing. He made it to the smoke and disappeared.

Once inside the smoke screen he ducked hard to the right and rolled until he slammed into a mud wall. He oriented himself, gained his feet, injected a new magazine and lowered his gun. "Cover fire directly up the middle for five seconds," he said into his radio. Small arms fire erupted behind him and he counted. One – two – three, the heavy machine gun opened fire, aiming straight down the road – four – five. He lunged forward as the smoke dispersed, his M-4 on three-burst automatic and aimed at the nest. He cleared the smoke and pulled the trigger again and again. Twenty-seven rounds spit out in three-round busts. His accuracy was perfect. The first shots cut into the men manning the gun and the remaining twenty were overkill. Andrew jammed a new magazine into his gun and jumped through the window the Taliban had been firing from. Three bodies lay splayed out on the dirt floor. One of the men was still alive and grabbing for a rifle. Andrew squeezed the trigger and the Talib's body jerked as the bullets slammed into his chest. He lay motionless on the floor. Andrew double-checked the room and the area outside the rear door.

"Clear," he said into his radio.

The smoke screen had blown off in the afternoon breeze and he looked out the window to see the remainder of his squad moving up the road. Bringing up the rear was Matthews, his camera bag banging against his side as he ran. He clutched the pistol firmly in his right hand, scanning the peripheral buildings for any sign of the enemy.

"You'd make a good soldier," Andrew said as Russell entered the house and fell against the wall next to the door. The reporter was sucking in deep breaths and his face was flushed. His hands shook with nerves and adrenaline.

"You are completely fucking crazy," Russell gasped.

Andrew grinned and checked the mag on his gun. "*Completely* fucking crazy gets you dead. *Sort of* crazy gets the job done."

Russell shook his head and pulled his video camera from the bag. He switched it to record and hit pause. He waited as the squad regrouped, radioed in their position and got the news back on the situation. With the threat in the center of town eliminated, the flanks were pushing to the canal and meeting limited resistance. The grenades from the stationary Strykers were raining down on the canal and the enemy was retreating, using the canal walls as cover.

"I'm almost out of ammo," Andrew said.

"One mag left," another man said. The others agreed. Everyone was low.

"Switch to single shot," Andrew said, adjusting his M-4 from three-round burst. The rest of the men did the same.

Andrew's squad exited through the rear of the house, five of them followed by Russell and Andrew bringing up the rear. Russell hit the pause button and the machine went to record mode. He taped the men ahead of him as they moved slowly up the alleyway toward the canal. There was gunfire on both sides and grenades were exploding almost directly ahead. Russell panned the camera 180 degrees and focused on Andrew, who was intent on keeping their tail clean.

Russell didn't see the Talib with the black turban until he was leveling the gun at Andrew. He came out of a doorway so narrow that he couldn't keep his gun parallel to the ground, and that gave Andrew a half second to react. The specialist spun fast, his finger tightening on the trigger. A single shot ejected from the barrel, the casing flying back and bouncing off the soldier's helmet. The bullet sliced through the hot summer air and smashed into the Talib's face, just above his nose on the right side. The bullet exited his head and took a massive chunk of skull and brains with it, splattering the mess across the door and the dusty wall. The man dropped to the rough stone, blood leaking into the sand and porous rock.

Andrew turned to Russell and stared at the camera. Neither of them spoke. The line of men ahead of them were stopped and looking back. Andrew gave the all-clear sign and jerked his head at Russell.

"Let's move," he said.

The final fifty meters to the north end of town was uneventful. Any Taliban who had been in the center part of town had melded back into the dust and rocks from where they came. Andrew sat on a short wall with a view over the canal. He held out his hand and Russell relinquished the pistol.

"Did you fire it?" he asked.

"No."

Andrew lit a cigarette and watched the troops moving out of the narrow streets to the west and east. The explosions had stopped and there was a spattering of small arms fire. The battle was over. It had been tense for a half hour, then training and determination had kicked in and swayed the outcome. If anyone in the company had ever wondered why they spent so many hours running drills, they weren't wondering anymore.

"Shit, I hate mowing the grass," he said.

Russell looked at him, away from the activity near the canal. "What are you talking about?"

"The FOB is our little garden. No weeds inside the wire. Lots of weeds and grass growing everywhere else. So we have to mow it. If you don't mow the grass, the weeds take over."

"And you have to keep mowing it," Russell said.

"Exactly. You have to keep mowing it."

"Like today."

"Yeah, like today." Andrew closed his eyes and sucked on the cigarette. He blew the smoke in the air and it slowly dissipated on the breeze.

The left and right flanks had secured the back end of the village and the Taliban were beating a hasty retreat down the irrigation canal. Going after them was out of the question. If the troops entered the canal and came up behind them, the Talibs only needed to turn and shoot to kill the first man. Chasing them by running alongside the canal wasn't an option. The entire stretch was likely mined on both sides. The company regrouped at the canal and established its losses.

Three dead, seventeen wounded, seven Strykers destroyed. They called in MEDEVACs and Armored Recovery Vehicles to bring out the salvageable Strykers. Three of them were beyond repair and the company commander called in a Blow In Place strike. The platoons pulled back from the village and cleared a space for the choppers to land to ferry out the wounded, leaving one squad in the village to mop up and ensure the enemy didn't return and start firing RPGs at the helicopters.

When the ARVs arrived to tow the disabled Strykers and the BIP strikes had destroyed the final three Strykers, Andrew and Russell returned to their vehicle and they retraced their way back to the road. The sun was low as they headed back toward Spin Buldak. To safety behind the wire in the FOB.

CHAPTER 22

Kandahar, Afghanistan

The request to meet the man from Peshawar came from Ahmad, with the promise that something good was afoot.

Early in the morning, Kadir hand-washed his shalwar kameez in a rusty bucket and hung it in the open air to dry. Afterward, he trudged back up the stairs to their apartment. A picture of Halima that had been taken about a year ago was propped up on the piece of scrap wood that he used as a chopping board. It was a gift from a nurse at a mobile medical clinic they had attended a month before the snow began to fall. It was his only picture of her, and the edges were dog-eared and smudged with dirt. Halima was smiling at the camera, and her eyes were bright with excitement. He treasured the photo more than anything else he owned. He tucked it into his shirt pocket and set about to making the girls a rudimentary breakfast.

When they were finished eating, he retraced his steps down the treacherous stairwell, retrieved his shalwar kameez and slipped it over his loose-fitting cotton pants. This meeting was beyond important. It was the opportunity of a lifetime – for Halima and her sisters as well. It held the potential for his oldest daughter to be in school, learning to read and write. It was a dream beyond anything he had hoped for. Perhaps it was a manifestation of Halima's dream that she had envisioned and shared with him a few days ago. What was it that she had said? People were talking about her. They had pictures of her. That she had changed the world.

"Yes, of course," Kadir mumbled to himself. "Halima wants to be a teacher. And students always talk about their teachers." He checked his garment for stains but there were none. He turned and waved to the girls who were clustered at the top of the staircase watching him. They waved back as he ducked out from the courtyard into the street.

The distance between the condemned building where he lived and Ahmad's house seemed greater today. Despite walking faster, the trip took longer. Or so it seemed. He arrived twenty minutes before the prearranged time. Ahmad immediately served *chai sabz* with sugar. Kadir sipped the green tea slowly, wanting more before the first cup was finished. When the last drops had wet his lips, he set the empty cup on the low table next to the cushion where he anxiously waited. Ahmad leaned over and poured a second cup and Kadir offered his thanks.

"When is this man arriving?" he asked.

"Soon," Ahmad said. "It's a long journey from Peshawar and the roads are dangerous. Many soldiers use the highway and the Taliban have been busy planting explosives."

"What is his name?"

"Tabraiz Khan," Ahmad replied, adding the Pashto word for mister to the man's first name. Respect for others was paramount in Afghanistan and there were few surer ways of insulting a man in a position of wealth or power than to address him solely by his first name.

"And you have met this man," Kadir said, phrased as a statement, not a question.

"Yes. Once. The day he came for the girl who lived in the tent. He was very polite. And well dressed."

Kadir's hands were shaking as he lifted the simple cup. The tea tasted so sweet. "Then I'm sure he is an honorable man."

A light knocking sound reverberated through the small room. Ahmad rose and opened the door. The hinges squeaked, a tiny detail that had never seemed important. Until now. Framed in the doorway was a tall man dressed in Western-style clothing. His white cotton shirt buttoned up the front and was fitted at his narrow waist. He wore beige dress pants, a brown belt and polished brown shoes. His hair was thick and recently styled, every strand behaving itself. He had a thin face, which suited his trim body, and dark brown eyes. Kadir thought he looked like one of the models in the magazines that were on display in the marketplace.

"Tabraiz Khan. Welcome to my humble house," Ahmad said. He backed up slightly and the man from Peshawar entered the room. His presence immediately dominated the small space.

"Good morning, Ahmad Khan," Tabraiz said. He bowed his head almost imperceptibly to his host, then looked at Kadir. "And you must be Kadir Khan," he said.

Kadir stood and bowed. He kept his useless hand tucked into the folds of his shalwar kameez. "A pleasure to meet you, sir."

"Some *chai sabz* or *chai siaa*?" Ahmad offered. He pointed to the largest and most ornate pillow in the room. "Sit, if it pleases you."

"*Chai siaa*," Tabraiz said, removing his shoes, then sitting and smoothing out the creases on his dress pants. "I much prefer the black tea to the green tea. Much more flavor." He smiled, an easy gesture that revealed slightly crooked but very white teeth. "Thank you for the offer."

Ahmad's wife, her face covered with a translucent scarf, served the tea and prepared a space on the low table for food. She disappeared into the rear courtyard without uttering a word. None of the men offered a salutation.

"How was the trip from Peshawar?" Ahmad asked. He sat, careful not to point his toes toward his guest, a sure sign of disrespect.

"Slow," Tabraiz replied. His voice was deep and didn't match his thin frame. "It's always slow now. ISAF troops are everywhere and the Taliban target their vehicles. I've taken to driving south through Quetta and crossing the border into Afghanistan near Spin Buldak. It's faster, but more dangerous."

"The Americans have a lot of men near Spin Buldak," Ahmad said. "Many tanks."

"It's a Stryker Brigade, not tanks," Tabraiz said nonchalantly. He turned to Kadir. "I understand you have a daughter who would like to attend school."

"Yes, Tabraiz Khan," Kadir said quietly. "She is very smart and would do well with her studies."

"Halima. Is that her name?" Tabraiz asked, then continued when Kadir nodded. "How old is Halima?"

"Eleven. She will be twelve in two weeks."

The Pakistani nodded his approval. "An excellent age to join a family with means. Young enough to learn new skills, and old enough to realize what an opportunity she has." He sipped his tea and leaned closer to Kadir, his eyes focused on Halima's father. "She will have to work hard for the family. Does she understand that?"

Kadir nodded. He knew without thinking that it would not be good to tell the man he had yet to discuss the issue with Halima. "Yes, she does. Halima is a very hard worker. On the days when I am working, she watches her two younger sisters. She fetches water from the well every day and buys our food at the market."

The man raised an eyebrow. "She negotiates with the sellers in the market?" he asked.

Kadir allowed a small smile. "She does. Last week I gave her two American dollars and she returned home with enough food for a week."

"So she is smart and capable."

"Yes," Kadir said.

Tabraiz finished his tea and held out the empty cup as Ahmad hoisted the pot and refilled it. "Tell me of your family, Kadir Khan. Your father and your mother. Your many brothers and sisters."

Kadir's chin fell to his chest. How could it not? A horrible disgrace was upon him. "I have no family. They are all dead."

"Everyone?" Tabraiz asked. His face registered surprise.

Kadir could barely raise his head to answer. Nothing mattered more in Afghanistan than family. Blood and tribal allegiances were the mortar that bonded a besieged population and defined who you were. Without family, without a tribe, you had no identity. At least, not one worth mentioning. Tragedy and death were his heritage. His father, dragged off to Pul-i Charkhi prison by the Russians and eventually shot in the head. His mother, raped and beaten to death by more of the same soldiers. His brother had died as a warrior, fighting with the mujahedeen against the Russian tanks and jets. Cousins, aunts and uncles, nephews – everyone murdered by one form of conqueror or another. He and his three girls were alone in a country that counted family before money.

"Everyone," he said, his voice nothing more than a whisper.

There was a brief silence, then Tabraiz said, "Then it is all the more important that Halima be given a chance to have a good and prosperous life."

Kadir swallowed and raised his eyes. A full minute passed, then he cleared his throat and asked, "What family would Halima be living with?"

"A good question. My client is an accountant for a large multinational company. He has a wife and four children. Two boys and two girls. The oldest child is nine, so Halima would spend a considerable amount of her working hours tending to the children and helping with meals. It is a busy house and with her in school four days a week, Halima would be very tired at the end of each day. Because of this, her wages will be considerable. About one hundred Afghanis a day. But she will have no expenses, so she will be able to save most of what she earns."

Ahmad's wife returned to the room with three plates heaped with food. *Borani*, fried vegetables covered in yogurt sauce, was the largest dish, with sides of *mantu* and rice. The men dug in with their fingers and Tabraiz commented on the high quality of the *mantu*, a ravioli-like pasta with lamb filling. The Pakistani asked about Ahmad and his family, and the conversation centered on the host while they ate. When they were finished, Ahmad's wife returned and cleared the dishes. More *chai* was served and the men settled back into their cushions.

Kadir was amazed at the money the family in Peshawar would pay Halima. The amount was incredible. If she was paid one hundred Afghanis a day, Halima would earn the equivalent of fifteen US dollars a week. A fortune for a twelve year old.

Almost as if he read Kadir's mind, Tabraiz said, "My clients are quite generous.

They feel that by offering their servant girl a decent wage that she can save, it will give her a chance to own a small house after ten years. I trust that seven hundred Afghanis a week is suitable."

"That would be fine," he said, trying desperately to keep his voice even.

"Did Ahmad Khan mention what sort of fee might be paid to you, her father?" Tabraiz asked.

Kadir phrased his answer carefully. The importance of the moment could not be underestimated. "My friend did mention a figure, but he also said that it would be negotiable."

"It could be, to a certain point. But only to a point, Kadir Khan."

Kadir's lips were quivering. The use of his name in the last sentence was a warning not to push any further. He was standing perilously close to the edge of a steep cliff and one wrong step could push him over and kill the chance of Halima having a decent life. He swallowed and lowered his gaze to the elephant-foot carpet adorning Ahmad's floor. The colorful medallions mocked the grayness that enveloped his heart. He was failing his daughter.

"What figure do you have in mind?" Tabraiz asked, a gentler tone in his voice.

"In Afghanis or American dollars?" Kadir asked, not looking up.

"Whichever you prefer."

He forced his eyes up from the carpet. "One thousand five hundred American dollars."

Tabraiz nodded slowly and rubbed his hand across his clean-shaven chin. "That figure is possible, if Halima is a hard worker." He paused for a moment, then added, "Do you have a picture of your daughter?"

Relief surged through his body as Kadir nodded his head. The negotiations were ongoing. He hadn't derailed things with his impertinence. "Yes," he said, digging under his robes. He pulled out the dog-eared photo and handed it to the Pakistani.

"I'd like to meet Halima," Tabraiz said. His eyes were focused on the photo, staring intently, unmoving. "Is that possible?"

"Yes. When and where?" Kadir asked.

"I'm in Kandahar for two more days," Tabraiz said. "Today is Saturday. Maybe we could meet here again on Monday. That would be August the 9th. Does that work for you, Ahmad Khan?"

Ahmad bowed his head slightly. "It is good."

"Kadir?"

The dates confused Kadir, but he understood Monday. Not tomorrow, but the next day. He nodded. "That is fine."

"Same time?" Tabraiz asked.

"Yes, the same time. On Monday."

"Can I keep this picture until we meet again on Monday?" he asked.

"Of course," Kadir said. Any apprehension that he might not get the photo back was beaten down by the opportunity that lay in front of him. Refusing to allow Tabraiz to keep the picture would be an accusation of mistrust.

Tabraiz stood up, as did Ahmad and Kadir. Without letting his eyes glance down, Tabraiz asked, "What happened to your hand?"

Kadir was taken aback by the question. He had kept his hand covered during the meeting. Somehow, the Pakistani must have caught a glimpse of it, perhaps when they were eating.

"I was accused of stealing and my hand was smashed."

"By whom?" Tabraiz asked.

"The Taliban."

Tabraiz eyed him carefully. "Were you stealing?"

Kadir shrugged. "I didn't think so. But he did and what he thought was what mattered."

Tabraiz looked down at Kadir's destroyed hand, now visible. "You must hate them," he said.

Kadir closed his eyes. Visions of his wife bleeding to death in the street flashed through his mind. The acrid smell of gunpowder stung his nose and the dust burned through his eyelids. He felt her blood, thick on his hands, and her last breath, a slight wisp of air against his cheek. He saw the rifle butt slamming down on his defenseless hand and cringed as the bones shattered and unimaginable pain coursed through his body. He opened his eyes.

"I hate what has happened to my country," he said.

Tabraiz walked to the door and paused, his figure backlit by the bright sun illuminating the street. “Maybe it’s time for things to get better. For you and Halima. For Afghanistan.” He bowed his head slightly and left.

Kadir stood, unmoving. It was possible that things were getting better. Tabraiz Khan had come into his life with the promise of a new life for Halima. And for him and his youngest daughters as well. A small house of their own, with money to buy food for months, maybe years. Clean water to drink and warm blankets in the winter. Shoes without holes that kept the water and snow from freezing tiny feet. So many intangibles that might now become realities. The future was opening in front of him with promise and purpose.

He could only hope.

CHAPTER 23

Soho, New York City

Carson woke early on Saturday morning and turned on the coffee machine. For the past two nights sleep had been elusive, the contents of Fleming's e-mail heavy on his thoughts. He had no idea what to make of it.

Received your fee. Team in place. Time frames are tight but should be okay. Crash inevitable.

He wasn't naïve. Nor entirely trusting. Wall Street wasn't populated with a bunch of Boy Scouts sitting around a campfire singing *Kumbaya.* It was a collection of the brightest, most ambitious and brilliant men and women in America who were involved in the most cherished of all commodities. Money. They shaped, or destroyed, the economy of the country, and to some degree, the world. When Wall Street pushed the limits, through derivatives and a host of other complex financial instruments, they were playing Russian roulette. It bothered Carson, but not enough to speak out. That was the last thing Carson was going to do. He liked his job. He needed his job.

He replayed the wording in Fleming's e-mail. *Received your fee.* Money had been paid for a service. Since the e-mail was addressed to Fleming, the money must have come from him. Carson was acutely aware that Fleming didn't hand money out for nothing, so whatever the service was, it must have had value. *Team in place.* Whoever was working the deal was not handling things by themselves. They needed other players, which meant it was something complicated. When you were treading close to the edge of the ethical or legal boundary, involving the least number of bodies possible was paramount. *Time frames are tight but should be okay.* Whatever was happening, it was coming down the pipeline soon. *Crash inevitable.* Without those two words, he would have simply ignored the communiqué. With them, it was impossible to ignore.

William Fleming, and Platinus Investments, held incredible sway over the markets. They were comparable to Goldman Sachs and Citigroup. They competed with the big boys and often came away the victor. If Fleming was planning on manipulating a specific slice of the market – causing some part of it to crash – then pouncing on the carcass before its true value was assessed, he could potentially reap tens of millions of dollars in profits. If that was his intention, it extended far beyond unethical. It was illegal.

The final few drops of water trickled through the filter and Carson poured a cup of coffee. He padded through the dated kitchen to the living room. Nicki was still sleeping and he was quiet not to wake her. The last few weeks had been a real struggle. Yesterday had been a good day, but she could slip backwards so easily and be dead in a week if the wheels came off. He didn't know how much more he could take, and wondered every day how she coped.

He leaned against the windowsill and watched the Saturday morning traffic. The world was so much easier to understand when it slowed down. Weekends, even in New York, were more relaxed. Especially in the summer. He sipped the coffee, savoring the taste and the warmth. The caffeine helped arrange the jumble of thoughts and ideas floating about his head. The one that rose to the top was Fleming's e-mail. It obviously wasn't going away.

The cordless phone was on an end table near the window. He picked it up and dialed Alicia's cell from memory. It rang three times and she answered. She sounded tired and he glanced at his watch. Nine o'clock. He didn't feel guilty – people should be up by nine.

"Hey, you awake?" he asked.

"Barely. It's Saturday morning. I don't feel like working today." The sound of rustling sheets ebbed through the phone.

"I need a favor. Nothing that has to be done right away. It can wait until Monday if you're not going to be near a computer."

"I'm always near a computer," she said. "What do you want?"

"Can you figure out who owns a specific e-mail address?"

"Usually, yes."

"Why usually?"

"You identify the IP Address and trace the owner. It's not hard unless the person on the other end doesn't want to be found, then it's difficult." She was awake now, and intrigued. "Why are you asking?"

"I need you to find out who sent an e-mail."

"I can try. What's the sender's address?" More rustling, this time paper.

"tm5397@gmail.com"

She repeated the sequence of characters carefully, one at a time. "Is that it?"

"That's it."

"I'll give it a try later this morning. I'll call you when I have something."

"Thanks."

"Hey," she said. "What's this all about?"

Carson watched a man and woman talking on the street corner as their dog sniffed a tree and peed on it. "International intrigue. Very dangerous stuff. Be careful."

She laughed. "Sure. If I see James Bond or one of the other MI-6 guys I'll let them know where you live."

"You do that," he said, then set the phone back in its cradle. The sound of pressure on a loose floorboard drifted through the room and he turned from the window. Nicki was coming out of the bedroom dressed in a thick bathrobe. No oxygen tank or hoses. He set the coffee on the sill and said, "You feeling better?"

She nodded and snuggled up against him. She was warm to the touch. "A lot better. My breathing is decent. I don't know what happened but I'm not complaining."

"Good news," he said, hugging her.

"My contact at Sympatico called yesterday. I'm on the top of the list. Priority seating, so to speak. They'll fly me anywhere in the country if they find compatible lungs."

"This is exciting. Your life is going to change."

She looked up at him. "*Our* lives are going to change, Carson."

Silence settled in for a minute, then she said, "I heard you talking to Alicia. Everything okay at the office?"

He made a split-second decision not to tell her what he had seen on Fleming's computer. There was no proof that he was involved in anything and worrying Nicki for no reason had absolutely no merit. "Just some details. One of the evils of being the boss."

She burrowed her head into his chest and they stood motionless. It was a moment when their world was all about them and nothing else. Not his job, not cystic fibrosis, not money or family. It was two people in love, touching each other on every level. It was a moment neither wanted to end.

CHAPTER 24

Outside Spin Buldak, Afghanistan

Decompression.

There was no other way to describe where Russell was. The events in Dabarey the previous day continued to rattle his body and mind. The acrid smell of burnt shells, the pandemonium of the fight for the village, the screams of death. It felt surreal – like it was anchored in the twilight zone and had never happened. One minute the world was in some sort of disjointed harmony – the next it was a demented version of hell.

The harshest moment, when the young Talib took the slug in the face, kept replaying like an image captured in high definition. Russell tried to tell himself the young man was a bad guy – one of the insurgents who planted IEDs in culverts and hid in the bushes, waiting to press the remote detonator and kill ISAF troops. That he was another bin Laden. Nothing but a sliver of human garbage that was intent on destroying any chance the Afghan people had of normalcy in their lives.

How old was he? Seventeen? Eighteen? About the same age as some of the US forces that had stormed the Taliban-infested town. Just a kid. One without a future. Like so many of the American boys who were shipped back to the mainland in sterile metal caskets. No future for them either. Or their families.

Parents, sisters, brothers – torn apart by a split-second action a world away. It worked both ways. This was war, and war provided casualties on both sides.

But the Taliban didn't fight fair. They hid behind cloaks of invisibility by melding into the population. They used their heritage, their skin color and fluency in the language and customs to their advantage. They terrorized the locals who wanted nothing more than peace and murdered those who stood up to them. They played the tribal card, intimidating the mullahs and elders and subjugating the young men. They raped or killed the women. The Taliban had controlled Afghanistan and during that time they had shown their true face. They were brutal, repressive animals, capable of murdering people in public for trivial crimes.

Any vestige of pity he had felt for the young man with the black turban was gone. A vile taste in the back of his throat was all that remained. He glanced up as Andrew James pushed open the door and let himself in.

"You okay?" the young specialist asked. He sat on a wooden chair next to the foot of Russell's cot.

"Yeah," Russell answered confidently. "I'm fine."

"You saw some pretty nasty shit yesterday."

"Nothing I haven't seen before," Russell said. His voice felt detached, like it was someone else talking and he was in the same room, listening. An out of body sort of thing.

"Still, kinda weird seeing someone die like that. Messy business."

"Yeah, it was pretty brutal," Russell agreed. Silence for a minute, then, "It went the right way, though. I'd rather see one of them face down in the dust than one of us."

"No shit," Andrew said, nodding. Another minute passed in silence, then the soldier asked, "Do you have any idea who they are?"

Russell tilted his head slightly, thinking about his answer. The story most North Americans knew, if they had any idea at all, was that the Taliban had formed from Mullah Omar's reaction when a local warlord raped two girls. The one-eyed religious teacher left his madrassa, amassed thirty students and went after the man. Somehow, the Talibs overran the warlord's home base and strung him up from the barrel of a military tank he kept on the property. Omar repeated the violent retribution against other warlords when they crossed the boundaries of what he considered to be acceptable behavior. His reputation grew and two years later, when he draped himself in the Cloak of the Prophet, the people bestowed on him the title of Amir-ul-Momineen, which translated to Leader of the Faithful.

The rest was history. Ugly history. The Taliban slammed the strictest version of sharia law the modern world had ever seen on the people of Afghanistan. No television, no radio, music or dancing. White socks and toothpaste made the list of banned items. Women were required to be veiled outside their home, and even wearing flared pants under their burqa was subject to severe and painful punishment. Men were publicly whipped for trimming their beards. Windows were painted black so no one could see women moving about inside their houses. The list was relentless and grew every week. Afghanistan reverted to the most basic tribal structure, with public beheadings and stonings in the sports stadiums.

Russell thought about the soldier's question. *Do you have any idea who they are?* Truth was, other than the party line he had been fed over the years, he really didn't know who the Taliban were.

"No," he replied.

Andrew grinned. "An honest answer. Cool."

"I take it you have an opinion."

"I do." Andrew relaxed into the chair and put his boots on the edge of a low table. "You probably know all about that Mullah Omar crap," he said, then kept going as Russell nodded. "Almost from day one, the Taliban have been about money. And drugs. Get this – they outlawed using opiates and manufacturing heroin, but allowed making and trading opium."

"That reasoning seems a bit conflicted."

"Very. Right from the start, back in '94 and '95, they were involved up to their necks in the drug trade. One of their first financial backers was Haji Bashir Noorzai, who was, and is, nothing more than a successful drug dealer. He's in jail in New York now – something to do with conspiring to import heroin worth about fifty million into the US. Total piece of crap, this guy. Come to think of it, if he's in jail, maybe he's not all that successful."

"At least they caught him," Russell said. "More than you can say about bin Laden."

"Oh, the whole bin Laden thing. What a complete clusterfuck that was. They had him, you know. Had him in their sights and let him go."

"I did not know that," Russell said.

"Bin Laden flew into Kandahar all the time in the late 1990's. He and his friends from Dubai and the UAE went falcon hunting in the desert. The US had teams in place that could have moved in and taken him out, but they didn't. It turns out that was unfortunate, given what happened."

"How could they justify killing him? He hadn't taken out the World Trade Centers back then."

"He was brokering deals between Arab drug lords and the Taliban and using the money – millions of dollars – to establish terrorist camps. The DEA knew what was going on and they fed information back to the intelligence guys in our government. The problem is, nobody acted on it." The army specialist lit a cigarette and blew the smoke up at the ceiling. "Bin Laden's a thorn in our side, but he's not the big fish."

"Who is?" Russell asked.

"Not who so much as what," Andrew said. "Have you heard of the ISI?"

"Of course. Inter-Services Intelligence. Pakistan's answer to the CIA."

"Now those are bad dudes."

Russell shifted on the bed. Andrew was a good conversationalist and this was a very good conversation. "Why do you say that?"

"The ISI was involved in protecting drug smugglers when the Soviets were in Afghanistan. That never changed. Even Pervez Musharraf said that agents inside the ISI were working with the insurgents. And he was Pakistan's prime minister for a number of years. So that intel is coming from the highest possible level. The ISI is dirty – they were back then and they are today. Those pricks are helping the Taliban, all the while their government is pretending to be our ally. It pisses me off."

"If I have my facts straight, the ISI was responsible for helping to form the Taliban," Russell said. "So this is nothing new."

Andrew shrugged. "They helped, but they never had control over the Talibs. Neither did Benazir Bhutto, who tried to nail down a monopoly on trade to the republics that had split off from the Soviet Union."

"I remember that. She and Naseerul-lah Babar went to the Taliban and brokered some sort of deal with a trucking firm that belonged to some arm of the military. Babar was even quoted as calling the Taliban "our boys" in a press conference."

The door opened and both men spun their heads. It was Captain Brian Hocking. Andrew James jumped to his feet and saluted.

Hocking acknowledged the salute, let the door bang shut behind him and said, "At ease, specialist." He turned to Russell. "I understand you were in the thick of things yesterday."

"Pretty much," Russell said.

"How are you feeling?"

"I'm fine. No problems."

Hocking stared directly into Russell's eyes for fifteen seconds, searching for any indication the man was lying. When he was sure Matthews had pulled through the firefight okay, he said, "You've done this before, I understand. Somalia. Iraq."

"That's correct."

"You outside the wire on those missions as well?"

"Yes, sir." The reference to the captain as sir sounded strangely normal.

The captain shifted a bit, moving his weight from one foot to another. Most people wouldn't have read his apprehension. Russell did.

"Our intel was wrong yesterday," Hocking said. "More than inaccurate, it was deceitful. We relied on a source who had given us some good stuff in the past, but this time he lied to us. We expected about forty tier three enemy forces. What we ran into were over three hundred entrenched tier two Taliban, and the whole area mined with IEDs. We were set up."

"I kind of figured that out."

"I wanted to apologize for dumping you in the middle of it," Hocking said.

His voice was sincere. “That wasn’t my intent.”

“It’s okay,” Russell said.

“Will you be writing a story on what happened yesterday?”

Russell looked at the floor for a minute, then glanced back at the captain and said, “What I saw yesterday – and the pictures I took – are important in reporting what’s going on over here. That said, I don’t see any reason to include graphic violence in the story. I can work with the footage I have that doesn’t show Talib being shot in the face. I can certainly report on the high level of professionalism I saw in our troops.” He paused, then added, “This has nothing to do with appeasing you or anyone else, captain. It has to do with the story. And that’s the story as I saw it happen.”

Hocking remained motionless, then nodded slightly. “That’s fair, Mr. Matthews.” He left through the door as unceremoniously as he had entered.

Andrew stood up. “I have some things to do. I’ll talk to you later.”

“I hope so,” Russell said. “You know a lot about what’s going on over here. Talking with you is a real pleasure.”

“Thanks.” The army specialist retreated to the compound.

Russell gathered his equipment and set to work on the video footage. He edited it down to a thirty second clip that showed the troops moving into position, taking some fire, and cleaning up after. He stored the shot of the Talib taking the bullet in a separate file. Then he sat down to his computer and wrote the copy. Once it was finished and edited, he sent it to his portable printer and read it for timing. With the text whittled down to exactly two minutes, he headed out into the sunshine and rigged his video camera up on a tripod. He positioned it so the front gate of the FOB was in the background. He touched record and walked to the spot in the sand where he had marked an X.

This is Russell Matthews reporting from Spin Buldak on August 8th, 2010. Yesterday, I accompanied three platoons of our troops as they mowed the grass. That’s their term for keeping the area around the FOB clear of Taliban. Mowing the grass. At 07:00 hours, they left the safety behind the wire and headed out on heavily mined roads for the village of Dabarey. What they found in the village was not what they expected. The Taliban had snuck in during the night. They mined the incoming roads and the dusty fields surrounding the village and dug in to wait with three hundred of their best fighters. Less than one hundred of our troops. They in hiding. Us walking into a trap. The fight was intense. Brutal, even. We lost three men. Seventeen wounded. We killed scores of Taliban. I witnessed bravery that I never knew existed. I saw men repeatedly put their lives on the line to capture the town. Then, at the end of the day, we pulled back and returned to the FOB. So why did we do it? Why did the soldiers of the 5th Brigade venture out from behind the wire and risk their lives? Because the soldiers look at Afghanistan as a garden. It's a garden that's choking on weeds and the Afghans don't have the gardeners to tend it. That falls to the US and Canadian and British forces working in the Kandahar and Helmand regions of southern Afghanistan. It falls on us to give the men, women, and children who live in villages like Dabarey a chance at a normal life. The right to attend school. The right to a life without fear and violence. The right to a stable and just government. There's a cost – an incredible cost – to this responsibility. But the men and women who venture outside the wire believe in their mission. They believe Afghanistan is worth saving. This is Russell Matthews, reporting from Spin Buldak, near Kandahar, Afghanistan.

Russell switched off the camera and returned to his bunk. He plugged in his computer, transferred the video files to his hard drive and spliced in some of the footage from the fighting in Dabarey with his voiceover. He watched it run, edited it a bit more, then saved it and sent the file to Anita in Boston.

CHAPTER 25

Kandahar, Afghanistan

Kadir brushed Halima's hair with a ratty comb that caught on the tangles and jerked her head each time he tried to force it through her thick curls. Finally he gave up and pulled her hair back and tied it with her scarf.

"Who are we meeting, father?" Halima asked.

"A man from Peshawar," he answered nervously. "A very important man."

Halima sensed the apprehension in her father. "Why are we meeting him?"

Kadir adjusted the scarf, then sat in front of her on a cinder block. His hands were shaking as he touched them to her cheeks. "This man may have an opportunity for you. The kind of opportunity that is very rare. We are most fortunate."

"What sort of opportunity?"

Kadir measured his words. He needed Halima on side and eager about the prospect of living in Pakistan. Taking her kicking and screaming to see Tabraiz was impossible. The man would walk out of the meeting and their lives would remain exactly as they were. Desperate.

"He can get you into a school."

Halima's eyes widened and she sucked in a sharp breath. She clutched her father's hands and said, "Oh, I *do* want to go to school. Badly."

Kadir looked at the dusty floor. "The school is not in Kandahar, Halima."

Her grip on his hands faltered. She sat back. "Where is it?"

"Peshawar. It's a city in Pakistan."

She managed a hint of a smile. "Maybe you can find work. And we can have a house."

"I won't be coming with you, Halima. Aaqila and Danah and I will be staying in Kandahar."

She pulled back from him and shook her head. "I don't want to live in Pakistan without you. It's impossible." Tears pooled in her eyes. "How can you watch Aaqila and Danah without me? You can't. And if you have to watch them, you can't work."

"I'll get by. So will your sisters. This isn't about us, it's about you. This opportunity is for you, Halima." He set his hands on her thin shoulders and lowered his head slightly so he could look directly into her eyes. "You will have a chance to live in a nice house, with a family, and go to school and get an education. Then, when you have finished school, you can come back to Afghanistan and get a job as a teacher or a doctor. And because you have a good job, Aaqila and Danah will be able to attend school. Everything will change, Halima. Everything. You will have a good life. *We* will have a good life."

She was crying, tears coursing down her cheeks and spilling onto the front of her embroidered blouse. She had seen her father like this in the past – his mind set and unwavering. She knew it was not possible to change things once he had made his decision. She was listening to him tell her that her life had changed. That her city, her country, her family, were soon to be nothing more than memories. She raised her hand and wiped away the tears. Afghans were strong people, and right now she needed to be strong.

"Where will I live?" she asked. She couldn't believe the words that were coming out of her mouth. The calmness with which she delivered them.

"A beautiful house," her father said. "And you will have your own bedroom. But you will have to work to earn your keep."

"What will I do?"

"Clean, and cook some meals. You are very good at both." He stroked her cheek. "We need to leave now to meet him." He wiped at the last remnant of a tear at the edge of her eye. "Are you okay?"

She nodded bravely. "I am, father."

They collected Aaqila and Danah, then made their way down the rubble-strewn staircase and into the street. Two blocks from their makeshift apartment, Kadir hailed a cab. They piled in, Kadir ensuring the driver that he had the money for the fare by showing it. Halima was going to ask why they could suddenly afford such an extravagance, but decided against it. Today was a strange day, filled with new things, and taking a taxicab was simply another one to tack onto the list. The trip to Ahmad's house was short, and cost thirty Afghanis. Kadir reluctantly handed over the cash, then herded the girls from the car and across the street to Ahmad's door. It opened before he could knock.

"Kadir, my friend," Ahmad said. "You are right on time. Five minutes to nine."

"It is rude to be late," Kadir said. He greeted the man with a firm handshake, then placed his right hand over his heart. His friend mirrored the gesture.

They entered the house and Kadir was shocked to see that Tabraiz had already arrived. He was seated on a pillow in a corner and stood when they came in through the door. He was dressed in business clothes again, with a suit jacket and a freshly pressed shirt. Ahmad's wife appeared in the doorway leading to the rear courtyard and at their father's bidding, Aaqila and Danah followed her into the mid-morning sun. Kadir and Halima sat next to each other, across from Ahmad and Tabraiz.

"So you are Halima," Tabraiz said. "Your father has told me so much about you." When the girl didn't respond, he continued. "He said that you want to attend school and learn to read and write."

Halima stared directly at him, and nodded.

Tabraiz waited for her to answer, but after a few seconds it was apparent she wasn't going to speak. "I have a family in Pakistan who are looking for a girl to help around their house. They have four children – the oldest is nine, almost your age. The mother and father are very busy, so they have need of someone to help with the household chores. Your job will be mostly cooking and keeping the house clean. And watching the children sometimes. In return, you will have your own room and you will earn one hundred Afghanis a day."

"When can I visit my father?" Halima asked.

Tabraiz's eyebrows pushed down a touch and slight wrinkles creased his face near his mouth. "That may not be possible for quite some time, Halima. You will be working every day and attending school four days a week. During the school holidays you will be busy with the children. It may be a few years before you see your father or your sisters again."

"My sisters will be grown. I may not recognize them."

Tabraiz smiled. "You will know them when you see them. Family is like that."

Kadir touched his daughter on the shoulder and said, "This is important for you, Halima. To have a chance at a good life. At an education. I am your father and I can tell you that you must do this, but I prefer for you to agree. To want this change in your life."

She stared straight ahead, her eyes fixed on some unseen and unimportant object. A sheen washed over her eyes – then abated before tears could form. Then, for a moment, she was gone. Unconstrained by reality, in a world where her imagination was the only cage. A world where, at least for a few precious seconds, no one else could intrude. Sitting by the Arghandāb River with her mother, a soft autumn breeze tussling her hair. The sound of water trickling across smooth, timeworn stones. The scent of pomegranate on the air. There were no words – none were needed. Love was not a word that needed to be explained. And everything was good in the world.

That life had been torn away years ago. She barely remembered the warmth in her mother's smile, the passion in her eyes. But tucked somewhere in a remote recess of her mind was a sliver of the distant memories. She drew deep from the well, reaching out, struggling to touch the ethereal cloud that could never again be anything more than a dream. Halima opened her eyes and stared directly at the man from Peshawar.

"I would be pleased to live in this house and to work for this man and his wife." There was no smile on her face, or in her eyes.

Tabraiz measured her response, then said, "Once you go, that will be your life."

"I understand," she said. She smiled and the life returned to her limbs. She brushed a hair back under her headscarf. "I will work very hard. In the house and in school. When I return, I will be educated."

Tabraiz smiled and nodded, very slowly. "Yes, exactly. You will be able to make a difference to your city, Halima." He turned to her father. "My terms are acceptable, Kadir Khan?"

"They are."

"Then I will be in touch. It will take some time, perhaps a couple of weeks. I will let you know when I have the agreement in place with the family." He slipped his hand inside his suit jacket and retrieved the photo of Halima, which he handed to Kadir. "Thank you for the picture, it was very helpful."

"You're welcome," Kadir said. Confidence surged through him. The Pakistani had said he would return the photo and he had. He was a man of honor and his word could be trusted. He tucked the photo safely away in a pocket.

"Kadir is difficult to reach," Ahmad said. "You can contact me and I will be sure that the message is delivered."

"Thank you," Tabraiz said. He took the appropriate amount of time to say his goodbyes, then left, closing the door behind him.

Safa appeared at the back door and Halima joined her, the girls distracted by looking at how her wounds from the shrapnel were healing. Safa's mother called and they disappeared into the rear courtyard leaving Kadir and Ahmad alone in the house.

"It is necessary," Kadir said quietly. He ran shaky fingers across the smooth metal of the teacup.

"Halima will return a woman of great importance," Ahmad said.

Kadir nodded, but wasn't sure. If this was such an incredible opportunity, then why wasn't Safa leaving for Pakistan? The question hadn't occurred to him until this moment. He pondered asking Ahmad, but decided against it. His friend had introduced him to Tabraiz and was responsible for brokering a life-changing deal. To question his motives would be the greatest insult he could hurl at the man. He must keep his doubts locked away.

"She will change the world," he said.

The words were charged with electricity and he realized that he absolutely believed them to be true.

CHAPTER 26

Kandahar, Afghanistan

Dusk was settling over the Governor's Palace, and across the street at the Mosque of the Sacred Cloak, the late-day sun glistened off the Helmadi marble and mirror tile. A sharply dressed man sat under one of the archways leading to the cloistered room containing the cloak that had once adorned the Prophet Mohammed. Armani sunglasses reflected the glare and hid his penetrating eyes from passersby. He watched the approaching police officer with a detached sort of amusement.

"Nice uniform," Tabraiz said when the man stopped in front of him. Sarcasm washed through his voice.

The Afghan National Police officer was sweating profusely and dark stains formed visible rings under his arms. Beads of sweat dotted his forehead. His eyes darted from side to side, and he shielded himself from the men entering the mosque by turning his back to them.

"It was foolish to meet here," the ANP officer said.

"*You* wanted to meet," Tabraiz said. "Not me."

"I wanted to meet, but not here."

His name was Kunar Lodhi, and for six years he had been Tabraiz's eyes and ears inside the ANP. Money was constantly moving from the Pakistani to the

Afghan – money that bought certain assurances of privacy and the opportunity to operate outside the law. But things were changing. The police force was morphing away from the practice of graft and incompetence and becoming a collection of men willing to enforce the law. A new connection to the Canadian military was shaping both the government police force and the army into working units, shocking some Afghans and pleasing others. It depended entirely on which side of the law you lived on. Kunar was a dinosaur who was still on another man's payroll with no intention of enforcing the laws. But his ranks were dwindling and it was becoming difficult to keep prying eyes at bay.

"What do you want?" Tabraiz asked.

"You are not safe," Kunar said. "The net is closing in on you. Quickly."

The arrogant posture Tabraiz had brought to the meeting left him. "What are you saying?" he asked.

Kunar licked his lips, dry from the relentless wind and sand. "They know who you are and what you're doing. I can't protect you any longer."

Tabraiz slipped off his sunglasses, his eyes burning with anger. "When did this happen?"

"We have weekly meetings on Friday. I was given an assignment on the south side of the city and kept out of the meeting. I only found out this morning that they were talking about arresting you. They know you're in Kandahar and are planning to throw you in jail."

Tabraiz did the math. It was Monday night, three full days since the ANP had sat around a table and discussed arresting him. He was surprised they hadn't been at his hotel, waiting for him. Maybe they had. He hadn't returned to the hotel since his meeting with Halima and her father earlier in the day. They could be waiting for him. They probably were.

"This changes everything," he said. He thought for a minute, then asked, "Who is looking for me?"

"The commander of my section. His name is Farouk. He has three men dedicated to tracking you."

Tabraiz wanted to scream at his informant. To demand why he was only finding out about this now. But it was useless. The man had reacted in a timely fashion when he found out. The only ones to blame were the ISAF forces that had brought their version of ethics and legality to a country that functioned perfectly well before they arrived. Now things were out of control – the police sticking their noses into things that had been the status quo for decades.

Tabraiz Masood traded in human flesh. For fifteen years he had provided young girls and boys to wealthy men in the United Arab Emirates and Saudi Arabia for sums of money that far exceeded what most people earned in a decade, some in a lifetime. The girl who lived in the tent south of Kandahar had netted him thirty-two thousand US dollars after expenses. Halima was a much better catch, and after e-mailing the photo of her to his client in the UAE, he had negotiated a fee of sixty-five thousand dollars upon delivery. Subtracting the fifteen hundred for her father, another one thousand to the ANP officer, two thousand to transport her, and four thousand to his contact in Peshawar who posed as a successful businessman with a lovely family, he would net just over fifty-five thousand dollars. Far too much to let slip through the cracks. He needed to make this deal work.

It would be his last transaction in Kandahar. His swan song. He was okay with that. He could rebuild the business somewhere else.

"I'll leave Kandahar immediately," he said to the cop on his payroll. "Today is August 9th. I'll be back in exactly two weeks, on August 23rd, to pick up the girl."

The policeman nodded, visibly relieved that his patron was leaving the city. "What do you need from me?"

"Two things. First, I want you to deliver fifteen hundred dollars to Kadir Hussein. I'll give you the name of another man who can contact him and set up the meeting. Assist Kadir to the bank and help him set up an account. Be of service to him. Be polite. Tell him that I had business in Peshawar and that I will return on the 23rd to get Halima. I want to meet just outside the south edge of the city, near Shakpur Darwaza Chowk-e. It's dark and deserted in that section of town. You can pick the exact place, but I want it surrounded by open fields with some valleys or rock outcroppings nearby. I can protect myself from an attack if I can see it coming. Do you understand?"

"Yes. This is not a problem. I know of a place that is only a few hundred meters out of the city, with a hill to the north and a narrow valley to the south. I'll scout it and make sure."

"Good," Tabraiz said. "The other thing we will need is a diversion. You must give Farouk a reason to be on the north side of Kandahar while we meet to pick up the girl. A shipment of drugs, something like that."

"I can arrange that," the policeman said. He wasn't sweating now, realizing that the situation was in hand. That Tabraiz was taking this threat seriously. "What time do you want this to happen?"

"At dusk. I need a bit of daylight so I can see what is happening around me, but enough darkness that I can slip away if things go wrong."

Tabraiz motioned to the police officer to follow him and they walked away from the mosque to the road. When they reached the parking lot, the Pakistani took an envelope from his pocket and counted out two thousand five hundred American dollars. He handed it to Kunar.

"One thousand five hundred for Kadir Hussein. One thousand for you."

"Thank you, Tabraiz Khan," the man said, taking the money.

"Make this happen. Exactly as I have told you."

"It is done."

"We'll see about that," Tabraiz said.

He left the parking lot in the same taxi that had brought him to the mosque. Sitting in the back of the car, he poured over his options. He could wait in Kandahar for two weeks and risk being discovered or he could slip over the border into Pakistan and travel back to Peshawar. He disliked traveling by car through the lawless regions that separated the two countries, but that was his only option if he left Afghanistan by one of the southern routes. Flying out of Kandahar wasn't possible. Farouk would have one of his men watching the outgoing flights. Driving north to Kabul and flying over the mountains to Peshawar was probably the best choice. It was a long trip but nowhere near as dangerous as trying to navigate the southern route, through Spin Buldak, which was crawling with ISAF forces. The final option was to leave Afghanistan and not return. Let Halima live out her life with her sisters and father. That option wasn't even on the list. He wanted the money.

Halima was a great find. She was pretty, with a strong spirit and quick mind. And the perfect age. Old enough to be menstruating and still a virgin. The kind of girl his client paid top dollar for. He wondered how long she would live. Two years, tops. Then the Arab would tire of her and either kill her or sell her into slave labor in one of the third-world factories that made much of the first-world clothing. He didn't care. The girl was expendable. She was nothing more than a commodity. The tiny gap her disappearance would make was indiscernible, and another girl would fill that space immediately. The world didn't care what happened to her. Only her father cared. And he was nothing. A man without family or a tribe. Useless and without influence or power.

Halima was in demand and he was going to broker the deal. It was that simple.

Tabraiz decided on heading overland to Kabul, then on to Peshawar by plane. He rattled off some instructions to his driver and settled back for the trip. In the grand scheme of things, this was nothing but an irritant. And certainly not the worst one he had ever faced.

CHAPTER 27

Frankfurt, Germany

Julie Lindstrom checked the list. It was concise and uncluttered – every item necessary to bringing off a perfect show. At the top of the page was a single word followed by a date.

Frankfurt – August 10, 2010.

U2 was in town and Frankfurt was in a frenzy over the concert scheduled for Commerzbank Arena that night. A local radio station was promising two free front row tickets for the show to the fan who could come up with the most original new lyrics for *Where the Streets Have No Name.* In German of course. An affiliated television station was giving up four of the coveted ducats for the cleverest clone of the band. Faux Bonos and Edges were everywhere. The whole thing was surreal.

It was business as usual for the woman heading up security for the world's most popular rock band.

Julie scanned down the list. All the different levels of personnel, including security, were listed. Crowd safety stewards. Front of house staff. Hospitality stewards. Back stage security. Gate auditors. Merchandise security. Night security staff. Concession checkers. The list ran on for two pages, showing the local security personnel needed for the gig and the name of each staff member who was overseeing them. Her staff, and no one else, handled the most crucial parts of the band's security once the stars arrived and were on-site. The extras watched over things before the band arrived and formed the ring of heavies around the stage when Bono and the boys were playing. The real security, the stuff that actually kept the band safe, happened behind the scenes.

She set the list on the table in her hotel suite and picked up the schematics of Commerzbank Arena. It was originally built in 1925 and updated over the years, but had been completely renovated from the ground up between 2002 and 2005. Her assistant had used a comprehensive set of the latest drawings to arrange the arrival and departure routes for the band and their immediate entourage, and she double-checked his work. There were two points on the route that worried her and she marked them in red. She would be at the stadium five hours prior to the concert and would walk every step of the proposed paths in and out of the stadium. Nothing was ever left to chance.

Her cell phone rang and she pushed the green button. A voice tinged with a Russian accent was on the other end. It was Dimitri Volstov, the promoter for the Moscow concert. He liked details and was treating the concert as if it were a business transaction inside Murmansk-Technika, his multi-billion dollar flagship company. He was professional and dealt with things on his end as they arose. She liked promoters who weren't constantly on the phone whining at her.

"Hello, Dimitri," Julie said.

She caught her reflection in the wall mirror and pushed her shoulder-length mousy brown hair back from her face. She hated the color. It was so nondescript – so vanilla. Tiny lines ran from the corners of her eyes and she touched her skin, applying just enough pressure to smooth them. The rest of her face was still young looking for her age and her eyes were bright green. She couldn't begin to count the comments – compliments, actually – she had received on her eyes. She was pretty. It wasn't ego, simply a fact. And Dimitri Volstov was handsome and rich. In fact, the man was ridiculously rich. And he was single. Every time they talked she wondered if he found her attractive. "How are things in Moscow?"

"Wonderful, now that I'm talking to you."

Volstov was one of her favorite people – anywhere. She had known him for about two years – their initial introduction had come when he was staging a benefit concert for Afghan refugees in late 2008. She seldom stayed in touch with concert promoters, but Volstov was different. He was generous and popular for the right reasons. She liked him a lot. Probably more than she should like a client. "What can I do for you, Dimitri?"

"We're getting close to the date and I wanted to know if there is anything you need of me."

"Not right now. I'll have an advance team in Moscow on August 22nd, three days prior to the concert. They'll be in touch with you and your staff and will go over everything. Until then, nothing. I already have the plans of the stadium that you sent me and we're completely staffed for security at all levels. We're good, but thanks for offering."

"You're organized." A pause, then, "Where are you today?"

"Frankfurt. Then we have two shows in Horsens and two in Helsinki, and after that…Moscow."

Volstov's voice grew serious. "How is Bono's back?" he asked.

"Better than it was a couple of months ago. It looks like the European tour will go ahead. This is only their second show after the cancelled North American tour, but he's feeling okay and wants to perform. Don't quote me on it, but I think your show in Moscow will go as planned."

"Fantastic. The city is getting excited and there are all sorts of competitions for people to win tickets."

"It's good when the city gets engaged. The band likes the energy."

"When are you flying in?" Volstov asked. "I'd like to have dinner."

"I'm not sure if I'll come in with the advance team or a day later. And of course we'll have dinner. I might even let you pay," she teased him. No one took their wallet out when they were with Volstov in his city.

"This is good. I'll let you go."

"I'll talk to you soon."

Julie hung up and walked to the coffee machine on the credenza. She poured a cup, added some cream and sugar, and sat on the couch, reflecting on the rollercoaster ride her life had taken to get her to this place and time. Thirteen years with the FBI, embroiled in domestic counter-terrorism, had given her the credentials she needed to open her own security firm. It had also cost her the chance to have children and finally, her marriage. She didn't blame her ex, he had taken a subservient role to the bureau for ten of the eleven years they had stayed together. The first year was the honeymoon, then the job had steamrollered both of them. In retrospect, she realized she had let it. She had made a choice and it had turned out to be a very bad one. Ryan was a wonderful man and she missed him. Everyday.

She was a fit, attractive thirty-eight year old who spent at least an hour in the gym five or six days a week. Other than that, her focus right now was her company. Details Matter was fast becoming the premier security firm for high-profile bands and celebrities on tour. She had built her business by establishing herself and her team as the one company that could think of every detail and ensure the event came off seamlessly. Three years and counting, and she now had U2 on her client list, among others. Having the Irish rockers really helped. Her marketing and business departments were in negotiations with heaps of big-name bands for their upcoming tours. Once you had the best, the rest followed.

The hotel phone rang and she plucked it from the cradle. It was one of the locals who were sub-contracting the muscle for the front of the stage. Problems. Nothing new. She listened, then jotted down the concerns and penciled in a name behind each line. Identify the problem. Come up with a solution. Assign a person to initiate action and carry through until the problem didn't exist. There was no such thing as a problem without a solution. She assured the man his concerns would be dealt with immediately. It disarmed him and when he hung up the phone, his voice was even and relaxed. She set the phone back in the cradle and pulled out her cell. Not a big deal.

Another day, another rock concert.

CHAPTER 28

Kandahar, Afghanistan

Kandahar Airfield was never without some sort of activity. It serviced a limited number of civilian flights, but the majority of the traffic in and out was military. Supplies and troops for forty-three countries funneled through KAF on their way to and from southern Afghanistan. Teams of logistics experts tagged and organized the massive shipments of food and arms that arrived daily. Among them were eighty-one crates of weapons from Bonn, Germany. The crates had been on the ground for five days, since Thursday, August 5th, and it was time to get them moving.

US Army Specialist Eric Strand was in charge of expediting specific shipments of armaments from the airfield to the Forward Operating Bases. This one fell under his jurisdiction. He checked the paperwork, noting that everything was in order and all the necessary spaces were complete with signatures. Sixty-two of the crates were filled with Javelin shoulder-fired anti-tank rockets. They were being assigned to the 5th Stryker Brigade. He knew the Stryker crews liked having the Javelins strapped to the sides of their vehicles. It made taking out an entrenched enemy position a lot easier. The rest of the shipment was fine. Two 81mm Mortars, a few crates of M134D mini guns and a couple of hundred M-4s. He signed off on the shipment and authorized it to be loaded for transport to the

FOB.

"The boys in Spin Buldak are going to be happy about this one," he said to the soldiers who showed up to move the crates. "Two hundred and fifty Javelins."

The man smiled. "Last time we delivered Javelins they gave us a bottle of Jack Daniels. And there were only about a hundred in that one."

"Lucky you," Strand said.

The driver checked the manifest and said, "Strange for these to be coming out of Germany." He glanced at Strand for a reaction.

Strand shrugged. "The paperwork is in order. That's all I care about."

"Okay. We'll have them to the boys sometime tomorrow."

"Don't forget to get a signature."

The man shook his head. "Not a chance."

Strand wagged a finger at the driver. "Make sure they get to the FOB and don't end up with the ragheads."

"Bastards could do some damage with these."

Strand didn't answer. He didn't want to think about it.

* * *

Midtown Manhattan, New York

"We're chasing at least three stocks," Chui Chang said. He was in the doorway of Carson's office on the forty-sixth floor at Platinus Investments, and he was not happy with the printouts he held in his hand. "It's not good. We need to back off or we're going to do some damage."

Carson ran his hands through his hair. They were shaking. Not much, but enough to warn him that the man standing in front of him was probably deadly accurate in his assessment. The stripped down algorithm was proving to be more dangerous than he thought. It was front-running stocks, driving them up beyond their tangible value. Other traders were jumping in, anticipating a bump in the limit price and looking to make a few million with a quick flip. The trouble was, the algorithm believed the frenzy it was creating to be true.

Without the additional iterations to smooth the bid-ask curve, it was unable to determine the difference between real value and perceived value. Platinus Investments was on the edge of a very slippery slope, and it was dragging a handful of stocks with it.

"Which stocks?" he asked.

Chui read them off the sheet. Carson knew all three by name, but wasn't positive what products or services they offered. If memory served him, one was involved in mining operations in South America and another was the parent company for a health care provider. Big business. Not to be rocked easily by a slight glitch in their share prices. He checked his watch. Three o'clock EDT. The market would be closing for the day soon, and there would be no more damage today. Maybe things would settle into place by Wednesday morning. It was a risk he was willing to take.

"We wait and see what happens when the market opens tomorrow," he said. "If things continue to move in the wrong direction, we shut it down and restart the old algo."

"Okay," Chui replied.

"How are things coming on building the new algo?" Carson asked.

"Fine, but it takes time. I don't need to tell you that. Writing these things is what you did before you got your ass transferred to that chair."

Carson couldn't help laughing. "I didn't get transferred, Chui, I got promoted. I'm your boss. Remember?"

"I think what you're doing is dangerous."

"William Fleming is happy. And right now, that's what counts."

"Careful serving a boss with a twisted agenda," Chui said.

"What's twisted about making money?"

Carson's phone rang and Chui shook his head and returned to the hallway. Carson checked the caller ID and picked up the phone. "Hi, Alicia."

"Chui talk to you yet?" she asked.

"He just left. You want to grill me as well?"

"I'd like to. The program is behaving badly, but I'm sure Chui told you that. I called about the e-mail address you gave me."

"What about it?"

"Who is this guy, Carson? And how did you get mixed up with him?"

Carson leaned forward, his senses perking up. Alicia's tone was beyond intrigued. It was cautious. Scared, almost. "What's going on?"

"His name is Trey Miller, and he's ex-CIA. When he was with the agency, he was in covert operations."

"He was a spy?" Carson asked. The word sounded so strange coming from his lips.

"I'm not sure *exactly* what he did, but he was definitely the type of guy who was responsible for getting the CIA's fingers slapped."

Carson gripped the phone tighter. "How do you know this?"

A pause, then, "I couldn't get past the firewalls so I asked a friend of mine to have a look."

"Who is this friend of yours?"

"A hacker. His name is Aaron."

"He hacked into the CIA's database?" Carson whispered.

Silence.

"Alicia? What did this guy do?"

"He took a quick look at Miller's dossier."

"Where's the information your friend dug up?" Carson asked between short breaths. There was no sense in ignoring the result of the intrusion. The damage was done, he might as well see what they had found.

"He downloaded it to a memory stick and gave it to me this morning."

"Can I see it?"

"Of course."

"I'm coming down." Carson hung up and grabbed his suit jacket. What the hell was going on? Why was Fleming mixed up with someone from the CIA? And now, with the algorithm driving stocks up beyond their true value, things were quickly spinning out of control. Today was Tuesday and Fleming was due back in New York on Friday. He needed answers by then.

No, that wasn't right. He needed answers before then.

CHAPTER 29

Outside Spin Buldak, Afghanistan

Andrew showered, dressed in his combat fatigues and went searching for Russell. He found the reporter near the south wire staring at the distant mountains that divided Pakistan and Afghanistan. A border drawn by one generation of men and ignored by all others. To the Pashtun tribes living on either side of the imaginary line, it didn't exist. They traveled back and forth between the two countries as they had for thousands of years, without the slightest hesitation. Their cultures, their families, their heritage trumped any divisions. Bottom line was, they didn't care it was there. It was life as normal.

It fascinated the journalist. It always had.

Russell turned at the sound of crunching gravel. He nodded to Andrew. "Good morning."

"And to you," the army specialist said. He sat on a crate and lit a cigarette. "Are you ready for an adventure?"

"Where to?" Russell asked. His pulse quickened at the thought of leaving the safety afforded by a handful of HESCO bastions and a few rolls of razor wire.

"Oh, you're going to love this. We're actually being shipped out on Friday for the next two weeks or so. We'll be staying at another FOB. Ma'sum ghar. It's on the west side of Kandahar. It's pretty crazy over there. Captain told me to let you know that you don't have to go with us. You can stay here if you want. It's totally up to you."

Russell set his empty coffee cup on the small table next to his chair. "Sell me on why I should go with you. I'm rather enjoying the security of this place after what happened in Dabarey."

Andrew sucked in some smoke and blew out smoke rings that dissipated in the slight breeze. "We'll be working almost hand-in-hand with the Canadians. A very polite group. Always say please and thank you. They even have a Tim Horton's coffee shop at KAF."

"You don't have me yet. What else?"

"The area is totally nuts. Like the Wild West. The road running out of Kandahar down to Mūshān is the most heavily mined road in the world. IEDs everywhere. It's in a valley and the Taliban wait in the hills for us. They target the convoys that keep our Combat Outposts supplied. If we're lucky enough to make it to Mūshān, we have to drive through the center of town to get to the final COP. It's the most insane place in the entire country. Dudes with snakes and little flutes, birdcages filled with exotic birds everywhere, and everyone has a gun. I'm not shitting you. That's deadly accurate."

"And this is your way of talking me into going?" Russell asked.

Andrew shrugged. He dropped the cigarette and ground it out with his heel. "I thought you were looking for a story."

"I am."

"If you want to see what's happening outside the wire, Ma'sum ghar is the place. And we'll be closer to Kandahar. If something goes down in the city, you can cover that as well."

"Okay, now you're talking."

A convoy of six trucks and four Strykers came into view over a rise to the north. Supplies coming from KAF. They rolled up to the gates and entered the compound. A group of local Afghans, hired to work inside the base, congregated at the trucks and began to unload them. Numerous long, narrow crates were placed on pallets then shuffled toward a heavily-fortified underground bunker.

Andrew grinned. "Javelins," he said. "Man, I love those things."

"I've seen them before. They're high-tech rockets, aren't they?" Russell asked.

"Yeah. They're great for clearing out the snipers. Not at all subtle. You press the trigger and the side of the building is gone. The problem is, they're expensive and we get read the riot act for using them." He counted the number of crates and mentally did the math. "There are somewhere between two and three hundred of them in that shipment. Somebody, somewhere, likes us."

They both watched two larger crates being moved by forklift to a central location in the base.

"They look like 81mm Mortars," Andrew mused. "But I can't imagine them giving us that sort of artillery here."

A few smaller crates were unloaded and stacked in the shade. Some small, very heavy wood boxes were the last to be unloaded, and the trucks returned to the front gate. They cleared the wire and headed back toward Kandahar.

"M-4s and ammo," Andrew said. "Strange that they'd ship those."

"You don't need ammo?" Russell asked.

"No, not the ammo, the guns. We bring our weapons with us and keep them for the duration of our tour." He turned back to face the reporter. "Well, what do you think? Want to come with us to Ma'sum ghar or stay here with the pussies."

"Well, put that way..."

"Thought so," Andrew said. He gave the journalist a loose salute and headed back into the center of the FOB.

Russell watched the specialist walk away. Andrew intrigued him. He was different from a lot of the other soldiers – more of a big picture guy. He really understood the issues that were at the root of the conflict. Chances were that James would make a good story. Maybe. He just didn't know how.

Not yet at least.

CHAPTER 30

Moscow, Russia

Five days had passed since Trey Miller and his team had set the wheels in motion to take down the U2 concert in Luzhniki Stadium. They had already made a substantial dent in the list of tasks Trey had prepared. But as they moved ahead, new obstacles were emerging.

The lease for the retail space on Usaceva was signed and they had taken possession of the unit. Dark paper covered the windows and it was impossible to see in from the street. The traffic on Hamovniceskij Val, a main artery to the north of the stadium, masked the noise and vibrations the team made cutting through the floor and the cast-cement pipes of the storm sewer system. The entire team had spent a few hours in the complex maze of pipes running under the street, and they all had a healthy respect for the complexity of what they had undertaken.

It was a horrible mixture of hundred-year-old, decrepit tunnels that felt like they were going to collapse, thirty-year-old sections covered in slime and new ones that hadn't been added to the latest drawings. The electrical conduits were helter-skelter and not properly noted on the schematics, making it difficult for Petr Besovich to locate the optimum places to splice into the system. If he only had to cut into the grid in one place, it would have been tough. But the electrical feed to the stadium came in on a handful of separate lines. It was simple to determine that there were six main conduits. Finding the right places to access a junction box on each of the six was a nightmare. Every time he found a place that looked good on paper, it wasn't the same when he was underground actually looking at it.

They met in the lobby of the Korston Hotel on Wednesday at two in the afternoon. Each of them wore a grim expression.

"This is a clusterfuck," Besovich said. "It's impossible."

"Nothing is impossible," Trey remarked. "Simply more difficult than we thought."

"I can't find one place to cut into the grid," Besovich snapped. "Not one. And I need six to take down the power. It's not working."

"You still have two weeks," Trey said.

"I need better plans."

"Alexi is working on it," Trey said calmly. He needed the team together on this, not pushing at each other.

"Work harder," Petr said, challenging Androv with a snide look.

Androv's eyes darkened. The dangerous side of the man cracked through the veneer for a moment, then disappeared as he smiled. "Yes, Petr, I'll do that."

Trey watched both men. He knew Androv's response had been solely for his benefit. Under the surface, the dapper Russian was seething. Trey could think of few things more dangerous than angering Alexi Androv. The man was borderline psychopathic. They needed to work together for the next fourteen days without killing each other. Literally.

"Maelle, where are you with getting into the computer systems for the stadium and the city?"

She shook her head. "It's not going well. I need a line to get in without being seen. A back door of sorts. I'm waiting on Petr to find me one."

Trey looked back to Petr.

"Plans. I can't function without an accurate set of working drawings." Besovich kept his eyes focused on Trey and didn't let them wander to Androv. No sense inciting the wolverine any more than he already had.

"Do you know what kind of equipment you'll need to splice into the grid?"

Trey asked Petr. "If you do, we can pick it up now so we have it on hand."

"Sort of. I'll give Alexi a list of things I need so he can start building the contactors. We've agreed on the basics of how it should work, so we have a good idea of what to buy and how to put it together."

"Alexi, any problems building the units?"

"None that I can see."

"Good." Trey pushed his chair back and said, "Alexi will have the plans soon. Then we'll be moving ahead on all fronts. Until then, make sure you familiarize yourselves with the tunnel system between our shop and the stadium." He paused for a second then added, "I have the travel route for the backup generator and I'll handle it. It looks like I'll be in Belarus in ten or eleven days. Only for a day, though."

Trey's phone rang as the meeting broke up and he took the call while standing at the window, looking out over the river and Luzhniki Stadium. The person on the other end of the line took him by surprise.

"Trey, it's Anne Sommer."

It took him a moment to process the fact that someone from Langley was calling him. "Anne, this is a surprise," he said. He checked the room as he spoke, ensuring the rest of the team members were out of earshot. "What's up?"

"Sorry to bother you. This will only take a minute."

"Take your time. It's been quite a while and it's nice to hear your voice."

"A few years," Anne said. "Listen, we have a bit of a situation here."

"What's going on?"

"A hacker managed to get into our system Monday night. They went directly to your file."

"*My* file?" he asked. "Are you sure?"

"Positive. Once they were in, they made a beeline for your information. Spent about two minutes searching through sixteen pages, then downloaded four megs of data and left."

"Any idea who it was?"

"Not really. That's why I'm calling. We spent all day yesterday trying to track them, but they bounced their IP address off so many servers and proxies that we can't find them. We think they might be in New York, but that's the best we can do. We thought you might be able to help."

Trey's mind raced at warp speed. Bill Fleming was headquartered in New York and had hired him for the job. But Fleming already knew some of what was in his CIA dossier. There was no reason for the billionaire to risk hacking into the database to acquire knowledge he already had. It wasn't Fleming. So who?

Did Dimitri Volstov know there was a team in place and was he digging for information? He ran that through a few scenarios and discarded them. Volstov had no reason to suspect anything to do with the concert. And the man was too busy to be looking for proverbial needles in a haystack. Plus, the hacker had most likely been in New York when he or she cracked the security. If Anne was telling him they thought the hacker was likely in New York, then that's where they were.

It all came back to Fleming. Someone had connected him to the billionaire.

"I might have an idea who was behind the intrusion," he said slowly. "I don't want to give you a name right now. I promise you that as soon as I find out, you'll find out."

"Fair enough," she said. "I'll give you my direct line."

Trey jotted down the number, thanked her and hung up the phone. He left the hotel and found a stretch of road on Leninskij Prospekt busy with coffee shops and boutiques. He browsed until he found what he wanted. A single, affluent-looking woman working on her laptop. Surrounding her on the small table were a pen, an electronic daytimer and a cell phone. He ordered a latte and sat at a table next to her. Inside ten minutes she left the table to use the bathroom. Trey stood up, pocketed her phone and returned to the street. He dialed a number with a New York area code. Fleming answered.

"Why are you calling on this number?" Fleming asked. The phone was registered to a non-existent person in New Jersey. Fleming kept it for times like this – when calls should be untraceable from both ends.

"Something is going on that I don't understand." He explained the call from his former co-worker at the CIA. "There's no reason for anyone to be looking at my file, unless it's related to what we're doing over here."

"Maybe it was a random hack into the system," Fleming said.

"Not a chance. Whoever managed to breach the firewalls is a damn good hacker. And they went directly to my file. This was a purpose-driven exercise. They were looking at me."

Trey waited while Fleming digested the new information. A minute passed, then the billionaire said, "Leave this with me. I'll dig into things on this end. You'd be wise to do the same over there."

"Of course."

"How are things going?" Fleming asked.

"Not bad. We're running into some snags, but that's to be expected. Nothing ever goes exactly as it should."

"Are you on schedule?"

"I think so, yes. We should be fine."

"Good." A moment of silence, then, "Call me if you need anything else." The line clicked over to a dial tone.

Trey wiped his fingerprints off the phone and dropped it in a garbage bin. The more he thought about it, the more he was sure. The intrusion into the CIA mainframe had to do with Fleming. Someone suspected something. And that left a few unanswered questions.

Trey hated unanswered questions. They were dangerous.

CHAPTER 31

Soho, New York

Carson stared at the information on the sheet in front of him on the kitchen table. It was like something out of a spy novel.

Trey Miller was ex-CIA, but lots of people had worked at the Central Intelligence Agency at one point in their lives. They typed memos. They collected information. They wrote software. Most of the jobs inside the agency were fairly mundane. But not Miller's. Not in the least.

Miller had been with the agency over twenty-one years – stationed in the Baltics for three years and Tajikistan and Uzbekistan for another five. During his stint, nine foreign agents had died and three more went missing. While the data inside the file never specifically linked Miller to the killings, the inferences were obvious. He was trained in hand-to-hand combat, knife-fighting, handguns, explosives and held numerous records for sharpshooting. He spoke six languages flawlessly.

And Trey Miller was somehow tied in with William Fleming.

Carson rubbed his hands over his eyes. He didn't need to look in the mirror to know they were bloodshot. His head hurt from pressure behind his left eye – something that happened when he succumbed to stress. The Advil he had swallowed an hour ago was kicking in, but the pain was still there, lurking, ready to spread. A floorboard creaked behind him and he instinctively slid a blank piece of paper over the page with Miller's photo.

"What are you doing?" Nicki asked. She sat across from him at the table. The dinner dishes had been cleared and low voices from the television drifted into the kitchen.

"Looking at a potential new hire," he lied. The last thing Nicki needed right now was stress of any sort. Telling her he suspected Fleming was embroiled in something shady wasn't going to help her already fragile health. "How are you feeling?"

"Better," she said. "My breathing is easier and I have more energy."

"Eating well, too." He stood and hugged her. Nicki's body was warm through her robe and there was a hint of strawberry fragrance on her skin from her bath oils. He held her for a minute, then said, "I have to go in to the office for a while. Do you think you can amuse yourself for a bit?"

She didn't pull away. "I think so." Her breathing was rhythmic and slow. "What's so pressing?"

"We're running a series of tests on the new algo. I want to see the results as they come in."

"Okay. How long will you be?"

"It's eight o'clock now, and I should be at the office about an hour. With travel time I should be home by ten."

"I'll wait up."

"Good. I'd like that."

He collected his briefcase, kissed her, then locked the door behind him and hailed a cab. He gave the cabbie the address on Avenue of the Americas and dialed Alicia's number on his cell phone.

"Can you come in for a few minutes?" he asked when she picked up.

"Carson, it's almost 8:30 on Wednesday night. I only got home an hour ago."

"You live five minutes from the office. What took you so long to get home?"

"I went for drinks in Bryant Park with friends," she said.

"Come back in, please. I need a favor."

A moment's silence, then she said, "All right. See you in ten minutes."

Carson hung up and closed his eyes. He always processed thoughts better when there were no other distractions. Fleming was tied in with Trey Miller. Miller had spent time working as a spy for the CIA. Fleming was in Cabo San Lucas and wouldn't be back until Friday. That gave him a window of opportunity that might not reappear for some length of time. A chance to find out what Fleming was up to.

Carson was worried about where he might stand legally if Fleming was gearing up to manipulate the markets. His latest promotion put him in a lead role inside the company. But along with the remuneration and the rest of the perks came a certain degree of risk. If the Securities and Exchange Commission investigated his division and found wrongdoing, he could be hung out to dry. How well did he know William Fleming? It was a simple question and an equally simple answer. Not all that well. He'd worked for Platinus for years but it was only in the last couple of weeks that he had interacted with Fleming with any degree of regularity. Maybe it was a coincidence that Fleming had received that particular e-mail from Miller at precisely this time. Maybe.

Carson hated coincidences. He didn't trust them.

The cab driver pulled him back from the quiet world of processing disturbing thoughts. The fare was nine dollars. Carson handed the man twenty and waved off the change. He swiped his card in the reader and signed in, calling the night security man by name and asking how his pregnant wife was faring with the summer heat. He let the guard know that Alicia would be coming in soon and took the elevator to forty-six. He unlocked his office and powered up his computer. Minutes later, Alicia appeared at his door.

"What's going on, Carson?" she asked. "Does this have something to do with the algorithm?"

Carson shook his head. "No. Chui and I were watching how it performed today and it was okay. Chased a couple of smaller stocks, but didn't drive anything beyond a realistic value. I think it'll be okay. We're going to keep our eye on it, though."

"Okay, then it's about that e-mail from Trey Miller that you asked me to trace."

He nodded. "Sit down, please," he said, pointing to the chair facing the desk. Behind them the skyline of Manhattan was darkening. Shadows danced off the buildings and the park was a huge black rectangle.

"This thing with Miller has me worried," he said.

"No shit," she replied. "The guy is CIA."

"Ex-CIA. He hasn't worked for the agency for a few years."

Alicia shook her head. "It hardly matters. Aaron sent me a copy of the file. He killed people, Carson."

Carson's hands were shaking slightly. "I know, Alicia. It's not good news." He leaned forward, his elbows firmly on the desk. It masked the tremors coursing through his body. "That's why I want you to pull every e-mail Miller has sent to Fleming off Fleming's computer."

She stared at him, wide-eyed. She didn't move for fifteen seconds, then shook her head. "That's crazy, Carson."

A strange calm settled in over him and he stopped shaking. "No, it's not. It's what we have to do. It's possible that Fleming is involved in something illegal, and whatever he's planning could easily filter down and bite you and me and Chui in our proverbial asses. We need to protect ourselves, and the best way to do that is to find out exactly what Fleming is up to."

She didn't look convinced. "You're talking about hacking into his computer. William Fleming's computer. I don't need to remind you that he's one of the richest men in the world. And powerful. And I doubt if he would be very forgiving if he found out. You, and I, could kiss our careers on Wall Street goodbye."

"So let's make sure we don't get caught."

"Not funny, Carson."

"Can you get in?" he asked.

She didn't answer for a minute, just stared out the window at the privileged view. Finally, she nodded. "Probably. I could go in through your computer and since it's on the same server I'd only have to figure out his password to have access to his e-mail. It's not difficult."

Carson's eyes bored into her. "Alicia, I'm worried and I can't sleep. If Fleming is planning something, we need to know. Breaking through firewalls and cracking passwords isn't my thing. I need your help."

"When?" she asked.

"Now. He's back from Cabo on Friday and his secretary told me that he never checks his e-mails while he's there. I'm not sure when we'll have another opportunity like this. When he's in New York he always has his Blackberry on."

She glanced over at Carson's computer, the screen backlit and casting a soft pall across the room. "This is dangerous," she said.

"So is doing nothing."

Alicia stood and walked to the window. There was no reason for her to do what Carson was asking. William Fleming was her boss – the man who ran one of the most prestigious and powerful trading firms in the world. He had the right to conduct business as he saw fit, providing it didn't circumvent the law. Pushing things to the limit was a trademark of almost every billionaire on the Forbes list. They didn't get there by being the nice guy on the block and allowing the competition to run roughshod over them. They set the pace and others followed. Fleming was no different.

But what Carson was suggesting was troubling. The reference to a crash being inevitable was like being hit in the gut with a sucker punch. The last thing Wall Street, or America, needed was another market crash. If Fleming was setting things up for a fall, with plans of swooping in and picking the meat off the carcass, then he had to be stopped. But it was a huge *if*. They had no proof. Nothing tangible. Not yet, at least. A quick look into his computer could change that.

She sucked in a deep breath and said, "Okay, but we're in and out. We find what we're looking for, download it and leave. The shorter length of time we're poking around in his e-mail the better."

"Of course." Carson slid out from behind his desk and Alicia took his place.

She started typing. "I need to capture the traffic inside the network. The easiest way to do that is to use EnCase to make an offline copy and analyze it later, or to insert a packet sniffer like WireShark to identify and capture e-mails. But both of those require foresight."

"Sorry about that," Carson said.

"It's okay, I have other ways." She worked for another couple of minutes, then pointed at the screen. "There it is. The e-mail from Trey Miller."

"Can you group all the e-mails from him together?"

"Easy." She hit the *from* tab and the computer ordered the e-mail alphabetically.

"Download all of them," Carson said, then added, "please."

There were four in total and she highlighted them and sent them to the memory stick. Another click and the e-mails went back to being ordered by the date they arrived. Alicia moved the curser to sign out, but Carson touched her hand.

"Open that one," he said, pointing.

She hesitated, then clicked on a mail from Jorge with *Arrived safely in KAF* in the subject line. It opened revealing a message only five words in length.

Crates at KAF. Submit invoice.

"Why this one?" Alicia asked.

"I think KAF is short for Kandahar Airfield. I have a buddy who spent some time over there and he always referred to it as KAF. He said it a lot and it stuck." He leaned closer to the screen, peering over her shoulder. "Can you reorder them so everything from Jorge is together?"

She glanced back at him for a second, then clicked on the *from* button. There were three from Jorge since July 27th. "You want me to save them?" she asked.

"Please."

Alicia sent them to the memory stick, reset Fleming's e-mail to its original settings and exited the program. She pulled the memory stick from the USB port and handed it to Carson.

"Thanks for doing that," he said, taking the stick and slipping it in his pocket.

"It's okay," she said. "Let's hope we're still employed next week."

CHAPTER 32

Kandahar, Afghanistan

Halima was beginning to see the upside to living in Peshawar. The days without food and clean water would be history. Watching her younger sisters go hungry was no longer something she would have to live with every day.

It had been a while since she'd seen her father happy. She couldn't remember the last time, but she knew it was while her mother was still alive. The Taliban had ruined his hand when they crushed it with the rifle, but they had ruined his life when they came back to reclaim the area around Kandahar. It brought more war and a never-ending stream of conflict. Finally, when he met the man from Peshawar, there was a glimmer of hope in him.

He wanted this so badly for her. And for Aaqila and Danah. He had told her that if she went to live with this family in Pakistan that he would be able to buy food and water for years. That the family would be so happy to have her that they would pay him. He cried when he told her this – and begged her forgiveness for selling her. She had touched his hand and told him that he wasn't selling her, simply making a good decision.

He left the room, the tears falling freely.

When he returned he was composed. He apologized for showing such weakness and asked her if she could refrain from telling anyone. She burrowed her head into his chest and held him as tight as her thin arms could. That was three days ago. Now, today, he had left a few hours earlier with a different man to go to the bank. She didn't understand what a bank was, but he told her it was a place to store money. She thought it was strange that he didn't keep it under the blanket. That was where he always kept his money, even as much as two or three dollars.

Footsteps from the stairwell echoed through the room and all three girls looked at the door with fear and mistrust. Seconds later their father shuffled into the room. He smiled and knelt down with his arms out.

"Aaqila, Danah, look what I have for you," he said. He thrust his hand into his tunic and pulled out a small bag of candy. They scampered over to him and he doled it out to them as they giggled. When each had taken their share and had retreated across the room to compare their treats, he motioned to Halima. "Come here," he said softly.

She sat beside him. He was trembling as he slipped a thin package from under his tunic. It was a plastic bag from a store in the center of Kandahar. One of her friends had brought a similar bag to the marketplace. Everyone was envious. The friend had never told what was in the bag, just having it was privilege enough.

"Open it," he said. His voice was so gentle.

She cracked open the top flaps and peeked in. "Oh, father," she whispered as she pulled out the book and pencil. The cover was bright red and inside the pages were lined and blank. Ready for writing. The pencil was emblazoned with multi-colored flowers and sharpened to a flawless point. She ran her hand across the book cover, feeling its strength and smoothness. She had never held such a treasure.

"It's for your first day of school," Kadir said.

Halima looked at her father. There was no mistaking it. Her father was finally happy. She slipped her hand around his waist and snuggled into him. His breathing was slow and rhythmic. She felt something she had never felt before.

She felt safe.

CHAPTER 33

Outside Spin Buldak, Afghanistan

"We've got something cool for you," Andrew said. He propped himself against the doorjamb. "If you want it."

Andrew's wiry frame was silhouetted against the bright afternoon sun and Russell squinted to see the soldier's backlit features. "What's that?"

"An interview. A meeting with one of the tribal elders from the Dabarey region."

Russell arched an eyebrow. "Now that's something I'd be interested in. When can we meet him?"

"Now. He's camped about three hundred meters outside the FOB."

Russell jumped to his feet. "He's here to see me?"

Andrew nodded. "Captain Hocking has spent a lot of time working with the people here and has a certain level of trust with the elders. He asked if one of them would meet with you and they agreed."

"Let's go," Russell said. He grabbed his laptop and stuffed some blank paper and pens in with his camera. "Can I photograph him?"

"I'm not sure, you'll have to ask. And this is your lucky day. The guy they sent to meet you speaks English."

"Thank God. I've worked with enough translators to know how tough it can be," Russell said.

A line of five Strykers was waiting near the front gate and Andrew and Russell piled into the third one, their heads poking out the rear hatch. Outside the wire the air was calm and the sun blistering hot. The eight-wheeled armored vehicles churned up clouds of dust as they tracked along the road leading west. Ahead, a group of three tents were pitched by the side of the road. The Strykers pulled up a bit short of the encampment and stopped. A soldier jumped to the ground and was met by four men in traditional Afghan garb, their tunics hanging limp in the dry, still air. A brief conversation ensued, then the soldier yelled up to the Stryker commander. A minute later the command came over the radio to set up a perimeter around the tents, and that the entire area had already been checked carefully for IEDs. The Strykers rumbled into position and shut down their engines. An eerie silence settled over the group.

"His name is Pacha Khan Zadran. Please don't insult him," Andrew said as they approached the tents.

"I'll do my best," Russell said, taking in the situation. The tent was open to the desert on the north side, from which they were approaching. Six men were in the tent, three seated and three standing. No weapons were in sight, but Russell wasn't naïve enough to think that the tribal men weren't armed. Baggy clothes were of great benefit for hiding handguns, even rifles.

The man sitting in the middle appeared to be in his mid-sixties, with a flowing grey beard and a light orange turban. He wore eyeglasses with large dark frames and Russell was struck with the ridiculous thought that if Buddy Holly had been alive and living in southern Afghanistan, it could be him. He reached the edge of the tent and bowed slightly to the elder.

"*Salaam aalaikum*," he said.

"*Pikheyr*," Pacha Khan Zadran replied. The tribal elder motioned to a pillow opposite where he sat and said in accented English, "Please sit."

"Thank you." Russell slipped off his shoes and sat with his legs crossed and his toes pointing away from the tribal leader. This seemed to please the man and the next fifteen minutes was filled with offers of *chai sabz* and sweets and proper introductions. Pacha Khan Zadran spoke proudly of his Pashtun heritage – he was descended from Qais, an influential man who was like a brother to the

Prophet Mohammed, and a member of the ruling Durrani clan.

"Why do you call it the *ruling* clan?" Russell asked. He sipped the *chai sabz* carefully, without making noise.

"Good question, Russell Khan," Zadran said, smiling. "Ahmad Shah Durrani was responsible for founding Afghanistan in 1747, and the Durrani clan has ruled Afghanistan ever since. As a member of the Popolzai clan, Hamid Karzai is a descendent of the Durranis. We have great influence over this country, both historically and today." The tribal elder adjusted his pillow slightly and said, "You are a journalist."

"Yes."

"For what newspaper?"

"It's not a newspaper. I work for a television station in Boston."

Zadran nodded approvingly. "Do many people listen to you?"

Russell laughed, but not too loudly. "Yes, I think so. But not my wife."

It was Zadran's turn to chuckle. "So this is a problem everywhere, not just Afghanistan." He sipped his tea and said, "You can ask questions if you wish."

"Thank you." Russell slipped his notepad and pen from his computer bag. There was no sense pushing things by pulling out a bunch of electronics. "The ISAF troops have been in your country for some time now. What do you think they have accomplished?"

Pacha Khan Zadran thought about the answer for a minute, then said, "I think the troops provided the Afghan people with a psychological sense that America is here. That the western world cares. For a time we felt protected. But that feeling waned with time. We, as a people, as a country, had high expectations. Perhaps too high. Now it is difficult. We bend and flex like the stem of a poppy, unsure who to stand behind."

"Us or the Taliban?" Russell asked.

"That's a very limited view, but if I were forced to answer it, I would say yes. Afghans want to believe the coalition troops will not only defeat the Taliban, but will also remain to help us rebuild. What happens if you don't? What happens if you leave? Having thrown our support behind you, we will face the wrath of the Taliban with no protection. That," Zadran paused, "is an alarming thought."

"Your government is ramping up its focus to protect you. The Afghan National Police and the Army are getting stronger every day."

"That is true, but the perception of the Afghan people is that our government is weak. We believe a firm and just hand is needed." He shifted to get comfortable on the pillow and waved for more chai. "Let me give you an example."

"Please," Russell said, his pen poised over the paper.

"The region between Pakistan and Afghanistan is almost lawless. There are many small villages, few roads, no border outposts and the government has very little influence. In one of these regions there is a man who everyone refers to as the commander. He is the acknowledged leader of the entire area. One day, a man is brought in front of him, accused of raping a local woman. The commander listens to all sides of the story, and makes a decision after all witnesses have spoken. The man accused of rape disappears and is never seen again." Zadran set his empty teacup on a small sliver tray and held out his hands. "Problem – evidence – solution." His hands moved like the scales of justice as he spoke. "What the people of Afghanistan want is a government that operates like the commander. One with benevolence, intelligence, and the strength to make difficult decisions."

"I understand," Russell said. He scanned the notes on his page, then asked, "You perceive that your government is failing you. Are we, the troops and the NGOs, failing you as well?"

"It's not that you're failing us, Russell Khan, it's that there are different agendas. Contradictory ones."

Russell looked puzzled.

"You have to ask, *What do the Afghan people really want?* and then decide if that is what you are trying to do. It's not the same. The guns and the bombs aren't a permanent solution. You're fighting the wrong war."

Russell shifted slightly on his pillow. "All right. What war should we be fighting?"

"The war to win the people. To gain their trust. We don't want your brand of democracy. Help us improve the simple things – safe streets, electricity, clean water. Everyone can agree on this. Stop imposing your version of what is right and help with the basics."

"That seems so obvious," Russell said, nodding. "Okay, here's a simple question. In one word, what's the answer?"

Pacha Khan Zadran smiled. "You are a crafty man, Russell Khan. That is anything but a simple question."

"True," Russell said.

"I will give you two answers. First – corruption. This is the root of everything wrong in Afghanistan. It is impossible to get anything done without bribing someone. I have heard that the average bribe is something like one hundred and sixty US dollars. Most Afghans earn between four and eight hundred dollars a year." He shrugged his shoulders. "How does this work?"

"It doesn't," Russell said.

"The government can't stop the corruption, but if they can slow it down then important issues like security can be addressed. Until then, nothing can change. Corruption breeds insecurity, and with insecurity comes the Taliban."

"You said there were two answers," Russell said.

Pacha Khan Zadran waved for more sweets and tea. He waited until both men had tasted the delicacies and their cups refilled. The wind picked up slightly and a touch of sand blew in through the open tent flaps. One of Zadran's men covered the food with an engraved silver lid and another man adjusted the flaps to keep the wind at bay.

"Education," Zadran said when the flurry of activity was over. "We have lost this generation. Any person who is thirty years old has seen nothing but war since they were born. First the Russians, then civil war, then the Taliban and now the insurgents. Thirty years of war." Zadran stared hard into Russell's eyes. "For thirty years all we've known is war. It has become what is normal. Peace is an unknown. Is it possible for you to understand this?"

Russell shook his head. "Honestly, no."

Zadran nodded slowly at the journalist's sincerity. "We must look to the next generation for change. And that change starts with educating them. Boys...*and* girls. The Afghan way has always been to view women on a different level from men, but for many of us that is changing."

"I've been noticing a lot of different attitudes," Russell said.

"Yes, that is true. Even among some of the elders there is a desire to educate our women."

"How can this be accomplished if the children can't risk going to the school? The NGOs build schools and the Taliban leave night letters on the doors threatening death to any teacher or student who attends."

Zadran waved his arm in a wide arc. "It all comes back to where we started. We need security, and to have this the corruption must be stifled."

They continued to talk for another hour, about drugs and intimidation, culture and expectations, tradition and religion. It was almost noon when Russell slipped his notebook back in his case and shook Pacha Khan Zadran's hand. He left the tent with a low bow. Russell was quiet on the short trip back to the FOB.

The guns and the bombs aren't a permanent solution. You're fighting the wrong war.

Zadran was right. Bombing villages or strafing convoys of insurgents and civilians would never win the war. Every time the troops killed a Talib or an innocent, three of their relatives or friends left their villages and picked up arms. The fight to win the country would be won by working with the villagers, earning their trust, rebuilding infrastructure and educating the next generation. This was not a short-term exercise.

He sequestered himself in his tent when they were back inside the wire and wrote his copy. It took three hours. There was so much to pack into two minutes of airtime. All of it important. When he was satisfied with how it read, he set up the video with the mountains in the background and pushed the record button. He walked to the small x in the sand.

Four days ago I reported on a vicious firefight in the town of Dabarey, only a few miles from our Forward Operating Base. We were ambushed, and three soldiers died in that fight. Today I met with the tribal elders from Dabarey. They wanted to meet – to talk about their lives – their country –and their future. What I heard were real answers to the problems that plague Afghanistan. Honest answers to difficult questions. The answer – according to one of the elders who wished not to be identified – lies in stemming the endemic corruption that is crippling this country. According to world statistics, only Somalia is more corrupt. Billions of dollars are siphoned off every year by a select few, while the masses suffer. Nothing new there. But in Afghanistan, there is little motivation for anything to change. The government of Hamid Karzai is often named as the most powerful thief in a dangerous nest of thieves. Corruption breeds insecurity. Stem it and you bring the insurgency to its knees. Then, stay – help the Afghans – some of whom have never known peace – to rebuild their schools, their hospitals, their police forces and the infrastructure necessary to provide water and electricity. And most importantly, provide education. Teach them to read and write – to build bridges and treat the sick – to design new buildings and open banks. These are an intelligent, resilient people, and if we gain their trust, we can help change lives. But we cannot gain this country's trust solely through military means. We need to help them rebuild. To stem the corruption. To educate the upcoming generation. That's the message I heard today. This is Russell Matthews, reporting from Spin Buldak, Afghanistan.

Russell tapped the *record* button and replaced the camera in its case. He wondered if the people in Boston who watched the nightly news would get what he was saying. He suspected some would, and knew some wouldn't. There was nothing more he could do than go outside the wire and chase the stories. Report the facts and make them impactful. After that, it was up to the people.

It always was. It was what they did with it that counted.

CHAPTER 34

Peshawar, Pakistan

The trip back into Pakistan from Kandahar city had taken Tabraiz two full days. He was angry at the inconvenience, but glad to be back in his country. Afghanistan was becoming more dangerous with every passing day. Not the levels of violence. That he could deal with. The real danger to him was the Afghan National Police. They were quickly becoming a legitimate presence in southern Afghanistan. He blamed the Canadian military for the increase in police and army efficiency in and around Kandahar. He despised them for making his life so difficult.

He waited by the open window of his ornately decorated hotel room overlooking Peshawar's Old City. A light knock on the door stirred him from the chair and he pulled the door open without checking the eyehole. He knew who was in the hall, and God help them if it was anyone else. The Glock pistol in his waistband wasn't there for show.

"Ismail," he said. "Please come in."

"Thank you, Tabraiz Khan." The man was slender with thick eyeglasses and short-cropped dark hair. He had a tic, the right side of his face twitching every few seconds. It wasn't a problem. It never showed up in the pictures Tabraiz took and sent back to the parents of the children he brokered to his wealthy buyers. Ismail was his front man – his accountant and the father of the wealthy family who lived in Peshawar and took in poor children. So far he had been a very temporary benefactor to thirty-seven girls and boys. It had allowed him to become quite well-to-do by Pakistani standards. Ismail followed Tabraiz to the table and chairs near the windows.

Below the renovated 18th century *haveli* that was now the exclusive Khan Klub Hotel, the Old City was waking up. The call to prayer drifted over the Khyber Bazaar as carpet merchants and kebab sellers arranged their wares for the day. The wails echoed through the Kabuli Gate and into the Qissa Khawani, where storytellers had recited tales of bravery and battles since the rule of Alexander the Great. The pungent scent of spice and tea hung in the still air.

"I wanted to speak with you about the next girl. Her name is Halima and she is quite special. I have a very generous offer from one of my clients in the UAE, and this generosity will be passed along to you. Your fee for Halima will be four thousand US dollars."

Ismail steepled his fingers and bowed his head. "You are most generous, Tabraiz Khan."

"We need to move more quickly with Halima than in the past." He locked eyes with his front man. "This will be our last girl from Kandahar. The police are watching me. I need you to take the pictures when she first arrives. Have her dress in three or four different pieces of clothing so I can send her father the groups of photos about two months apart. It will look like she is still at your house."

"I understand."

"I will have other girls and boys for you, Ismail. But there will be a break. Kabul is a good source of children, but they are mostly orphans, ill-kept and covered with lice. Girls like Halima are hard to find in Kabul."

"I will have great patience," Ismail said respectfully.

Tabraiz smiled. "Yes, my friend, I'm sure you will. You have always been loyal to me, and that is something I will remember." Tabraiz stood to indicate the meeting was finished. "I'm bringing Halima from Kandahar ten days from now, on August 23rd. It will take one or two days to get her across the border. Be ready for me."

"Of course."

Tabraiz didn't walk the man to the door. He sat staring over the cityscape. Peshawar was the place of his birth and he owned two houses. But when he arrived back from Afghanistan, he always spent the first two or three days sequestered at the boutique hotel tucked away in the heart of the city. If the police were after him, they would visit his house and his housekeeper would phone to tell him. So far that hadn't happened, but being careful was gravely important in his line of work.

The thought of delivering Halima brought a smile to his face. She was so innocent. So pure. So perfect.

* * *

Outside Spin Buldak, Afghanistan

Russell recognized the soldier walking toward them in the early morning shadows. He was about the same age as Andrew, had ridden with them in the same Stryker on one occasion, and had been introduced as Bobby. No last name, no rank, just Bobby. He was less than six feet, lanky, and moved with an easy gait. Despite the relentless scorching sun, his skin was pasty white with a touch of sunburn. He had a quick smile and disarming blue eyes. He nodded to Andrew as he approached.

"Hey, Andy," he said. His voice carried a strong Southern accent. "How y'all doin' today?"

"Okay." Andrew jerked his thumb toward the journalist. "You remember Russell Matthews? He rode with us to Dabarey."

"Yeah, sure, I remember. You're the writer guy."

"That's me." Russell extended his hand and they shook. He leaned back into the sandbags surrounding their bunk.

"Robert K. Sullivan. But you can call me Bobby."

"Bobby it is," Russell said.

Bobby sat next to Andrew and held up his M-4. "Check this out. Brand new, baby."

Andrew showed an interest in the gun. He took it from Bobby and held it in both hands as if weighing it, then sighted on some point outside the wire. He checked the magazine and handed it back.

"Nice. You get it from the shipment that came in a couple of days ago?"

"Yeah, sure did."

"What was wrong with your gun?" Andrew asked.

Bobby shrugged. "I dunno. Just wanted a new one, man. Nothin' wrong with that."

"Nah, nothing wrong with a new gun."

"Where you from?" Russell asked.

Bobby offered both men a cigarette, then lit his and Andrew's. "Augusta. Wrong side of Broad Street."

"Augusta," Russell said. "The Masters. Great tournament."

Bobby looked away and said, "The Masters ain't what it's about in Augusta, man. It's about survivin'." He wagged his finger at Russell. "You thinkin' about Augusta National and all the magnolias and shit that goes with one weekend in April. But I'm all about workin' a min-wage job and worryin' about my momma's health. That's what's real for fifty-one weeks a year if you live there. Then there's that one week when all the rich folk come into town and pay shitloads of money to rent houses and eat in restaurants. So what you see on television ain't nothin' close to the truth of what Augusta's all about."

"Sorry, man. I didn't know," Russell said.

"It's okay." He pointed at Andrew. "Can't all have rich parents."

It had never occurred to Russell that Andrew might have come from a wealthy family. In fact, he hadn't asked the specialist any personal questions. "Is that true?" he asked. "Your parents rich?"

Andrew gave off a sheepish grin. "Yeah. Not excessive, though."

Russell looked off to the horizon, where the morning sun was cresting the mountains. He was a fool. If this were school, he'd be flunking out of first-year journalism. Never assume. It's one of the first things eager wet-behind-the-ears reporters are taught. And he had committed the cardinal sin by stereotyping Andrew James. It had never occurred to him that Andrew might be from a wealthy family. There usually wasn't a lot of incentive for young men and women with influential doors opening in front of them to choose the army as a career. This was Andrew's second tour. He'd returned knowing the incredible toll it took to survive on the front line of a war zone. He understood, and now he was back.

Returned to the hell that was war.

"Are you going to college when you finish this tour?" Russell asked.

Andrew sucked on the cigarette and shrugged. "Maybe. I'm not sure. I need to know what I want to do."

"Any ideas?" Russell asked.

"I think I'd like to stay here on the ground and work for an NGO. I want to be part of the rebuilding."

"Rebuildin' what we're takin' apart," Bobby said. "Shit, man, that's good stuff. First you blow it up, then you get a job with an NGO puttin' it back together."

Andrew laughed. "You think *we're* the ones who are taking this country apart?" he asked the other soldier. When Bobby shrugged the question off, Andrew said, "It's the Taliban, man. They're the ones with their fingers on the destruct button. We're only trying to patch things up." He turned to Russell and said, "You know what these guys are. We talked about it."

Russell nodded. "Sure. Drug dealers."

"Yeah, exactly," Andrew said. "The Taliban are nothing more than a group of well-financed drug dealers. They've been moving heroin and opium through the Baluchistan Province into Iran and Turkey for years. They want to control Helmand and Kandahar for one reason and only one. They want the drug money from the poppy fields. Fuck religious idealism. These guys are greedy bastards who could care less who they kill or what they destroy so long as they get paid."

"Sorry," Bobby offered. "Didn't mean to push your buttons so early in the morning."

"It's okay." Andrew settled back against the wall of sandbags. "I don't like to see people caught in the middle of this mess."

"You got that," Bobby said. "We better get fed. We're rolling out of here at 0800." He shouldered his new gun and headed off to the kitchen for breakfast.

Andrew followed a minute later, leaving Russell alone in the shade with his thoughts.

Russell closed his eyes and mentally stacked up the obvious differences between the two men. Andrew was from an upper-class family in California, Bobby from a dirt-poor upbringing in the deep south of Georgia. He liked to think people were above things like money or skin color or gender, but the divisions still lingered. Here, in a world where the man next to you was the guy who could save your life, no one cared if you were rich or poor or white or black. Just do your job and get your buddy's back. There was the occasional thing about working and living in a war zone that made sense. Equality was one of them.

He wondered how he could have misjudged Andrew so badly. He had assumed the young soldier was from a middle-class home. Where his father drove a bus or fixed cars. Maybe his mom worked as a receptionist at the local Ford dealership. Who knew. Who really cared. Over here he was just another grunt, M-4 resting on his chest and ten full magazines in his vest pockets. He wanted to apologize, but there was no reason. He leaned back and tried to get comfortable against the sand bags. There wasn't much time to rest, as they were leaving for Mūshān in about an hour. What was it the soldiers called the town? The Wild West. That was it. He shook his head at the absurdity.

Talk about jumping out of the frying pan and into the fire.

CHAPTER 35

New York

The meltdown started at six minutes after ten on Friday morning. It took one hour and nine minutes to run its course, and in those sixty-nine minutes, almost unimaginable damage was done to five highly valued stocks.

The Platinus algorithm, now stripped of most of its pattern recognition software, began seeing trends in the market that did not exist. It started placing flash orders on an exchange, valid for less than half a second, then terminated them before the orders could be matched on a competing exchange. That made Platinus a poster, not a responder, and put it in a position to collect the rebates offered by the exchange. But flash orders generated by the ultrafast computer with a shaky algorithm had their downside. The computer began chasing its own orders.

The moment that happened, the stock prices on five companies the Platinus computer was chasing began to rise. The bid-ask raced upwards and the high-frequency feast was on. The computers at Getco, Renaissance, Citadel and Goldman immediately spotted the trend and added to the feeding frenzy. In just over an hour, the value of the five stocks the computer targeted had soared between thirty-five and eighty percent. At 11:15 the regulatory boards stepped in and suspended trading on all five stocks. But it was too late. The damage was done.

Carson was aware that the algorithm had gone rogue within three minutes of when it started to chase its own tail. He watched the carnage on the screen, aware that pulling the algorithm would immediately identify Platinus as the company responsible for the meltdown. That was something he was not willing to do. When trading was suspended, he called Chui and Alicia and told them to have someone rein in the algorithm and reinstate the old one. He asked them to meet him in his office. They were standing in front of his desk in less than two minutes. Both were showing obvious signs of stress.

"What's the damage?" Carson demanded.

Chui shook his head. "We won't know for sure until trading ends for the day, but it's not good. The algo ran five stocks way past their true value. They're going to crash when the market opens on Monday."

"Are we visible?" Carson asked.

"I don't think so," Alicia answered. "The trades were all under naked sponsored access. We should be okay."

Carson nodded. Naked sponsored access was a method by which traders used a broker's identification to trade directly on the exchanges. It allowed anonymity and saved the traders time. The problem was, with the trading happening in faceless trading arenas known as dark pools and a variety of traders using the broker's ID, there was no way of tracing back what company was front-running the stocks. Bad for the companies whose stocks had just been overvalued, but in this case, lucky for Platinus Investments. Chances were good that Platinus could sidestep the puddle they had created and not get their feet wet.

"Monday is going to be ugly," Chui said. "One of the companies, Benediem Inc., is up almost eighty percent. It's going to dive big time."

"I don't know the name. What are they?" Carson was sweating now.

Chui checked his file and said, "An umbrella company for a bunch of health care providers. Shit's going to hit the fan on Monday when the execs get in front of the cameras and tell them they have nothing to substantiate the increase in the stock price."

Anger flashed across Carson's face. "I know what the fallout will be, Chui. I hardly need to be reminded."

Chui snapped. "The algo was dangerous. We should have waited for the new one."

Carson leaned onto his desk, his face taking on more color. "Do you *want* to be unemployed?" he asked, civility lacking in his voice.

Chui matched his glare. "You wanted to make a splash when you took over the department, Carson. We warned you. Shit, you *knew* this could happen, but you pushed ahead. You caused this. So don't sit behind your desk and threaten me because you made a huge fucking error. I'm watching your lips moving, but all I'm hearing is that you know you screwed up and you're taking it out on us." He stood up and closed the file. "Unless you're going to fire me on the spot, I'll be at my desk."

Carson watched him leave without twitching a muscle. He was right. So right. He had pushed the limits and then some. Gone too far in an industry where the fallout was huge. Right now, in offices across the country, men and women who held important positions in large corporations were meeting behind closed doors, trying to figure out what had happened and how to repair the damage. Damage they had neither caused nor anticipated.

"He's upset," Alicia said quietly.

"So am I," Carson whispered. "It's true. I really fucked up."

She didn't respond for the better part of a minute, then said, "We can't be timid in this game – we'd get steamrollered. When everything works, we make the investors a fortune. When they don't, well, things get a bit ugly."

He let out a long breath and shook his head, almost imperceptibly. "Yeah. Tell that to all those people whose savings just tanked."

"I need to get back to eighteen. It's chaos down there right now. No one is going to want to move on anything without Chui or I okaying it."

Carson nodded and she left. He checked a number on his Blackberry, dialed it on his office phone and swiveled about in his chair to face Central Park. Overhead, the sun shared the sky with a handful of popcorn clouds. Beneath, trapped by a fortress of buildings on all four sides, the park remained its staid self. Verdant green, peaceful, unchanging. The ringing stopped and Fleming answered.

"It's Carson Grant. There's something you should be aware of."

CHAPTER 36

Moscow, Russia

The water in the labyrinth of tunnels under Moscow was a few degrees above freezing. The sun never penetrated the layers of concrete and dirt above, where people walked and cars drove. The damp air cut through their clothes and chilled Trey and his team to the bone. Locating the electrical lines necessary to cut the power to Luzhniki Stadium was turning out to be quite the ordeal.

Petr was wearing knee-high waterproof boots as he slogged through ankle-deep water carrying a new set of plans for the sewer system. It was early Saturday morning and the constant rumble from the cars and trucks overhead was considerably less than usual. Behind him, Trey held two flashlights, one illuminating the drawings and the other focused on the twisting section of tunnel ahead of them.

"Is the new set better?" Trey asked.

Alexi had secured a new set of drawings of the underground sewer system that showed the original tunnels and many of the changes up until 2004. On the same set were the electrical conduits, which usually ran immediately adjacent to the sewers, with openings in the concrete at specific intervals to access the junction boxes. No new plans had been drawn inside the last six years, and if they had, they were not available.

Petr nodded. "A bit. Alexi was very resourceful to get his hands on these, but even with them it's difficult. Many of the things we're looking at are not the same as the drawings indicate."

"It's frustrating," Trey agreed, keeping the lights pointed exactly where Petr needed them.

"This way," the stocky Russian said, motioning to a narrow tunnel that forked sharply to the left.

The section of tunnel they entered was crumbling in on itself. Chunks of old bricks and mortar, slippery with algae and slime, had fallen into the water, making their footing unstable and dangerous. The tunnel was too narrow for them to walk side-by-side, and Trey passed one of the lights to Petr, who alternated between checking the plans, his handheld GPS and their position in the tunnel. Trey, also dressed in waterproof boots to stay dry, followed behind, rubbing his hands and his chest in a vain attempt to keep warm. They reached a fork in the tunnel and Petr chose the right track. The width was even narrower and his broad shoulders touched both sides as they waded through the stagnant water. Thirty meters into what was beginning to look like a dead end, Petr turned to Trey and shone the light on his own face. He was smiling.

"Look what I found," he said. He angled the light so it illuminated the tunnel ceiling a couple of meters ahead of them. A newer metal conduit, sandwiched amongst two dozen other older ones, disappeared into a large junction box.

"Is that what you need?" Trey asked.

"I'd say it is. I'll know in a minute, but I think this is one of the places I can splice in and kill the power."

He removed some equipment from a harness on his chest and went to work on the box. Trey kept the flashlight focused as Petr removed the cover. Inside was a mass of wires and Trey was suddenly very glad he had chosen the Russian for the job. He had no idea what any of them were for.

"This is a pull box," Petr said as he set about determining whether the wires inside the newer conduit were the incoming service to the stadium.

"What's a pull box?" Trey asked.

"You can only pull so much wire through a conduit before friction and weight make it impossible. Then you need to cut the conduit and start fresh. When you do that, you need to encase the conduit in a junction box."

"So the incoming wire was never cut," Trey said.

"No, but because it's only 600 volts, the thickness of the wire should be manageable."

It took almost an hour for Petr to determine that he had located the right conduit. He flagged several of the wires with bits of fluorescent tape and closed the box. He noted the exact location by jotting GPS coordinates on a pad of paper, which he then carefully tucked back in his shirt pocket. He replaced the cover on the box and tightened the screws.

"Why did you use two different colors of tape to mark the wires?" Trey asked.

"We need to activate the contactors remotely, but the wireless technology doesn't exist to turn off circuits greater than twenty amps. These ones are three hundred. So what I'm going to do is hardwire in the switch activator and use a remote to turn on its power. I used red tape to identify the power source into the stadium and green for the line that will run between the remote and the contactor. It's complicated, but it'll work."

"I hope so."

Petr put away his tools and said, "Okay, we only need to find five more of these and a backdoor line for Maelle so she can tap into the city computers," he said.

"When are you going to splice in the contactors?" Trey asked.

"Probably two or three days before the concert. Any sooner is too early and I don't want to shut down the power to the stadium while the roadies are setting up U2's stage."

"Yes, of course. Good thinking."

"We're in a bit of a race," Petr said, motioning for Trey to turn around and start moving back toward the main tunnel.

Trey did the simple math as they trudged back through the water. They were eleven days from the concert, so if Petr wanted to cut into the systems three days in advance, that only gave them eight days to do the groundwork. The odds of succeeding were still in their favor, but he was aware that the closer they got to the concert without locating all the junction boxes, the greater the chances of failure. He envisioned the meeting with Fleming, telling the billionaire that the million dollars he had spent on the team was wasted. That they had failed to cut the power and disgrace Dimitri Volstov. That was one meeting he did *not* want to have.

But Trey wasn't sure Fleming's wrath was his biggest problem. The hack into his file on the CIA computer three days ago was front and center on his mind. Who had risked getting caught and possibly going to jail in order to see his history with the agency? He was fortunate Anne Sommer had taken the time to call and inform him of the situation. There was nothing deadlier than getting blindsided by something you never expected.

He wracked his brain, asking himself again why the intrusion had happened, but came up with nothing more than it being tied in somehow with Bill Fleming and the U2 job. Something was brewing – somewhere. He needed to find out what, but he was at a horrible disadvantage. He was out of his element in Moscow, without any support network. As a foreigner, his actions were already under a certain degree of scrutiny by the authorities. He couldn't get to the right people and start asking questions. Not without risking someone listening in on unsecured phone lines or e-mails.

Fleming was aware of the problem. He was watching things from New York. Maybe he would solve the problem and that would be that. Maybe. Then again, maybe not. It might blow up in his face and people might die. That would be unfortunate, but such was the nature of his work.

CHAPTER 37

Soho, New York

Carson woke on Saturday morning with a splitting headache, which might have something to do with the bottle of red wine he'd had with dinner. He swallowed two extra-strength Advil and locked himself in the shower.

The water invigorated him and the Advil kicked in. By the time he was finished showering he felt better. Two or three on a scale of ten, but much better than a zero. He fixed breakfast for Nicki and delivered it to her in bed. She swallowed a handful of pills to help her digest the food and picked at her eggs and toast.

"You seem a bit stronger," Carson said. He finished his breakfast and pushed his plate to the other side of the bed. He traced the shape of her leg through the duvet.

She smiled. "I feel okay. Definitely stronger, but I still don't feel much like eating."

"Curse of CF," Carson sighed. She could eat whatever she wanted and not gain a pound. Trouble was, eating had become too much work and she dreaded food. "But you certainly don't mind drinking coffee."

"Love coffee," she grinned. "And if you keep making it, I'll stick around." She pushed her plate back and asked, "You seem a bit stressed. Are things okay at the office?"

"Things are fine," he lied. The terseness in Fleming's voice kept replaying as he remembered the telephone conversation from yesterday afternoon. Where he had told the owner of Platinus Investments about the meltdown. That his computers were responsible for grossly inflating the value of five solidly performing stocks. It had been every bit the nightmare Carson thought it would be. Until Fleming asked if the Security and Exchange Commission knew Platinus was the guilty party. When he found out the entire series of transactions had happened in a black pool, he relaxed a bit. He was still angry, though. "The boss arrived back from Cabo late last night. Everyone is on their toes."

"Do you have to go in today?" she asked.

He shrugged. "If he calls. Otherwise, probably not." That was total bullshit. He knew Fleming would be calling. Soon. And he would be going in to explain how the algorithm went rogue. He kissed her and took her plate. "I'll be in the living room looking over a few things from work."

"See you in a bit," she said.

Carson sat in the chair by the open window and listened for the shower to start. Everything was so difficult for Nicki. Showering. Eating. Tying her shoes. The CF was more than life altering. It was life consuming. He heard the water and settled back in the chair with his coffee and the file folder containing the e-mails from Fleming's private computer.

There were four from Trey Miller and three from the man named Jorge. He had taken a quick look at all of them on Thursday, the day after he and Alicia had downloaded them from Fleming's computer, but with the algorithm running amok on Friday morning he hadn't had a chance to pull them out again. He set the ones from Jorge aside and concentrated on the four from the ex-CIA operative.

Miller kept his communiqués short and to the point. The first one, sent on July 30th, appeared to do with banking. *Bahamas account # 973-4462-8812.* It seemed reasonable that a billionaire would have incoming e-mails that dealt with banking details. Fleming must have been expecting the e-mail, as there was no indication of what was expected once Fleming had the account number. Which meant Miller and Fleming had talked beforehand. The second one, dated August 1st, was not so straightforward.

Assembling team. P today. M tomorrow. Worried about Lindstrom.

Why did Miller need a team? And who was Lindstrom? No first name, simply Lindstrom. No gender, no location, no indication of why Miller was concerned. Carson set the document aside, picked up his laptop and Googled *Lindstrom*. There were 6.2 million results and he scrolled through the first couple of pages and gave up. Without more to go on, he would never figure out who or what Miller was referring to. He went on to the other e-mails, the next one originating on August 3rd.

Have Maelle. Meeting Alexi and Petr now. Should be in business by later today.

More names. None of which where familiar. Maelle, Alexi and Petr – they sounded more Eastern European than American. Again, no surprise that an extremely wealthy man would be involved in international business. But what sort of business? None of it gave any sort of a clue. He compared the second and third e-mails. Perhaps P was Petr and M was Maelle. But that didn't make sense. Miller's August 3rd e-mail indicated that he already had Maelle on the team and had yet to meet with Petr. In the e-mail from two days prior, he said *P today* and *M tomorrow*. That didn't work. Carson went on to the last one.

Received your fee. Team in place. Time frames are tight but should be okay. Crash inevitable.

This one made sense. He was receiving a fee, which explained the information for the Bahamian bank account sent on July 30th. The team he talked about was now in place. And they were under some sort of time crunch. His eyes focused on the last two words. Crash inevitable. The two words that had initially captured his attention.

What were they crashing? Was it the stock market or something else? Why would Fleming want to crash the market? What was the financier's upside to a market meltdown? The more he ran the question through his mind, the less it made sense. After ten minutes of playing out every scenario he could envision, he knew there was no solid reason for Fleming to want a market crash. So it was something else. His brain was whirling and he finally set the list from Miller aside and picked up the one from Jorge. This one was equally as interesting.

The first incoming e-mail was dated July 28th. *Account number for payment.*

8863-742-9915. Half now, half on delivery. Carson scanned it a couple of times. It was pretty straightforward. Fleming owed this Jorge character money for some reason and the man was providing a bank account for the transfer. Simple. What was the money owed for? That was the million-dollar question.

The second e-mail, sent two days later, on July 30th, was much more sinister.

W crated in G, then leaving for KAF.

He felt strongly the reference to KAF was Kandahar Airfield. This – was bothersome. He knew that Fleming owned a number of companies outside Platinus Investments, and that one of them supplied weapons to the US military. There was no chance that Fleming would be depositing cash directly into someone's account if the deal was legit and being brokered through the company. If KAF stood for what he thought it did, then Fleming was up to something. The word *crated* was suggestive of weapons. Perhaps that's what the W stood for. Weapons. Carson pulled out a pen and jotted the line down on a blank piece of paper.

Weapons crated in G, then leaving for Kandahar Airfield.

Unfortunately, he thought, this chain of e-mails was beginning to make sense. He scanned the final e-mail, sent on August 4th. *Crates at KAF. Submit invoice.* Again, it didn't take a rocket scientist to piece together what was happening. Fleming was shipping weapons to Afghanistan under the radar. Why he was doing it was also pretty simple. Money.

The phone rang and he checked the caller ID. It came as no surprise that it was Fleming calling from his office. The time had come to head in and face the man himself. To explain how the algorithm had taken off and driven five stocks into the ozone. And to wonder what the man sitting across the desk from him was up to. He picked up the phone.

"Good morning, Mr. Fleming," he said.

CHAPTER 38

Midtown Manhattan, New York

William Fleming's penthouse overlooked the mid-section of Central Park West, with a view of the back side of the Metropolitan Museum. He loved the building, the art, the sculptures, everything about it. Except the crowds of tourists. Occasionally he spotted another true New Yorker, perusing the exhibits, thoughtful and cultivated. He enjoyed sharing the space with them – everyone else could go to hell.

Sunday mornings were the worst. He could see them from his balcony, milling about, families with young children who were probably so out of control they would try to touch the art. He turned his back on the sight and retreated to the quiet luxury that twenty million dollars buys. The penthouse afforded him a three hundred and sixty degree view. One-way reflective glass darkened the room a bit, but it was a small price to pay to keep out prying eyes. He settled into a chair with a west-facing view and set his coffee on the table.

His meeting with Carson Grant Saturday afternoon was on his mind. The young MBA had risked taking down the exchanges in order to out-game the other high frequency trading firms. He had mixed feelings about that. Carson was brash. Perhaps too brash to be managing the HFT division. But he was also capable of making gutsy decisions unbothered by the threat of a meltdown. He had let the stripped down algorithm loose on the markets in favor of buoying profits. When the computers had run out of control, he had jumped in and stopped them before too much damage was done. Best of all, Carson had ensured all the trading was in dark pools in order to protect their identity. Smart. Very smart. At the end of the day, the carnage was untraceable.

On one hand, he wanted to fire Carson. On the other, he felt a massive bonus was warranted. The middle ground was probably the most logical. Do nothing. Watch him and see how he reacted to the fallout which was coming tomorrow morning. At least five companies were going to see their stocks plummet once they reported there was nothing tangible to justify the huge increase in Friday's stock price. What goes up must come down. That cliché was never truer than with an overvalued stock.

Fleming wondered how Carson was faring. When they had met in his office yesterday, he had seemed fine. But much of that could be an act. Under the skin his emotions could be churning like surf in a hurricane. He'd find out tomorrow.

What Trey Miller had said to him on Wednesday was still bothering him. Some unknown person had hacked into the CIA computer and looked in Miller's file. Trey felt the intrusion had something to do with the U2 concert. It was obvious that Trey didn't believe in coincidences. Neither did he. Someone was poking around in things that didn't involve them.

The phone rang and he answered it. A man's voice asked if he was speaking with William Fleming.

"Yes, this is Fleming. With whom am I speaking?"

"Mr. Fleming, this is Greg Stanfield. I work in the security department at your Platinus office on Avenue of the Americas."

"All right, Greg. What can I do for you?"

"I was wondering if you accessed your private e-mail when you were in Cabo San Lucas?"

Every cell in Fleming's body snapped to attention. "No, why are you asking?"

"Someone logged into your e-mail, sir. There is a note on our records that indicates you do not check your e-mail when you're in Cabo or southern France."

Fleming's mind was moving at warp speed. "When was the intrusion?"

"Last Wednesday, at 9:16 pm."

"How long were they in?"

"Four minutes."

"What did they look at?"

"E-mails from two different senders." He rattled off the addresses, which Fleming immediately recognized as Trey Miller's and Jorge Amistav's.

"Do you know who it was?" Fleming asked, his grip on the phone getting tighter by the second.

"No, sir. It's impossible to tell exactly what computer was used, but I can tell you for a certainty that the intruder was on the Platinus server. The intrusion came from inside the building."

"Are you sure?" Fleming asked. His hand was shaking and his grip threatened to crush the phone.

"Positive," the security man said.

"Send me a report on this with everything you have. I want to know exactly what you know."

"I'll deliver it myself, sir," Greg said.

Fleming gave him his address and set the phone back in its cradle. He sat unmoving for thirty seconds, then he reached out and grabbed a cut-glass sculpture from the coffee table and threw it across the room. It hit the credenza and split the wood front. Shattered glass flew in all directions. Within seconds the doors from an adjoining room flew open and two men rushed in. One was holding a pistol, the other had his shooting hand close to his chest. Their eyes searched the room for an intruder.

"It's fine," Fleming said tersely. "I dropped something."

The first man in the room nodded. "Of course, sir."

"Send someone in to clean up this mess," he snapped.

He was seething. There was a rat inside Platinus. Someone had intruded in his private e-mails, targeting the communiqués between him and Miller. All this coming three days after someone had hacked into Miller's CIA file. He picked up the phone and dialed Miller's cell. He picked up after five rings.

“Is it okay to talk on this phone?” Fleming asked.

“Yes. What do you need?”

“Have you received any updates on who was in your file at the agency?” Fleming asked.

“No, why?” Trey said.

“Someone was prying into my e-mails last Wednesday. They went directly to the ones you sent me. Whoever it was, they accessed my computer from inside Platinus.”

Silence for a few seconds, then, “That’s not good.”

“No shit,” Fleming snapped. “Does anyone know what you’re doing?”

Again, a few moments of silence. “Not that I know of. I certainly didn’t tell anyone.”

“We may need to take care of this,” Fleming said. “You mentioned Alexi in one of your e-mails. Is that who I think it is?”

“Yes,” Trey answered. “Alexi was with me on the Minsk job. He’s the same person.”

“He has certain talents,” Fleming said.

The length of time it took Trey Miller to answer told Fleming that Miller knew exactly what he was talking about. Alexi Androv excelled at eliminating people. Violently. In fact, he enjoyed it. Which meant he was the perfect choice to remove whoever was becoming a problem.

“I told you, I don’t want to be involved in that sort of thing.”

“You won’t be. Alexi will.”

“What do you want me to do?” Miller asked after a long pause.

“Have Alexi ready to move on a moment’s notice. I’ll send my private jet to pick him up.”

“All right, I’ll mention it to him.”

“Tell him to invoice me for two hundred and fifty thousand.” Fleming knew the amount was high, almost double what he needed to pay, but he didn’t want the Russian to turn it down.

“I’ll do that.”

“How are things going over there?” Fleming asked.

"Slow. The storm sewers are like a rat's nest. We're moving ahead, but it's tough slogging."

"I need this to work," Fleming said.

"We'll get it done. Anything else?"

"No."

"I'll be in touch." Miller cut the connection between New York and Moscow.

Fleming rubbed his temples to keep the blood flowing smoothly and the oncoming headache at bay. The stress was beginning to build. Business problems he could handle, but this was different. He had just discussed having someone killed, without even knowing who. It bothered him, and at the same time, exhilarated him.

Surprisingly, he liked the feeling.

CHAPTER 39

FOB Ma'sum ghar, Afghanistan

Russell had never been so glad to look out and see wire surrounding him. Protecting him from the rest of the world.

The trip from Spin Buldak to the Forward Operating Base of Ma'sum ghar the previous day had been nothing short of a nightmare. The first ambush happened when the convoy of sixteen vehicles was halfway across the bridge between Kandahar Airfield and the city. The terrain created a perfect environment for the Taliban to direct an attack at the road. Cliffs towered over the bridge and the road narrowed to two thin lanes with no shoulder. There was nowhere for a disabled vehicle to pull out of the way. Nowhere to hide.

The fourth Stryker in the line took a direct hit from an RPG. It sliced off the gun turret with almost surgical precision and peppered the inside of the vehicle with razor-sharp pieces of shrapnel. They slammed into the commander's flak jacket and cut through his pants and his shirt sleeves. He screamed in agony as the hot metal tore into his flesh and muscle and snapped bones. The soldiers returned fire and peppered the ridge with small arms fire. They pinned down the location the RPG had come from and one of the men sighted in with a Javelin. The shoulder-fired missile hit the target and they followed up with a thundering grenade barrage. The gunfire stopped as the insurgents retreated. A recovery vehicle pulled onto the bridge and hooked up to the destroyed Stryker while the medical personnel worked on the injured soldier. It was almost an hour before they resumed the eighty-mile trek.

They reached Kandahar city at one in the afternoon. The streets were crowded, and getting from the east edge of the city to the west side took the better part of two hours. They exited Kandahar on the Ring Road, then cut south on Route Fosters, a secondary highway that Andrew James described as the most heavily mined road in the world. It had already been cleared but the lead Stryker driver stopped at each culvert and a team jumped out to check for IEDs. The Taliban had proven many times that they could slip in and plant an IED in the short time between the advance team and the convoy. It was slow going and they were under constant small arms fire from the surrounding hills. They kept the hatches on the armored vehicles closed and the inside temperature was in excess of one hundred and twenty degrees. Darkness was setting in as they pulled through the gates into the Canadian military compound.

As Russell was learning, the coalition forces shared things in Afghanistan. Helicopters were used by whoever needed them and were often multi-tasked. It wasn't uncommon for a chopper to take Canadian or US wounded into the city and return with fresh troops and weapons. The ISAF forces worked together. Strangers in a hostile environment. And right now, what the Canadians needed to augment their FOB was a Stryker force. Holding Ma'sum ghar and the Combat Outposts on Route Fosters was key in controlling the area. If they were to hand control of the roadways to the Taliban, everything would quickly fall apart. That was not going to happen.

The American command at Spin Buldak was reluctant to give up sixteen of its coveted armored vehicles, but the situation warranted it. The Canadians were under constant attack from insurgents on their south and west sides. To the north, things were better. A couple of miles from Ma'sum ghar was Patrol Base Wilson, manned almost entirely by US troops. From here they controlled a vital section of the Ring Road and their influence carried far enough south to ensure the Canadian FOB didn't suffer heavy attacks on their northern flank.

By ten in the morning on Monday, August 16th, Russell was up to speed on the situation. He had met a handful of Canadian soldiers and was impressed. They were well equipped, professional and friendly. And they had the best coffee he'd had since leaving Boston. Andrew showed up with two steaming cups of java and sat next to him on a bench overlooking the Arghandāb River. He handed one of the cardboard cups to Russell.

"Thanks," Russell said. "This is good stuff."

Andrew grinned. "Tim Hortons. It's the best there is. If you like cream and sugar, you just tell them you want a double-double. Timmy Ho's is one of the reasons we don't mind being embedded with the Canadians."

"Any other reasons?" Russell asked.

"Lots. The Canadian women are cute. And who wouldn't like a bunch of guys who name the roads after their favorite beer?"

"Beer?" Russell said.

"Sure. Route Fosters. We came in on it yesterday. It's an Australian beer. There's Route Molsons – that's Canadian – and a whack of other ones."

"Interesting." Russell sipped his coffee, mulling over the different ways the ISAF soldiers tried to bring some normalcy into their lives. He finished the coffee and said, "What next?"

"There's tons of stuff on the go," Andrew said. "We're heading for Mūshān tomorrow."

"The place you called the Wild West?"

"That's it."

"What are we doing?"

"Providing support for a resupply convoy. The Combat Outposts need food and ammo. It's a full day outside the wire with more chances to be ambushed than anywhere else in the country."

"That sounds dangerous."

"Seriously dangerous." Andrew stood up. "I've got stuff to do. See you later."

Russell nodded and settled back onto the bench. The FOB was slightly higher than the surrounding ground, giving him a decent view of the adjacent countryside. North of Ma'sum ghar was the river; lifeblood to the crops and vegetation that followed its winding path through the rocky wasteland of southern Afghanistan. Without water, there was nothing but rocks and sand. A desolate wilderness where the Afghan people somehow had managed to carve out an existence for centuries. An old Afghan proverb came to mind, one that had been told many times to the long list of invaders who had tried unsuccessfully to conquer the country.

You may have the watch, but we have the time.

Russell had seen resistance to invasion in many different forms. In the case of the Afghans, it was best to fight their battles with patience. Why try to outgun your foe when you can simply outlast him? Afghans were tied to a country with strategic military importance. The piece of rock that was constantly being overrun, then ignored. He felt for the people, torn apart by thirty years of war. The ground was inundated with landmines and unexploded shells, and the Taliban moved about freely, focused only on the power and wealth from the opium and heroin trade.

Stem the corruption. Education. Pacha Khan Zadran's words floated back to him on the hot, desert air. The answers were so simple, yet so difficult to provide.

He stood and stretched. Tomorrow they were leaving the safety of the FOB. Heading into the most dangerous part of the country. This was why he left Boston. To be on the edge and taste the dust and feel the fear. To see what the soldiers and the civilians see, and then show the world.

He was ready.

CHAPTER 40

New York

On Friday, August 13th, Benediem Inc. shares had shot up from $32.14 when trading opened, to $56.46 when trading was suspended at 11:15 am. On Monday, August 16th, the company issued a statement that there was no reason for the jump in share price. There was no new technology or miracle drug hiding in the wings. Nothing that they were planning to release would change the industry. Their stock plummeted to less than eight dollars.

By 1:00 EDT, with their shares hovering around $9.12, the executives at Benediem had given up any hope of a quick recovery. They called a second press conference from their headquarters in Chicago. Jack Ashton, the CEO, faced the television cameras, saying that they were in serious trouble. Over sixty percent of the company's net worth had been wiped off the board in a matter of hours. Their creditworthiness was being reevaluated. Doors to seed capital for new research were slamming shut. The reservoir of cash that covered their bi-weekly payroll was drained. The company's foundation was creaking under the weight of the financial drubbing they had suffered.

And there was no rescue in sight.

Carson switched the flatscreen off and slumped forward, his head in his hands, his elbows resting on his desk. This was his doing. A solidly performing company had been reduced to a simmering mess of ashes in less time than it took to play a professional baseball game. How many people had he impacted? He had no idea. There was a light knock on his door and he looked up. William Fleming was standing in the doorway.

"You've been watching the meltdown," Fleming said. There was little emotion in his voice. Actually, there was none.

"I have," Carson said. His head was screaming for an Advil, the banging threatening to push his eyeballs out of their sockets. He ignored it.

Fleming entered the room and leaned on the back of the chair facing Carson's desk. His eyes were dark and searching. More inquisitive than angry. Watching his department head – looking into his mind and dissecting how it reacted to acute pressure. "Benediem is the worst. I don't know if they'll survive."

"I know. It's ugly," Carson said quietly.

"No," Fleming corrected him. "Ugly would be if the SEC knew we had caused this mess and it was costing us money."

Carson didn't respond. Not verbally or with any sort of body language. He kept his eyes focused on the CEO and tried not to show his disgust.

Fleming cocked his head slightly and peered at Carson. "You're thinking that this isn't just about money." Fleming's tone made it clear it was a statement of fact, not a question and certainly not open to dissension. "Well, it *is* about money. Entirely. This is all about money and nothing else." He released his grip on the chair, like a hawk easing its talons from its prey. "Money doesn't care who owns it, Carson. It waits for someone to come along and claim it. If it's not us, it's someone else."

Carson swallowed. His throat felt like someone had poured a cup of sand in his mouth. He kept his eyes locked on Fleming. Neither man wavered. Finally, he said, "Shit happens."

Time screeched to an absolute stop. Fleming was judging him, looking for the slightest chink in the armor. Willing the younger man to show he was lying. That he *did* care. Carson gave him nothing. His eyelids didn't flicker. His lips didn't quiver. He was a heartless rock that made decisions and ignored the carnage those decisions inflicted.

Fleming smiled. Slowly. It started almost as a leer, then spread across his face until his lips pulled back revealing even, white teeth. "It does," he said. He turned and walked back to the door, then paused. "Have you noticed anyone in your department acting strangely?"

Carson responded, "What do you mean?"

"Someone acting differently. Suspiciously."

Carson shrugged. "I think everyone is a bit stressed over what happened with the algorithm, but other than that, no. Why do you ask?"

Another pause. Assessing him. "No reason," Fleming smiled again, this time a coldness crept into the gesture. "Keep an eye on Benediem and the other stocks. Watch how they respond."

"Of course."

Carson's gaze stayed fixed on the empty doorway for a full minute after the CEO had left. Fleming suspected something. He probably knew someone had hacked into his e-mail, but was unsure of their identity. If he knew who it was, he would have come out and said something. He was fishing – looking for a reaction. The question was unexpected and had caught him off guard. He wondered if he had given anything away. He had no idea. It had happened too quickly.

One thing was certain. The shine was fading fast on William Fleming. The Wall Street icon was a snake. Carson was beginning to despise him.

No, that was wrong. Not *beginning* to despise. He already did.

He was finished with Platinus Investments. He needed an exit strategy. Some way to bleed himself out of the organization without raising any red flags. It would take a bit of time, but his decision was made. There was no future here. In his world, people trumped the almighty dollar. A calmness settled in as he came to terms with the gravity of his decision. It was okay to back off from something that was wrong. It was better than okay – it was the right thing to do.

The only question that remained was whether Fleming had the resources and the tenacity to track down whoever had hacked into his computer. And if he did, then what?

CHAPTER 41

FOB Ma'sum ghar, Afghanistan

Outside the wire.

Russell was starting to wonder about the sanity of heading beyond the security of the Forward Operating Base. They hadn't been outside the main gate more than three minutes when the small arms fire started. It pinged off the armored Strykers as harmlessly as the stones churned up by the tires. But it kept them tucked inside the vehicle and peering at the hills through the three narrow slits on each side. The slits were mostly covered by kit – the equipment hanging on the outside of the armor. It allowed a very limited view of what was happening around them and blinded them to the threat of IEDs hidden in culverts and hastily buried in the roadway.

"This is insane," Russell yelled over the roar of the engine and the thuds of stones and bullets. "Why are they so close to the FOB?"

Andrew tightened his helmet and laughed. "If they were any closer, they'd be inside the wire. This is their turf and we're on it. Remember, Helmand and Kandahar are poppy-ville. This is where all the drugs originate."

"Where the bad guys live," Russell said.

"Not all of them live here. Hell, the central government is in Kabul. There's more corruption there than anywhere else in the country. The ISI are in Pakistan, and they're a bit like the CIA, except dumbed down. The big difference is, the guys who are here are the ones shooting at us."

"Man, it seems like everyone's shootin' at us over here," Bobby said. He had tagged along with Andrew and Russell and suggested to the journalist that he, Bobby, would make a great character when some studio picked up Russell's story for a movie script.

Russell thought Bobby was probably right.

The convoy was a mixture of Canadian Leopard 2 tanks and LAVs, which were similar to the Stryker, and American Strykers and supply trucks. It numbered over a hundred vehicles and kept a steady pace as it wound its way westward along Route Fosters. Despite the fact that the road had been cleared that morning, three vehicles hit IEDs before they reached Mūshān. As they pulled up to the outskirts of the town, a Canadian LAV hit a bomb and flipped on its side. The front end was blown completely off the vehicle and smoke poured from its motor. Minor injuries was the good news. The bad news was that it was straddling an extremely narrow throat of road and had stalled the convoy. Almost ninety vehicles were stranded behind it, many of them in compromised positions near buildings, irrigation canals and grape-drying huts.

Troops poured out of the vehicles and secured the nearby areas with only sporadic incidents of small arms fire. Andrew poked his head out of the Stryker and motioned for Russell to join him. They scrambled out and hustled to one of the huts the locals used to dry their grape crop. The building's walls were a meter thick and made of dried mud, with slits to allow for airflow. They were a favorite for Taliban snipers as bullets from an M-4 couldn't penetrate the walls. It took a tank to mow one down or a well-placed RPG to blow a hole in the wall. Andrew entered the structure first, M-4 level and ready for action. Bobby followed, then Russell. The building was empty, save for a few pieces of wood and some cloth. It smelled dank and moldy, and the temperature was fifteen degrees cooler than outside. Andrew radioed in his position.

"If we're stuck here more than ten minutes, they'll be lobbing mortars on the trucks," he said, his eyes watching what was happening on the road.

"How do they get here so fast?" Russell asked. He was leaning on the edge of the entrance with his camera focused out the door.

"They have guys watching when we leave the FOB and they call ahead on their Motorola cell phones to their buddies, who then drive their Toyotas to where we're going to be in an hour or so. Then they sit around and drink Coke and make sure their guns and mortars are ready to fight the Western influence on their lifestyle."

"Okay, that sounded a bit jaded," Russell said.

"Oh, I forgot. A couple of them rush into town and plant an IED in the middle of the road so one of our lead vehicles hits it and slows or stops the convoy. And none of the villagers think it's a good idea to let us know where it's buried."

"Crazy shit," Bobby said, nodding his head hard.

"They're scared," Russell said. "What happens to them after we leave if they tell us? The bad guys come back and kill them."

"They gotta make a stand," Bobby said. He checked his window, then sat back and lit a cigarette. He dropped the match on the ground and glanced back out the window. "What the fuck?"

Andrew and Russell both reacted without hesitation. Andrew by dropping to one knee and sighting on the door near the slit in the wall. Russell by switching on his camera and touching the shutter so the camera light-metered the room. A moment later a man, accompanied by a woman in obvious distress, entered the grape-drying hut. She was grasping at her extended stomach and waves of pain coursed across her face.

The man screamed at the soldiers in Pashto, but both Andrew and Bobby raised their hands and shook their heads. The man gestured wildly at the woman, who had collapsed against the wall, shaking and moaning. Fear gripped her dark brown eyes, and her hair was soaked and plastered to her head.

"Shit, man, she's pregnant," Bobby said. He kept a watchful eye out the slit. Time was becoming the enemy as they waited for the line of trucks and armored vehicles to get moving. "Really fucking pregnant. She's ready to pop."

"She's in labor," Russell shouted back. He snapped off a couple of shots, then slung his camera over his shoulder and knelt beside her.

Andrew was on the phone asking for an interpreter. He got an affirmative

– one was only a couple of vehicles behind their location. He poked his head out the door and waved the Afghan in when he came running up the street. It took a couple of minutes to get the story. The woman was from a village two hours north and they had just arrived in Mūshān. She needed a doctor, but had been told that the only medical person who lived and worked nearby was more than two hours away. The baby was not going to wait. She wanted one of the Americans to deliver her child.

"Tell her we're not doctors," Russell said.

"She doesn't care," the interpreter said. "You're educated people. You know these sorts of things. You can do this."

"Get on the radio and see if you can get a medic up here," Russell said to Andrew.

The soldier hesitated, then called it in. The response came back fast, almost as the first mortars began falling. The disabled LAV had been pushed aside and there was absolutely no way the convoy was staying put any longer. The mortar fire grew in intensity as the Taliban artillery found the range. Calling in fast air or attack helicopters was impossible. The Taliban were dug in with the civilian population and the collateral damage would be significant. They were on their own, a thin line of vulnerable vehicles spread out over the better part of a kilometer.

"Let's go," Andrew yelled over the noise of exploding shells. "Now."

"We can't just leave her," Russell yelled back.

Andrew reached out and grabbed Russell by the front of his vest and pulled. Strength and adrenalin yanked the reporter to his feet so their faces were almost touching.

"You didn't get her pregnant," he said. "Neither did I. This is not up to us to fix."

"She's in trouble. It'll only take a few minutes."

"One minute is all it'll take right now to get twenty of us killed." He pushed the journalist toward the door. Outside, the vehicle in front of their Stryker was moving. "I'm not fucking kidding." He kept a vice-like grip on Russell's vest and broke into a run.

There was nothing Russell could do but try to keep his feet under him and match Andrew's strides. Dust kicked up as they ran, Bobby bringing up the rear behind them and the interpreter. They reached the Stryker and piled in the back hatch. It was moving the second they were in. Behind them the entire line of vehicles was under attack. Mortars were blasting holes in the already pothole strewn road, making it even more difficult to navigate. An armored LAV took a hit but the mortar didn't have the penetrating power to disable it. The driver countered his steering and the blast failed to tip the vehicle. The column kept moving forward.

Small arms fire was coming from closer now. Muzzle flashes lit up some of the windows and there was no mistaking the bullets rattling off the Stryker for rocks. They reached the edge of Mūshān and regained the advantage of open terrain as they pushed ahead to resupply the Combat Outposts.

Radio reports kept coming in. Miraculously, they had made it through the town almost unscathed. The first Canadian LAV was totaled and had been blown in place to keep the Taliban from cannibalizing parts for making IEDs. Two other vehicles, one Stryker and one soft-top truck, had taken hits but were mobile. Casualties were zero, except for a couple of minor bullet wounds. A far cry from what would have happened if they had been trapped any longer by the ruined LAV.

The sound inside the Stryker settled down to a deep, steady rumble. The commander opened the hatch and fresh air poured in. The soldiers sat in silence for a while, checking their weapons and snapping in fresh magazines. They were half an hour out of the Mūshān before Russell spoke.

"She's probably going to die," he said. Despite how quiet he spoke, the words carried throughout the enclosed space.

Andrew sat with his rifle on his knee, moving with the rhythm of the vehicle. Finally, he said, "Probably."

"We could have saved her. We could have saved the child."

"Maybe. But I'll guarantee you that men would have died. One, two, ten – no idea how many. Guys like Bobby and me would be bleeding out in that shithole and a whole bunch more would be wounded. Shattered bones. Shattered lives." Andrew leaned forward on the bench, his eyes alive with raw energy.

"Here's exactly how that would have played out," he said. "Bobby and I dig in on the far wall while the medic works on delivering the baby. Mortars and RPGs start crashing down on the convoy and they make a decision to leave one vehicle to bring us out after we're finished. The Taliban fall into the void that's left once the vehicles move on. They fan out through the town, target on the lone vehicle and RPG the shit out of it. They pour into the hut where we're waiting. We take out a few of them at the door, but there's too many. They get inside and kill Bobby and me. Then they turn the guns on you and the medic. The woman's husband begs for them not to kill him and his wife. They see that she's asked us for help to deliver her baby and pump an entire magazine into her and the guy who's thrown himself on top of her."

He leaned back against the metal wall, his body swaying with the movement of the vehicle. "And that's how it goes if we stay and help deliver her baby."

Russell swallowed hard and stared at the soldier. The young man's eyes had lost their intensity and he looked relaxed sitting with his M-4 across his chest, his forearms resting on the stock and barrel. Russell knew he was right. They had gone with the only decision that made sense. If they had stayed to help, chances were that everyone would have died.

He closed his eyes and pushed his head back against the pulsating armor. How had this happened? How had Afghanistan slid into such a horrible state of despair? People living without the most basic services. Women and children dying in childbirth because there were no doctors or clinics. No medicine. No diagnostic machinery. No electricity to run it even if they had the tools. How could this be happening in 2010?

He wanted to fix it, but knew he couldn't. To stop the insanity and give these people what everyone deserves. Peace. A life with purpose and promise. Security. Simple things that most of the world takes for granted. It wasn't going to happen today, or tomorrow. The worst-case scenario. Maybe never.

CHAPTER 42

Soho, New York

There was no future for him at Platinus Investments. Regardless of what came out of the two sets of e-mails he had found on Fleming's computer, Carson didn't trust the man and had no desire to work for him. There were plenty of firms that would take him on.

He sat in his favorite chair, Jorge Amistav's e-mails on his lap, listening to a CD with trickling water and soft music. Nicki was sleeping soundly in their bedroom, even snoring occasionally. She seldom managed a decent sleep for any length of time and was always tired. It was early for her to be turned in, but anytime she could sleep was good.

He checked his watch. It was a bit after eight on Tuesday evening. Certainly not too late to call someone in Washington DC. He slipped his Blackberry out and scrolled through until he found the name he wanted. He hit the send button and the wireless device dialed the number. A man's voice answered. Businesslike.

"Terry, it's Carson Grant in New York."

"Hey, Carson, how are things?" The voice changed immediately, taking on a friendly tone.

Terry Palmer was an old high school friend who had joined the military after graduation. He had done a couple of tours in Iraq before moving into procurement. If anyone understood how the military moved its weapons and men, it would be Terry. He had left the military and was in DC working as a lobbyist, but the knowledge of how things worked would still be tucked away.

"Things are okay here," Carson lied. "Nicki's doing pretty well and I'm crawling my way up the ladder on Wall Street. How are things in DC?"

"Okay, but not great. I feel like a used car salesman selling a lemon to a blind man."

Carson chuckled at the thought of Terry's commitment, or lack or it, to his new position as a lobbyist on Capitol Hill. "It's much the same here. Wall Street has its moments."

"I'm sure it does. What can I do for you?" he asked.

"I need a bit of information. I thought you might be able to help."

"I'll try. No guarantees, though."

"If someone was talking about KAF, they'd probably be referring to Kandahar Airfield. Is that right?"

"Sure. I don't know any other meaning for it."

"And if someone wanted to supply weapons to KAF, what's the procedure?"

"Through the established channels." He took a minute to skim over how the procurement procedure worked. "Despite the volume of stuff they move, the military is pretty good about keeping tabs on things."

"What about weapons not going through those checks and measures? Could someone circumvent this and still get the shipment to KAF?"

There was a long silence, then, "You're fishing, Carson. What's going on?"

There was no upside in lying to his friend. "I stumbled across something." He went on to describe what he had discovered.

"They could have been stolen," Terry offered. "Or rejects."

"That happens? That kind of stuff can get through the system?"

"The problem is that they don't go through the system. They find a way around it. There are lots of arms dealers out there who will pass along whatever they can get their hands on. The guys in the field are getting new guns and grenades, so they don't complain. The key to making it profitable is to have someone who can get their invoices through all the red tape and actually get paid."

"Where would the weapons be shipped in from?" Carson asked.

"Lots of places. The US mainland or Germany. Sometimes they hub through Kyrgyzstan and head on to KAF from there."

The conversation shifted around to what was happening in their personal lives. They spent another fifteen minutes talking, then said their goodbyes and both men promised to stay in touch. Carson checked his Blackberry for any e-mails that might have come in while they were talking, then switched it off. He needed to think.

There was little doubt in his mind that William Fleming was shipping weapons to Afghanistan without following the proper procedures. The only reason why he would do it was to make money. Money that he didn't need. And according to Terry Palmer, the weapons were probably either stolen or defective. He set the e-mails from Jorge Amistav on the coffee table and picked up the ones from Trey Miller. He took a minute to scan the contents and the date they had arrived.

Bahamas account # 973-4462-8812. July 30th. *Assembling team. P today. M tomorrow. Worried about Lindstrom.* August 1st. *Have Maelle. Meeting Alexi and Petr now. Should be in business by later today.* August 3rd. *Received your fee. Team in place. Time frames are tight but should be okay. Crash inevitable.* August 4th.

When he had last looked at the e-mails on Saturday, he had decided that the dates didn't work for *P* and *M* to be Petr and Maelle. So if they weren't people, then what were they? He opened his laptop and powered it up. He clicked on the Internet and typed some keywords into the Google search line.

Maelle Petr Alexi Lindstrom Trey Miller

Miller was a known, but he was also an ex-CIA spy who would probably do whatever he could to stay off the radar. His name was adding a lot of unnecessary hits to the total. He dropped Trey Miller and tried again.

Maelle Petr Alexi Lindstrom

He hit enter. The results still ran into the millions and were all over the map. None of the keywords worked together and the first five pages of hits were random pairings of the words. He switched his train of thought and concentrated on the letters. What could *P* and *M* mean? If Miller was putting together a team of specialists for a job, maybe they were in different places. Different cities or countries. Alexi and Petr sounded Russian. *P* could be St. Petersburg. *M* might be Moscow. Another try, this time adding the two words to the list.

Maelle Petr Alexi Lindstrom St. Petersburg Moscow

Still too many results. He removed the first three names. They were too common and most of the results were from the names embedded in by-lines and text.

Lindstrom St. Petersburg Moscow

He scanned the lines intently, looking for how the Google algorithm was pairing the keywords. The first few pages were filled with tourist attractions for St. Petersburg and Moscow. The ballet, lists of museums and parks, and restaurants and hotels. The first mention of Lindstrom was on the seventh page. It had something to do with a woman named Julie Lindstrom who owned a company that was providing security for the upcoming U2 concert in Moscow. He read a few lines then went on to the next page of results.

His eyes were sore from staring at the screen and he killed the connection to the Internet and shut down the computer. Two hours of poking around and he'd uncovered nothing of any value. He needed some sleep. Tomorrow, Thursday at the latest, was going to be a tough day for him. Benediem, and the other companies whose stocks had fallen prey to the runaway algorithm, would be forced to address their shareholders and reveal the extent of the damage as well as their plan to deal with it. None of it was going to be pretty and some of it could easily end up on his plate.

One thing was now set in stone. He was leaving Platinus. He had to be careful how quickly he handed in his resignation so he didn't raise any red flags. Breaking into Fleming's e-mail account was risky and he wasn't sure if the intrusion had been noticed. If it had, and he handed in his notice immediately, the suspicion would fall on him. He had to pace himself – be careful.

He pushed himself out of his chair and headed for the bedroom. He may have wasted two hours of his time on the computer, but at least Nicki was getting a good night's sleep.

Sometimes you had to celebrate the small victories.

CHAPTER 43

Kandahar, Afghanistan

"I'll be in school soon," Halima said to her friend.

Safa slid into the small alcove that set the doorway back from the street. In stark contrast to the rough stone under her feet and the prickly mud her shoulder rested on, the carved olivewood door was smooth against her back, The two girls barely fit in the small space half a block from the Old City market. Overhead, the midday sun flooded the narrow street between the buildings.

"When do you leave?" Safa asked.

"Five days." Halima recounted the days to make sure. Her father had told her that today was the 18th and she would be leaving on the 23rd. She was quite sure the difference between the two was five.

"You're lucky," Safa said.

"Why am *I* lucky?" Halima asked. "You go to school, and you didn't have to leave your family. I have to leave Kandahar."

"That's why you're lucky. I hate it here." Resentment simmered in her words.

Halima looked at her friend with worry. "This is where you live. Where you grew up."

"I hate the war," Safa said. "It's dangerous here. You and I were playing with the goat and look what happened." Her finger traced the scar on her face and she started crying. “I’m scarred. No one will ever want me.”

Halima touched the other girl’s arm. “That’s not true, Safa. You’re going to be a beautiful woman. You’re already beautiful. You’ll be even prettier when you’re older.”

“I hate it,” Safa snapped. “I wish I lived in America.”

“What do you know of America?” Halima asked.

“Lots,” Safa replied. “They have stores with shelves so long that when you stand at one end you can’t see the other. And that’s just for food.”

Halima tried to imagine such a sight. It was impossible. The stores that dotted the twisting side streets in Kandahar had short, wooden shelves that were often empty. Maybe it was like the market. She glanced down the street at the rows of men selling vegetables and rice and naan bread. Chickens with their throats sliced open hung from their bony legs, the last of their blood dripping on the dusty soil. A goat, staked to the ground with a short piece of wood and a fraying rope, watched her with a modicum of interest. The scent of spices was thick in the air and there was a constant hum of voices and motorcycle motors. Tea boys darted through the crowds, hurrying from one customer to another.

“How do you know so much about America?” Halima asked.

“From talking with the soldiers.”

“They speak Pashto?” Halima asked. “I didn’t know that.”

“No, silly, they have interpreters. If you ask them questions, they’ll usually answer.” Safa held her pointer finger in the air. “They have a big white house in a city called Washington.”

Halima was getting tired of Safa’s descriptions of places she had never visited. “There’s a white house near where I live,” she said.

“This is a *big* white house,” Safa countered.

“So is the one on my street.”

They lapsed into silence as two heavily bearded men emerged from the market and walked toward them. They both wore black turbans and loose clothes that could easily hide automatic weapons. Their dark eyes constantly scanned the road and the surrounding buildings, searching for what they deemed to be danger. They passed the girls with only a perfunctory glance and continued down the street to the first corner. They turned left onto the cross street and disappeared from sight.

Taliban.

Halima let out her breath. They scared her. She knew it was the Taliban who had crushed her father's hand and that her mother had been caught in a gunfight between the Taliban and the foreign soldiers. There were so many stories about their brutality that she had become numb to them. She liked the soldiers and wished they could keep the Taliban from coming into Kandahar, but that wasn't happening. Maybe it never would. There were always so many of them.

"Is that a new blouse?" Safa asked. She ran her fingers across the embroidery on Halima's sleeve.

"Yes. My father bought it for me." She couldn't keep the pride from her voice. Her father had picked it out especially for her and she knew it had cost him at least one day's wages. "He wants me to have something nice to wear when I meet my new family."

"I like it," Safa said. She tucked into the doorway even tighter as a merchant pushing a cart went past. The wheels were almost touching the girl's exposed legs. "I hope you have a nice family in Pakistan."

Halima smiled as a warm sensation poured through her. She was leaving her friends and her father and little sisters, but for all the right reasons. She had a chance to make something of her life. To get an education and learn to read and write. She knew her numbers, but in school they would teach her to add and subtract them. Not easy numbers like 18 and 23, but really large numbers. Her father told her that the teachers knew all about the sun and the planets, and why the snow on top of the mountains didn't melt even when it was hot outside. There were so many things to learn.

"You're right, Safa," she said. "I am lucky. Very lucky."

Five days until she left Kandahar city. Five days until the start of her new life. She was filled with a sense of wonderment at the upcoming change in her world. At what she felt in her heart. It was something different and exciting. She'd felt it before.

Hope.

CHAPTER 44

Moscow, Russia

The team was beginning to fracture.

Trey could see the foundation crumbling and he was determined to stop it. Petr was all over Maelle, making derogatory remarks about her and calling her out for not responding to his advances. Maelle, in turn, had threatened to drug him and cut off his testicles while he slept. Alexi was like a pot simmering on the stove. Ready to boil over at any moment. Trey realized that if Alexi had a meltdown, someone would die. Who it was didn't matter, but it would attract the police and that was something they didn't need right now. He called a meeting at the shop to read them the riot act.

Three blocks away, walking on Usaceva Street on his way to the meeting, his phone rang. He ducked into a doorway for relief from the incessant road noise. He knew from the call display that it was Anne Sommer at CIA headquarters in Langley.

"Hello, Anne," he said. He cupped his hand around the mouthpiece. "Do you have something for me?"

"I do. Are we okay to talk on this phone?"

"Yes."

"I'll be quick," she said. "Do you know a man named Aaron Hall?"

"No. Is he the guy who hacked into my file?"

"Yes. But we don't think he's a player. He's a nobody living in a dumpy basement suite in Queens. Someone else is working him."

Trey noticed her choice of words. *We*. Whenever someone with the agency talked about what they had found, it was always *we*. Never I. Always *we*.

"Who are you working for, Trey?" she asked.

"Do you need to know?" he asked.

"It would help. We have a line on something and it would be nice to know if we're moving in the right direction with this."

Trey considered his options. There was no upside to keeping Anne in the dark. "William Fleming."

"The Wall Street billionaire, William Fleming?" she asked.

"Yeah, him."

He caught something in her voice. Recognition, perhaps.

"I have to check on something. I'll call you back in a bit."

"When?"

"An hour, maybe two."

He touched the end button and slipped the phone back in his pocket. He poked his head out of the doorway and scanned up and down the sidewalk. Nothing. Old habits died hard. He continued on to the retail space they had rented on Usaceva. He unlocked the front door, then closed it behind him. The brown paper on the windows kept out more than prying eyes. Barely any sunshine found its way through the well-sealed paper and it felt dreary inside. He made his way to the rear of the shop and opened the door that led to the office and restroom. Sitting around a rickety card table were the rest of his team. The silence in the room was noticeable. He slid back the last chair and sat.

"Did you find a line for Maelle to hack into the city computer?" he asked Petr Besovich. No preamble. Not with this group. It showed weakness.

"I did. She's working on it."

Trey looked at Maelle. "When will you be in?"

"Tomorrow."

Trey nodded his approval. "Tomorrow is Thursday. If you're inside the city computers by Friday, you can begin sending messages that look like they are coming from the city's electrical division advising the maintenance crews at the stadium of the upcoming power outages." He thought for a second, then asked, "Will you be able to intercept any calls from the staff at the stadium to the city?"

"Yes, but we have to be careful that we don't cut in on unrelated calls. We won't be able to patch them through to other departments or answer their questions. If they get suspicious, we're in trouble."

"Only monitor the calls immediately after you send them the notices. Ten minutes, max. If you get a call that isn't related, pretend they've called a wrong number and hang up." He turned back to Petr. "Do you have all six locations yet?"

"I've located all six. The contactors Alexi built are perfect. Small and easy to hide behind the junction boxes. No one will ever find them. I have the hardware in place on four of the six."

"Excellent. So there's nothing to keep you from having all six power conduits into the stadium rigged to fail."

Petr wiggled his head back and forth a bit. "Should be okay," he said. He rotated his body so he was facing Maelle. "I'll be ready for my bonus soon."

"Not now," Trey shot at the Russian. His voice was a step up from terse and one down from threatening. He had to stop this in its tracks before it got physical. "Have you tested Alexi's hardware?"

Petr reluctantly turned back toward the team leader. "The contactors are fine, and the switch to turn on the remote is excellent. He did a good job. I can trip the power remotely, then bring it back up after the crowd has left."

"Good work," Trey said. He offered a rare compliment. "You're a master with electronics, Alexi."

The thin, elegant man shrugged. His eyes were unemotional – pure ice. "I'm bored."

Trey changed the subject. "I'm leaving for Belarus early Saturday morning to take care of the backup generator. I should be back later that day, Sunday at the latest."

"Any problems with that?" Maelle asked.

Trey shook his head. "Not yet. The crew moving the generator are with a union, so it's simple to track them. The union stewards call the drivers a couple of times a day and their cell phone records are easy to access. Each time they connect it gives me a location. I track it on my map. They'll be in Orsha on Saturday. I don't think the truck will be leaving there for a week or two."

Trey's phone vibrated and he glanced down at the call display. He excused himself from the table and walked back to the front of the shop, out of earshot.

"Go ahead, Anne," he said.

"We have the connection, Trey, but before I give you anything, I need you to promise you won't do anything stupid."

Trey couldn't help smiling. Amazing how a reputation could stay with you for so many years. "All right, Anne, I promise I won't do anything that will get you in trouble."

"That's not what I said."

"It's the best I can do. What did you find?"

Silence, then, "Aaron Hall is a friend of a woman named Alicia Crane. She works for Platinus Investments, which, of course, is owned by William Fleming."

"Alicia is our gal?"

"We don't think so. We have a trail of other cell and landline calls. Our guess is that she was helping someone else."

"Who?"

"His name is Carson Grant, head of the Platinus High Frequency Trading division. Grant is on the inside track and would have known Fleming was in Cabo San Lucas and wouldn't be checking his e-mail."

"Opportunity," Trey said quietly.

She didn't acknowledge the interruption. "He swiped into the building at 8:36 on Wednesday, August 11th. Sixteen minutes later, Alicia Crane arrived. Grant went directly to his office on the forty-sixth floor and Alicia followed when she arrived. The elevators only went to forty-six. No other floors."

"And Alicia Crane's office isn't on forty-six."

"It's on eighteen." A brief pause and the CIA agent continued. "Twelve minutes after Crane arrived on forty-six, someone hacked into Fleming's computer. They downloaded two groups of e-mails. Four from you and three from a man named Jorge Amistav."

"Who is that?"

"Amistav is a mid-level arms dealer. He brokers deals. Usually stolen or damaged weapons. We'd love to take him out but he never does anything quite bad enough to justify it."

"Pity," Trey said.

She ignored him. "Now you're up to speed. Do not do anything that links the agency to this."

"Promise. Sort of." He waited a second, then added, "I owe you one, Anne."

"You did a lot for us when you were here, Trey. It's payback."

"Cool. Thanks."

He replaced the phone in his pocket and took a couple of deep breaths. Carson Grant. Who the hell was this guy and why had he opened up this can of worms? Why would a Wall Street golden child with a seven-figure income care about what his boss was mixed up with outside the office? It made absolutely no sense. Yet Grant had talked a friend into hacking the CIA mainframe and looking through a highly classified file. Then he had downloaded e-mails that tied William Fleming into an illegal act in a foreign country.

Fleming was going to go ballistic when he found out.

Trey briefly considered not passing the information along, but discarded that path as dangerous and stupid. There was no reason to protect Carson Grant from his own curiosity. The bottom line was, the man had poked his head into a place where it could get cut off. That decision on how to handle Grant was up to Fleming. Trey dialed a New York number on his cell phone and waited. Fleming answered.

"We found the intruder," Trey said.

"Who is it?" Fleming's voice was terse. And anxious. He wanted to know.

"Carson Grant."

At least thirty seconds passed before another sound passed across the line. "Are you absolutely certain?" Fleming asked.

"Of course."

Another long pause. "Take care of Mr. Grant," he said. The line died.

Trey shuffled back to the group. All eyes were on him as he sat down. He looked at Alexi. "I have a job for you," he said.

"Excellent news," Androv responded. Excitement crept into his eyes. More than excitement. Desire.

CHAPTER 45

FOB Ma'sum ghar, Afghanistan

Russell had never felt inadequate in front of a camera. Until now.

He sat on the pile of sandbags that rimmed his bunk and stared overtop of the video camera – outside the wire at the vast expanse of desert to the south. The sand dunes were so close he could see the ripples scarring their smooth peaks. Beyond the massive sand waves were more of the same. Unending, like the ocean, but barren of life. Even the Taliban steered clear of the wasteland that extended south from Kandahar to the border with Pakistan.

The resupply trip from the FOB to Mūshān was vivid in his mind. He was stunned at the vulnerability of the convoy and the speed at which the Taliban were all over them. There was no doubt about the viciousness of the response to their presence. But nothing impacted him more than the pregnant woman and her husband.

What had happened after they left? Was she alive? Did the baby survive the birth? He had asked himself the same questions a hundred times over the last twenty-four hours. And he was still without answers. The scene haunted him now, and he knew that it would stay with him forever.

Russell dragged himself off the sandbags and checked the settings on the camera. He had to film the report. That was the reason he was here. To show the world what insanity looked like in the first person. He scanned his notes, then touched the record button and took his spot on the x in the sand.

Yesterday, we ventured outside the wire. A hundred vehicles left our new home at FOB Ma'sum ghar and headed for the combat outposts on the road to, and just beyond, the town of Mūshān. American and Canadian soldiers working together to resupply troops who are dug into the rocks and sand that permeate every corner of Afghanistan. Tanks. Stryker armored vehicles. Trucks. Hundreds of troops. An impressive force.

Yet the advantage still lies with the insurgents. They waited for us. Patiently. When we hit the edge of Mūshān they took out one of our lead vehicles, then laid down an unrelenting barrage of mortar and small arms fire. The convoy was under threat of annihilation.

In the midst of the battle, a human tragedy unfolded. A pregnant woman and her husband came to us in crisis. She was in labor and ready to deliver her baby. There was no doctor for hours in any direction. Her only chance was for one of our medics to assist in the birth. To ensure the woman and the child had a chance at life.

But that didn't happen. If we had stalled the convoy for the time it would take to help her, we would likely have been killed. The moment the disabled vehicle was removed from the road, we left. Chances are – we left her to die.

This is the tragedy of Afghanistan. We want to help. To change lives and bring stability to a country that hasn't known peace for thirty years. Normal does not exist in Afghanistan. If there is a traffic jam it's not because there was a fender bender, it's because an IED exploded somewhere ahead on the road. Electricity and clean water are luxuries, not necessities. Medical facilities are non-existent. Guns are everywhere, and trust is nowhere. Hope has been erased from the average Afghan's dictionary. They exist in a constant state of strife. Conflict surrounds them on every corner. Death and suffering are constant companions.

So how does Afghanistan rise out of this mess? It's a good question, and one that does not have an easy answer. Perhaps, there may not be an answer.

Yesterday – outside the wire – we couldn't help one woman in crisis. How are we supposed to help an entire country in crisis? This is Russell Matthews reporting from FOB Ma'sum ghar, Afghanistan.

Russell retreated to his bunkhouse and replayed the video. Satisfied, he compressed it and sent it to Anita Greenwall in Boston. He sat in front of the computer for a couple of minutes, thinking about Andrew James. There was a nagging doubt in the back of his mind about the soldier's story. Something about the man and the picture he painted of his life in the US was bothering him. Finally, he gave in to his curiosity and keyed in a message to Anita, asking for some back-story on Andrew. He shut down the computer, packed up his gear, and stashed it in his bunk. He went to the kitchen and ate sitting by himself in the corner. The scene kept coming back to him. The woman, pleading in foreign words to save her baby. The husband, desperate for someone, anyone, to save his world from collapsing. The mortars crashing down. Andrew pulling him back to the Stryker before they were killed.

Some days he loved his job. Today, he hated it.

CHAPTER 46

Midtown Manhattan, New York

Benediem bottomed at 2:15 EDT on Thursday, August 19th. The company's CEO faced the television cameras in Chicago for the second time in four days and broke the bad news. They were preparing to file for Chapter 11 bankruptcy. All operations for the parent and subsidiary companies had ceased, effective immediately.

Carson watched the death of a giant corporation from the quiet luxury of his office. He had orchestrated the collapse and was struggling with both remorse and loathing. The loathing was for William Fleming – for Wall Street – and for himself. They not only chased the American dream on Wall Street, they manufactured it. When the markets weren't aligning, they adjusted them. When people were scared, they assured them the new derivatives were sound. When they needed growth, they stimulated financial investments based on smoke and mirrors, not value.

But while the loathing was distressing, the remorse was much more difficult. He didn't know who to feel sorry for. They were all out there. Families who had saved their hard-earned money and entrusted their portfolio to the investment brokers. The institutional investors who had picked Benediem as a solid performer and were now watching their mutual funds plummet. He didn't even want to think about the people who relied on Benediem for services.

He switched off the television and went back to the pile of work on his desk. Chui had the new algorithm ready for a test run. They were still at least three weeks from implementing it even if the tests went well. No more pushing the envelope. That decision had come from his desk and he didn't care if Fleming liked it or not.

Six o'clock rolled around and he packed up and headed home. Nicki had supper ready and they ate as she talked about her friend in North Carolina who was getting married in September. Exciting times. The message was sparklingly clear. She would like to be suffering the same excitement as her friend. And soon.

Carson cracked a beer and retired to the living room after supper. He poked around on the Internet while Nicki watched television. The thing with Fleming and Trey Miller was driving him nuts. The two men were connected and up to something. He Googled new strings of keywords but nothing was working. He went back to the final words he had tried on Tuesday night, but dropped St. Petersburg.

Lindstrom Moscow

He touched the enter key and worked his way through the Moscow listings for major attractions. The first good hit he got was for Julie Lindstrom and the U2 concert in Moscow. He went to the website for her security company, Details Matter. She provided an all-inclusive service to bands and celebrities while they were on the road. The site was short on exactly how she did that. In fact, the site was short on most things. It was a slick place that catered to the rich and famous and couldn't care about impressing anyone else. Like him. He killed the link and went to U2's site. The band was an icon – everything they did was somewhere in the stratosphere. Massive concerts that sold out the moment tickets went on sale. Multi-million selling CDs and DVDs. Huge philanthropic gestures. They were the real thing. He Googled the Moscow concert and added the stadium name and date so he would pick up related articles. A few came up in Russian, but one had been translated. He read through it.

The concert was the brainchild of a prominent Russian, Dimitri Volstov. He had enticed the band to visit Moscow and the copywriter was gushing about him like he was the second coming of John Lennon. He entered the Russian's name and scanned through the first few pages of information. Volstov was a player in Russia. He was the majority shareholder of international energy giant, Murmansk-Technika. He also owned steel mines and mills, oil pipelines and coveted real estate in Moscow, St. Petersburg and Paris. His yacht was four hundred and seventy-one feet – eighty-nine feet shorter than Roman Abramovich's, and eighteen feet longer than Larry Ellison and David Geffen's. Volstov was a regular on the Forbes top 100 richest people list.

Impressive.

Carson set the cursor back on the Google box and added William Fleming behind Dimitri Volstov. That would give him the Forbes list and their rankings. Interesting to see who was richer. He hit enter and froze.

The first article that featured both men was not the Forbes list. It was a newspaper story from March, 2002. He read every word of the article. Then he read it again. When he was finished, he sat back in the chair, his hands shaking so hard he could barely hold his beer.

Volstov and Fleming knew each other. And there was nothing friendly about their relationship. They had both invested in a pipeline to move oil from Russia across the rugged terrain of Turkmenistan to Russia, via Kazakhstan. Midway through the project the Kazakhstan government had decided they didn't want American interests in their oil shipping industry and had cut Fleming out of the deal. Fleming publicly blamed Volstov for inciting the anti-American sentiment in the country and causing the deal to fall apart. Fleming sued Volstov for $2.3 billion. He netted nothing for his trouble, except forty-two million in legal fees.

The pieces were falling into place. Knowing Fleming, his resentment was probably still festering. It was a stretch, but Carson instinctively felt there was a connection between Lindstrom, Miller and the concert.

Carson spent another hour on the computer, then followed Nicki to bed. Sleep was more than elusive, it was impossible. He lay in bed until a few minutes after three, then got up and made some tea. He paced the small apartment like an animal operating on instincts, but not sure quite what to do. Finally, he powered up the computer and returned to the Details Matter website. There was an 800 number and he dialed it, not sure what he was going to say. To his surprise, a live voice answered.

"Details Matter. Can I help you?" It was a man's voice, with a cultured English accent.

"Um, sorry, I thought I'd get voicemail at this time of night."

"The Baltimore office has the phone forwarded to our crew. We're in Europe. It's morning here. What can I help you with?"

"Um, you provide security for bands while they're on tour. Is that correct?"

"Yes. If you want to book us for your tour, call back when the US office is open. They do all the booking. We're on location with a band right now."

"Weird that you actually answer the phone," Carson said. He was floored that he had a real person on the other end of the line.

"Our CEO is a people person. She insists we answer calls whenever we can. I am busy though, sir. Is there anything I can help you with?"

"I just happened to notice that your firm is supplying the security for U2."

"Yes." Even one word was enough to catch the change in the man's voice. Suddenly cautious.

"I was wondering…if there were…any problems."

"Not that we're aware of, sir. Are there any problems that *you* are aware of?" There was no mistaking the difference in the tone and cadence of his words. He was on the offensive, looking for information.

"No. I don't think so."

"Who is calling, please?" the voice asked. More pleasant now. Not challenging.

"Um, I'd rather not say." Carson walked over to the window and stared out into the vacant street. The city was always so calm at this time of night. So deceptive. "With all the problems Bono has been having with his back, I was wondering if the Moscow concert is still on."

"Yes. You can find the information on our website. I would really like to know your name, sir."

"Thanks for your time. Sorry to have bothered you."

Carson hit the end button and dropped the phone onto the window ledge.

Why the hell did he phone them? That was dumb. There was absolutely no upside to making that call. The only saving grace was that he had a permanent block on his number so the other party couldn't see where the call had originated. He was glad of that now.

A wave of exhaustion swept over him and he tiptoed into their room and slid into bed next to Nicki. She stirred but didn't wake. He pressed his body against hers and even in her sleep she snuggled into him. He closed his eyes as his mind shut down and he was asleep in seconds.

CHAPTER 47

Helsinki, Finland

The man dialed Julie Lindstrom's number and waited.

His name was Evan Lucas and he took care of business when Julie was elsewhere. Which was often. Right now, she was in Miami signing a new band and wouldn't be back in Europe until Monday. That was far too long to let something like this sit unattended.

Every call that came into Details Matter was saved to a hard drive at their main office, and he had retrieved the digital recording of the conversation with the man asking about the U2 concert in Moscow. He replayed it twenty times, listening to the intonations and the pauses between the man's words. He knew something. Evan was sure of that. Once Evan deemed the call to have value, he had traced it. The phone line had a block on the number, but it was rudimentary and easy to bypass. It took less than five minutes to pull the caller's name.

Carson Grant.

Another half hour and he had Grant's life printed and sitting on the desk in front of him. He lived in New York – Soho. He was engaged to Nicki Parkins, who suffered from cystic fibrosis and no longer worked. He had recently been promoted to the head of High Frequency Trading at Platinus Investments. The information ran on for three pages of single-spaced, eleven-point font. His bank accounts, his credit cards, his purchasing habits over the past five years. The amount of data available if you had the means was incredible. And Lindstrom's company certainly had the means.

"Hello." Julie's voice was tired.

"It's Evan."

"Is everything okay?" she asked.

"Things are fine here. We're set for the Helsinki show and Horsens went off without a hitch. Bono is holding up well. His back isn't causing him much pain. That's not why I called. There's something else going on that I think you should know about."

"What?" She was awake now and her voice all business.

"I sent you a link to a call I received about two hours ago. It's on your mobile. You should listen to it and call me back."

There was a brief pause while she checked her Blackberry, then she said, "It came through. Give me a few minutes."

Julie touched the power button on the coffee machine and it instantly began brewing a fresh pot. She was not a morning person and had learned a long time ago to prep the machine the night before. Especially in hotel rooms where the machines were always different. She had a quick shower and doctored her coffee as she liked it, then sat down and listened to the audio file Evan had sent. She replayed it a few times, made some notes, and called Evan's cell number.

"He knows something," Julie said.

"Definitely. And whatever it is, it involves the Moscow concert."

"Agreed." Her computer beeped as an e-mail arrived. It was from Evan. She clicked on it and Carson Grant's profile popped up on her screen. The picture was from the DMV and hardly complimentary. A link to his Facebook site was on the lower left portion of the screen and she clicked the cursor on it. A much better picture appeared. She studied his face, his eyes, the innuendo on his home page, then returned to the data file. "Why would a Wall Street MBA be interested in the security at a rock concert in Moscow?" she asked.

It was a rhetorical question and Evan countered back with more data, not an answer. "He has a very sick fiancée. Maybe he needs money and he's looking at extortion."

"Maybe..." Julie was scanning Grant's file. "This isn't adding up."

"No, it's not. He doesn't fit any sort of criminal profile I've ever seen."

"There's a tone in his voice," Julie said. "He's onto some little morsel, but he doesn't know what to do with it. He could be an innocent who stumbled onto something that's completely outside his comfort zone. It has to do with the concert, so he called us because he didn't know who else to call."

"Makes sense."

"Did he call from New York?"

"Yes. From his home number. It was blocked but it didn't take much to get around that."

"I think I'll change my flight, take a detour to New York and pay Carson Grant a visit."

"Do you need anyone for backup?" Evan asked.

"He's a Wall Street geek. I should be okay," Julie said. Her tone was easy-going, but she had learned better than to assume people were exactly who they appeared to be, no matter how harmless they looked. "I'll send you my new itinerary. Would you mind reserving a room at the Dylan?"

"Done. You want the suite?"

"Always."

"When should they expect you?" Evan asked.

She mentally calculated the times, allowing for the flight, checking into the hotel, then waiting for Carson to get home from work, which could be late. Wall Street execs often worked long after quitting hours. "I'll call by nine o'clock New York time. If I don't, send the posse."

"You got it."

"Thanks, Evan. Good work."

"Sure. Let's hope it's nothing," he said.

Julie hung up and dropped the phone on the bed. She stared at Carson Grant's Facebook photo. Clean cut, with well-groomed sandy-brown hair and a disarming smile. His eyes were different. Blue, but with a touch of grey. He looked to be younger than the thirty-six years on his computer profile. Probably from living the good life – cashing his bonus checks and heading for the local Ferrari dealership. She wasn't a Wall Street fan. Like many, she had been hit hard by the 2008 crash.

"So what are you up to, trader boy?" Julie asked, tapping the screen on her laptop.

She went online and booked a flight to New York departing Miami in three hours and was out the door exactly sixty-three minutes after Evan had called. Her schedule for Friday, August 20th had changed substantially. It was now an evening meeting with Carson Grant.

It occurred to her as she took the elevator to the main floor of the hotel that she lived a very strange life.

CHAPTER 48

Newark, New Jersey

William Fleming's Gulfstream flew direct from Moscow, with one stop to refuel in Prestwick, and touched down in Newark at 5:32 Friday morning. Alexi Androv was reluctant to deplane. He had spent time on private jets before, but never a Gulfstream G500. The sleek exterior with its powerful Rolls-Royce engines couldn't begin to do justice to the interior space. The leather seats were a dream and the scotch was 30-year-old Brora Cask Strength, with a deep oaky taste. The flight attendant had appeared exactly when he needed a refill and the meal she served was better than most five-star restaurants in Moscow.

Customs and Immigration for Newark International Airport came onboard and cleared him for entry with only a perfunctory check of the plane and his documents. He thanked the pilot and walked the short distance to the private terminal where a gunmetal grey Audi A-8 with a driver was waiting. The early morning air was invigorating and he cracked the window slightly as the car drove across the river into Manhattan. Once on the island they headed south toward Soho. It was busy, but most of the traffic was heading into midtown and the northbound streets were far more congested than the south ones.

They arrived at the address on Spring Street and the driver found a spot across the road with a good vantage point. Alexi checked the time – 7:12. They'd made excellent time from the airport and there was a chance of catching Carson Grant before he left for work. He really didn't care whether he saw the man leave or not. His focus now was to understand the nuances of where Grant and his fiancée lived. The entrances and exits to the building and to their suite. The amount of foot and vehicular traffic on the roads in front of the building and on both side streets. And most important, the layout of the apartment where Carson and his fiancée would die.

He opened the file Trey Miller had given him and glanced at Grant's picture. He didn't need to look at the photo, he was merely filling time. He knew every line on the man's face, the intensity in his eyes, the bone structure underlying his cheeks and forehead and chin. Nothing Grant could do to alter his appearance would keep him from being recognized. Not that the Russian was expecting the banker to act differently than any other day. He would have no reason to suspect one of the faceless people on his street was there to kill him.

The front door opened and a man wearing an expensive suit stepped out, turned left and walked quickly toward West Broadway. When he reached the corner he held out his hand and a cab pulled up to the curb. He slipped into the back seat and headed north for midtown.

Alexi noted the time that Grant had left his apartment.

He waited twenty minutes, then crossed the street to the front door of the building. He picked the lock in under six seconds and let himself into the small foyer. The door closed silently behind him. To either side were doors, one marked 1A the other 1B. Ahead was a staircase leading to the upper floors. He took the stairs one at a time, his feet quiet on the treads. He reached three and stood in the foyer for a minute, then rapped lightly on Grant's door. The intel he had received from Miller assured him that Grant's fiancée was in the suite. If she came to the door, he would simply beg forgiveness for knocking on the wrong suite. If not, she was likely sleeping. He could enter, get the layout of the apartment and be back out without waking her. If she did wake and see him, then she died now rather than tonight. He could care less.

The woman didn't answer and he inserted his lock-picking gear in the slot and fished for a few seconds until he felt the tumblers drop into place. He opened the door and waited. Nothing. He let himself in and closed the door. Locked it. Slipped the security chain in place. If she woke, it was game over.

The interior of the apartment was quiet. A smattering of noise came in from the busy street through an open window. He moved through the tiny foyer into the living room. It was a decent size, maybe four meters by five. A beaten-up couch sat against one wall, facing a forty-two inch flat-screen television. A Blu-Ray player and expensive home theatre system looked out of place amidst the modest furniture. A *Vanity Fair* magazine and yesterday's *Times* sat on the coffee table. He moved silently through the living room to the galley kitchen. A couple of freshly rinsed dishes were drying in the rack. He opened one of the drawers and selected a carving knife from the offered selection. He closed the drawer and left the kitchen, the knife firmly planted in his hand. A short hallway led to two doors. The first was the bathroom. He peered in as he passed, but it was dark and deserted. One room left. He knew the layout. He could leave now – back up and retrace his steps to the door and let himself out into the hallway.

That didn't happen.

Androv continued on into the bedroom. The woman was sleeping. She was curled in the fetal position and her breathing was steady. Her hair was pushed back from her face and he could see her features. She was attractive. Sexy in an average sort of way. Not the blonde bombshell type, but more like the girl next door. He put one foot in front of the next until he was standing next to the bed, almost touching the sheets. He wanted her to wake up. He willed her to wake up.

How can you sleep with death so close? he whispered so low he couldn't hear the words himself.

Nothing. Her eyelids rippled slightly as her eyeballs moved rapidly back and forth. REM. She was in deep sleep. Perhaps she was dreaming. Maybe she would wake up with some recall of a man in her bedroom. A man with a carving knife. He slowly backed up, still wanting her to wake. She refused. Apparently, it was not her time to die. Later tonight, but not at this moment.

Androv contemplated replacing the knife in the drawer, but decided that it might come in handy later. He could make the crime scene look like Carson and the woman had surprised a burglar and the perp had grabbed a weapon of convenience. He wrapped the blade in a small towel and tucked the knife in his shirt, then let himself out of the apartment. He felt exhilarated – alive – like he should spend some money. And he certainly had money. He had the original eighty thousand for the U2 gig coming, plus another two-fifty for killing Carson Grant. He'd include the woman in the price – a freebie of sorts.

He walked down the street to the Audi, a smile on his face. Just another person happy to be alive and in New York City.

CHAPTER 49

Moscow, Russia

Maelle had falsified the headers and IP addresses on the e-mails she forwarded to the staff at Luzhniki Stadium late Friday afternoon. The messages were simple and to the point. They were to expect power outages on various lines at specific times over the weekend. She and Petr activated the software rerouting all outgoing calls between the stadium and the city. Maelle would receive them in the empty retail space. Then they waited.

The call came through in less than five minutes. It was the building superintendant for the stadium, checking what the outages were about. Maelle connected the man to Petr, who reassured him that it was simply upgrading on the systems leading into the stadium and that the off-hours timing had been picked so they would not conflict with any events. They agreed that next week, after the upcoming U2 concert, Petr would stop by with a case of vodka for the inconvenience.

He hung up and glanced over at Maelle. "I'll arrange to send the vodka. If I don't, he'll be calling back to find out where it is."

"Don't leave a paper trail," she said.

"Of course not." He stood up and stretched, then checked the time. Nine in the evening. Time to get back into the tunnels and tie in the final contactor that Alexi had designed to cut the power. He tucked the hardware into a small backpack that contained the tools he needed and flashed a smile at Maelle. "I'm off to work, honey. See you later."

"I can hardly wait," she replied.

Petr pushed back the furniture covering the access to the subterranean tunnels and lowered himself into the hole. The section of underground he was working in today was dry, so having Trey or Maelle with him wasn't necessary. Trey had bought Princeton Tec headlamps, a favorite with cavers, and rigged them up on their helmets so they could work alone. Today he was splicing the final piece of equipment into the conduit, and once that was in place his job was essentially done. There would be details to take care of over the last five days leading up to the concert, but the tough stuff was out of the way.

He oriented himself directionally and switched on the GPS. It tracked his movement as he made his way through the maze of intersecting tunnels. He had already located the final junction box, but it had been too late to wire in the contactor. The water was only ankle deep and he made good time, arriving at his destination about an hour after leaving the retail space. He found the box and attached the contactor so it wasn't visible. It was difficult – the worst yet – as he had expected. The space behind the junction box was tiny. It was large enough to fit the electronics, but left him no space to wedge in a stone cover. He scraped at the cement and rock in the back of the hole but it was impenetrable without a special drill, small enough for the gap. He swore under his breath and started reassembling the city equipment.

"What are you doing?"

The voice came from behind him. He jerked around at the noise and saw a light bobbing along the tunnel toward him. A solitary light. One man. Petr had no idea if the man was armed security or simply a worker who had happened to end up in the same tunnel at the same time. He turned to face the oncoming person so that his light was shining in the other man's eyes, blinding him.

"I'm completely lost," Petr said. "I'm looking for the Usaceva Street telephone junction."

"Why are you in here? This is not a place for telephone lines."

The man's tone was confident, like he knew what electronics the conduits contained. That ruled out the police or security personnel. Petr relaxed a bit as the approaching figure came into the beam from his light and began to take on a shape. He was a large man, and he looked overweight, which would be a definite disadvantage in a small space.

"I told you," Petr said. "I have no idea where I am. I'm probably in the wrong tunnels."

"If you're looking for phone lines, you definitely are."

Now Petr could see the man's face and make out his features. He was about fifty years old and carrying an extra forty pounds on his belly. His cheeks and chin were fleshy and round, with little definition, and his hairline had pushed back considerably from his forehead. He wore a brown uniform that needed pressing.

"And who are *you*?" Petr asked, changing his tone and going on the aggressive. "And why are *you* here?"

"I'm with the city. We check these tunnels regularly."

Petr waved his hand about. "But there are so many. How do you keep track of where you are and where you've been?" He was fishing to see if anyone knew exactly where he was, or if they would send a search party directly to this section of the tunnel.

"I do as I want," the man said, a tinge of arrogance in his voice. "And I check in when I want."

"Like being your own boss," Petr said.

"Yes."

"Most unfortunate for you."

Petr was within a meter. Inside the killing range. His arm shot out and his extended fingers hit the man's windpipe with a staggering amount of force. A sick cracking sound reverberated through the tunnel for a second, and then a gurgling noise as the man dropped to his knees, unable to breathe. He grasped at his throat with a bewildered and frightened look in his eyes. He remained upright for thirty seconds, his skin turning a delicate shade of blue, before he dropped face first into the shallow water.

"Dumb, fat fuck," Petr said. Anger was etched into each word. "Now what the hell am I supposed to do with you?"

He grabbed the man by his collar and dragged him for forty meters until he reached a narrow offshoot of the main pipe. He managed to squeeze the man's body into the crack behind him and pulled it about thirty meters before letting go and stepping over the corpse. He retraced his route to the shop on Usaceva and knocked on the access panel under the back room. There was the sound of furniture being moved and Trey's face looked down at him.

"Everything okay?" he asked.

Petr hoisted himself out of the hole and set his backpack on the floor. "I couldn't get the contactor in and cover it properly. The hole is too small for the drill I had with me. I'll have to take a smaller one and gouge out the rock a bit so I can make it fit. I'll have it done by tomorrow night."

"Good. Maelle told me you sent the message to the stadium about the power outages."

"We did and we had one call back."

Trey nodded. "You promised him some vodka. Good move. Just don't forget to send it."

"I won't."

"Anything else?" Trey asked.

Petr shrugged. "Nothing on my end."

He pushed by the team leader and opened the little bar fridge and cracked a beer. He had decided not to tell anyone about the city employee he had met in the sewer. That way, if someone came looking for the missing man, Trey and Maelle could honestly say they had no idea. Lying was so much easier when you didn't know you were doing it.

Tomorrow was Saturday. He would get the last one in place, then, while they were still offline, remotely test all six units. If they all responded to the wireless test he would be ready to attach them to the grid. When Maelle's power outages started on Monday, he would begin the job of physically splicing them into the network. They were cutting it close, but if nothing went wrong they would make it. In fact, he was sure they would get it done.

One thing was certain. When U2 took to the stage in Luzhniki Stadium in five days, the power was going out and not coming back on. Not until the crowds were long gone and the timer in the remote turned the power back on. The whole thing was brilliant. Simply brilliant.

CHAPTER 50

Soho, New York

Julie Lindstrom spotted the well-dressed man almost immediately.

He was walking slowly eastward on Spring Street, smoking a cigarette and pausing occasionally to look in the L'Occitane and Chanel showcase windows. He reached a point halfway down the block, then turned and strolled back at the same speed. Other people were either stopped and talking, sitting at one of the small bistros, or moving at a normal pace. Aside from an outing in Central Park, Julie knew that New Yorkers seldom meandered when they walked. They went from point A to point B with purpose. All except him.

Julie took one of the tables facing onto the street a block east at the Manhattan Bistro and ordered a sandwich and sparkling water. She had a clear view of the street from her seat – perfect for watching the pedestrians as they ebbed and flowed past. The man who had captured her attention had slid into the back seat of an Audi with tinted windows, but had not pulled away from the curb. He was still inside, and the vehicle was parked in a spot that allowed surveillance of Grant's apartment building. Twenty years of experience told her that this man was a problem.

She hadn't expected to walk into a situation. The flight from Miami had landed at La Guardia on time, putting her in New York a bit after lunch. She took a cab to Grant's address in Soho intending to wait and speak with him when he arrived home from work. But things had changed. Meeting Grant and talking with him was important, but finding out who this new man was now took priority.

An hour passed. She ordered a latte and handed her server a twenty-dollar tip, then pulled a paperback from her bag and read a few chapters. The Audi's back door opened and the man stepped out, lit a cigarette and walked slowly toward her. Julie popped her cell phone out of her purse and held it to her right ear. She angled her body so she was looking at the buildings directly across from her, pointing the camera up the sidewalk. As he walked closer, she adjusted her shoulders slightly and began snapping pictures. She took about twenty shots as he walked past, then shut the phone and set it on the table. When he walked back she was immersed in her book, the phone sitting idly next to her plate. He continued up the sidewalk, smoked another cigarette and got back in the Audi.

Julie knew how easy it was for an amateur to make a mistake. Like snapping photos of someone, then immediately looking at the pictures. If the person being photographed is a professional, they see the phone pointing toward them and watch what happens after they pass. They use storefront windows or glance back to see if traffic is coming before crossing the street. They have their ways, and if they see something suspicious, they're onto you. She gave him nothing. To him, she was simply another woman having lunch at a sidewalk deli.

When enough time had passed, Julie retrieved the photos, zoomed in on the best one until only his face was on the screen and sent it to Evan Lucas as an attachment. In the e-mail accompanying the photo, she asked him to use facial identification to see if the subject was in any of the international police databases. She ordered a salad and settled in with her book.

Another half hour ticked by, taking the time to five minutes past three before Evan's e-mail came in. She flipped open her laptop and viewed the attachment. A picture of the man she had seen on the street came up on the screen. Alexi Androv. He had pleasing features – welcoming eyes and a warm smile. Three pages of written text followed. He was a contract man, splitting his time between designing complex electrical components for covert operations and killing people.

Androv was a hired assassin with an extensive client base. In addition to a number of private contractors, numerous government agencies, including the CIA, SVR, and MI-6 regularly used his services. His CV was a global road map of shallow graves. Julie counted at least sixty known contracts and stopped. She got the picture. Alexi Androv was an extremely dangerous man.

So why was he here, watching Carson Grant's apartment? There really could only be one answer. Someone had hired him to kill Grant. And this was happening a few hours after Grant had called her company and asked if there were any problems with the U2 concert in Moscow. There was no possibility of this being a coincidence. The likelihood of Carson Grant dying bothered her in an offhand way, but the idea of someone targeting one of her client's concerts was much more alarming.

She had to intercept Carson before Androv did. Once he entered Grant's building, it was over. She packed up her computer and paid the bill, then walked down the sidewalk away from where Androv was parked. The thought of catching a cab to Carson's Midtown office occurred to her, but the traffic was building and she might miss him if he left early. She discounted that possibility and concentrated on how to intercept him at his apartment. She rounded the corner and stopped, looking for a back entrance to the building. When Grant arrived home from work there would be a very short window to save his life and she needed to be ready.

Then she would put together how all this involved her upcoming concert.

CHAPTER 51

Soho, New York

Carson slipped his key into the lock on the front door and pushed. He took the stairs to the third floor one at a time. He was tired and discouraged. Spending nine or ten hours a day at Platinus Investments making more money for William Fleming was the last way he wanted to spend his day. He hated it and could hardly wait to get out.

He opened the door to the apartment, then closed and locked it behind him. Cooking odors drifted through the short hallway and he made his way to the kitchen. Nicki was at the counter dicing vegetables and didn't hear him. He snuck up behind her and grabbed her around the waist.

"Gotcha," he said as she jerked at the unexpected touch.

"Carson," she gasped. "Don't do that. You scared the shit out of me."

He twisted her around so she was facing him, wrapped both arms around her and grinned. "Sorry."

"No you're not."

He motioned to the counter by tilting his head slightly. "What's for dinner?"

"Chicken Marsala, roasted veggies and rice pilaf."

"Mmmm. Lucky me."

"How was work?" she asked.

They separated and Nicki turned back to the chopping board as Carson opened the fridge, grabbed a beer and took a long sip. "Okay. I'm not all that impressed with Platinus. Might start looking for something else." He leaned on the counter next to her.

Nicki stopped in mid-chop. She looked sideways at him. "What are you talking about?"

He shrugged. "Fleming is a bit shady. I don't like some of the stuff that's going on."

"That's not good," she said.

A sound from the door leading to the living room caused them both to jerk their heads in that direction. Framed in the doorway was a figure. Carson sucked in a deep breath and pushed Nicki behind him, instinctively protecting her.

* * *

Soho, New York

Once Carson had come into view on the street, Julie was on the move. She walked to the intersection of Spring and Wooster, then angled across the vacant lot to the rear of Carson's building. There was a narrow gap between Grant's building and the one to the south and the fire escape was tucked between the two buildings. She yanked on the bottom rung of the fire escape. The metal ladder slid down on its track and she was climbing the rungs before it was fully extended. She reached the second floor and pushed up hard on the window. It opened, as she knew it would. Two hours before she had determined the best way to access Grant's apartment without using the front door. She was in the building and on the stairwell leading to the third floor two minutes after Grant had entered the building.

She reached his door and took a couple of seconds to listen. She could tell he was already deep inside the apartment. She worked on the lock and pushed and the door open. Voices came from somewhere inside the unit. She could smell cooking odors and assumed they would be in the kitchen. She moved quickly through the living room and stood in the doorway to the narrow kitchen. Both

Grant and the woman swiveled their heads to look.

* * *

Soho, New York

"Who the hell are you?" Carson asked. He had pushed Nicki behind him and reached for the chopping knife on the counter.

"Julie Lindstrom," she replied. "You called my company and spoke to one of my employees about the upcoming U2 concert."

He stared at her. Mouth open. And widening. "What the hell?" He composed himself and asked, "What are you doing here?"

"I need to speak with you, but not here. We have to leave. Now."

"I'm not going anywhere until I know what's going on," Carson said. Defiance crept into his voice and he raised the knife.

"Put that thing down," Julie said harshly. "There's a man across the street who is here to kill you. If he'd arrived before me, you'd both be dead. I don't know if he's coming for you right away, but I'll guarantee he saw you go in the front door. He's coming – I'm just not sure how quickly."

"To kill me?" Carson asked. The color drained from his face. "Why?"

"We can figure that out somewhere else. Right now I need to get you out of here."

"Carson," Nicki said, her fingers wrapped tight on his arm. "I think we'd better do what she says."

He thought for a few seconds, then said, "Okay. We can go to another apartment on the second floor. The people who live there are on holiday and we have a key so we can water the plants."

"That works," Julie said. "Let's move. And lock the door behind you."

They filed out into the small, third-floor landing and Julie started down the stairs as Carson locked the door. He met them on the second floor and opened a door. They entered and locked it behind them. Julie pointed to the couch and Carson and Nicki sat. Julie didn't waste any time.

"You called the main line for Details Matter. Is that correct?" she asked.

"Yes."

"Why?"

Both women were watching him. Julie, wanting an explanation and Nicki, expecting no less. "I work for Platinus Investments, a Wall Street firm owned by William Fleming."

"I know more about you than *you* know," Julie said. "Keep it to the reasons you called and give it to me in bullet points. We are really pushed for time."

"I saw some e-mails to Fleming indicating the sender had put a team together and there was a crash coming. At first I thought it was about rigging up some sort of stock market crash, but the more I looked into it, the less sure I was. I had a friend figure out who sent the e-mail, then find out a bit about them. Turns out the sender was Trey Miller, an ex-CIA agent who does contract jobs for Fleming. Your name was mentioned in one of the messages, along with Alexi and Petr. The names sounded Russian, so I Googled some keywords and came up with your name and Luzhniki Stadium."

"And you tied Fleming to U2?" Julie asked.

Carson nodded. "Fleming and Dimitri Volstov, the concert promoter, were involved in some pipeline deal back in 2002 where Fleming was embarrassed and had his financial ass kicked. He's not the kind of guy who likes to lose face or money. He doesn't like to lose – period."

"So you thought Fleming might be trying to get back at Volstov."

"Yes."

"How did you get your information on Trey Miller?" Julie asked.

"A friend of a friend hacked into the CIA database."

"Shit," Julie said. "That's how they found you." She shook her head in disbelief. "What made you think that you can break into their computer and not get caught?"

"Carson," Nicki said, staring at him. "Is this true?"

"It's true. I didn't tell you because I thought it might upset you."

"Well, you would have been right." She was struggling to breathe now, the CF jamming her lungs with phlegm. She looked at Julie. "Who is this person trying to kill Carson?"

"His name is Alexi Androv. He's a professional assassin and from what I've read in his dossier, he never misses or gives up."

"Alexi," Carson said. "One of the names of the men on Miller's team." He took a deep breath. "What now?"

Julie took a few seconds, then said, "You need protection, Carson."

"Or I'm dead."

She didn't bother telling him he was right. They all knew it. Instead, she turned to Nicki. "You're in Carson's file. You have cystic fibrosis."

"Yes."

"That affects your lungs, doesn't it? Makes it tough to walk or climb hills."

"That's pretty much simplifying it – but yes."

Julie's face took on a softer look for a moment. "Is there somewhere safe you can go? Somewhere off the radar until we can sort this out."

Nicki looked confused. Then what the woman was saying sunk in. They needed to split up. "I could visit my aunt in Virginia. She lives in Richmond."

"Good. But don't call her from your cell phone. The call could be traced. You should just jump on a train and then call her once you're in Richmond."

"What about Carson?"

This time Julie didn't answer for the better part of a minute. She was quickly processing what had just happened, looking at all the options, eliminating the bad ones and whittling the good ones down until she had only one remaining. When she reached that point, she said, "I'm leaving for Moscow now. I think you should come with me."

Carson was about to object, but stopped. She was right. What were his choices? There was a professional killer outside his building intent on eliminating him. What were his chances against someone like that? And Nicki would be in Virginia. He was finished at Platinus. The life he knew was basically screwed. He swallowed and nodded.

"I'll need my passport. It's in our apartment."

"And I need my medicine," Nicki said.

"Tell me exactly what you need and where it is," Julie said. "I'll get it."

She listened closely, then took his key and made her way back up the stairs. She entered the apartment and tiptoed through to the bedroom and retrieved

Carson's passport from his bureau. Nicki's was with his and she grabbed it as well. She hurried to the bathroom and slid the mountain of pills into a plastic bag. She stopped as she neared the door, returned to the kitchen, removed a pot from the stove and turned off the element. She hustled to the front door. She checked the hallway, then let herself out and took the stairs down to the second floor. She knocked lightly and Carson answered.

"Okay, we're out of here," she said, letting herself into the suite and heading directly for the window that overlooked the alley. She lifted the glass and stepped out onto the fire escape. Standing on the metal ribs she could see directly below her and had a clear view of both ends of the narrow lane as well. Androv was nowhere in sight. She motioned for Carson and Nicki to follow. They made their way down the rungs, Nicki gasping for air as she neared the bottom. When their feet were on the asphalt, Julie unhooked the bottom section and it slid back into place a couple of meters above ground. She glanced at her watch. Thirteen minutes had passed since Carson had walked in the front door of his building. They were lucky Androv wasn't already inside.

Julie ran across the narrow lot that bordered Carson's building, checked both ways, then waved for Carson and Nicki to follow. They turned south on Wooster Street. At the next cross street they cut back west and headed for Avenue of the Americas. In less than a minute they had hailed a cab and were lost in the sea of yellow heading into Midtown Manhattan. They had dodged a bullet. She knew it, and from the looks on Carson and Nicki's faces, they knew it too. Getting Nicki on a train to Richmond was easy. There was little to no way of tracking her if they paid cash for the ticket. But Carson was a different story. He would have to purchase a ticket in his real name and swipe his passport at the airport. She was positive Miller and Androv would be watching. They would know Carson had accompanied her to Moscow. And if they had decided Carson needed to be killed, they weren't about to quit when they missed him in New York.

Then there was the most pressing question. What sort of disruption or violence were Trey Miller and his team planning to unleash on Luzhniki Stadium in five days?

This was far from over.

CHAPTER 52

Soho, New York

Androv was in no hurry. He preferred that his victims have time to eat before his visit. Food slowed response times and every second counted. Even amateurs could be dangerous. Perhaps even more so because they were unpredictable.

Forty minutes after Grant arrived home from work, Androv strolled across the street and let himself into the building. He took the stairs to the third floor and waited by the door for a minute, listening for activity. Music, the television, pots clanging – anything that would tell him what Carson and his fiancée were doing. Where they were in the apartment.

Nothing.

He inserted the lock-picking tools and aligned the tumblers. A slight pressure on the door and it silently swung open. The knife appeared in his hand and he moved through the foyer into the living room. Empty. His grip tightened on the hilt as he rounded the corner and stepped into the kitchen. There were pots on and beside the stove, dishes laid out on the counter, but no people. He continued on to the hallway leading to the bathroom and bedroom. They must have decided to have a nap before supper. Or sex. He grinned at the thought of killing them when they were naked.

His feet were soft on the floorboards as he approached the closed door. He set his palm flat against the wood and pushed hard. The door flew open and he rushed the bed. Then stopped. It was empty. He checked the closet and under the bed, then the bathroom. A quick look in the hall closet confirmed his suspicions.

Carson Grant and the woman had fled.

He touched a pot on the stove, feeling warmth in the metal. They hadn't been gone for long. The escape routes from the aging apartment building were limited, only one exit to the front and the fire exit in the rear. He had relied on that detail to ensure he would see them if they tried to leave. It was no accident that they had slipped by him. Leaving by using the fire escape was not an option unless they wanted to get out without being seen. Somehow, they knew he was watching. He briefly wondered how, but filed that thought in the deal-with-it-later envelope.

Androv scoured the apartment for any sign of where they might have gone. He checked the phone for the last incoming and outgoing numbers, and jotted them down. A search of the kitchen drawers netted him a stack of bills. He rifled through them, taking a copy of their monthly cell phone bill and the most recent bank statements. Conspicuously missing, although he might not have found their hiding place, were passports and money. He powered up their laptop and clicked on their contact list. He created a file, inserted a flash drive into one of the USB ports and downloaded it. There was nothing else readily accessible on the computer and he shut it off and snapped the lid closed. He took one last look about the apartment, then let himself out and locked the door.

Once on the street and moving with the pedestrian traffic, he dialed Miller's cell number. He calculated the time difference between New York and Moscow – seven o'clock Friday evening on the eastern seaboard was 3:00 am in Moscow. Trey would likely be pissed at being woken.

"That was quick," Trey said. His voice was groggy, like his head was in a fog.

"My name isn't supposed to appear on call display," Alexi said.

Trey yawned. "I have a very smart phone. How are things?"

"Not good. They got away."

A long stretch of dead air, then, "So what are you going to do about it? You need to find them."

"*We* need to," Alexi said. "You have a lot more resources than I do."

"Resources that I don't like using," Trey snapped. "*You* fucked up. Why don't *you* call in some favors. I don't see how this is my problem."

"Just find them, Trey. I'll take care of the rest."

"Where are you?" Miller asked.

"New York. A couple of blocks from their apartment. They know I'm here. I was waiting outside their building and they used the fire escape at the back and disappeared."

"Maybe they're still in the building. Visiting friends in another suite."

"I read the file. The woman has cystic fibrosis. I was in the apartment earlier in the day scoping things out and there was medicine on the bathroom vanity. When I went back, it was gone."

"Okay."

Alexi remained quiet while silence dominated the international phone line. He knew exactly what Trey was doing. Assessing the damage and deciding on whether to cut his killer loose or hold onto him and try to find the target. Figuring out how pissed off Fleming would be if he found out Grant had escaped. Deciding whether to fly to America and take care of things himself.

"All right, Alexi," Trey said. "I'll try to find him for you."

"You can call me on this number when you do. I won't miss twice."

"I'm sure you won't," Trey said. He ended the call.

Alexi pocketed his phone and returned to the Audi. He slipped into the back seat and asked the driver to take him to Times Square. Since he was in New York, and probably would be for the night, he might as well check out a Broadway play.

CHAPTER 53

Peshawar, Pakistan

Tabraiz was apprehensive about the trip to Kandahar. Something about it felt wrong.

He contemplated not going, but the financial rewards were too great. Fifty-five thousand dollars was a small fortune for one quick jaunt into Afghanistan. Today was Saturday and he had a flight booked for Kabul. He had arranged for a driver to take him south to Kandahar on Sunday. His accommodation in the city was in place and Kunar had the meeting with Kadir and Halima set for dusk on Monday. Everything as it should be. Everything perfect.

Afghanistan worried him. The country was fractured and dangerous. The Afghan National Police were beginning to function as a cohesive force and they were now a threat to him. The days of paying the police to look the other way were lessening. Corruption was still endemic, but change was happening, and those changes were not going to work to his advantage. He was done with Afghanistan. This was his last deal.

Tabraiz slid out of bed, the tile floor cool on his feet. It was good to be back in his house. He liked the Khan Klub, it was an elegant and safe place to stay when he returned to Peshawar from his business trips, but it wasn't home. This was. Five thousand square feet of marble and stone with Persian tapestries and carpets adorning the walls and floors. Three-meter-high walls surrounding the house and gardens kept the undesirables out. Trafficking in human beings was a lucrative trade, and he was good at it.

Halima was a jewel. She was a snapshot of everything good in a country that had been laid to waste by a long trail of invaders. Her heart and her body were pure and she was full of life. The plight of her city had not disheartened her. Not yet, at least. It would happen eventually, Tabraiz thought. The country, the city, the people – were dominated by whatever or whoever was holding court in Kabul. It didn't matter if it was the Russians or the Taliban or even the Afghans themselves – the men in power were like jackals, picking the flesh off the bones. Leaving nothing of value for the villagers who spent their lives eking out a meager existence from the harsh, dry land.

She would be rid of the dust and the hopelessness soon. Her life was about to change, and while it would be a difficult transition, Halima stood a chance of carving out a decent life in the United Arab Emirates. A small chance, but one nonetheless. She had no future in Kandahar. School was a dream that would never happen. Her father was a man of no means with a useless hand. He could offer her nothing. At least when she was in the UAE she would be fed and kept warm.

He stepped into the shower and turned on the water. It pounded against his skin, tiny darts of energy that invigorated and empowered him. He imagined Halima's life with her new owner. At his beck and call every moment of every day. The man forcing himself on her. And when he was finished…

When he was washed and had tired of the sensation of the water, Tabraiz quit the shower and toweled off. It wasn't his place to judge people. There were many whose opinion of him would be harsh. He understood there was the possibility that Halima might die at her keeper's hand. Perhaps she would be sold into industrial slavery in India or Pakistan. The child's future was in the stars, not in his hands. If he didn't take advantage of her, someone else would. Or she would fade into nothing, left to the life she had now. What he did, or didn't do, held no importance.

He dressed and checked the mirror. Stylish, but not flashy. After all, it was Kabul he was flying into, not New York. He slipped on his shoes and left the house. The game was on. There was a young girl to be sold.

* * *

Orsha, Belarus

Trey sat in his rental car, watching the traffic pull in and out of the fueling station in the center of the motorway. The semi carrying the backup generator would be getting low on diesel, and the driver would want to be sure he had plenty of fuel before heading into Russia. It was simply a matter of patience.

He checked his watch. Eleven o'clock on Saturday morning. There were flights from Orsha to Minsk every hour on the regional carrier, and his return flight to Moscow wasn't leaving Minsk until nine o'clock that night. Plenty of time to disable the truck's motor and make his flight, providing the truck was on schedule. If it wasn't, he'd simply book another flight. He continued to scan the trucks coming and going from the station. There was no marking on the truck to link it to U2, but he had seen a picture of it on the union website. It had a unique logo on the side and he'd know it when it arrived.

He preferred not to spend any more time in Belarus than was absolutely necessary. The issue with Alexi missing Grant in New York was troubling. Fleming was going to be pissed. And he had enough on the go right now without having to help Alexi find Grant. Incompetence irritated him. Not that he was going to be the one who told Alexi that he had screwed up. The man was a borderline psychotic.

He ventured out of his car and into the rest stop. Families in cars on summer vacations. Truckers fueling up. Businessmen driving to appointments in other cities and towns. Normal lives. All except him. No one else was hanging around waiting to sabotage a truck. *What a strange life you lead*, he thought as he exited the confection building and walked back to his car with a bottle of water and a chocolate bar. A truck pulled in and cruised past him. He recognized the markings. The backup generator had shown up.

He returned to his car and watched the driver fill the tanks. The man jumped up into the cab, pulled the unit in with the other parked semis and headed in for some lunch. Trey waited until he was sure the man hadn't forgotten something, then strolled over to the truck. It was parked between two similar trucks, which obscured any possible view from the restaurant. He opened the hood and found the housing for the main computer chip. He pried it open and pulled out the chip, then used a needle to make tiny, almost invisible lacerations in the processor. He replaced it, closed the housing and the hood and walked back to his car. He waited until the driver was finished lunch and came back and tried to start the truck. The moment Trey saw the driver get out and lift the hood, he pulled onto the motorway. That truck wasn't moving for a while.

CHAPTER 54

FOB Ma'sum ghar, Afghanistan

"Do you feel like another adventure?"

Russell looked up from his computer and shielded his eyes with his hand. The figure was backlit by the morning sun and he couldn't see the man's features, but he knew Andrew's voice.

"Maybe. What do you have in mind?"

Andrew shifted to the side and sat in a folding chair next to the journalist. "Today's Saturday. We're heading out tomorrow. This is a good one." The specialist leaned back in the chair, an unlit cigarette in his hand. "Could be a good story."

"What about?"

"We're putting together a big push on one of the Taliban strongholds north of Kandahar. It's called Kāneh Gerdāb."

"Nice place?" Russell asked.

"Yup, a real shit hole. You'll like it. It'll be great for filming."

Russell glanced again at the e-mail that had come in from Anita Greenwall about twenty minutes ago. He saved it to a Word file, and closed it. "My network contact in Boston likes the footage from outside the wire," he said. "She said it's very raw. Very real."

"Well, man, it is real. This is what happens over here. They try to kill us and we try to kill them."

Russell shook his head. "This is me you're talking to, Andrew. You know that's not the way it is. Save the clichés for someone else."

Andrew's face changed. Darkened. He thought about his next words carefully. "You think I like killing them? You think for a minute that I wanted to kill that Talib in Dabarey?"

"No," Russell answered.

"No, I didn't want to. I hate it. It sucks. Whoever that guy was, he had a family. A mother, a father, sisters, brothers. He got mixed up with a bunch of drug dealers and look what happened. He got his face shot off."

"It was you or him," Russell said.

"It didn't have to be. There's other ways to resolve this mess."

Russell tilted his head and lowered an eyebrow. "Are you saying the ISAF troops shouldn't be here?"

Andrew shook his head vigorously. "No, man, I'm not saying that at all. We need to be here. But we have to fix things, not blow them up. And that's going to take time. Right now, the mission is to control the situation and get the Taliban out. It's when they're gone that they really need us."

"To rebuild," Russell said.

"Yeah, exactly. The schools, the medical clinics, all that."

"I talked about that in my last report. I said we wanted to help them change things. Lots of people watch the news, Andrew. They saw the pictures, heard the words. It makes a difference, me being here."

"I never said it didn't." He stood up and slung his rifle over his shoulder. "I'm glad you're here, Russell. I like you and I like what you're doing. Just be ready for tomorrow. It's going to be crazy."

"I'll be ready," Russell said, tapping the camera bag next to him. "I have my weapon right here."

He watched the soldier walk away, then opened the file that contained the e-mail from Anita Greenwall in Boston. He read it again.

Russell – here's the info on Andrew Malcolm James, Specialist, 5th Stryker Brigade, 2nd Infantry Division currently deployed in the Kandahar region of

Afghanistan. I think it's the same guy, but his story is different from the one he gave you.

He's from Pismo Beach, California, but his family background is pretty sketchy. It doesn't jibe with what you gave me. His mother was a crack addict who was constantly in trouble with the local police. She was busted six times for possession and did time for possession with intent to traffic. She dabbled in prostitution but the cops never charged her.

His father is worse. He had some questionable business dealings and ended up owing his "associates" a few thousand dollars. They caught up to him outside a tire store and shot him twenty-one times. No witnesses, at least no one willing to speak up against the shooters.

Andrew was in and out of foster homes, but he always kept his marks up in school. He graduated with honors and went straight into the military.

Take care over there and keep sending the stories. They are great.

Anita.

He closed the file and shut down his computer. Why was no one who they said they were? Andrew James ran when he graduated. To a place where the men and women fighting next to him didn't question his back-story. Where he could be whoever he wanted, and be judged on what he was capable of now. Not surprisingly, his version of his life before the army was a warped variation of the truth. His father didn't own a chain of tire stores – he was gunned down in a parking lot next to a tire outlet. His mother was a drug addict. Now Andrew was in Afghanistan killing drug dealers. Christ, the irony of it all.

Russell packed up his computer and his camera bag and slung them over his shoulder. Time to head back outside the wire. If Andrew was right – and he probably was – this one was going to be a test.

CHAPTER 55

Frankfurt, Germany

Carson fiddled with his Blackberry. It was sporadically receiving e-mails where he and Julie were sitting in the Frankfurt airport. Its lack of reliability might be because he was on the other side of the Atlantic from his New York server, or maybe it was simply from being in the airport. He had no idea.

He slid the device back in its case and strolled down to view the massive departures board, scanning it until he found their flight. Lufthansa from Frankfurt to Stockholm, departing in a little over one hour. Booked at the last possible minute. Their itinerary was Julie's idea. She had immediately rejected flying directly from Frankfurt to Moscow. The moment immigration officials swiped Carson's passport through their machine, Androv and his partners would have their destination. If there was a team on-site in Moscow, they would send someone to meet the flight. That was not an option. Instead, once they were in Stockholm, they would book a flight to St. Petersburg, then one to Moscow. The last time his passport would be put into the system was the arrival in St. Petersburg. After they were in Russia, he would no longer need to show his passport. The more circuitous route would likely take them an additional twelve hours, but Julie had deemed it necessary.

Carson stood in front of the giant screen, wondering what had happened to his life. On Friday night he had arrived home from work and everything was normal. Now, Saturday afternoon, eighteen hours later, Nicki was in Virginia and he was in Germany, running from a trained assassin. His career with Platinus, and probably all the Wall Street firms, was in tatters. William Fleming had deemed him dangerous enough to hire someone to kill him. He had stumbled onto something of significance, but neither he nor Julie understood the scope of what Miller and his team were planning. Tucked in the back of his mind were the e-mails between Fleming and Jorge Amistav. Proof that Fleming was involved in an illegal arms deal. His life had unraveled at an unimaginable rate.

His traveling companion was constantly on the phone, communicating with her people on the ground in Moscow. They were trying to locate Miller but having no luck. As Julie described it, finding an ex-CIA spy who didn't want to be found would be next to impossible in a city like Moscow. Her crew had checked with the stadium staff for any unusual occurrences, but the only thing out of the ordinary was a series of scheduled electrical outages over the next few days. Red flags had gone up immediately, but Julie had learned that the building superintendant had called the city and confirmed the disruption was legitimate.

Carson walked back to the departure gate and sat a couple of seats from Julie. From what he could hear of the conversation, she was talking to someone in Moscow. The band's equipment was en route from Horsens and was expected in Moscow early on Sunday. The initial prep for the stage was already underway and when the trucks arrived, the stage, sound and lighting would be together in twenty-four hours. That gave them a forty-eight hour window to deal with any problems that might arise and she seemed okay with that.

Julie snapped her phone shut and shuffled over two seats so she was in the one next to Carson. "I've been talking with Evan. This is still a stretch, but if we make the assumption that Fleming and Miller are targeting the U2 concert to get back at Volstov, then they're not going to use anything like a bomb. If Fleming wants to settle a debt with Volstov, that's not how he'll do it."

"Makes sense," Carson said. "Maybe he'll make it impossible for the band to enter the country."

Julie gave the idea a few moments to settle in, then shook her head. "Too difficult. He'd have to trump Dimitri Volstov with Russian immigration and that's not likely to happen. We already have their visas in place. And even if the band *did* get stopped from coming into Russia, Volstov wouldn't take the hit for it, the authorities would."

"Of course."

"I suspect this will have something to do with the concert itself."

"Like what?"

She looked worn out. "There are so many possibilities. Admissions, lighting, sound – anything that would prevent the concert from happening. It's hard enough to put on a smooth concert at the best of times."

"Could they cut the sound? That would ruin things pretty quickly."

She shook her head. "I can't imagine how. The band has their own crew to set up the stage and all the sound and lighting. Miller would have to be in the thick of things as the crew was rigging the gear in order to sabotage it. I don't think that's possible."

"You said lighting and sound. They both require electricity. What about an electrical failure?"

"The electrical systems coming into a stadium that size are extremely complex. It would be difficult – probably beyond what a small team could do in such a short time frame.

"Sure would screw things up, though," Carson said.

"If that was their intention and they managed to crash the power grid, it would be complete bedlam."

"People panicking in the dark."

Julie shook her head. "It wouldn't be completely dark. The emergency lighting would kick in. Each of the emergency lights is on its own backup battery."

Julie returned to her paperwork, but the conversation with Carson had twigged with her. The issue of scheduled power outages was suspect. What were the chances of that happening at exactly this time? Slim to none. She made a note in her electronic daytimer to check with the city when she arrived in Moscow and verify that the outages were legitimate. She glanced back at Carson, who was fiddling with his Blackberry.

"Are you okay?" she asked.

"Sort of," he said. "There's a lot of stuff happening right now."

Carson's Blackberry vibrated and he checked the e-mail for the sender's name. When he saw who it was from, he excused himself and walked over to an empty boarding gate. He sat in a chair overlooking the jetways and stared at the sender and the subject line. It was from Sympatico, Nicki's heath care provider. It was marked high priority and the subject line said, *Your upcoming lung transplant*. Carson opened the file with shaking hands. This was it. The news that would give Nicki a new lease on life. There was no reason for Sympatico to send a high-priority e-mail unless they had found a donor. The file downloaded and the text appeared on the screen. The color drained from Carson's face as he read the words.

It explained that Sympatico was a subsidiary company of Benediem, which had taken a huge hit on its stock price in the last week. The meltdown had wiped out billions of dollars in value and the parent company had filed for bankruptcy protection. There were no longer funds to pay for surgeries and until they reached an agreement with their insurance company, all scheduled transplants had been indefinitely postponed. Nicki's surgery was on the attached list. The communiqué ended with a sterile apology.

Carson slumped back in the chair, his chest pounding, his head threatening to explode from the pressure. He grabbed his temples and pushed, trying to stop the throbbing. Nothing worked. He was hyperventilating and the room began to spin. He tried to stand, but the ground was unsure and he teetered for a moment before crashing to the carpet. He lay on the airport floor, unable to move, darkness flooding over him.

His last thought before he passed out, was that he had killed his fiancée.

CHAPTER 56

Kandahar, Afghanistan

They pulled out of Ma'sum ghar at dawn Sunday morning and took Route Fosters to Kandahar. Andrew and Russell's Stryker was fifth in a column of armored vehicles. The force was evenly split between US Strykers and Canadian LAVs. Empty pop bottles were lashed to the antennas in distinct patterns that identified which armored squadron the vehicle belonged to. The soldiers inside the armored vehicles were serious and conversation was rare. This one was going to be tough.

Their mission was to jar the Taliban loose from their entrenched positions in and around Kāneh Gerdāb, about ten miles north of Kandahar. Another armored division, with tanks and infantry, was joining them on the north side of Kandahar city. Then they would roll up the Arghandāb River valley together. The time of arrival was slated for eleven in the morning. As things were, they hadn't even left Kandahar by eleven.

"We'll never make it back in time. We're gonna get stuck outside the wire overnight," Bobby said, chewing on a fingernail. "Shit, I hate spendin' time out there. Fucking spiders and snakes everywhere."

"Taliban, too," Andrew said.

"Nah," Bobby grinned, "they'll all be gone by then. Dead or running like hell."

"Wishful thinking," Andrew yelled over the hum of the tires on the asphalt.

They were making good time now that they had linked up with the other division on the main road. It had been cleared earlier that morning and they were averaging forty miles an hour. To their left was the river, a jagged line of blue water fringed with green on both sides. Pomegranate and grape fields dominated the foliage. Conical-shaped grape-drying huts punctuated the farmland – perfect places for the Taliban to hide and take potshots at them. Harmless enough so long as it was small arms fire and they weren't bogged down and crawling along the road. As Russell had found out, very dangerous if they stalled long enough for the enemy to bring in mortars or artillery.

"What tier are these guys?" Russell asked.

"All Tier One. These are some of the best they have. And they're well armed. Lots of shoulder-fired missiles and RPGs. If we don't secure our position quick, we could be in some trouble."

"It seems you're always in trouble," Russell remarked.

"Just like at home." Bobby checked the magazine on his M-4. "I was always in trouble in Augusta. That's why I ended up here. It's a good way to stay out of jail."

"What sort of trouble?" Russell asked.

Bobby grinned and opened his mouth to reply. A second later the Stryker in front of them hit an IED. The force of the explosion lifted the armored vehicle two meters off the ground and folded it almost in half. The concussion wave from the explosive hit Andrew and Russell's Stryker and threw them into the walls like dice in a cup. Their driver slammed on the brakes and all eight soldiers in the back were thrust into the wall at the front of the cavity.

The Canadian LAV directly behind their Stryker swerved to avoid rear-ending them and veered onto the sand and rocks next to the road, its front tire hitting the second IED. It flipped on its side and slid sideways for thirty meters before grinding to a halt. Smoke poured from both damaged vehicles and tongues of fire licked at the underside of the Stryker. The rear hatch on the overturned LAV opened and Canadian soldiers slithered out onto the dirt. Soldiers from nearby vehicles were on the road, wielding fire extinguishers and setting up a perimeter. The gunners on the LAVs and Strykers swiveled and locked in on the strip of green bordering the river. Moments later the small arms fire started, followed by the first mortars. The US and Canadian troops returned fire, their 25mm cannon chewing into the Taliban's defensive positions.

Inside Andrew's Stryker, the men were slow to react. The explosion had concussed the four soldiers sitting closest to the front and they were in shock and bleeding from their ears. Both Russell and Andrew had substantial ringing in their ears but no bleeding. Andrew levered open the hatch and he and Bobby helped the other men out. They huddled against the sheltered side of the Stryker on the side facing away from the river. There was a constant sound of bullets pinging off the armor.

"Are you all right?" Andrew asked Russell.

"I think so." Russell checked himself up and down to see if he was bleeding. Nothing. "Yeah, I'm good."

"I'm going over to the disabled vehicles." Andrew snugged his M-4 against his chest and motioned for Bobby to follow him. "Let's go." They rounded the front of the Stryker and ran the short distance to the crumpled mess blocking the northbound lane of the road.

The fire was under control and two Canadians were working on the hatch. They managed to pry it open and a thick stream of smoke drifted with the breeze. They waited for a minute until the cavity was clear enough to see and to breathe, then one of the men lowered himself in. Andrew followed. The interior was quiet. It was covered with blood and it took Andrew and the Canadian a minute to assess the situation. Two dead, four injured and unconscious and one severely injured and trapped. Andrew radioed in the information and asked for a MEDEVAC. They handed the injured first, then the dead up through the hatch to Bobby and others who were waiting, then turned their attention to the soldier who was trapped.

When the Stryker folded, it had collapsed like an accordion, crushing the man's legs just above the knee between two sheets of metal. The damage was catastrophic. The bones were smashed and the flesh pinched down to a quarter of its thickness. The only positive aspect of the injury was that the pressure of the metal pressing against his flesh sealed the arteries and stemmed the blood flow.

Without that, he would have died. Andrew took stock of the situation and knew he had to wait. Relieving the pressure would start the blood flowing and kill the man. The response to his request was answered – medics were on the way. He sat next to the soldier in case he came to. Outside, the sounds of bullets and mortars peppering the convoy were diminishing, then it stopped. Return fire continued for a few minutes, then silence settled in. The Taliban had hit them while they were stalled, then run back to their caves. At least two dead and the man next to him forever changed.

Andrew loosened his helmet and ran a dirty hand across his forehead. The temperature inside the damaged Stryker was intense and rising quickly. He hoped the docs arrived soon – he needed to get out. Away from the shattered body and the smell of death.

The injured soldier stirred and opened his eyes. He was disoriented and his eyes flicked about the destroyed cabin, trying to understand what had happened. He looked down and saw the metal across his legs.

"Hey, buddy," Andrew said. He cradled the man's head in the crook of his arm and tried to get him to focus on his face. Anything but on the damage. "You're going to be okay."

"What happened?" His voice was thin and quivery and his body started to shake. Shock was setting in.

"You hit an IED," Andrew said. He held the man tighter.

"Shit, man. Look at my legs." Some level of coherency was returning, and with it, reality. "Look at my fucking legs."

"The medics are on the way. They'll get you out of here."

"I can't feel anything." Panic was in every word and growing. "I can't feel my legs." He reached down and grabbed at the sheet of metal that had pulverized the flesh and bones in his thighs. He ripped at it with his bare hands, trying desperately to free himself.

Andrew hugged the man's upper body against his. The soldier thrashed about, trying to break free, but Andrew kept his grip. He could feel the man's heart beating wildly. Blood started to seep out of the wound. The harder the soldier struggled, the tighter Andrew clutched him. Sweat poured off Andrew's brow and he could barely breathe in the hot, confined space. His strength was waning, his grip on the man loosening. Then, as if someone had flicked a switch, the man stopped writhing about. He lay still, letting Andrew hold him. His eyes stared up at Andrew, fear and confusion in command.

"Medic."

The voice came from the open hatch and Andrew looked up. A face was framed in the opening. Young. Too young to be a doctor, Andrew thought. He let up on his grip, reassured the man everything was going to be okay and pulled himself up and through the hatch. The open sky, with its sunlight and a soft breeze felt strange after the dark, scorching confines of the destroyed Stryker.

Andrew leaned against the twisted metal and stared down at his feet, his breathing fast and shallow. He knew that only a few meters away, the medics were cutting through flesh and bone, taking off the man's legs. He wanted to scream. To run pell-mell into the grape fields and flush out the cowardly bastards who had done this and empty his magazine into them. To kill them with the same savage indifference they showed the foreign troops who opposed them. To slaughter them without the slightest tinge of guilt or remorse.

Instead, he simply stood up, looked at Russell and Bobby, and said, "Let's go."

CHAPTER 57

Nearing Moscow

The train was a milk run and took seven and a half hours to cover the distance between St. Petersburg and Moscow. Its estimated time of arrival was 05:30 on Sunday morning.

Despite Carson's passing out in the airport, Julie and he had made the flight out of Frankfurt. Julie's quick reaction to the situation, explaining to the security personnel that he suffered from low blood pressure but would be fine in a minute or two, defused a potential disaster. They flew into Stockholm and took a quick cross-border flight into Russia. After arriving in St. Petersburg they cleared Customs and Immigration and caught a cab to the train station and purchased two tickets to Moscow. Having missed the Express, which took less than four hours, there was only one option –Daily Train #29. The upside to traveling by rail was that, unlike flying, no identification was required. That ensured their trail, which Androv would be following, went cold in St. Petersburg.

They were sharing a private coach with a polite couple from Belarus, and as the train neared Moscow Carson stared out the window at the moonlit countryside, wondering how he had been so foolish as to put Nicki's life at risk. It would have been easy to rationalize his behavior and tell himself that Wall Street demanded certain things of people at high levels. But that argument didn't fly.

He had screwed up and now the woman he loved was going to pay.

The economic meltdown from the sub-prime mortgage fiasco had swept across the country and then the world, but the traders on Wall Street had skimmed overtop the carnage, mostly untouched. Average people had lost their houses, their businesses, their savings. The people he worked with came out just fine. He had survived with barely a scratch. Not anymore. Pushing the computers too far had backfired and this time he was personally affected. The faceless masses had come home to roost. He closed his eyes and drifted into a tormented sleep.

Julie woke him when they were twenty minutes from the main station. He used the time to splash some water on his face and pound back two cups of coffee. They talked for a few minutes about the situation with Nicki – which explained the panic attack in the airport – and Julie was surprisingly sympathetic. Her stance was that things always happened for a reason. That life's challenges had ways of working out. He was not at all convinced.

They reached the station and hurried through the throngs to the main entrance. A car was waiting for them at the curb and Julie introduced the man in the front seat, next to the driver, as Evan Lucas. One of her senior associates, Evan was capable of handling anything, no matter what. Evan was quiet and thoughtful as Julie explained why Carson was with her. Carson was content to settle into the back seat and listen as the two security experts talked.

"We've asked for permission to look in the tunnels around the stadium, but getting clearance is almost impossible," Evan said when Julie had finished.

Evan was mid-thirties and dressed in expensive jeans and tailored shirts that were fitted at his thin waist. Every hair was in place and he was clean-shaven. His home city was London, and when he had first applied for the job Julie had been reticent to hire him, given the distance from the United States, where most of her work was at the time. She had decided to give him a shot and considered it one of the best decisions she had ever made.

"What else do we have?" Julie asked.

"They could use gas. Nothing fatal, maybe a mild nerve agent that incites vomiting. Doubtful, as it doesn't really make Volstov look like the bad guy. We have three other possibilities." He pulled a file out of his leather briefcase, flipped it open and reviewed the final three scenarios.

"No," Julie said when he finished going through the list. "I have a feeling this has something to do with the main electrical feed. First thing tomorrow morning we need to check on the power outages the city scheduled for the area around the stadium. It's too coincidental."

"The superintendent at the stadium already called."

"*He* called. *We* didn't. Not yet. First thing tomorrow. I want to hear from the city that they ordered the outages."

"Okay," Evan said. He made a note in the small notebook he carried with him at all times.

"We need to get into the tunnels near the stadium, but if they're planning on taking down the substation that feeds it, we may need to expand our search area."

"Maybe not," Evan countered. "The further from the station they are, the more area they black out. Then it looks like the city screwed up, not the promoter. And, if you're talking about a substation, you're talking about very high voltage. That gets very dangerous."

Julie mulled it over. "Good points. Still, get some plans showing the main feed into the stadium." She glanced at her watch. "Shit, it's already the 22nd. We have three days until the concert." She was starting to show signs of the panic she was feeling.

"One more thing," Evan said, consulting his notebook. "The truck with the backup generator broke down in Belarus."

Julie cocked her head a bit to one side and stared at him. "And when the hell did you find out about that?"

"Last night, about midnight. The driver pulled in for fuel and a bite to eat and when he went to leave, the truck wouldn't start. The computer is shot."

"How long will it take to get it fixed?"

"At least a week by the time they can get a part through Customs and to the truck."

"Can we bring in one of the other generators?" she asked.

Evan shook his head. "We don't have one close enough to Moscow."

"Damn it," she said.

Carson listened as they dove into the rest of the details. Julie was intelligent and focused. She peppered Evan with questions about the security setup at the concert, from the turnstiles to the front-row seats and every step in between. Backstage routes of getting the band in and out – always with an alternate. Food, water, dressing rooms, flowers, seating areas for family and friends, bodies to man the gates, the aisles, the access to the floor, the stage – the list was long and arduous. For every question she threw at Evan, he had an answer. But underlying the back-and-forth banter, their tone made it obvious that they were worried. Carson could tell from the intensity of their conversation that the threat was real.

He closed his eyes, blocked out their voices and tried to force the image of Nicki's face into the blackness. He wanted to call her, to tell her how much he loved her and that things were going to be fine. That she would get healthy and they would have a long and wonderful life together. Aside from the fact that he loved her, everything was a lie.

The driver pulled up in front of their hotel and they piled out onto the sidewalk. Julie motioned for him to come and he followed them through the lobby to the elevators. Evan already had a key for him, and he and Julie stopped and checked out his room before heading up to the suite they had rented.

"Stay in the room until we come back for you. We'll call first, then come to the door a minute later. Don't open the door for anyone. No one. Not the hotel manager, or the cleaning staff. Do you understand?"

Carson nodded. "Yes."

"We'll be at least two hours. Probably more. Get some sleep."

The door clicked behind them and he clamped the security bolt in place. He fell onto the bed and within seconds he was asleep.

CHAPTER 58

Moscow, Russia

Trey listened to his contact inside Langley with great interest. Grant's passport had been scanned late Saturday evening on an outgoing flight from Stockholm – destined for St. Petersburg. It was now Sunday afternoon, and Grant was already in Russia.

Trey picked up a pad of paper with the Korston Hotel logo at the top and sat in a wingback chair near the window. He started a chronological list of Grant's apparent involvement in Fleming's private affairs. At the top of the list was the intrusion into Fleming's e-mail account at Platinus Investments. There was no doubt that he had read all four e-mails concerning the Moscow gig. Which meant he had certain keywords to work with. *Team. Lindstrom. Maelle. Petr. Alexi.* Plus, Grant had the e-mail header, which was how he sourced out the sender.

Once Grant knew who had sent the e-mails, he had some bit player named Aaron hack into the CIA database by inserting a Trojan Virus in an employee's computer. That gave Grant Trey's entire CIA file. Grant also had three other names to work with. Of the three, Lindstrom was the most damaging. Somehow, Grant had managed to connect Julie Lindstrom to the chain of evidence he was building. Then he eluded a killer who seldom, if ever, missed a target. The fact that Grant ran out with a sick fiancée and didn't use the front door indicated he knew Androv was waiting. But how?

He stood up and paced the room. Grant had flown from the US to Frankfurt, then caught a flight to Stockholm, which was a short hop from Russia. From there he flew over the border to St. Petersburg. Grant was no fool. He knew if he flew directly into Moscow, Androv's team would be waiting for him. He was thinking and acting like a professional, which meant the Wall Street trader wasn't working alone.

Trey sat at the table and pulled out his file on Julie Lindstrom and her company, Details Matter. Everything he had learned about the woman was inside and he read through it. The fact that she had spent fifteen years with the FBI pretty much explained everything. Lindstrom got to Grant and his fiancée first and spirited them out the back of the building. And they weren't heading for St. Petersburg, they were on their way to Moscow. Lindstrom had connected Fleming's e-mail to the concert. He picked up the phone and dialed Maelle's room.

"We're checking out," he said when she answered.

"Problems?" Maelle asked.

"Maybe. Probably. Get packed and come down here. I'll fill you in."

He called Petr's room but it went to voice mail. He tried the Russian's cell number with the same result. He left a message. *Check out and keep your cell phone turned on. Do not return to the Korston under any circumstances.* Then he made one more call. Alexi answered after a few rings.

"He's in Moscow," Trey said.

"Who? Grant?" Alexi asked.

"Of course." Trey was having trouble keeping his anger in check. The Russian should never have missed. This was causing problems that were going to escalate. "You need to be back here, now."

"Is Fleming sending his plane?"

"Are you fucking nuts?" Trey spat into the phone. "If Fleming had you in his sights right now, he'd kill you. Get a commercial flight and do it now. Call me on my cell when you arrive in Moscow."

"You're worried about some Wall Street schmuck?" Androv asked.

"He's with Julie Lindstrom. I'm worried about her." Trey was seething.

"She's just a bitch. We can take care of her."

Trey's angered boiled over. "Don't underestimate her, Alexi, or she'll take you out before you even know she's in the room." Hand-to-hand combat, small arms and explosives weren't things a typical female was familiar with, but they were in her file. "She spent fifteen years with the FBI in counter-terrorism."

"Whatever."

"Get back to Moscow. And don't come to the Korston. We're checking out."

Trey slammed the phone in its cradle and started working on dismantling their communication and work center. He rolled up the plans of the tunnels, taking time to mark which grid each one covered. The transmitter to trip the low amperage remote that would then send power to the contactors was carefully stored in a padded box. Without it, the mission was a complete failure. It operated on a specific frequency and was encrypted so no one could start or stop the process without the password. It was Alexi's work, and it was brilliant.

There was a knock on the door and he looked through the peephole. It was Maelle. He opened the door and she pushed in dragging her suitcase behind her.

"What's happening?" she asked.

He filled her in on Grant's escape and Julie Lindstrom's appearance on the scene. "Her job is to protect the band," he said. "By now, she knows what Grant knows. It's not going to take her long to figure out what our plan is."

"So we're dead in the water?" Maelle asked.

Trey shook his head. "I don't think so. Petr should have the last contactor in place by now. Everything is live and ready to go. They're well hidden behind the panels, so unless Lindstrom and her team know where to look, they'll have no idea where we've cut into the system. All we need to do now is stay under the radar for three days then push the button."

"Where are we going to hide out?" Maelle asked.

"The Hotel Akvarel. It's central and they don't ask questions. I'm worried that Lindstrom is going to search the area for new leases or purchases and find our retail space. If she finds that, she finds our access to the storm sewers."

"That's not good," Maelle said.

"Not good at all," Trey agreed. "C'mon, it's almost noon. Help me pack."

CHAPTER 59

North of Kandahar City

The armored column met light resistance as they neared Kāneh Gerdāb at 15:00 hours on Sunday afternoon, and the joint US-Canadian force cleared out the few Taliban hiding in the grape-drying huts on the near side of the river.

Across the Arghandāb, the village of Kāneh Gerdāb was engulfed in vineyards, cornfields and olive trees. Beyond the village were a series of rocky peaks, thrusting another thousand meters above the fertile valley. The terrain was dangerous to the attacking troops on all levels. The low mountains provided an ideal spot for the Taliban to dig in their artillery, and the heavily foliated fields next to the river were a breeding spot for the insurgents to lie in ambush. The armored LAVs and Strykers were targets for RPGs and any routes in and out of the town were guaranteed to be rife with IEDs. The column slowed as it approached the access to the bridge. Crossing the river was going to be a challenge.

A team moved ahead of the main column, checking the surface of the road and underlying culverts for explosives. They found four IEDs and blew them in place. The craters the explosions left in the road were a couple of meters deep, but the vehicles had no problems navigating through or around them. They reached the river and the first vehicle started across the bridge. Taliban artillery from the hills to the west opened up immediately. Shells were dropping everywhere, and the stalled column took a couple of direct hits. One was a shaped charge, the copper cone transformed into a hot, molten jet on impact. The liquid metal pierced the half-inch armor on a LAV and sprayed the inside of the vehicle. The soldiers' flak jackets protected their torsos, but their legs, arms and faces were severely burnt. Screaming and the putrid smell of burning flesh erupted from the LAV as the men threw back the hatches and piled out. Choking smoke poured from the openings, staining the clear, blue sky. Medics raced up the column and were at the disabled vehicle in less than a minute.

The column thrust ahead across the bridge and moved into the town. The fire coming at them intensified. Infantry leaped from the Strykers and LAVs and spread out into the town, moving from house to house, clearing the way for the advancing line of armor. The slower-moving tanks, which had dropped back on the highway, caught up to the rest of the force and started shelling the artillery position in the hills. Puffs of smoke gave the tank gunners targets and they were deadly accurate with their return fire. The barrage of artillery slowed to a trickle. Choppers landed on the east side of the river to MEDEVAC the injured men. What had been a quiet Afghan village was now a vicious battleground. The house-to-house sweep by the infantry was proving costly, and radio reports were coming back with the casualties. There were numerous more injured and one killed. The Taliban were entrenched and not giving up ground without a fight.

Andrew, Bobby and Russell were part of the force flanking the village on the south side. They had six other soldiers with them and their objective was to get through town quickly and circle back on the Taliban from the rear. Bobby was in the lead, two other men directly behind him, then Russell and Andrew and the final four men. They kept to narrow alleyways. If the enemy tried to come up in front or behind them they could only get one man in position to fire. Bobby was moving fast, his shoulders rubbing on the rough stone walls until the alleyway widened, then he slowed. Now, the buildings on both sides had windows and doors where the Taliban could hide and take potshots. The men split into two lines and moved cautiously. A door opened and eight guns jerked around. A woman stood in the doorway, a look of shock on her face. They waved her back inside and kept going.

They rounded a sharp curve and Bobby threw himself backwards into the wall. A split-second later, bullets chewed into the bricks on the opposing side of the street. Bobby held up three fingers, then motioned for the four men in the rear to cut into an alley leading to their left. Flank them. Come up from behind. Bobby spoke quietly into the radio. Watch for trip wires on the detour. The group divided into fours, Russell staying with Andrew and Bobby.

The street was bordered on both sides by single-story mud houses and Andrew backed up five meters to a door and tried the knob. It was locked. He stepped back a couple of paces and kicked the door. It flung inward on its hinges and he disappeared into the dark hole. Thirty seconds passed with no sound and he poked his head out.

"Clear," he said. "And it has an access to the roof. I'm going up to have a look."

Bobby nodded that he understood. "Radio us once you're in position."

Andrew ducked back into the house and a minute later he called down to them from the roof. He was directly overhead, leaning over the edge. "These houses are all joined, and there are stub walls all over the place up here so I should be able to stay out of sight. I'm moving forward."

"Not alone," Bobby said. "I'm coming up."

He motioned for the last two men to stay put, then glanced at Russell as he headed for the door. "You comin'?"

With his camera in hand, Russell fell in behind him. Little sunlight penetrated through the small windows, and the interior of the house was dark. A woman grasping two small children huddled against the far wall, watching but not making a sound. Russell wanted desperately to capture the look on her face – her eyes told him she would die to protect her children – but he let the moment go. This was her house and they were already violating her space. They spied a rudimentary ladder, constructed of scrap wood lashed together with dried hemp. Bobby went first, then waved for Russell to follow.

The sunlight was blinding. Russell's pupils had adjusted to the darkness inside the tiny house and he squinted to cut down the glare. Bobby was motioning for Russell to keep his head down below the level of the short mud walls that delineated each rooftop, and the journalist dropped onto his knees. Cisterns for storing water stuck above the walls at irregular intervals and laundry was hung out to dry, flapping in the low breeze. Andrew had cleared a couple of the short walls and was visible only when he stuck his head up. He waved them to come ahead.

They joined him on a roof a few houses ahead. He pointed due west. "Check this out," he whispered. "There's about five guys hanging out up here. I think they're working the remote detonators on the IEDs."

"Can we get them?" Bobby asked.

Andrew stayed focused on the area where he had seen the Taliban. A head popped up, stayed in sight for ten or fifteen seconds, then disappeared. A minute passed and it happened again. The spotters were watching a specific location, ready to detonate the IED when troops were overtop.

"It's going to be tough to get close," Andrew said. "If they look this direction when we're going over a wall, they'll see us."

"Shit, man," Bobby said. "This is bad. We gotta get close or they'll duck behind the wall and take shots at us."

"If we don't take them out, they'll blow up our guys."

"Let's split. I'm over there," Bobby pointed to the right, to the edge overlooking the road. "You're over there." He jerked his head to the left, into the warren of walls and cisterns. "When you're ready, I'll lay down some fire. They'll be all over me and not noticin' you."

"In theory," Andrew said.

"Don't be theorizing' nothin' with me, dawg. This is gonna work."

"On three."

Bobby settled back into the wall, breathing fast. "Why always three? Why not two?"

"Okay, on two.'"

"Naw, I'm just fuckin' with ya. Three's good."

The adrenalin was pumping and the quick one-liners helped with the incredible stress. "Okay, on three," Andrew said. "You're sure."

"I'm sure. On three."

They split, Bobby angling toward the edge and Andrew scampering over the walls leading into the maze. Each time they cleared a wall, they waited until the Talib lookout peered down to the street then ducked out of view. It took almost five minutes for them to get into position. Andrew checked with Bobby on the radio.

"I'm about twenty meters to the southeast of their position. There are three more walls between me and them, including the one they're hiding behind."

"Roger that," Bobby said. "One, two, three…"

Both men emerged over the walls, Bobby in firing position with his M-4 and Andrew running hard toward the enemy. They felt the impact of his boots on the rooftop and five heads popped up. Their bodies started twisting toward Andrew, their guns leveling off. Bobby pulled the trigger. Nothing. The M-4 jammed. He pulled once more with the same result, then let go of the automatic weapon, his right hand moving at an impossible speed, yanking his pistol from its holster. The Talib had a clear shot on Andrew, who had reacted quickly to the lack of cover fire and was bringing his M-4 to bear. Bobby raised the pistol and started firing. The distance was over fifty meters, the targets mostly hidden by the mud wall. The bullets from his pistol slammed into the first Talib, then the second and a third. The fourth shot missed, but the fifth was deadly accurate, the bullet tearing a hole in one of the men's chests.

The lone remaining Talib tried to react to Bobby's fire, but Andrew had him in his sights and opened up with his M-4. Half a magazine riddled the man's body and he dropped to the roof. Andrew kept running until he reached the wall and peered over. All five Taliban were dead. He ensured the area was secure and waved for Bobby and Russell. They gathered at the gruesome site.

"What the fuck kind of cover fire was that?" Andrew asked. "I almost got my ass shot off."

"Fuckin' thing jammed," Bobby said, lifting up the M-4.

"How many bullets in your mag?" Andrew asked.

"Twenty-eight. Never put thirty. Things jam if you load them to the max." He pulled the clip and checked the bullets. They were fine. He pushed another magazine into the gun, aimed it away from them and pulled the trigger. It fired three shots in rapid succession. "Now it works. What a piece of shit."

"You get that from the new shipment that came in the other day?"

"Yeah. And this ain't the first time it jammed. Once on the firing range yesterday."

"Get another one."

"No shit."

"Hey," Andrew said as they gathered around the detonator. "Nice shooting with the pistol."

"Thanks."

They checked out the remote detonator and the street below. The vantage point from where the insurgents were stationed was a major intersection with a small square, a well, some trees and a few wooden benches. Andrew called it in on the radio. They were going to blow an IED. They gave a description of the square and any troops nearby melted back into the adjoining streets. When they were all clear, Bobby pushed the detonator.

The explosion ripped apart the square, sending fragments of lethal shrapnel in a 360-degree arc. The house they were sitting on shook and threatened to collapse. The smoke cleared, revealing a three-meter deep crater. Surrounding buildings were scarred with jagged pieces of smoking-hot metal. The collateral damage from the bomb, if set off when troops were gathered in the square, would have been devastating.

"Whooee," Bobby yelled. "Holy shit, that was fuckin' amazing."

"You get that on film?" Andrew asked.

"Oh, yeah." Russell was shaking with adrenalin. "I got it." He sat on the roof, his camera in his lap.

Andrew broke into a wide grin. "Yeah, that was fun."

Andrew stomped on the remote and ground it into the baked mud. "Let's get back down to the street."

They retraced their steps to the opening in the roof they had come up through. The woman was still sitting against the wall, her children tucked tight to her. There was something else in her eyes now. Fear. There was no mistaking it. The same emotion showed in her children's eyes. Russell tried to imagine what it was like, cowering in your house while armed soldiers from the other side of the world kicked in your door. Nowhere to go that was any safer, and hoping – praying—that it would all simply stop. Knowing that it wouldn't.

He tried to imagine. But he couldn't.

CHAPTER 60

Sheremetyevo II Airport, Moscow

The flight from Heathrow arrived twenty minutes early, putting Alexi in Moscow a few minutes before six on Monday morning. On a commercial flight, New York to Moscow in eighteen hours was fast. It was morning and he had slept all the way from London. He was rested and ready to begin the search for Carson Grant.

He powered up his cell phone and headed directly for the main entrance, a small carry-on bag in his hand. Traveling without checked luggage was the key to catching last minute flights and making tight connections. He slipped into the back of a cab and asked for the Tverskaya Ulitsa district. There would be coffee shops open and catering to the Monday morning crowds in the upscale shopping and business district. He started when his cell phone rang at such an early hour. The number was prefixed with a 212 area code, which was even more unexpected. New York.

"Is this Alexi Androv?" the voice asked.

"It is."

"William Fleming."

"Good morning, Mr. Fleming," Androv said politely.

"It's ten at night over here," Fleming shot back at him. "But you're in Moscow and that gives you one day less to find Carson Grant."

"I'm working on it," Alexi said. His tone was not quite as civil.

"I'm disappointed. Trey recommended you. He said you were reliable."

Alexi was quickly losing his cool. "I said that I would take care of it."

A few seconds of static swept across the line, then Fleming's voice was back. "Your word is of very little value to me right now. I expect you to be wrapped up in Moscow before the 25th."

"Or what?" Alexi asked. He was sick of the condescending tone in Fleming's voice. He was baiting the billionaire for a response.

"Or nothing," Fleming said after a moment's silence. "No paycheck. No further work. You get nothing."

The slight pause before Fleming's response spoke louder than the words. Fleming was not saying what he was thinking. Not in the least. Alexi stared out the window at the city of his birth. A city stripped of its relevance by Peter the Great in the seventeenth century when he declared St. Petersburg the Russian capital. Two hundred years passed before Moscow lived up to its pedigree and was again the center of state. Patience and guile were second nature to Muscovites. Attempting to deceive a Russian was dangerous. And stupid. As Alexi saw it there were two ways to play this. One was to be polite and pretend he didn't understand what was going on in the man's mind. The other was to be blunt. The choice was easy.

Alexi stopped the cab in front of a favorite bistro, paid the driver and stood on the sidewalk. "Threatening me is extremely foolish," he said quietly. "If I think for one moment that you've hired someone to kill me, I'll be through your security and in your bedroom while you're sleeping. I am not the kind of person you ever – ever – want to threaten."

A long silence filled the line. Finally, Fleming said, "Find Carson Grant and kill him." The line clicked over to a dial tone.

Alexi shoved the phone back in its leather case. Fleming didn't bother him. Being stiffed on the quarter million dollar fee did. He had two days to find the American. Not much time, but he was on his own turf now. He knew the city, and his well-placed contacts could find almost anything or anyone, including

Carson Grant. He would take great pleasure in killing him, and, if necessary, William Fleming.

He found a nice table facing the streetscape and ordered an espresso.

CHAPTER 61

Kāneh Gerdāb, Afghanistan

One hour until sunrise. Soon, the hell would be over.

Russell sat with his back against the cool metal of the Stryker. Above him, thick clouds obscured the moon and left the attack force in an inky blackness that limited vision to less than three meters. It was like being in a closet, where fear was the only thing more pressing than the dark.

They had pushed the Taliban out of Kāneh Gerdāb at about eight o'clock. Far too late to attempt the trip back to Kandahar city or the FOB. They were stuck outside the wire for the night. Every soldier's worst dream.

The blackness prevented the Taliban from targeting the ring of vehicles with their artillery and mortars and it restricted their movements on foot and in their ratty Toyotas. But it also provided them with the ultimate cover. Without their night vision goggles on, it was impossible for the troops to see anything coming at them. The desert night was a scary place even without men with guns running around. Vipers, rats, scorpions. Camel spiders were the worst, with bites that had the potential to be fatal.

"You get any sleep?" Andrew asked as he sidled up next to Russell.

"None. You?"

Andrew laughed, the sound a disembodied chortle coming out of the blackness. “Nobody ever sleeps out here. We get our turn, but it never happens. You lie there staring at the black, wondering if one of them is five meters from you with a knife. It’s a bit unnerving.”

“Like you have to tell me,” Russell said. “I’m out here hoping that something doesn’t crawl in my pants and bite my dick.”

“Oh, man, that would be bad. If one of those fuckers bites your bad boy, it’d probably fall off.”

“I’ve spent time in some shitty places and I’ve been scared, but this is the worst. Every second is total stress. I can’t even start to tell you how wound up I am,” Russell said.

“It’ll be over soon,” Andrew said. “Look at the sky to the east.”

Russell stood up so he could see over the Stryker. The sky was lightening, a crescent of pale yellow pushing into the black palette. Soon, the snakes and bugs would be crawling back into their holes. The Taliban were dug into the hills to the west and the troops’ directive was to hold the town, not chase the bad guys into their lair. That was the sort of thinking that got people killed.

“What now?” Russell asked.

“We’re heading back to the FOB. But we need to stop in Kandahar to pick up some medical supplies.”

“Is everyone heading back?” Russell asked.

“Nope,” Andrew said. He leaned against the Stryker and watched the sun crest the eastern horizon. Light skimmed the sky and visibility increased until an ambush was impossible. The tension melted out of his shoulders and his grip loosened on his gun. “Most of the guys are here for another night or two until the village council gets control of the town.”

“I’m glad we’re leaving.”

“Yeah, me too. About half the guys will be heading out, but most of them are rolling right back to base. Us and two Canadian LAVs are headed into Kandahar.”

“That’s not much of a presence. Are we okay with only three vehicles?” Russell asked.

“Sure. There are a few Taliban running around the city, but we control it.

Once we have the medical supplies loaded, we'll be on Route Fosters to the FOB. We should be in easily before dark.

"Good. I don't want to spend another night out here."

"No shit."

Andrew shuffled off to talk over the route into Kandahar with his driver and the two Canadian LAV commanders. Russell stretched and walked around the armored vehicle a couple times to get his blood flowing. Surrounding him, in a huge circle, was the entire strike force, the armored vehicles and tanks on the exterior and the soft-skinned trucks on the inside. The area was active – men moving about having breakfast and drinking coffee – everyone alert, knowing they were inside enemy territory.

Russell watched them, wondering if anyone would die today. Young men and women stuck in an insanity you had to see to believe. Back home, parents and loved ones praying for their safe return. He tried to describe it in his reports. He knew it didn't work. Understanding the intensity of Afghanistan, or Iraq, or Somalia, required feet on the ground. Sleeping overnight surrounded by armed insurgents and camel spiders. Busting into mud houses not knowing if a woman and her children were inside, or an automatic weapon aimed at the door. Driving on a road that could erupt any second with enough force to destroy a tank. Understanding the reality required being here with the troops.

For most people that would never happen. He wasn't sure if that was fortunate or unfortunate.

CHAPTER 62

Kandahar, Afghanistan

Tabraiz sat in the back of the taxi with dark sunglasses and a pakol hat. His pashmina scarf was pulled up on his neck and covered part of his face. The last thing he needed was for a member of the Afghan National Police to spot him. He was probably being overly cautious – Kandahar city was bustling and the police had a multitude of other problems to deal with. A man in town to buy a young girl wouldn't be at the top of their list.

Still, Kunar, his informant inside the police, had warned him that his section commander was on the lookout and had other officers watching as well. They knew Tabraiz was coming to Kandahar to pick up a young girl and take her to Pakistan, but they didn't know when. If he could keep a low profile for the next four or five hours, he would have Halima and be gone. Out of Kandahar. Out of Afghanistan. Never to return.

The taxi driver slowed as he entered the Shakpur Darwaza Chowk-e and stopped next to a teashop. He jumped from the car and entered the ornately decorated doorway, reappearing a minute later with two steaming cups of *chai siaa* and fresh naan. He delivered the tea and bread to his passenger, then piled back into the driver's seat and pulled away from the curb. They drove for about five minutes in silence.

“Another three blocks, then turn left,” Tabraiz said as they reached an intersection.

The man followed the order. They were on the last road on the southernmost edge of the city, with single-story mud buildings to the right and desert to their left. Tabraiz ordered the man to stop, and got out carrying his tea. He walked half a block in a westerly direction and waited until a car pulled around the corner and stopped. A swarthy man dressed in khakis and a baggy T-shirt stepped out of the back seat and walked toward Tabraiz.

“Are you ready for tonight?” Tabraiz asked when they were standing opposite each other.

“Yes. I have two other men. Both trustworthy, and good shots.”

“I don’t want any shooting unless it is absolutely necessary,” Tabraiz cautioned. He sipped the tea with a slight slurping noise. “You’re for backup only. In case something goes wrong.”

“We still get paid, even if everything is okay?” the man asked. He appeared worried about that.

“Yes, of course.” Tabraiz dug in his pocket and handed the man a wad of bills. “This is half of what we agreed on. The other half tonight.”

“Thank you, Tabraiz Khan,” the man said, taking the money a bit too quickly.

Tabraiz ignored the social faux pas and said, “Let’s walk.”

The two men left the road and walked south toward the crest of a small rise. They reached the top of the hill and both men took in the lay of the land. Behind them was Kandahar and stretching out in front of them was a vast expanse of sand and rock, punctuated on occasion by scrub brush. A hundred meters down the gently rolling slope was a narrow valley that sliced through the barren land. Between them and the valley, about eighty meters down the slope, was an outcropping of rocks.

“I will be standing there, midway between the rocks and the edge of the valley. The girl and her father will likely come from the street where my taxi is parked. They will walk by this spot where you and I are standing.”

The man nodded his understanding. Tabraiz was arranging the meet so that if the police showed up, he could disappear behind the rocks or into the valley, depending on which direction they approached from. The city was only a hundred meters to the north, but out of sight. That eliminated the possibility of the police sneaking up on them from behind the buildings, yet put the maze of narrow streets close enough for Tabraiz to meld into if necessary. The meeting spot was well chosen.

"You should position yourselves behind the rocks," Tabraiz said. "If the police do show up, it won't matter which direction they come from. If they come from the top of the hill, you can slide over the rocks for protection. If they attempt to flank us, which is more likely, then you're already out of sight."

The man surveyed the land. Tabraiz was correct – the police would be too exposed if they came straight down the hill from the city. They would flank the situation from the east. If he and his men were behind the rocks they would be well protected.

"Agreed," he said. "We'll position ourselves behind the rocks."

"Good. Make sure they know not to shoot unless they are being shot at."

"Not unless we are threatened," he agreed.

"More than threatened," Tabraiz snapped. "Shot at. You do not fire your weapons unless you are shot at."

"I understand. We will not fire."

"That's all for now. Be here tonight at eight o'clock. The father and his daughter will be here about fifteen minutes after that."

They walked back to the road that skirted the edge of the city and shook hands. The man returned to his car, started the motor, ground the gears and sped off, a plume of dust rising behind the car. He turned a corner and headed back into the city.

Tabraiz stood in the middle of the deserted road, the afternoon sun baking his face and arms. This was it. The place where Halima would leave her world and move on to a much darker, more dangerous one. This was the end of her life as she knew it. He could care less. To him, she was fifty-five thousand US dollars after expenses. Nothing more, nothing less.

Business was business.

CHAPTER 63

Moscow, Russia

Three in the afternoon on Monday, August 23rd, and Julie was no closer to gaining access to the intricate series of tunnels under the roads and parks near Luzhniki Stadium. She was beginning to panic.

Sunday, Julie had split her team into two groups. The team charged with finding other ways for Trey Miller to ruin the U2 concert had not come up with one other viable option. That confirmed her initial suspicion that Miller would interrupt the power to shut down the stadium as the most likely scenario. The clues that supported her theory were still intact. Plus, more were appearing as they moved forward. They had confirmed that Alexi Androv was involved, and aside from killing people, he was an electronics expert. The truck with the backup generator breaking down in Belarus was starting to look like more than just a coincidence.

She picked up the phone and dialed Sergei Berensko's line at MosEnergo. Berensko was the supervisor in charge of the city's electrical system in the quadrant that housed Luzhniki Stadium. She had called him earlier in the day to find out if the city had issued any e-mails about scheduled power outages in the last week. He answered the phone and she tried talking with him in rudimentary Russian.

"Miss Lindstrom," Berensko said in heavily accented English. "We can speak English. It is good practice for you."

"For you," Julie corrected him.

"Yes, as I said, for you."

Julie let it slide. "What did you find out Mr. Berensko?"

"I checked our records and there were no scheduled power shutdowns," he said.

"You're positive?"

"Yes."

"Okay, thank you."

"It's okay. Enjoy Moscow."

Julie set the phone in the cradle and went back over the growing list. Androv on the scene. The backup generator stuck in Belarus. Fake calls about power outages to the stadium. And there was one more. A very disturbing one. The disappearance of a city inspector who was working in the underground tunnels near the stadium. No one had seen him since Friday, August 20th. The man had no history of drinking and not showing up for work, and the police had opened a missing persons file. Julie and Evan had little doubt that the man's body was crammed into a recess somewhere in the labyrinth of tunnels.

The hotel door opened and Evan entered Julie's room. He nodded to Carson, who was staying close to Julie at her request. "We found Miller," he said.

"Where is he?"

"The Korston Hotel. Alexi Androv used his credit card for a single transaction in the bar. He must have slipped up and used it by mistake. I have three men on the way over. They should be there by now, or really close. We'll know in a few minutes what's going on."

"The guys you sent – are they armed?"

"Yes."

A shiver ran down her spine. This was getting out of control. "Is that what I think it is?" Julie asked, pointing to a roll of paper under Evan's arm.

"Sure is," he said. He spread it out on the table. "Pretty rudimentary, but they're plans of the tunnel systems near Luzhniki."

"Excellent," Julie said. She flipped the drawings around so they were properly oriented to her and Evan. "It's like we thought. The access to the electrical conduits is through the storm sewers."

"Right. Especially the junction boxes." He stabbed at the drawings in three different places. "These are some of the places where the incoming power splits off from the main line. The tunnels where the power conduits run are much narrower than the adjoining storm sewers. It will be much easier to navigate through the sewers and then link in with the electrical system when we're close to the junction boxes."

Julie nodded. "Agreed. And we're pretty sure they'll be targeting the junction boxes. They're the easiest places for them to splice in." She glanced up. "How are we doing with getting permission from the city for access to the tunnels?"

Evan shook his head. "Not good. They don't see any reason to let us in, and they're in no rush to let us talk to anyone else. I tried offering them money, but it didn't work."

"Well, whether it's okay or not, we're going in."

"I had a couple of guys look for a way."

"And..."

"There's a metal grill embedded in a concrete slab in the park, about two hundred meters north of the stadium. It's locked, but I can't see that stopping us."

"Excellent. We'll need lights and some gear."

"I already thought of that. We picked it up a couple of hours ago."

Evan held his hand up to curb her response, pulled out his vibrating phone and answered it. "Did you find him?" he asked. He listened for a few seconds, then grabbed a piece of paper and jotted down a name – *Petr Besovich.* He grunted a few times then killed the call.

"That was one of the men calling from the Korston. Miller was registered as Adam Stewart. The desk clerk recognized his picture. They ran the fake name just to be sure and found it's one Miller used when he was with the agency. They managed to get the name of another member of his team; Petr Besovich. His expertise is electrical circuits and detonating devices."

"Great," Julie said under her breath.

"Let's hope Miller brought him in to focus on electrical circuits and not detonating something," Evan said.

"You want to take the risk?" Julie asked.

"No."

"Neither do I." She ran her hands through her thick, wavy hair. "But I'm not going to push the panic button."

Evan agreed by nodding and said, "We won't mention the alternative yet, but we could look around a bit. Just in case. If we're careful and don't raise any red flags, the staff at the stadium wouldn't suspect we're looking for explosives."

"Okay, shift the secondary crew onto it. They're wasting time looking for other scenarios. We know what Miller and his team are up to – we just need to figure out how they're going to do it and stop them." She checked the time. "Three-thirty. I highly doubt the city is going to get back to us. Looks like we're breaking into the sewer."

Julie stood up and walked over to the window. In the distance, Luzhniki Stadium reared over a solid wall of green. What Trey Miller was planning was dangerous. A dark space, tens of thousands of people, and no show. Many of the concert-goers intoxicated or high. It was a bad mixture. It could be a full-scale disaster for Volstov.

She wasn't going to let it happen. But time was slipping away and she had a litany of problems. The city authorities were hampering her efforts and she was filled with frustration and anxiety.

"Carson, are you up to skulking around in a sewer?" she asked. She wanted him close by where she could watch him. The last thing she needed right now was to come back to the hotel and find a body. Besides, he was the one who had dug up the plot to derail the concert. She owed him.

He shrugged. "Sounds gross."

"It's not a waste sewer. No crap and toilet paper. It's a storm sewer. It takes rainwater from the gutters and channels it into the river."

"Sure."

"Great. I don't feel comfortable leaving you here alone. Androv may show up."

"That wouldn't be good," Carson said. He tucked into the corner of the couch a bit tighter.

"Get some rest if you can. It's going on four o'clock. We'll be heading underground by ten."

He nodded. "I'll try," he said. But in his mind he already knew that there was no chance of sleeping.

CHAPTER 64

Kandahar City

Kadir smoothed the wrinkles from his shalwar kameez with his good hand. His appearance was important. He wanted Tabraiz to think highly of his choice of families – that he had made a good decision in picking Halima to live in Peshawar. So many young girls in Kandahar, and Tabraiz had seen the most potential in Halima.

Kadir could barely hide his pride.

His happiness was tempered with apprehension. Would Halima enjoy living so far from her family? Would she work hard enough to satisfy her wealthy sponsors, and would she do well in school? He knew his daughter – how hard she worked and how well she negotiated with the traders in the marketplace. She always came home with more onions and tomatoes than she should. Maybe the traders liked her – maybe she was good at bartering. He didn't really care. His daughter was competent and intelligent. That was all that mattered.

When she returned as an educated woman, her world would be so different. He pictured her standing at the front of the schoolroom, writing the alphabet on the blackboard, the children watching her with respect and adoration as they learned their lessons. The pride returned, and his chest puffed out slightly as he envisioned her.

Halima climbed the staircase leading from the courtyard to the lone room the family called home. She stood quietly in the doorway.

"Are you ready?" he asked.

"Yes, father." She looked down at her clothes, at her new blouse with embroidery on the sleeves, intricately stitched, with red, blue and yellow thread. The design was abstract, but beautiful. To cover her legs, she wore loose white pants, comfortable for traveling. "Do I look alright?"

Kadir sized up his eldest daughter. Barely twelve years old and already a woman. A pretty one with a wonderful future and a thoughtful smile. He focused on her eyes, hazel more than brown, and saw the determination. "You are perfect," he said. "Absolutely perfect."

She blushed slightly, then said, "I'll check on Aaqila and Danah. They're playing in the courtyard."

Kadir reached out and picked up a ratty knockoff watch he had found almost three years ago. Despite a cracked glass front, it kept good time. It was five minutes to seven. "I have a taxi picking us up at seven o'clock. He will drive us to Ahmad's house and your sisters can wait there while we meet with Tabraiz Khan."

"I'll make sure they're ready," Halima said. She retreated back down the stairs.

Kadir rose from his cushion. His joints ached with arthritis and sharp barbs of pain shot through his knees and fingers. This was the tangible pain, but it was not the most intense. Sending Halima away – selling her – was infinitely more agonizing.

He glanced back at the threadbare room knowing it would soon be only a memory. He thought of their new lodgings, bought with the money from the Pakistani. Twenty blocks closer to the market and almost twice the size, with a separate bedroom for the younger girls. He wasn't sure whether he should be proud of his new home or if he should hate it.

It had come at such a high cost.

He put one foot forward, then the other. He reached the top of the stairwell and started down. The journey he had both hoped for and dreaded had begun.

* * *

Kandahar City

Tabraiz met with the swarthy man and his two accomplices at ten minutes to eight. They were armed with Kalashnikovs and had revolvers tucked into their belts. Tabraiz handed the man the other half of his fee and reminded them no shots were to be fired unless someone was shooting at them. They disappeared behind the rocks, close to where the exchange was to take place.

Twenty-five minutes.

He placed a call to Kunar on his cell phone. "Is the diversion working?" he asked.

"Exactly as planned," Kunar said. Crashing sounds emanated from the phone. "Farouk and his team are busting a drug dealer. I called in his location and the whole department ran out the door and raced up here. We're on the north side of the city. Even if they knew you were in the city and what was happening, they could never get to you in time."

"Well done," Tabraiz said. "Expect a bonus soon."

"Thank you, Tabraiz Khan."

Tabraiz hung up and pocketed the phone. The ANP were busy, the sun was moving close to the western horizon and his backup muscle was in place in case something went wrong. A block to the north was a car, waiting to take them across the border into Pakistan.

Everything was right. All he needed now was the girl and her father. And he knew they were coming. He slowly walked to the top of the rise, looked about, then headed down the hill to the meeting place.

* * *

Kandahar City

"They're finished. Let's get out of here," Andrew yelled. He entered the Stryker through the rear hatch and Russell and Bobby followed. They left the hatch open to allow the air to circulate.

"It took forever to get all those medical supplies loaded on the truck. Are we going to make the FOB before dark?" Russell asked.

"Shit." Bobby leaned back against the metal sidewall. "You shouldn't ask that, man. Like sayin' he's got a no-hitter goin' into the bottom of the ninth. You're jinxin' it."

"Jinxing what?" Russell asked.

"Getting' back inside the wire."

"Ahh, I don't want to do that," Russell said. He was absolutely serious.

Andrew chimed in. "We'll make it. We're at the southern edge of the city and we'll be on the highway in no time. They've just finished sweeping it for IEDs. We're good."

"Thank Christ," Russell said. "Last night was a fucking nightmare."

"You should try living on one of the Combat Outposts," Andrew said. "They can get overrun any time in those things."

"Crazy business, this war," Russell said.

The Stryker lurched forward and picked up speed as they cruised through the southernmost tip of Kandahar city. Russell pulled his video camera from its case and checked the battery. He'd had it plugged in while they were loading and it was almost full. He wouldn't have to charge it tonight. Straight to bed when they got inside the gate.

Above, the fading light streamed in through the hatch as the sun sank to the horizon.

CHAPTER 65

Kandahar City

Kadir directed the taxi driver to the nearest street to where Tabraiz was waiting. They turned the corner and cruised slowly down the road that divided the final row of houses from the rocky desert stretching endlessly to the south. Kadir ordered the man to stop, got out and paid the fare. He would take a bus back to pick up Aaqila and Danah from Ahmad's house. The cab drove slowly to the next intersection and turned right, headed back into the city.

Kadir took Halima's hand and squeezed gently. "I'm going to miss you," he said softly. The air was still and there were no other sounds to drown out his voice.

"I'll miss you too," Halima said. "And Aaqila and Danah. Make sure you tell them. Everyday."

He smiled. "I will, Halima. I'll tell them every morning and every evening before they go to bed."

She clutched a tiny bag that contained a single change of clothes. The bright red notebook and flowered pencil her father had given her stuck out the side pocket of the bag. She held her father's hand as they walked southwest, toward the mountains and away from the city. They crested the hill and began the trek down the gentle slope. Kadir scanned the rocks on his right, anxiously looking for the Pakistani. Nothing. They reached the spot where Kunar had instructed them to wait, midway between the rock formation and the edge of the valley, and stopped. The sun had almost disappeared behind the mountains and the oncoming darkness bothered him. A figure emerged from the edge of the valley and walked toward them. He was dressed in tailored pants and a white fitted shirt, with polished black shoes, now covered in fine dust. He smiled as he approached and his dark hair caught the last rays of sun and glimmered in the dying daylight.

Tabraiz.

Kadir felt Halima's grip tighten. He could only imagine what was going on in her mind. The uncertainty of the moment mixed with hope for her future. Kadir pushed back his shoulders and took long strides. This was a proud moment in his life.

They were ten meters from Tabraiz when they heard the low rumbling that resonated off the buildings and floated to them on the evening air. It increased in volume and the ground trembled slightly. Kadir turned to look behind him. He knew exactly what it was. They all did. There was no mistaking the growl of armored vehicles. They were quickly moving closer, and Kadir pulled Halima tight to him and covered her with the loose folds of his tunic. A second later, an eight-wheeled armored vehicle came into view on the hilltop.

He froze. Tabraiz stopped moving. The vehicle rolled to a halt and the dust settled. The air, the clouds, the world – everything was suspended in the moment.

* * *

Kandahar City

Andrew and Russell's Stryker was the lead vehicle in the convoy. The soldiers sitting inside the vehicle could hear the chatter between the commanders coming across the radio. The truck carrying the medical supplies was having trouble navigating one of the bends in the road and needed to back up and make another attempt. The commander of Andrew's Stryker came on the radio, telling the others he was continuing to the edge of the city. He estimated it to be two, maybe three blocks.

The Stryker rolled on, leaving the rest of the convoy with the supply truck. Thirty seconds passed, then they took a sharp turn to the right. Their speed began to increase, then the driver's voice came over the radio.

"Checking out some movement to the south."

The Stryker was bouncing more now as the driver steered off the road. They rolled for less than fifty meters, then the driver was back on his mic. "I've got something here, guys. You'd better take a look at this. The action is to the south, halfway down the hill."

Andrew, Bobby and RJ, the other specialist, checked their guns and exited through the rear hatch. Russell grabbed his video camera and followed. Outside, daylight was failing fast. They had precious little time to identify the risks before they were cloaked in blackness.

Andrew was in the lead and reported the situation over his radio. "I've got two men about eighty meters downhill. One in pants and a shirt. The other guy is in loose clothing. Looks like he's hiding something under his clothes."

"Shit, man," Bobby shot back. "Who knew we were comin' this way?"

"Nobody," Andrew said. "We have a problem." A slight pause, then, "Bobby, head straight down the hill. I'm going around on the east. RJ, take the right side and skirt those rocks."

"I've got them from the turret," the commander said from the Stryker.

"Hold on," Andrew said. If the Stryker gunner opened up with the .50 caliber there would be precious little left of the two men. "We don't need to shoot the crap out of this. Not yet, at least."

The three soldiers spread out and approached the two men standing midway down the hill. Russell followed behind them and shouldered his camera. He pushed the record button and began feeding images to his hard drive. Andrew was moving quickly now, circling the two men and coming in from below them. He and Russell stopped within twenty meters, and the man in the shirt and pants began backing up toward the rocks, his hands out to the side, in plain sight. They were empty – no gun.

"What have you got there?" Andrew yelled at the man in the tunic. "What's under your clothes?"

The man yelled back in rapid-fire Pashto. He waved his free hand around wildly and gestured at his midsection.

"What's he sayin'?" Bobby yelled, his M-4 leveled at the man. "What's he sayin'? I don't understand a word."

"It's Dari or Pashto. I don't have a clue," RJ yelled back.

"Shit," Andrew said, watching the man in the shirt and pants slowly recede into the dusky streetscape. "I can't see much. It's getting too dark."

The man in the tunic continued to yell. Frantic. Excited. Manic.

"This guy is freaking me out," RJ yelled. "I think he's got a bomb under there."

"More trouble," Bobby yelled. "I got guys with guns at nine o'clock. At least three. Behind the rocks."

"I see them," RJ yelled back. He jogged down the hill, away from the rocks where the men were dug in.

"Oh…fuck," Andrew yelled. The figures were moving away from them, rifles in hand, the barrels barely visible in the failing light. "We might have an ambush."

"Firing a warning shot," Bobby yelled. He aimed his M-4 low, at the rocks and to one side of the figures and pulled the trigger.

The first three-round burst fired properly. Bobby squeezed the trigger to send a second burst, but a flaw on the inside of the barrel caught the bullet and it jammed in the chamber. The gunpowder exploded with the round still inside the breech. With the bullet stuck and the gun unable to expel the spent cartridge, the trapped hot gases exerted immense pressure on the bolt carrier. It shattered and a chunk of shrapnel flew back, striking Bobby in the right eye and penetrating his brain. Bobby dropped, dead before he hit the ground.

"Shit, Bobby's hit," RJ screamed. He trained his M-4 on the figures behind the rocks. They scattered when they saw the soldier target them. "I got the guys with guns, you take the bomber." He opened fire as the men scampered up the short hill toward the city. The man in the shirt and pants dove over the rocks and disappeared.

Andrew sighted on the man in the tunic and fired. Two shots. Both hits. The man dropped to the ground and stopped screaming. He lay in a heap, moaning in pain. Silence settled over the scene. The men behind the rocks and the man in the pants and shirt had made the short run to the edge of the city and disappeared over the rise and into the labyrinth of houses and alleys. Andrew and RJ slowly approached the crumpled figure in the dirt. They looked for the explosive he had hidden under his clothing.

"I don't see any wires or shit," RJ said as they neared the man.

Above them, the remainder of the convoy lurched around the corner and soldiers piled out. Everything had come across their radios as it played out and they had a grasp of the situation. They ran forward, fanning out to secure the area. A medic headed directly to where Bobby lay motionless.

Andrew kept his gun trained on the figure lying in the dirt, his finger tight to the trigger. Half an ounce more pressure and a killing shot would leave the barrel. He was ten meters, then eight, then six. Darkness was closing fast, but as he drew closer the scene became visible. The man was on his side, in the fetal position. His head was resting on the ground and his arms were wrapped around something. One of the shots had hit him in the right arm, just below the shoulder. Five meters. Four. Andrew stopped, and silence descended on the darkening scene.

He could make out the form of another person curled next to the man. Smaller, with girl's shoes and a scarf wrapped around her head. Three meters. Two. One. Andrew stood silently, staring down. A bag was ripped open and clothes scattered on the ground. A red notebook and a pencil lay in the dust. The man was crying, cradling the girl's head in his arm. He was whispering something. A name. Andrew knelt down.

"Halima." His voice was a whisper, like a tiny gust of wind.

The girl wasn't moving. Andrew's eyes scanned her body. Blood was leaking from her chest and she had stopped breathing. Her eyes were closed and the color was draining from her face. He knew the signs. He'd seen them too many times to mistake what this meant.

"Halima," the man wailed. "Halima."

Andrew's head dropped onto his chest. His eyes teared up and he let the drops fall on the dusty road. "No," he said. "No, no, no." He closed his eyes and gripped his rifle until his hand went white. "Please, God, no."

He looked up. Russell was standing above him, the camera resting on his shoulder. The journalist slowly lowered the camera and touched a red button. The camera stopped recording.

CHAPTER 66

Boston, Massachusetts

The time difference between Kandahar and Boston was eight hours. That was enough time for Russell's film to reach the television station and be edited for the nightly news on August 23rd, the same day it was shot on the other side of the world.

There were hard decisions to be made about the video. It was graphic and clearly showed a US soldier killing a young Afghan girl. The light levels were adequate for viewing the images and understanding them in a general sense, but not substantial enough to make out all the details. The audio on the film was crude and needed to be censored for content, but its rawness gave it a powerful punch. The images of the M-4 backfiring and killing Bobby were deemed too bloody for network television. The decision came down from the top at ten minutes before the top of the hour. It was a go. The remainder of the video, minus Bobby's death, was put on the air at six o'clock.

The video went viral almost immediately. Once the network had aired it across the US, the edited footage was released to CNN and the other major networks. The moment it was in the public domain, it hit YouTube and a host of other video sites. By midnight on the east coast, the video had been viewed over twenty million times and the number was growing exponentially.

Chat rooms on the Internet were busy, people engaging in the incident. It was early in the discussions, but the trends were already establishing. Most viewers' sympathy extended not only to the father, but also to the soldier who had fired the killing shot. There was considerable talk about the unforgiving conditions the soldiers were facing. The more viewers waded in on the issue, the hotter it got. Halima's death was becoming a world-shaking event.

* * *

FOB Ma'sum ghar, Afghanistan

Russell lay on his cot in the FOB at Ma'sum ghar, staring at the ceiling. His computer was shut down for the night, but not before he had seen the reaction to his footage. Closing his eyes was useless. His mind continued to replay the images of what had happened. The quickness and brutal reality of the young girl's death. The senselessness. He turned his head slightly toward Andrew's bunk. The specialist was lying on his back, his eyes wide open.

"You okay?" Russell asked quietly.

Andrew slowly rolled his head to the side. "Not really." His voice cracked with emotion. "She was just a little girl."

Russell could see the tears in the low light that filtered in through the windows. "Andrew, no one is going to believe you meant to kill her."

"But I did."

Russell didn't respond. What could he say to that? It was a simple and irrefutable truth.

"I didn't sign up for this," Andrew said. There was a hollow resonance in the words. "I just wanted to make a difference."

"You tried," Russell said. "You're here for the right reasons."

"Yeah." A long pause, then, "This is going to hit the fan, isn't it."

"It already has."

Andrew rolled slightly and propped himself on his elbow. "The press will dig into my life, won't they?"

“Like vultures on a carcass.” Russell read Andrew’s expression and continued, “It doesn’t matter what they think. It’s the guys inside the wire who matter. None of them are going to judge you.”

Andrew remained propped up on his elbow for a minute, then slowly lay flat on his back. A tortured voice broke the silence. “I killed a little girl, Russell.” The words could barely make it out between the sobs. His body was wracked with convulsions. “I killed her.”

“You had no choice once Bobby went down.”

“Fucking defective gun. If it hadn’t jammed and backfired…”

“Yeah,” Russell said. “Bad luck, that.”

They lay alone in the darkness while the world watched their story unfold.

CHAPTER 67

Moscow, August 24th, 12:45 pm

"Have you seen this?" Carson asked.

Julie looked up from the diagram of the underground tunnel systems and focused on the television. It was tuned to the English-speaking CNN channel and a talking head was centered on the screen with a picture of a young girl inset on the upper right hand corner.

"Turn it up, please," she said. "I can't hear it."

Carson adjusted the volume until the woman's voice was audible through the hotel suite.

"Her name was Halima, and this video was shot by Russell Matthews, a freelance journalist embedded with troops in the Kandahar region of Afghanistan. This footage is graphic and it is real. It was shot yesterday, August 23rd, just before sunset on the southern edge of Kandahar City."

The screen changed. Gone were the uniform studio lighting and the carefully applied makeup. Instead, the cameraman was moving and the picture was grainy and shaking. The low light made it difficult to discern exactly what was happening. The voices coming through with the images were clear – at least three soldiers, all yelling at each other. The cameraman providing an ongoing commentary. An Afghan man in a tunic shouting frantically. A man in a white shirt next to him. Shadows moving in the background – silhouettes of men with guns hiding behind an outcrop of rock. Then a shot. One soldier down and another firing at the man in the tunic. More yelling. Then silence. The soldier moving in on the fallen man with the camera following. The first images of a young girl lying next to the man. The blood pouring from a wound in her chest. Her eyes closed. The man saying her name.

Halima.

The camera shifted to the soldier's face. He was bent over the man, then fell to his knees, whispering one word over and over.

No.

The screen returned to the studio and the anchor.

"The soldier has been identified as Specialist Andrew James, from Pismo Beach, California. This is his second tour in Afghanistan and he has seen action many times throughout southern Afghanistan. The girl was Halima Hussein, and information on why she and her father were on the hillside just outside the city is only starting to filter in. What we're hearing, and this has yet to be confirmed, is that Halima had been sold and was being delivered to the man in the white shirt when the troops stumbled on them. We will update this information as things become clearer. In the meantime, one thing remains certain. Halima, who had recently turned twelve, was shot and killed yesterday in a tragic turn of events in Kandahar, Afghanistan."

"It's on every station," Carson said, hitting the power button. "All the Russian networks are carrying it."

"Horrible," Julie said. "What was that about her father selling her?"

Carson shrugged. "No idea. It's the first I heard about it."

Julie shook her head and looked back at the drawings. "Today is the 24th. We have until tomorrow night at eight to dismantle Miller's handiwork." She glanced up at Carson. "Evan and one of my field crew are taking the tunnels west of Eframova Street. You and I will concentrate on the ones to the east."

"Got it."

Julie pushed her hair back from her face and straightened up. "Are you sure you're up to this?

He nodded emphatically. "Getting out of here and doing something is exactly what I need."

"It's illegal." She glanced at him. "Do you understand how dangerous this is? If we get caught, we'll be in prison. Dimitri Volstov can probably get us out, but there are no guarantees."

"I understand."

The door opened and Evan entered, accompanied by another man who would be heading into the tunnels with Evan. They gathered around the table. Evan set a cloth bag on the table.

"It's exactly what you asked for," he said.

Julie picked up the bag and slipped her hand inside. She pulled out a Glock 17C pistol. She set it on the table and shook the bag. Four clips, loaded with bullets, spilled onto the drawings. She picked up the gun, looked to see if it was loaded, then spent a minute checking the trigger pressure, the slide and the other working parts. Satisfied, she set it on the edge of the table.

"Good work," she said. "Did you manage to find one for yourself?"

"I sure did," Evan said. "Glocks are easy to find in Russia."

"How about me?" Carson asked. "I'm feeling a bit left out here."

"Nice try," Julie said. "Not a chance."

"We have the rest of the equipment. Bolt cutters, portable GPS units, backpacks, waterproof boots, walkie-talkies and halogen lights. And," he held up a small screen about the size of an iPad, "I bought this as well. It's a mobile tracking unit so that someone on the surface can see where our GPS units are at all times. That way, you won't get lost. Or if you do, we'll be able to find you."

"Well done." She checked her watch. "It's one o'clock. Thirty-one hours until the band steps on stage. Let's go."

They bundled up the plans, tucked the guns in their backpacks, shouldered the rest of the gear and headed down to the street where an SUV with a driver was waiting. They drove to a park near the sports complex, parked in a remote corner of the lot and suited up. The grate was set back into a large group of shrubs, which hid them from view as they cut off the padlocks. Once they were in, the driver closed the metal grill and slipped the severed locks back in place. Only a close examination would reveal they had been cut. The driver remained above ground with the vehicle and the GPS tracking unit.

They paired up, switched on their lights and Julie led the way underground. A steep set of stairs led down, the temperature dropping quickly and the light fading until it was completely dark. The two groups went in opposite directions at the first fork in the tunnel. Carson followed Julie, who was moving at a fast clip, GPS unit in hand. She seemed to know where she was going and didn't slow through the dark and confusing maze. Finally, she stopped and had Carson help her unroll the drawings.

"Okay, we're here," she said, marking a spot on the paper with a fine-tip red felt pen. "The tunnels that handle the electrical conduits converge with the storm sewer we're in right now in about a hundred meters. From here on, we should be looking for any recent activity. New or disturbed mortar, or bricks sticking out a bit so they can find them again. Things like that."

"Okay."

Carson adjusted the light so the beam splayed out a bit more, illuminating the sides of the tunnel better. Julie concentrated on the left side of the underground channel and he scanned the right. They continued at a much slower pace until they reached the convergence point. It turned out to be a solid wall of concrete between the two tunnels – there was no chance Miller and his team had used this point to tap into the electrical system.

"Damn," Julie said. She pulled the drawings out and checked for the next place where the two tunnel systems ran parallel. "This way," she said, starting out down a fork to the left.

Carson fell in behind her, wondering if she knew where they were and how to get out. Water dripped from the ceilings and in places their footing was treacherous. Entering the tunnels had only increased the danger in his life. Now, in addition to being tracked by a psychotic killer, he was at risk of running afoul of the Russian police or getting lost in the concrete and brick labyrinth.

At least he had a chance. He couldn't say the same of Nicki. Her chances of survival had dropped to zero, thanks to him. He had played his cards for an uncaring and greedy man. He only had himself to blame. Of everything, that was the most difficult to take.

CHAPTER 68

Moscow, August 24th, 1:30 pm

Thirty hours had passed since he had arrived in Moscow and Alexi had yet to locate Carson Grant. It was making him crazy.

He sipped an espresso, smoked a thin cigar and watched people walk past the trendy bistro as he played out the situation in his mind. Grant would stay off the radar, but Julie Lindstrom would show up somewhere. And when he found her, he would find the Wall Street banker. He wasn't worried about locating Grant, but he was worried about running out of time. They were less than thirty-six hours from crippling the U2 concert and he needed Grant dead before then.

He had spent an hour setting up travel arrangements to New York for ten o'clock tomorrow night. A back up plan in case he missed killing Grant in the allowable time frame. A quick flight to the Big Apple and Fleming would be sorry he had ever started this whole mess. Actually, Fleming would be dead and dead people didn't care about much.

Alexi's phone rang. He glanced at the caller ID. He answered and a man's voice rattled off some names and addresses while he jotted them down on a piece of scrap paper. He thanked the man, promised to send money and hung up. He had her. Julie Lindstrom had booked her hotel rooms at the Ararat Park Hyatt through Evan Lucas, an employee of Details Matter. But his source had dug up more than simply their location. He had delivered the mother lode.

Evan Lucas had also used his credit card to make some very unusual purchases. Two portable GPS units, halogen lamps and waterproof boots among other things. They were heading into the tunnels. Lindstrom was a smart woman and he had little doubt that she was keeping Carson Grant close to her. Which meant that they would be in the tunnels together. That put them underground, in the dark and away from witnesses.

Lindstrom had a modicum of training with the FBI and Grant had no idea what he was doing. They were no match for him. Lindstrom and Grant would die like sewer rats in the tunnels under Moscow. Alexi paid his tab and hailed a cab. He gave the driver the address of the Ararat Park Hyatt. Patience was the key now.

* * *

Moscow, August 24th, 2:45 pm

The television in the luxury hotel suite was tuned to BBC.

Four men sat and watched the latest news on Halima. There was mounting proof that the gun belonging to the deceased soldier was defective. And that no one had fired on the troops. The reporter was checking on where the gun had been shipped in from, but so far had been unable to determine its origin.

Kadir, Halima's father, was interviewed from his hospital bed. He held her picture, the one that was on every television worldwide, in his good hand. Through an interpreter he tearfully told the reporters that he had sold his daughter to a man from Pakistan for fifteen hundred US dollars with the promise that she would be attending school in Peshawar. He held up his crushed hand and told of how he was unable to work, and that supporting his three children was impossible. The reporter, a serious-looking woman in her thirties with an English accent, thanked him and walked out of the room. In the hallway, she faced the camera and spoke.

"*What Kadir Hussein did not know,*" she said, "*was that Tabraiz Masood was not taking Halima to a family in Peshawar to live in their house as a servant. There was no school waiting for her. No chance to work hard, graduate, and become a teacher. Tabraiz Masood was a slave trader and Halima was destined for the United Arab Emirates, where a wealthy businessman was waiting for her. That was the future awaiting this young girl. The same future that awaits many.*"

The reporter signed off.

The talking head from the London studio came on. "*This story is gaining momentum with every hour,*" he said. "*It has been nineteen hours since Halima's death, and people worldwide are listening, connecting, and getting involved. There is sadness. There is outrage. There is bewilderment. And…there is understanding for Andrew James, the American soldier who fired the shot.*"

The man's face faded and the screen went to the now-familiar video. The audio on the film was notched down a few decibels and the anchor's voice-over dominated. "*Sentiment is on the side of the troops, whether they are US, British, Canadian, Australian, or any of the other forty-three nationalities on the ground in Afghanistan. The conditions under which decisions are made are somewhere between difficult and deplorable.*"

The rest of the story unfolded and the video ended. The picture reverted to the London studio. "*We will follow this story as it unfolds. In other news…*"

The mood in the hotel room was somber. One of the men walked over and picked up a guitar. He strummed some chords. Another found some drumsticks and tapped out a beat on the table. A bass guitar was leaning against the wall and the third man brought it into the mix. The most recognizable of the four hummed in tune to the chords and added an occasional string of words. They stopped and started, changed the key, added richness to the chords, then cut it back to give the sound a raw edge. For the next two hours they hammered away at the song and the lyrics. By suppertime, U2 had written the song they would use to open the concert in Moscow.

One Child.

CHAPTER 69

Moscow, August 24th, 10:15 pm

They had uncovered nothing of value in the tunnels.

Julie and Carson spent a full seven hours underground before reuniting with Evan and returning to the hotel. Combining the portable GPS system and the schematics gave them a reasonably accurate picture of the tunnel network and they had found two of the junction boxes where they felt Miller and his crew could have tapped in. Both had proven to be dead ends.

Carson showered, made some tea, then hovered near the edge of the dining room table where Julie and her crew were reviewing their strategy. The consensus was that they were on the right track and just needed a break. They were sure that the circuit breakers were already in place, set to cut the power. If they could find one of them, and the attached remote, they could dismantle it and determine the frequency Miller was using to activate them. With that, they could jam the signal and stop the devices from cutting the power.

That was Plan A. But as everyone around the table knew, Plan B existed for a reason. The problem was, they didn't have one.

Carson refilled his cup with hot water and swirled the teabag about. The television was in the adjoining room and he plopped onto the sofa and flipped through the channels. Most were in Russian and he stopped on the BBC feed.

The top story of the day was still the death of the young girl in Afghanistan. He turned up the volume a few notches.

"*...it is now confirmed that authorities have arrested Tabraiz Masood, the slave trader who bought Halima, as he was attempting to flee Afghanistan. He is being held in prison in Kandahar city and has been cooperating with the Afghan National Police. He has admitted to paying Kadir Hussein fifteen hundred American dollars for his daughter and confirmed that she was en route to the United Arab Emirates.*" The screen shifted from the news anchor to the video. "*Bobby Sullivan, the US soldier killed in the incident, died when his gun backfired and struck him in the face. Mr. Sullivan had taken possession of the standard-issue M-4 ten days earlier, on August 13th, and speculation is that the weapon was defective. With more on the story, this is Lisa Ambridge in London.*"

A woman appeared on the screen, framed by the British parliament buildings in the background. Hundreds of people were in the street, many holding placards.

"*Thank you, Liam. As you can see behind me, the country is reacting to Halima's death in many different ways. There are calls for the international community to crack down on slave traders targeting destitute families in hopeless situations. There is a greater understanding of the plight of Afghan girls, many who find themselves without a voice in their own country. Schooling is out of reach for the vast majority, and the lack of education is condemning them to lives of subservience and monotony. Grass roots organizations are springing up, raising money to fund schools and for desperately-needed medical clinics.*"

Carson muted the volume and picked up the telephone as the images moved from London to Rome and Washington DC. The iconic picture of Halima was omnipresent. He asked the operator to connect him with the BBC in London, England. It took a few minutes, but she found the number and put his call through. Carson asked the receptionist for the newsroom and waited. A woman answered, identified herself and asked the reason for his call.

"I may have information about the gun that backfired and killed the soldier in Afghanistan," he said.

"Yes, go ahead," the woman said. Her voice was interested, perhaps a bit excited.

"I believe a well known New York businessman was involved in shipping defective arms to Kandahar Airfield. They would have arrived on August 4th. Some of the weapons were M-4s."

"Can you identify this man?" she asked.

"William Fleming."

"That is a very serious allegation, Mr…"

"Grant. Carson Grant." He gave her his home address, phone numbers and date of birth. "You can quote me on this."

"Do you have any proof?"

"Yes. I have e-mails sent from an arms dealer named Jorge Amistav to Fleming that discuss the details. One deals with bank information for transferring funds. Another is about crating the weapons in Germany and shipping them to Afghanistan. The final e-mail has the weapons arriving at the airfield and an instruction for Fleming to submit the invoice."

There was no mistaking the anxiousness in her voice now. "Is there anyone who can corroborate this, Mr. Grant?"

"Yes."

"Who?" Even the single word was tinged with relief.

"Alicia Crane. She and I both worked for Fleming at Platinus." He gave her Alicia's contact information. "I haven't had a chance to speak with her about this, but you can call and tell her to phone me at the Ararat Park Hyatt in Moscow if she needs to. She has a copy of the e-mails on her computer."

"Can we contact you again, Mr. Grant?" she asked.

"Anytime," he said. "You have the number for the hotel in Moscow and my cell number. If there is anything else you need, please call."

"Thank you."

Carson set the phone down and sipped his tea. Fleming was a sick bastard who deserved to be brought down a few notches. Fitting that he was the one to initiate the process.

"Go ahead and try to kill me, you prick," he whispered to himself.

* * *

Moscow, August 24th, 11:15 pm

Alexi sat smoking a cigarette in the lobby of the Ararat Park Hyatt. He liked the hotel, from the massive stone pillars at the front entrance and dark-stained wood that dominated the reception desk, to the large, elegant rooms. He had attended many functions and stayed overnight numerous times. It was the perfect place to eat, lodge or wait for a victim.

Ninety minutes earlier Lindstrom and Grant, with two unknown men in tow, had marched through the lobby and taken the elevators to the twelfth floor. He followed on the next available lift and saw which room they entered. He could wait until they were asleep, enter their rooms and kill all of them. Messy, and sure to have the international media and police all over it. Or, he could wait until they revisited the unforgiving underworld, follow them in and take care of things in the dark. It was a no-brainer.

He was quite sure they wouldn't be coming out again tonight. Their backpacks were heavy with gear and the looks on their faces told the story of how things had gone. They had failed to find the circuit breakers. *Good luck*, he thought. His design was ingenious. The small contactors, tucked behind the main junction boxes, were impossible to find. But one thing was certain – they would try again in the morning.

This time, he would be close behind.

CHAPTER 70

Moscow, August 25th, 8:10 am – 12 hours until the concert

Preparations for U2's arrival at Luzhniki were proceeding as usual. Julie's onsite team was setting up security barriers, running over detailed procedures with the local security staff they had hired, and checking the band's route in and out of the stadium. Dressing rooms were stocked according to the rider, and the sound and light technicians were running their final checks. It was business as usual on the surface.

Julie and Evan were up at six reviewing the sections of the underground they had covered the previous day. Despite having two teams, almost eighty percent of the tunnel system had yet to be checked. The task was daunting and time was quickly running out.

"Is the jamming apparatus ready?" Julie asked as they prepared to leave the hotel.

Evan nodded. "They both are." He pointed at two cases that traveled everywhere with the band's security. One was considerably larger than the other. "The crew is going to take the Patrol-PX to the stadium and we'll keep the Patrol-BJX with us."

Julie nodded. "It would be best if they could jam the signal from the stadium. Their antenna and range will be far better than the remote unit we'll have with us at the tunnels."

"Way better. The PX uses a high-gain antenna and the BJX has a simple external one. That said, the small unit we'll have with us has 300 watts of power and can jam both VHF and UHF frequencies."

"If we can nail down the frequency and call it in to the guys working the machine at the stadium, that's best. The second option is to use the mobile unit and jam it from wherever we are."

"Right, but we have to be above ground. No sense taking it with us into the tunnels. The jamming signal from the machine can't penetrate ten or twenty feet of concrete and dirt."

Julie leaned back in her chair and ran a hand across her forehead. Her eyes were bloodshot and worry lines creased her face. "Are we on the right track?" she asked. "What if we're out in left field somewhere?"

"You think we are?" Evan asked.

She reconsidered the possibilities and shook her head. "No, I don't."

"Then let's go find whatever they hid in the tunnels. I'll send the large unit to the stadium and have a man standing by once we get the frequency."

"Okay, let's do it."

Carson was in the adjoining room, having a quick breakfast. The television was on and there was more on the Afghan situation. The American government had waded into the frenzy surrounding Halima's death with a promise of two hundred million dollars that would be targeted at building schools. The deal assured the funds would be managed by existing NGOs with strong ties to the local communities. The government viewed it as a new approach – grass roots rather than top down – one that would have tangible results.

Carson was reaching for the buttons to turn the TV off when a picture of William Fleming appeared on the right side of the screen. His name was emblazoned under his photo in block letters, and under his name was a caption. *Billionaire brokered defective arms.* He turned up the volume.

"*William Fleming, one of the richest men in the world, has been identified as an integral link in the chain of events that saw defective weapons shipped to Kandahar. One of the weapons from that shipment backfired two days ago, killing*

Bobby Sullivan, and the ensuing firefight resulted in the death of twelve-year-old Halima Hussein. BBC news has determined that the weapons, which included Javelin missiles in addition to M-4 rifles, were classified as defective by the US military and sent to Germany for disposal or remediation. Instead, the weapons were resold to the US government by Jorge Amistav, an Armenian arms dealer, and the deal was financed by William Fleming. Thirty-five million dollars was deposited into one of Mr. Fleming's Caribbean bank accounts. Mr. Fleming has refused our repeated requests for an interview."

Carson thumbed the power button and the screen went dark. It served the son of a bitch right. He pushed himself off the couch and joined Julie, Evan and the fourth man in the foyer. They took the elevator together to the main floor where the SUV was waiting at the curb. Eleven and a half hours remained until the concert.

It was panic time.

* * *

Moscow, August 25th, 8:30 am – 11.5 hours until the concert

Alexi watched the black SUV leave the hotel and told the driver to tail them. He noted every detail on the vehicle – chrome trim on the side panels, low-profile tires, the license plate number. The taxi pulled into the busy morning traffic and settled in a couple of cars back and one lane to the left. Five minutes into the drive, the cab driver sped up and ran a red light to keep the SUV in sight. Alexi pulled a wad of bills from his pocket and dropped them on the seat next to the driver.

The Sig Sauer P226 was uncomfortable tucked up against his rib cage. The gun was loaded, and he had a silencer in his blazer pocket. Using the metal cylinder to suppress sound was a good idea in close quarters, but it was heavy and affected the degree of accuracy at distances over fifteen meters. He didn't expect to be working with a shot over three to five meters, and he was deadly accurate inside that range. The silencer shouldn't factor in. In fact, he may not need the gun. He had a small, razor-sharp knife in his other pocket.

The sound of a siren filtered through the traffic and the car immediately ahead of the taxi slowed, leaving a growing gap between it and the delivery van it was following. Alexi leaned forward a bit so he could see what was happening. Concern tugged at his stomach as the distance increased and the wail from the siren intensified. Another siren joined what was now a cacophony of noise echoing off the four-story buildings on either side of the road. Alexi yelled at the driver to get around the car and make it through the upcoming intersection. The man frantically looked to both sides, trying to find a space to shift lanes but there was nothing but solid lines of traffic. They were trapped. Brake lights flashed and the car ahead lurched to a stop. A police car and an ambulance raced through the intersection. Another siren blended in and none of the cars moved. A second police car pushed its way through the intersection and disappeared down the cross street.

Alexi slumped back into the seat and waited. The light had changed from green to red and a full minute passed before the cab could move again. The SUV was nowhere in sight. He ordered the cabbie to drive to Luzhniki Stadium and he sat quietly in the back seat for the twenty minutes it took to make the trip. When they arrived, he asked the driver to wait. He got out and walked about the empty parking lot, wondering how he could find one vehicle in a city the size of Moscow. He knew Lindstrom and her crew were heading for an entrance to the tunnel system. Which meant they would be close to the stadium. Maybe there was a chance the SUV would be parked nearby.

He returned to the taxi and told the driver to travel in a north-south grid starting close to the stadium and working outward. He informed the man that they were looking for the SUV they had lost in the traffic. Alexi checked his watch. It was 9:15. Less than eleven hours until U2 took to the stage, and Lindstrom's chances of derailing their work were growing dimmer with each passing hour. The odds were heavily stacked against her. Still, he wanted to find Grant and Lindstrom. Partly for the quarter million dollars Fleming was paying, but mostly for the rush that would come from killing them.

CHAPTER 71

Moscow, August 25th, 5:00 pm - 3 hours until the concert

Carson was covered with algae and caked-on cement dust from almost eight hours underground. His back ached from standing on bricks and his shoes and clothes were soaked from the constant drips of water that percolated through the stone ceilings. The chill in the dank air had sunk into his bones, his lungs were congested and he was starting to cough. Julie wasn't faring much better. Her matted hair was plastered to the sides of her head and she was wheezing from breathing in the mold and mildew. And they were no closer to finding the handiwork of Miller and his team.

"This is going nowhere," Julie said. She found an outcropping of rock and sat down. She used the walkie-talkie to call Evan, telling him that they had nothing to report except a lot of tunnels and rats. His response was that they had found much of the same. She clicked off the walkie-talkie and used her cell phone to call their driver. The reception was poor, but she got the latest news on the concert. Everything was in place. People were arriving and the stadium was beginning to fill. She flipped the phone shut and slipped it into her pocket.

"I'm freezing," she said.

Carson leaned against the wall, alternating his weight from one foot to the other to rest his legs and knees. "Yeah, it's awful down here. And I thought New

York had rats. I've never seen ones this big."

"I hate rats," Julie said.

"You're sure about this?" Carson asked. "About Miller using the tunnels to cut the power?"

She nodded. "This is how he'll do it. We're missing it somehow."

"We keep searching for junction boxes that are ridiculously hard to find, but when we open them, everything is intact."

"So?" she said.

Carson's mind was racing now. "So…Fleming wants to discredit Volstov. If they were to tamper with the boxes in a way that could be discovered, then the blame would fall away from Volstov and onto some unknown saboteur. Mission not accomplished. But if they were to hide whatever they're using to divert the power, no-one would notice."

"We looked closely at the boxes," she countered.

"*In* the boxes, not behind them."

"They're set into brick and cement."

"Are they?" he asked. "We've spent hours looking for them and we know where they are. It wouldn't hurt to look again."

Julie considered the idea and said, "Let's check the closest one. It shouldn't take us more than fifteen or twenty minutes to get back there."

"Do you want to call Evan?" Carson asked.

She shook her head as she stood up. "No, we can call him if we find something."

They checked their bearings on the portable GPS and headed out.

* * *

Moscow, August 25th, 5:20 pm – 2 hours 40 minutes until the concert

"Stop," Alexi said sharply.

The taxi driver hit the brakes and the cab screeched to a halt next to the curb. Tucked between two large shrubs in the far edge of the parking lot was the black SUV with chrome trim on the side panels.

"Wait for me," he said.

He slipped out of the back seat and skirted the edge of the parking lot, cutting through the stand of trees north of where the SUV was parked. The back of the vehicle was flush to a small grove of shrubs and he had to get quite close before he could see the license plate. He read the series of numbers and letters and smiled. Finally. Five hours of driving the area had paid off. He returned to the cab and paid the driver, adding a substantial tip to the amount.

"You never saw me. You never drove me here. Do you understand?"

The driver nodded emphatically as he pocketed the windfall. "I understand absolutely."

Alexi waited until the cab had left the parking lot and was back in traffic before retracing his steps to the parked SUV. He approached it and waved to the driver, who was sitting in the front seat. He walked up to the window.

"I'm lost," he said, looking around the lot. "I'm looking for Luzhniki Stadium, but I think I got off at the wrong metro stop."

"That's Luzhniki over there," the man said, pointing but not moving from his seat.

Alexi looked in the direction the driver pointed. "How the hell can I get there from here?"

A pained look washed over the man's face and he opened the door. He walked a couple of meters in front of the vehicle and pointed again. "You need to take this road, because there is a..."

The knife severed the man's throat, cutting through the larynx, the jugular and the carotid arteries. Blood spurted from the open arteries, spraying in thick bursts with each beat of the heart, then faded to a light mist as his blood pressure dropped to near zero. He slumped to the asphalt, clutching his neck.

Alexi waited until the man bled out, then grabbed him under his armpits and dragged his body back into the bushes. He hopped into the front seat of the truck and glanced around. There was a cell phone on the console between the seats, and a thin computer screen that resembled an iPad next to it. A series of light blue lines crisscrossed the screen and two blinking lights were embedded in the grid.

"GPS tracker," he whispered under his breath. "How fortunate."

He searched the truck for extra gear and found two halogen lights and a stack of waterproof jackets and boots. He slipped a set of protective clothing overtop his suit jacket. A quick flip of the switch ensured the halogen light was working and had a full charge. He pocketed the cell phone and carried the GPS screen with him as he started searching the area for access into the tunnels. It took less then five minutes to find the grill. The padlocks had been cut and put back in placed with a smidgen of grease on them. He put the cell phone on vibrate and started down the stairs. As he moved through the tunnel, the blips on his screen adjusted slightly. He was moving toward one, away from the other. Choosing the closest one, he set a course through the underground maze. His hand instinctively touched the gun.

Soon. Very soon.

CHAPTER 72

Moscow, August 25th, 6:00 pm – two hours until the concert

Trey adjusted the transmitter and pushed the test button. The light flashed green. He checked the remote sensors. All six remotes attached to the contactors Petr had placed on the junction boxes responded that they were still functional. He set the time for two hours and five minutes and armed the device.

"Enjoy the first song," he said to no one. "That's all you're getting tonight."

He set the transmitter in the garbage dumpster and placed a crumpled newspaper over top. Then he shut the lid and padlocked it in place. There was no chance a homeless person could happen along looking for food and find the machine. The company that emptied the bins had a weekly routine, and this one was scheduled to be picked up forty-eight hours from now, on Friday. Trey returned to the street from the alley and settled into the back seat next to Maelle. He asked the driver to drop them at the International Terminal at Sheremetyevo II Airport.

"Well done," he said as they navigated the congested traffic on Leningradskij Prospekt. "And you managed to get out of this without sleeping with Petr."

"The man is a pig," she said.

"But he's a brilliant pig." He smiled at her. "Everything is a go."

The driver changed the channel on the televisions in the seatbacks to suit his

English-speaking fare. The anchor was talking about flooding in South America that had caused mudslides and wiped out numerous villages.

"Are you heading back to New York from Paris?" she asked.

Trey shrugged. "Maybe. I'm not sure. I like Paris. I might stay for a few days."

"Need a place to crash?" she asked. A seductive smile spread across her face. Trey returned the grin. He was about to say something, when Maelle pointed to the television. "Check this out."

A picture of William Fleming was on the screen and the anchor went live to a reporter in New York. He was standing on the Avenue of the Americas outside the high-rise that housed Platinus Investments. Trey asked the driver to turn up the volume.

"*. . . the allegations by Carson Grant, head of High Frequency Trading at Platinus Investments, and another employee working in the same division, were a one-two punch for Fleming, and this latest development confirms Grant's allegations. Jorge Amistav, an Armenian arms dealer, has told police in New York that Fleming was involved in a shipment of defective arms to Kandahar Airfield, and that Fleming netted thirty-five million dollars from the sale. Fleming has numerous criminal charges pending. Further to this, the M-4 rifle that backfired and killed US Army Specialist Robert Sullivan is thought to have been among the defective weapons, and there is talk of possible manslaughter charges. Fleming's flagship, Platinus Investments, is in a financial freefall. It opened the day at just over thirty-two dollars and when trading was suspended two hours later, it had dropped to under six dollars. This is Rory Black, reporting from New York.*"

"Hope you got paid upfront," Maelle said.

Trey shook his head. "Unbelievable." He was thoughtful, looking out the window as the car sped toward the international airport. "I almost wish I could put a stop to it."

"You can't?" she asked.

"Unfortunately, no. The transmitter is locked in a garbage bin and I threw away the key. There's no way we have enough time to get back there, disarm it, and make our flight."

"We could take a later flight," she said.

"This thing could completely blow up in our faces if the Russian police tie us in with Fleming. We need to get out of this country now."

"Any chance Lindstrom will figure it out?"

Trey didn't answer. He thought about the nearly hundred thousand people who were now crowding into Luzhniki Stadium unaware of the potential danger. "I hope so," he said.

CHAPTER 73

Moscow, August 25th, 7:15 pm – 45 minutes until the concert

Carson opened the junction box and stared inside at the maze of wires. He set the cover on the ground and pushed at the stone surrounding the box.

"It has some give to it," he said.

Julie slid in beside him and watched as he applied more pressure on the rock wall. It was moving. Ever so slightly, but compressing inward with each push. He gave it everything he had, getting his arms and shoulders and back into the thrust. The rock split and caved inward. He grabbed the pieces that were still attached to the wall, broke them off and threw them behind him on the ground. He shone his halogen beam in the hole and they peered in.

"Oh my god," Julie said. "That's it." She snugged up between him and the wall and traced two thick wires running from the back of the box into the hole. "These are the wires to divert the current, and the rest of the gear is to cut the power." She poked around for a minute, then said, "There's no remote, but there *is* a wire connected to this mess."

Julie traced the wire to where it entered a small, rusty conduit. She glanced in the direction it headed and followed the metal tube with her flashlight beam. The conduit faded off into the darkness that permeated every inch of the tunnel. She kept the beam angled upwards and carefully picked her way along the slippery stones as she tracked the thin-diameter pipe for fifty or sixty meters. It truncated in a small grey box tucked up near the ceiling. The latch was secured with a small padlock and she used a screwdriver to snap it open. Inside was a small rectangular piece of plastic with a tiny flashing light on one end.

She turned to Carson and gestured to the flashing green light. "This is the remote. The signal will come in through here."

"And it's activated," Carson said, staring at the flashing light.

"It's activated all right." She stepped away from the wall and slipped off her backpack. "I need to get in there, and I'll need lots of light. Can you stay to one side and shine your halogen in there for me?"

"Of course." He watched her unload some strange looking gear.

"What is all that?" he asked.

"I'm going to use what's called a patch antenna and micro strip method to determine the frequency. When I insert some EBG structures between the radiator and the detector and measure the transmission between them, it will identify the electromagnetic band-gap."

"I have no idea what you just said."

"Hold the light."

"That…I understand."

It took twenty minutes to nail the frequency, and when she was positive she had the right one, she reran the test. They were rewarded with a second positive response and she jotted the frequency down on a scrap of paper and stuffed it in her pocket. "They're using 117 MHz to transmit on. I'd never have guessed that. Never." She pulled her cell phone from her pocket and called their driver. It rang, then went to voice mail.

"Why not?" he asked.

"From 108 to 137 MHz is reserved for air traffic control. Nobody ever messes around with those frequencies. If you get caught, you're in a shitload of trouble."

"Like they care," Carson said.

Julie was scrolling through her address book, looking for the number of the tech waiting at the stadium with the other jamming machine. She found it and her finger moved to the send button. It never connected.

The bullet hit her in the left shoulder and she spun sideways and slammed into the wall. The force of the impact ripped the cell phone from her hand and it bounced on the stone and landed in the water. She slid down the wall, grabbing at the wound. Alexi appeared out of the darkness, a silenced pistol in his hand.

"You think you're pretty fucking smart, don't you?" he said as he neared her. He angled the Sig Sauer at Carson. "And you," he fired a shot that caught Carson in the arm. "Ever been shot before?" he asked.

Carson's nervous system went into overdrive. The pain from the bullet tearing through his skin, muscle, and nerves was excruciating. He clutched at his arm while blood seeped up through his fingers. It felt warm to the touch, soothing in the coldness of the tunnels. He looked up at the hired killer. The man was staring directly at him with disdain.

"You embarrassed me," he hissed, his finger tightening on the trigger. He caught a movement out of the corner of his eye and swiveled the gun toward Julie. She froze. "Give me your gun. Carefully or I'll kill you now, in front of this Wall Street Boy Scout."

She reached inside her jacket and pulled the Glock out with two fingers. She made a motion to drop it in front of her, but Androv shook his head.

"Throw it to me."

She heaved it in his direction as best she could from her stance lying in the water and sludge on the tunnel floor. The gun clattered on the ground, a meter in front of Androv. He moved forward slowly, the pistol trained on her, and picked it up.

"I love these guns," he said. "Thank you." He turned back to Carson. "That was nothing. It went right through. When a bullet sticks in your muscle, or shatters a bone – now *that* is painful."

He was close to Carson, his eyes raging with excitement and desire. "I don't want this to end," he whispered. "It's just too much fun." The sound carried well in the closed environment. He laughed and sighted the pistol on Carson's leg.

The retort from the gun was loud, reverberating through the tunnel like a sonic boom. Carson lay prone against the wall, not understanding the noise. Androv's gun had a silencer. Then he realized there was no pain – that he hadn't been shot again. Androv staggered slightly and blood dribbled out the corner of his mouth. He tried to bring the gun around and sight on Julie.

Another gunshot. The bullet hit Androv in the center of his chest and he teetered back and forth for a moment, then fell face first into the thin layer of water covering the tunnel floor. Carson flopped his head to the side and looked at Julie. She was holding a pistol, almost identical to the one she had thrown to Androv.

"It was nice of Evan to find me a gun, but I already had one," she said. She struggled to her feet, her injured arm hanging limp as she pushed by him. "We need to move. The concert starts in less than ten minutes."

Carson fell in behind her, amazed at the speed at which she was moving. The loss of blood had left him feeling strangely cold. He concentrated on putting one foot in front of the other and somehow managed to keep up with her.

CHAPTER 74

Moscow, August 25th, 7:58 pm – 2 minutes until the concert

They walked together through the concrete hallways leading to the stage. Four men whose music defied convention and defined the direction of rock.

The house lights dimmed and tens of thousands roared approval. Moments separated them from the instant when U2 belonged to them, and them alone. The band was in their town, playing for them. Fans took ownership of U2's early struggles and their relentless rise from talented, obscure musicians to greatness. Many felt a connection to Africa, and to the barefoot children who stood beside Bono as his equal. Every heart beat with anticipation.

U2 was here. In *their* stadium.

They walked onstage, veterans ready to play like it was the first time. The giant screens above and around the circular stage slowly came alive. Murky and indistinguishable at first, an image began to take shape as the screens brightened. It was a person. A face. A girl. The corners of her lips curled down – in thoughtfulness, not sadness. Her scarf covered her hair – in respect, not subservience. Her eyes looked out from her world to another – in wonder, not want.

It was an iconic image that had spread across the globe over the past forty-eight hours.

Halima.

The first riffs from The Edge's guitar cut through the air and Moscow went crazy. The chords were haunting – fitting for a girl who had lived with nothing, in a country with less. Bono stepped up to the mic and his lyrics told a story of hunger – for a better life. Of need – for those around her. Of desire – to change her world. Of hope – for her country.

The song drifted on the still Moscow air. It diffused through hundreds of high-resolution microphones and ran along the fiber optic cables that captured every note and every word, then shot it up to satellites streaking through the airless space above earth. From the sterile abyss of space, the music rushed back down to millions upon millions of people, all waiting for the new song by U2.

All waiting for *One Child.*

The band delivered, and the band played on.

CHAPTER 75

Moscow, August 25th, 8:03 pm – 3 minutes into the concert

Julie and Carson struggled with the grate and managed to push it to the side. They crawled out of the tunnels and staggered across the grass to the SUV. In the distance, Luzhniki Stadium was brightly lit and the sound of U2 playing floated across the parking lot. The signal to divert the power had yet to be sent. But it was coming.

"Oh, damn." Carson pulled back as he saw the driver's body under the bushes.

Julie pushed past him, opened the rear doors and climbed into the cargo area. She was dangerously dehydrated and her left shoulder was screaming for her to stop. She ignored the throbbing pain and pulled out the portable jammer. She had run this drill a hundred times.

Power on, antenna up, input the frequency. 117 MHz. She double-checked the frequency and hit the button.

Nothing happened. Nothing changed.

The stage lights from the stadium continued to dance across the sky and the opening staccato-like chords from U2's *Where the Streets Have No Name* ripped into the night air. Julie slumped back against the side of the SUV and stared at the jamming unit. She couldn't remember how many times she had lugged the machine in and out of a concert without using it. It was a key component of their anti-terrorism gear, purpose-built for incidents that might involve a bomb. Never once had she regretted having it on site, and this was why it was one of the first pieces moved into place and the last to be removed.

Carson was framed in the open rear doors of the truck. Moonlight reflected off his face, showing pain and relief. He pulled himself into the vehicle and sat opposite Julie. They both stared at the machine – listened to the songs from Luzhniki. Neither spoke for a few minutes.

"That's quite the machine," he finally said.

She nodded. "It is." Her head drifted slightly to one side. "I think I need a doctor."

Then she fainted.

* * *

Moscow, August 25th, 11:45 pm – one hour after the concert

It was almost midnight when Dimitri Volstov came looking for him.

Carson was in Volstov's study, sitting on an overstuffed leather chair and surrounded by walls filled with leather-bound books. He took a handful of them off the shelf and leafed through them. There were first editions of Tolstoy – in Russian. And first editions of Mark Twain and Edgar Allen Poe – in English. He replaced them and retook his seat, looking around and taking in the details. Volstov's desk wasn't large and Carson wondered what sort of business deals had been struck in the room. Outside the closed doors were the sounds of a party in full swing. He turned as the study door opened.

"I'm Dimitri," the man said, offering his hand, then sitting in a chair next to Carson. He was thickset with bushy eyebrows atop lively eyes. His hair was deep brown and thick for a man in his early fifties. "And you are Carson Grant." His English was almost perfect.

"I am," Carson said.

"How is the arm? Did the doctor take care of things properly?"

"Yes. Thank you." Carson hesitated, then asked, "How is Julie?"

Volstov's face remained serious. "She's in the hospital, stable, but they're keeping her overnight. I'll visit her once my guests leave. This is very serious – what you and she were involved in tonight." His face grew dark. "Fleming."

"Yes. He came very close to pulling it off."

"So I hear. Julie gave me all the details over the phone." He pulled a package of cigarettes from his jacket pocket and offered. Carson shook his head. Volstov lit one and blew out a heavy cloud of smoke. "I understand you were the one who caught on to Fleming."

Carson kept his answer simple. "Yes."

"Androv was sent to kill you."

"He was."

A couple of party guests opened the door and started into the room, but Volstov barked something in Russian and they turned and left. He waited until the door was closed. "You risked a lot, my friend."

Carson didn't answer, simply nodded slightly.

"This night could have been a complete disaster. People might have been seriously hurt. Or killed." Volstov settled back in the chair. "I'm indebted, Mr. Grant."

"There's nothing I need, Mr. Volstov."

"Please, call me Dimitri."

"Carson."

Volstov remained serious, and said, "Perhaps there is one thing."

"What's that?"

"Your fiancée, I believe her name is Nicola."

"Nicki."

"Nicki has a terminal illness and her medical coverage has been dropped. She needs an operation."

Carson stared at the Russian billionaire, wondering how he knew. Then he remembered telling Julie the story. "That's true."

"I can make this operation happen."

Carson's eyes locked on the man, frozen, unblinking. "How?" he asked, his mouth suddenly dry.

Volstov smiled. Benevolence simmered through the tough exterior. "I will simply pay for Nicki to have her new lungs. We will have to wait for a donor, just as you would in the United States, but Nicki will be first on the list. My plane is at your disposal and I have a house in Moscow for you to use until the operation. Anything you need will be provided."

Carson sat, speechless.

"You have earned this."

"Thank you." Carson said.

"Good." Volstov stood. "I have many guests who have come from the concert. Please stay here with me and we'll talk again in the morning." He started out of the room, then stopped and picked up the television buttons. He pressed the volume control. "This story is amazing," he said.

The newsfeed was from Washington DC. The reporter was a pretty English woman with a cultured accent.

"*...and Halima continues to capture our hearts. Money is pouring in – destined to help the most disadvantaged in Afghanistan, with ample funds to build new schools and medical clinics, and to create jobs and infrastructure. So many changes are in store for a country that has suffered for so long. And tonight, in Moscow, the Irish rock band, U2, opened their concert with a song for Halima. The name is* One Child, *and it is being transmitted globally across the Internet tonight. The band only asks that if you wish to download the song, you make a donation to help in Afghanistan. But what is truly incredible, is that little Halima, destitute and with no hope for the future, has made such a difference. That one child could change the world. This is Selma Black, reporting for BBC News, Washington, DC.*"

"Amazing," Volstov said, handing the buttons to Carson. "Absolutely amazing."

CHAPTER 76

Ma'sum ghar, Afghanistan, August 25th, 11:55 pm

Russell found Andrew sitting by himself on a stack of sandbags fifty meters inside the wire. He was smoking a cigarette and staring south to the desert.

"Hey," Russell said. He sat down next to the soldier.

"Hey." There were a thousand words he could have responded with, but using the same one seemed easiest.

"You okay?" Russell asked.

Andrew flicked the spent cigarette butt onto the ground and nodded. "Yeah. Actually, I'm fine." A minute passed, then he said, "Your video sure did well."

"It's been played a lot," Russell conceded. "People seem to be responding to it."

"It's important," Andrew said.

They both sat staring at the night sky, then Russell said, "It must be tough on you."

"No, it's not. I'm okay with it." Andrew shook his head and was quiet again. Finally he added, "It was necessary."

"You think?"

Andrew lit another cigarette and settled back into the sandbags. He sucked in some smoke, held it in his lungs for a few seconds, then blew it out slowly. It hung in the still air, a tiny cloud against a black sky. "I came back to Afghanistan because I wanted to make a difference here. I really wanted to do something of value. But the longer I stayed, the deeper I sank into the realization that it was impossible. That the country was beyond repair." He stared straight up at the sky. "But you know, I'm beginning to think that this is fixable. It's going to take time, and it won't be done with guns."

"Are you saying you shouldn't be here?" Russell asked.

"No, we should be here. We *need* to be here."

"Not everyone agrees with that."

"Then they should come to Afghanistan and have a look around." He took a deep breath. "Any one of us could have shot that girl. It just happened to be me."

"I suppose you're right."

Andrew shifted a bit so he could see Russell. "I heard you're leaving tomorrow. Heading back to Boston."

"I am."

"Are you looking forward to it?"

Russell considered the question carefully. "I want to see Tina. I miss my wife. And I miss having chicken wings with the guys on Wednesday nights, but other than that, not really."

Andrew smiled. "This place kinda gets to you."

"Yeah. I don't think much of the weather. It's mostly the people."

"It's always about the people."

Russell stood and stretched. "It sure is." He gave the specialist a small wave. "I'm off to bed. See you in the morning."

"Good night."

Andrew stretched out on the sandbags. The moon was alone in the sky, no clouds for company.

He let his mind drift and it went back to a time when he had been naïve enough to think his life was normal and his mother and father were happy. He was about Halima's age and it was summer. School was out and the days on the beach with friends were long and lazy. They were digging for clams and talking about what they were going to do after high school. Everyone had a vision of where they were going. He remembered his friend's faces, bright with smiles and trying to look serious as they shared their hopes. Racecar driver. Professional baseball player. Doctor. Scientist. He wondered if any of them had followed those dreams.

When they had asked him, his answer was simple.

I'm going to be important.

He closed his eyes and the moon vanished.

Jeff Buick

Jeff Buick is passionate about writing.

He has five previous bestselling thrillers, *Bloodline, Lethal Dose, African Ice, Shell Game* and *Delicate Chaos.*

Jeff is a natural storyteller, and has taken this talent into the world of public speaking, inspiring and entertaining people with his tales from the publishing trenches.

His one rule when he sits down to write, is to entertain the reader.

And Buick is his real surname. It's Scottish.

You can keep in touch with Jeff through Facebook, Twitter or through his website at Jeffbuick.com

Find out more about *One Child* at www.onechildonline.com